A Nye of
PHEASANTS

PREVIOUS BIRDER MURDER MYSTERIES

ABOUT THE AUTHOR

Steve Burrows has pursued his birdwatching hobby on seven continents. He is a former editor of the *Hong Kong Bird Watching Society* magazine and a contributing field editor for *Asian Geographic*. Steve now lives with his wife and muse, Resa, in Oshawa, Ontario.

A Nye of
PHEASANTS

STEVE BURROWS

POINT
BLANK

A POINT BLANK BOOK

First published in Great Britain, the Republic of Ireland and Australia
by Point Blank Books, an imprint of Oneworld Publications, 2024

ISBN 978-0-86154-177-5
eISBN 978-0-86154-178-2

Typeset by Geethik Technologies
Printed and bound in Great Britain by Clays Ltd, Elcograf S.p.A.

Oneworld Publications
10 Bloomsbury Street
London WC1B 3SR
England

Stay up to date with the latest books,
special offers, and exclusive content from
Oneworld with our newsletter

Sign up on our website
oneworld-publications.com/point-blank

MIX
Paper from
responsible sources
FSC® C018072

For Briar and Miles:
For whom the world is still a blank page on
which to write your stories

1

Autumn. If death had a season, thought Lindy Hey, it would be this one. Not the cold finality of winter, when the matter was settled, locked into its frozen state of permanent loss. But this time, when life could almost be seen leaving once vibrant, living things, could almost be observed leaching out and dissipating into the cooling autumn air. As it had done so recently from the body at her feet.

'Natural causes?' she asked.

Detective Chief Inspector Domenic Jejeune looked up and nodded solemnly, his hand still on the body. No warmth rose back through his outstretched fingers. He straightened from his crouch, turning to take in the surrounding woods. 'I don't see any evidence to the contrary. The vegetation is completely intact.' Jejeune pointed to the undergrowth. Apart from their own trail leading from the main path, the tangles of bracken and leafy ferns lay undisturbed. 'There would be some signs of disturbance if there had been an attack, or any kind of pursuit. Plus there are no obvious signs of trauma on the body.' Lindy saw his brows furrow in thought. 'In fact there are no signs of any cause of death at all.' He gave himself a moment to assess the evidence and then nodded thoughtfully. 'So yes, natural causes, I'd say.'

Lindy looked down again at the prostrate form, limp and still. It was as if an invisible veil had been draped over it, sealing it away from the world of the living. Though he hadn't voiced it, she knew Domenic was taking consolation from the fact that this life had not been taken by violence. He spent so much of his time investigating deaths from unnatural causes, many of them horrifically so. But this one hid no sinister secrets, no ugly human failings like greed or rage, nothing that might reveal the darknesses lying within people. While it was unfortunate that death couldn't leave him alone even on a quiet country walk on his day off, at least this one would require no further investigation.

A harsh call split the quiet of the moment and Jejeune looked up. 'Carrion Crow.'

Lindy nodded. Even she knew that one. 'It didn't take them long, did it?'

'It never does,' said Jejeune. 'It's why they're such successful scavengers. First to the kill get the spoils.'

Except this wasn't a kill, it was a natural death, one where life had just escaped the body like a sigh in this tranquil, peaceful place. She looked around her. Dappled light fell like threads of spun gold onto the tangled undergrowth beneath. Only the gentle tremor of the leaves on the trees disturbed the stillness. 'How sad,' she said, 'to die in a beautiful place like this. Still, I suppose if this woodland was going to be your last sight on Earth, you could do worse. Should we cover up the body, do you think? I know it sounds silly, but it seems like the decent thing to do.'

'If it makes you feel better.' Jejeune understood that people reacted in their own way to death, and he knew the need to make a gesture, any gesture, to acknowledge the passing of a life was necessary for some. He was not one of them. It might have been supposed it was the frequent exposure to the sight of dead bodies that had hardened this response out of him, but he had felt this way for as long as he could remember. He felt deaths keenly, and they wounded him, but he knew that no gesture, no matter how sincere, could affect the unrelenting finality they represented.

The shattering report of a shotgun echoed through the air, and Lindy's eyes widened in alarm. 'That sounded close.'

'A shooting party.' Jejeune pointed off into the distance. 'The Cleve estate borders this woodland. Don't worry. They're far enough away that they don't pose any danger.'

'You know my rule on gunfire, Dom. If you can hear it, you're too close.'

The crows, stirred perhaps by other memories of shotgun blasts, had lifted silently from their perches, and begun circling on outspread wings, like a host of black angels mourning the death in the clearing below them. Lindy looked down at the body. 'You don't think it had anything to do with this, do you?'

He shook his head. 'There's no blood, no evidence of any wounds. I don't think a shotgun was involved.'

'I'm glad you don't go in for that,' said Lindy, linking her arm in his. 'Shooting things.'

'Growing up where I did, it was all around me,' said Jejeune. 'Moose, deer, even bears. Hunting is a part of the culture there.' He shrugged. 'It just never appealed to me.'

'So you never hunted, then?'

'When I was a boy, before I knew any better. An uncle took Damian and me out once or twice. I fired at a couple of things, but I don't think I ever hit any of them.'

She looked at him now, staring into the sun-dappled clearing, and past it, into his memories. But the possibility that you might have done stays with you to this day, doesn't it? she thought. 'And that was the last time you fired a weapon?'

'I fired one last week, as a matter of fact. I had to retest to maintain my Authorised Firearms Officer designation.'

'It's funny, you and Danny Maik are the only AFOs I know, and I can't think of anybody less likely to shoot someone than you two. He doesn't hunt, does he?'

Jejeune shook his head. He knew that, like many with a military background, his ex-sergeant's experiences had taught him the value of life. 'I would guess that when you've seen enough death at close quarters, killing for sport just doesn't have that much appeal.'

'I wonder how he's doing over in Singapore. He's back soon, isn't he? Will you see him before he starts his new posting?'

Jejeune shook his head. 'Probably better to wait a while.' Something in the undergrowth seemed to catch his eye, and he turned his gaze away from her. The distancing had already begun, she thought. She hoped they could maintain contact with Danny. Before his departure from Saltmarsh station, he had been the closest thing Dom had to a friend, unless you counted his mercurial relationship with his chief superintendent, DCS Colleen Shepherd.

Another gunshot rang out, the echo rumbling across the sky like the roar of a wounded animal. Lindy flinched again, and leaned in towards Domenic. 'If you're uncomfortable, we can go,' he said. He looked around the treetops once again and paused, listening. 'Things are pretty quiet around here anyway, bird-wise.'

'Ones you can enjoy seeing, anyway.' She looked down again at the body at her feet, nestled on a bed of tawny bracken that surrounded it like a shroud. There was still vibrant colour in the face, shiny red cheeks, the metallic green sheen of the rest of the head. The beauty seemed to heighten the sense of loss for her. Was it the death of the bird itself she lamented or was it something more selfish? Would she have felt the same kind of regret at the sight of a female pheasant, with its drab brown plumage blending into the foliage around it, or was it the loss of this male pheasant's splendour to the world that made her so sad? It troubled her slightly that she couldn't say for sure. It would not be long, she knew, before this fleeting beauty disappeared. Even without the crows, the insects and soil microbes that lay beneath the body had already begun their work. How long would it take? Hours? Perhaps a day? How would she feel about this death when it was marked by nothing more than a few bleached bones and tufts of feathers, when all that remained of this magnificent bird was her memory of it, and the tragedy of its loss in this quiet, sunlit glade on this gentle autumn afternoon, with the sounds of gunfire rolling across the skies like distant thunder?

'I don't want to be here any more,' she said.

Jejeune curled an arm around her shoulder. 'Okay. Did you want to cover the body before we leave?'

Lindy shook her head. 'Better to just let nature take its course,' she said. 'Let's go.'

2

The heat hung in the room like a threat. Above the table, the blades of the solitary ceiling fan laboured though the heavy air without disturbing it. Through the half-drawn window blind, bars of coloured light flickered onto the opposite wall. From somewhere across the street, a neon sign was flashing. Perhaps it was a reminder that, outside, life went on. But if so, the message being morse-coded onto the dingy green paint in this room was also that, for the foreseeable future, any life beyond this one was out of reach.

From his chair at the steel table, the police officer looked up from his paperwork. Darkening patches on his blue uniform showed the effects of the humidity in the room, but he gave no signs of discomfort. He stared at the face of the man seated across the table from him. He seemed to be taking in the details: the clean dressing above the eyebrow, the fresh Band-Aid on the cheek, the gel that had stemmed the bleeding from the cut lip.

'You have received treatment for your wounds, I see. I trust it was administered with appropriate care and attention.' The man opposite him said nothing, but the officer nodded anyway. 'This is good.' He slid a single sheet of paper across the desk. 'You may bring charges against the officers who caused you these injuries, if you wish.' His tone bordered on insouciance. 'The charges will be dismissed, of course. Your injuries came about as a direct result of your violent attempts to resist arrest. We have many witnesses to this. The officers were authorised to use necessary force to subdue you.' He waved a hand airily. 'But we are keen that you should be accorded the due process of law, should you choose to pursue it.'

The man reached out a hand and set it on the paper. His knuckles were raw and bruised but, unlike his face, these wounds had not been treated. Until recently, the hands had been encased in plastic bags. He slid the paper back across the desk. The officer set it aside. The matter was closed.

There would be other offices in this building, the man knew, suites of them upstairs, large, well-lit spaces, fully air-conditioned. Holding him here was for effect; another message, more unequivocal than the one being flashed onto the wall. You are here, in this tiny, stifling room, they were telling him, because this is where we choose for you to be. We decide what happens to you now. We control your fate, and you are powerless to change it.

'But where are my manners?' asked the officer. He fished a business card from the top pocket of his shirt and set it on the desk in front of the man. He lowered his eyes to read it, then snapped them up again suddenly and set his hands on the edge of the table with enough force to jolt it forward slightly. The guard stationed at the door behind him took a step forward, but the seated officer held up a hand and, after a second's hesitation, the guard retreated to his post.

The officer nodded slowly. 'Yes, homicide. The victim was pronounced dead upon arrival at the hospital. He never regained consciousness. You were responsible for causing that death and so,' he spread his hands and looked around the room, 'here we find ourselves.' He looked down at the

7

arrest report. 'You claim the victim came at you aggressively, but none of the witness statements support this. What they saw was you adopt a combat stance and strike a blow to the victim's throat. Now, admittedly, none of these witnesses are experts in martial arts. But there are a number of people on this police force who are, myself included. From the description of the stance, we have concluded they saw the *kamae* position. This is an offensive stance, not a defensive one. And we are all in agreement, furthermore, that the blow the witnesses describe you delivering was *tettsui uchi*; a kill strike to the throat. So we have lethal force, delivered deliberately and with some degree of expertise; a compelling case, not for manslaughter, but for murder.'

The other man said nothing. But it was a different kind of silence now, watchful and wary. His body held a new tension. A rivulet of sweat trickled down his temple, but he made no move to brush it away.

'If you choose to retain the services of legal counsel, you will undoubtedly be told your cooperation may result in a more lenient sentence.' The blue-uniformed officer shook his head gravely. 'I cannot confirm this will be the case. Should you wish to make a statement at this time, we shall of course be willing to take it, but in truth we do not need your assistance. We have eight independent witnesses who are willing to testify they saw you deliver the fatal blow. You were arrested at the scene, fibres from the victim's clothing were found on your hand, and your DNA will be found on the body.' The officer allowed himself a small, satisfied smile. 'I have been doing this job for many years, and I have rarely known the luxury of such compelling evidence.' He let the statement hang in the sultry air for a moment before continuing in the same measured tone. 'The victim, as you are aware, was a serving police officer. He was also a foreign national. We owe it to his friends and colleagues in in his home country to see that justice is done. Indeed, we owe it to him.'

The bead of sweat had reached the man's cheek, but still he refused to acknowledge it. Perhaps he was concerned it might be taken as a sign of panic. He needn't have worried. It was hard to read this man's emotions, but the officer could tell fear was not among them.

'I want to exercise my right to legal representation,' said the man quietly.

'A wise decision, I think.' The officer nodded with seemingly genuine satisfaction and leaned back like a man who had already won his contest. 'From our point of view, a guilty plea under the advice of counsel is always the preferable option. Without it, a confession can be subject to so many questions at a later date. Even with the cameras covering these rooms today, there is always the chance a lawyer can claim it was obtained under coercion, or some form of intimidation...' He paused, as if to acknowledge such claims would be unlikely in this case. 'Far better, I think, to hear the evidence we have in the presence of a lawyer, and then decide the sensible course of action. We will make a request on your behalf immediately.' He leaned across the desk confidentially. 'Though I have to say, it might be necessary to accept the services of a public defender. A private defence lawyer's reputation is built on successes. Few, I think, would risk theirs on such an unwinnable case as this.'

The observation was met with more silence from the man on the far side of the table. Only his eyes moved, warily assessing the officer's position, the size of the room, the distance to the guard behind him. The paint on the walls wore a shiny skin of condensation from the moisture-saturated air. It made it look as if the walls were weeping. But were the tears for the victim, he wondered, or for him?

'Of course, it would not be prejudicial to your defence if you wished to disclose the nature of your relationship with the victim at this time. There are certainly those in this station who would welcome some insight into this.'

There was a pulse of hesitation as the man seemed to consider the offer, but ultimately he remained silent. The officer nodded. 'This is your right.' He waved another dismissive hand in the air. 'It will make no difference. We do not need to present any compelling evidence as to why you killed this person. We merely need to prove that you did. And that, as you are aware, is something we are able to do. So, you will be found guilty of murdering this police officer, this foreign national, and you will be sentenced accordingly. I should warn you to expect a lengthy term. A Singapore judge will be keen to send a message that violence against the police will be harshly punished, especially when the officer is unarmed.'

This time, the suspect started forward enough to raise himself from his chair. His hands grasped the edges of the table and he hauled himself upright. The guard rushed towards him, but he had recovered his composure and retaken his seat before the other man reached him. The seated officer had remained impassive throughout the outburst and now looked the guard back to his post, where he continued watching the man carefully.

The officer looked across the table. 'Since you have been in our custody, your wounds have been tended, you have been offered food and water.' He checked a sheet of paper. 'You have made no requests, therefore none have been denied. I think you will agree that your rights as a prisoner have not been violated in any way. This will continue while you await the arrival of your counsel.' The officer looked beyond the man towards the guard. If it was a message to the rest of the station, there was little doubt it would get through. The officer returned his gaze to the man seated on the other side of the table. 'It is my view that a dismissal of the case against you on some sort of technicality is your only way of avoiding conviction. I, and all of the other officers here, intend to ensure that this final glimmer of hope is extinguished, too.'

He lifted a laptop from a bag on the floor and set it on the table, opening it with exaggerated care as if to deflect any sense of drama from the moment. 'Now, we shall get a few formalities out of the way before your lawyer arrives. Let us start with your name. Here in Singapore, we are required to ask whether there is a Chinese, Malay or Tamil name as well as an English one. Forgive the presumption, but I'm assuming we can skip that part. So, just your English name then, please.'

The man leaned across the table slightly to make sure his softly spoken reply would be heard.

'Maik,' he said. 'Danny Maik.'

3

'What would you say to a restoration project, Domenic?' DCS Shepherd inquired, as soon as Jejeune entered her office. 'An individual who might need a bit of help getting a promising career back on track?'

'Sounds like quite a challenge,' he said. 'With everything else you have going on at the moment, I'm surprised you feel this is something you've got the time to commit to.'

'Not me, Domenic, us, we, the department.' Shepherd fixed her gaze on him over her steel-rimmed glasses. 'You.' He'd seen the look numerous times. It could convey many things, but none of them, to the best of his recollection, was ever positive. He took a moment to stare out of the window. A male Wood Pigeon strutted along the edge of the field boundary a few metres away. Despite the lateness of the season, the bird's plumage looked fresh and bright. It was a strikingly attractive creature and the detective reflected for a moment on how familiarity could sometimes cause us to overlook the inherent beauty of things. Having bought himself as much time as he could, he turned to address his superintendent.

'I'm not sure I'd be the best guy for something like that, you know, given everything.' He tried for a look that might remind her his own career had veered dangerously near the cliff edge on occasion.

Perhaps it had, thought Shepherd, but she would be hard pressed to find an officer in the division with a better closure rate. Policing was most definitely a results-based business, but success meant more than just a few points on somebody's scorecard. Every case successfully closed meant one more criminal behind bars, and a safer society for everyone. As long as the collars were lawful, and resulted in safe convictions, if Jejeune wanted to show the new man a few shortcuts to success, she could live with the headaches such an approach might bring. But she recognised that people only ever highlighted their own shortcomings when they wanted to avoid doing something.

'I understand your reluctance, Domenic. You've come such a long way in a short period of time, it's easy to feel that you still don't know all the questions yet, let alone that you're in a position to pass on any of the answers.' She paused. 'But I can tell you, no matter how long you've been in this job, you will always feel that way. We can't faff about looking for the ideal replacement for Danny Maik any longer,' she added impatiently. 'We need someone in, and this is a strong candidate. By far the strongest we've had, in fact.'

Jejeune twisted his lips thoughtfully. He knew once he began asking for details, the matter would be settled. He wanted to hold on to his escape route, however illusory, for a heartbeat longer. 'Did Eric get to see the Ring Ouzel up at Kelling I called him about?'

Shepherd was an expert at the long game herself. She knew where the meeting was going to end, so she could indulge her DCI for a few more moments. 'He did. And photographed it. Repeatedly. From every conceivable angle. I think it's fair to say I'd be able to recognise a Ring Ouzel now from a single feather.'

Jejeune smiled. Shepherd's partner was a fairly recent recruit to birding, and still pursued the hobby with a beginner's enthusiasm. Recently, though, he had adopted the associated pastime of capturing his sightings on camera. Like most partners of photographers, Shepherd seemed to mind less the exorbitant amounts he had spent on high-end equipment than the prospect of being forced to view the reams of images when he returned from his photo-safaris.

Shepherd waited patiently, and Jejeune knew his grace period was at an end. 'Do I know the officer?' he asked finally.

To her credit his DCS kept any hint of triumph from her expression. 'I don't believe so, but you'll have no doubt heard about the case. It was the one that happened while you were away in Colombia. A surveillance op that went badly wrong. Two officers had a warrant to search the premises of a known drug dealer and when they arrived, an officer who'd been dispatched to watch the place told them there was no one home. They went in, and the suspect opened fire on them. Two down; one recovered, one paralysed. The review board put the blame squarely on the surveillance officer. He had no business declaring the house clear if he wasn't absolutely certain. They threw the book at him.'

She paused to see if there was any flicker of recollection in Domenic's expression. His features were impassive at the best of times. When he was trying hard not to show any commitment like this, they were more impenetrable than ever.

'The thing is, Domenic, he was a high-flyer. Great things were expected of him before all this happened. I think he'd be able to relate to you more than most. You understand the pressure of living with high expectations, especially at an early age. I'm not saying that's what caused the wheels to come off in this particular case, but it would certainly be something you'd have in common.' She paused for a second. 'I'd be behind you all the way on this, Domenic. It would be made clear to him that he was on a tight rein, with no room for error. If it did turn out to be an inherent negligence or carelessness in him that can't be resolved, then we would cut him adrift without a second thought.'

'It's been a while since I was in Colombia,' said Jejeune. 'Surely this officer hasn't been suspended all this time?'

'Six months,' Shepherd told him, 'plus another six for all the prescribed counselling and courses. But then he took a further year off; personal leave. I dare say the expectation was that he wouldn't come back at all.' Her look was that of a supervisor used to dealing with officers who had failed to meet expectations, in one way or another. 'But when his leave was up, there he was, reporting for reassignment.'

And you offered to take him in, thought Jejeune. It was the kind of project Colleen Shepherd had built her career on. But it was not for any personal glory or bragging rights at the superintendents' conferences. She genuinely believed in second chances. And if you were part of her team, that meant you did, too. He sighed. 'I'd need to see his personnel file,' he said, trying to keep a note of defeat from his voice.

'Check your email. I've already sent it.' This time she did allow the faintest hint of satisfaction to creep into her smile. 'I've told him to be ready to report for duty at 0800 tomorrow.'

'Your very own fixer-upper,' said Lindy delightedly. She was standing at the window in the conservatory, staring at the inlet beside the house. 'And you, the elder statesman, dispensing the wisdom of your years.' She turned to him. 'Shall I fetch your pipe and slippers?'

'As my partner, wouldn't that make you the matronly homebody, pottering round the kitchen covered in flour?'

'*Au contraire*,' said Lindy, tossing her hair in faux dramatic fashion. 'I shall be the comely older woman who will gradually become the object of his desire, no doubt. Not to worry, though, I promise I shall always remain tantalisingly out of reach. Seriously though, Dom, even though I can tell you're not keen, I think you'd be perfect for this.'

'That's what Shepherd said.'

'I'm sure she took all your objections into consideration.'

He nodded. 'She did. Before I'd even had a chance to raise them.'

Lindy smiled. She knew it was a particular skill of DCS Shepherd to leave Domenic unsure whether her meetings had been an invitation to further discussion, or simply a declaration of a decision already taken. She looked out over the inlet again. She found the moods of the water mesmerising. Earlier in the day it had been churning dangerously beneath a gunmetal sky. Now the weather had brightened, only a few intermittent waves rippled gently towards the shoreline. 'I remember that case,' she said. 'The promising young officer's tragic fall from grace.' Whether she was quoting a headline she had seen or composing one she might have used wasn't clear. 'It came out at the hearing that there had been talk of fast-tracking him. It only seemed to add to the sense of tragedy surrounding the incident; that the force had lost two good officers through it, not just one. As I recall, he offered nothing whatsoever by way of a defence. What was his name?'

'Summer,' said Jejeune. 'Detective Constable Noel Summer.' He looked up from his phone to check the water for birds before returning to the PDF of the personnel file. 'He accepted the punishment without comment and declined to request an appeal. The board took it as a sign of the overwhelming remorse he felt.'

'Given that another officer was left paralysed, it's not hard to see why,' said Lindy. She looked at him earnestly. 'It would be hard to live with that sort of guilt, wouldn't it?' I imagine that has got a lot to do with why he wants to come back; to make some useful contributions that might overwrite those terrible memories. This could all work out, you know. Noel Summer's early press was striking. If you can recover the best of what was there before, I get the feeling you will be getting a good one. Would Danny be familiar with him, do you think?'

'It's possible. The incident was investigated by a multi-unit task force. Danny was our liaison for a while. He recused himself because he knew the injured officer, Bob Ferris, but he may well have run across this Noel Summer before he did.' Jejeune nodded thoughtfully. An insight into the type of personality they'd be inheriting would be no bad thing. And there were few officers around who could offer a more astute assessment of a person than Danny Maik. 'It couldn't hurt to ask,' he said. 'I'll give him a call as soon as he gets back.' *A good one*, he thought, looking out over the calm water one more time. It was just as well. To fill the gaping hole left by Danny Maik's departure, a good one was exactly what Saltmarsh station was going to need.

4

It was unusual to find an establishment where the rules were set by the patrons, but to all intents and purposes that's what had happened at the Board Room. During the morning breakfasts, the cosy interior of the handsome Georgian pub had evolved into an oasis of quiet contemplation. The locals read a paper or phone, or pondered over a studious game of chess. There was no music, no television, and the conversations rarely rose above low murmurs. There was no alcohol either. Though there was nothing preventing its sale, by convention the locals all settled instead for a steaming mug of tea with their full English.

Despite the increasing popularity of these morning sessions, there was plenty of room at the tables. Jim Loyal, however, had chosen to sit at the bar. Kenny, the landlord, looked between Loyal and the woman who had just entered to take the bar stool next to him. 'Play nice, you two,' he said.

'Game pie today, is it?' said the woman. 'Or just an assortment of pig parts for breakfast?'

'Give it a rest, Tara. I've just come in here for a quiet breakfast. The emphasis there would be on the word *quiet*.'

'You know you can get all the protein you need from a plant-based diet, and not a single animal has to die.'

'I don't eat food for the protein.' Loyal checked the phone he had laid on the bar. Another convention of breakfast at the Board Room was that phone calls were taken outside. His tone suggested he might have welcomed the opportunity. Loyal had long since become accustomed to Tara Skye's startling appearance but there was something different about her today. The blonde hair was the same, shoulder length at the back and on one side, shaved on the other, and he'd seen the eyebrow rings many times, too. The calf-length gingham dress was familiar, as were the shiny black combat boots. *Make-up*, that was it. Tara Skye was wearing mascara and vivid red lipstick.

'All dolled up for the weekend, I see,' he said. 'Just make sure you tell your people to stay off the land. It's posted and I won't hesitate to have the law on them if they trespass.'

'It'll all be law-abiding and peaceful,' she told him, 'and there won't be anything you and your lot can do about it.'

Jim Loyal didn't have a *lot*. He was a gamekeeper who preferred the company of the outdoors to people. The lot she was referring to, he knew, were the loose mishmash of protesters who would be assembled at the gates of Cleve Hall to counter Tara Skye's group. He could see how people might assume his own interests were more closely aligned with theirs than Tara's, but that would be a mistake. His own interests ended with the ongoing business of the estate. Any disruption to that, from either side, was unwelcome and would receive no support from him.

'So who'd you lend your quad bike to, then?' she asked.

'What?'

'Your bike,' said Tara. 'I saw somebody driving off with it when I got here. Whoever it is, I hope they know what they're letting themselves in for. It's a death trap, that thing. It shouldn't be allowed on the roads.'

'What are you talking about?' asked Loyal.

But the landlord had picked up on the woman's point already. He had rounded the bar and was heading towards the front door before the light finally dawned for Loyal himself. 'Somebody's nicked your bike, Jim,' he said as the other man joined him at the doorway.

Loyal burst past him and looked along the lane that ran past the front of the pub in both directions. The landlord left him to his fruitless survey and went back inside.

Loyal had his hands to his head in despair when he returned. 'God almighty. What am I going to do?'

'Want me to call the police?' asked Kenny. 'Nobody's accusing anybody of anything, you understand, but Tara here thinks it might have been Pete Estey she saw driving away with it.'

'He was a long way off over the fields,' she said guardedly, 'but it did look like him.'

'What? Estey? No.' Loyal shook his head. He seemed confused and disorientated. 'It wouldn't have been him. It wouldn't have been Pete Estey.'

'Makes sense,' said Kenny reasonably, 'given the history you two have. A bit of mischief, just to cause you some grief.' He held up his hands, a glass in one and a bar towel in the other. 'Nobody's making any accusations here, though.'

From the far corner, a pair of chess players looked up in contempt at the commotion coming from the bar. Tara Skye gave them a defiant glare. 'Oh, get over yourselves. The bloke's just had his bike nicked, okay?'

The players returned their gazes to their board. 'The more I think about it now,' she told Loyal, 'it did look like Estey, that ratty old green shooting jacket he always wears.'

'No,' he said firmly. 'I saw him. Earlier. On his bike, on the way to Cromer. He was miles away from here. He could never have got back in this time. It must have been somebody else.' He ran his hand through his hair again. 'Bloody hell.'

Jim Loyal had always struck Tara as someone who'd have no particular affinity for possessions. The things he owned would be tools only, fit for purpose or otherwise. That said, in her experience it wasn't unknown for older men to become attached to some odd item, regardless of how decrepit and beat-up it was, perhaps even because of it. Maybe even a grizzled outdoorsman like Loyal had some sliver of sentimentality about him. 'Well, whoever took it, you'd better report it to the police.'

Loyal shook his head. 'No need for that. It'll show up. Whoever it was, they'll abandon it somewhere around here soon enough. Like you said, they're not going to get far on it, the shape it's in.' He looked at Tara and tried a grin, but he seemed out of practice, and it turned out closer to a grimace.

'You expecting a ransom demand?' asked Kenny, nodding towards the phone Loyal had just checked again.

'The time's getting on,' he said. 'I should be going. Can I borrow your van, Kenny?'

He shook his head. 'Need it today. I'll call you a taxi though. Uber do you?

'On second thoughts, I'll walk. Do me good. Clear my head, give me time to calm down a bit.'

As he reached to gather his phone from the bar, it began to ring. Loyal answered it, inured from further disapproving glances due to his recent misfortune. 'Mr Loyal, it's Evan Knowles. How close are you to the Nye?'

If Kenny was searching for a word to describe the tone of the inspector from the Livestock Smallholding Agency, the eavesdropping bartender would have gone for *agitated*. No, on second thoughts, more than that – *worried*, closer to *frantic* even.

'I'm in the Board Room. Why?' Loyal cinched the phone close to his ear and gave a single short nod. He hung up and stretched his hand across the bar. 'Keys, Kenny. I need to get to the Nye right away.' His voice was taut with the effort of remaining calm, but it was clear he'd received alarming news.

'I can give you a lift,' said Tara Skye. 'What's up?'

'Come on then.' Loyal stood up sharply and strode towards the door, turning as he reached it. 'Call the police, Kenny. Tell them to get over to the Nye right away. Evan Knowles has just received a text. He thinks Abbie Cleve is going to kill herself.'

5

Selena Lim was young. There was no judgement attached to the observation, at least as far as Danny Maik was aware. He had simply reached the age where it was one of the things he noticed first, registering even before the person's attire or personality. In Selena Lim's case, both of those might have been described as crisp.

The drab beige walls of the consultation room seemed to be doing their best to suck the life out of the atmosphere. The venue was a step up from the dingy basement cell where he had been held until now, but that wasn't the highest of bars to clear. At least the air conditioning was working in here. Selena began by introducing herself formally. She extended her arm fully for the handshake, as if to preserve maximum distance from him. After they were both seated, she wasted little time in getting to the point. She looked down at the documents neatly arrayed on the table between them, scooping her dark, shoulder-length hair back behind her ears as it fell forward.

'Well, Mr Maik, there doesn't seem to be a lot of grey area here. Eight independent witnesses have testified that they saw you deliver a blow to the victim's upper thorax area, after which he fell to the ground. No one ever saw him move again. Your DNA was found on the victim's shirt up near the throat, and fibres from the shirt were found on the knuckles of your right hand.' She looked up like someone who had been told eye contact was important, and Maik tilted his head slightly to show he found no fault in her summary.

'I suppose you want to hear my side of the story,' he said.

Selena nodded slightly, but not in agreement. 'I understand that as a police detective back home your first priority would be to try to establish the facts. But my job is to assess whether there is some element of reasonable doubt in what appears to be an iron-clad case against you. Unless the facts can help me with that, I'm afraid they're of little use at this stage.' She fixed him with a frank gaze. 'It's important you understand there's no possibility of bail here,' she said firmly. 'You're a non-resident with no ties in Singapore. You've spent enough time around the criminal classes to know how to avoid detection, and you're resourceful enough to find a way off the island even if you have surrendered your passport. Plus, of course you're charged with a Class One indictable offence: the murder of a serving police officer in the Singapore Force. Bail is out of the question.' She gave her head a small shake, as if convincing herself of her earlier assessment.

She was considerably more engaged than most public defenders Maik had seen. They were typically on the younger side, too, many of them getting their first experience in defending clients. But that wasn't to say they were particularly invested in their role. Strangely, despite Lim's dire prognosis, there was no hint of defeatism in her tone, no sense that she saw her role in this matter as simply facilitating the inevitable. The uninspiring surroundings notwithstanding, Maik found himself buoyed for the first time since his arrest. He wouldn't allow himself the luxury of hope just yet, but even the prospect that such a capable, committed young woman would be looking into the case was more encouragement than he'd known for days.

'The police are offering a liaison officer,' she told him. 'It's up to you whether you want to accept, Mr Maik.'

He smiled at her. 'Danny will do. I wouldn't have thought they'd be too keen to cooperate with the defence in a case like this.'

'They aren't. This would meet their minimum requirements for keeping us informed of developments at all stages. They don't want to risk giving you grounds for appeal.'

Maik nodded. Only those found guilty needed to appeal. She was telling him in her own none-too-subtle way that she wasn't seriously considering that the case would result in an acquittal. 'I don't suppose it can hurt to hear what he has to say.'

Selena inclined her head. 'It's your decision. I'll let them know we'll agree to meet. Nothing more, at this stage. Okay, so let's get to your relationship with the victim, Titus Chupul. How did you know him?'

'I didn't. Prior to the attack, I'd never seen him before.'

'Never?'

There was no ambiguity in Maik's head-shake, no *as far as I am aware* or *not that I recall*. He meant never. She gave him a quizzical look and he was struck for a moment by her natural, unaffected beauty. Selena Lim would have no trouble getting respect from the men she dealt with, but few of them would be likely to overlook the fact that they were dealing with a stunningly attractive woman.

'So you're expecting me to believe a man you've never met travelled halfway across the city to attack you?'

'No. I'm not expecting it to make any more sense to you than it does to me, but it's what happened.'

'There is no one who can attest to the assertion that he approached you in an aggressive manner. The witnesses are saying that by the time they became aware of the altercation, you had already assumed a combat position.'

'I knew what was coming. A quiet word wasn't going to solve it.'

'Still, couldn't you have just subdued him, a man half your size?'

'He knew how to handle himself. He was a Gurkha.'

For the first time since she had entered the room, Selena Lim looked distrustful. It was as if a switch had flipped off behind her eyes. 'How could you know that? I thought you'd never met him.'

'I recognised his fighting style.' Maik looked at her evenly. 'You need to access this man's medical records. He must have had an underlying condition. That blow shouldn't have been enough to kill him. I know the difference.'

'Yes,' said Lim dubiously, 'your expertise in this area is not something we will be keen to point out to a jury. Even if it was not your intention to kill him, if he subsequently died of injuries sustained in your attack, you would still be responsible for his death. You struck an unarmed man with lethal force and he died. In the eyes of the law, Danny, you did kill him.'

'No.'

The vehemence of Maik's denial stunned Lim for a moment. 'Not unarmed. He had a knife. A kukri, they call it. They're standard issue for Gurkhas serving in the Singapore police force, I believe.'

'There's no mention of a knife in the police reports. And your hands and clothing showed no signs of having been cut by a blade.'

'When you're defending yourself against a knife attack, that's generally the idea.'

She consulted her notes, written longhand on a legal-size yellow notepad, which for some reason Maik found strangely reassuring. 'No knife was found at the scene or among the victim's possessions. And no witnesses reported seeing one.

At this point, as far as the police are concerned, that knife doesn't exist.'

The force of Maik's silence was the only response required.

'Very well. Tell me more about this knife. I'll start looking for it right away.'

'It was quite a bit smaller than a regular kukri, probably meant to be more ornamental than a service weapon. But it had all the same features: spring steel blade, with an inlay carved into the handle. They generally have some kind of Nepali symbol. This one was a bird. I'd say a pheasant.'

'Are you sure?'

'I know somebody back home who has an interest in birds. The handle was in the regimental colours of the Gurkha Infantry.'

'So a person unknown to you came out of nowhere, armed with a knife, with the intention of attacking you.' She stared directly into Maik's eyes for a moment and then lowered her head in thought. 'I believe we have a problem here, Danny,' she said. 'I know you think I'm young, but I've got enough life experience to recognise a liar when I see one. I don't think I see one sitting here before me now.'

'How is that a problem?'

'Although you're telling the truth, none of this makes any sense to me. And it won't to a jury, either.'

Maik nodded. For Selena Lim to solve her problem, as she put it, and convince a jury to believe his unlikely version of events, she would need to build a case for self-defence. And to do that, she would need to provide some proof that the knife existed.

'Can I ask you, Danny,' she said cautiously, 'why you didn't mention this knife, this kukri, to the police?'

'Because they clearly didn't have it. And since they're not the ones who are going to be defending me, I thought I'd wait and tell the person who is.'

Selena Lim's expression was everything a defendant would want to see: engaged, resolute and sincere. 'I don't defend people, Danny. I defend their actions. And if I'm going to defend yours, we have a lot of work to do. So let's get started. You can begin by telling me your side of the story now.'

6

Domenic Jejeune wheeled his Range Rover to a stop beneath a sign that read THE NYE. Tony Holland was emerging from his silver Audi TT as he got out.

'Sergeant Salter isn't with you?'

Holland shook his head. 'Called me as I was on my way to pick her up. She said she had to make an urgent call. She was trying reach some government department before they closed. Something to do with Max would be my guess. When it's your kid, everything else takes a back seat, doesn't it?'

Jejeune nodded. Even death, apparently.

'New bloke's already here, though, I see.' Holland pointed in the direction of a tall, slender individual leaning forward to examine something on the ground. 'He's keen.'

Holland continued to watch the man while Jejeune took in the surroundings. The property was enclosed by a high red-brick wall on three sides, leaving only the frontage to the road open. A large, gabled house of whitewashed brick stood near the road, while along the perimeter walls ran a series of low concrete pens, fenced in with chicken wire. The entire fore-court to the property consisted of fine white gravel, giving the place a neat, manicured appearance. In the centre of the fore-court lay the body of a woman. From long, shallow cuts on her wrists, pools of dark blood were soaking into the white pebbles beneath her outstretched arms.

'Abigail Cleve. Thirty-two years of age. Birthdate thirty-one twelve.' The voice beside Jejeune startled him and he spun around to find himself staring into the lean features of the man he had seen on his arrival.

'Noel Summer, I take it?' Jejeune extended his hand. 'Chief Inspector Jejeune,' he said. 'Domenic.'

The man's handshake was unexpectedly robust and Jejeune realised the detective's build was sinewy rather than simply undernourished. The man withdrew his hand but still held his shoulders hunched forward slightly, as if he was anticipating having to ward off a blow. Jejeune suspected, however, that the world had already delivered it. Summer joined him in looking at the body. 'You don't recognise her, then?'

'Should I?' asked Jejeune.

The question seemed to take the man aback. 'She's a member of a prominent local family, that's all. They own the Cleve estate, bordering this property.' He nodded in the direction of a row of stately oak trees that stood behind the red-brick wall.

'We tend to concentrate more on previous form than bloodlines,' said Holland, joining them.

'She doesn't have a criminal record,' Summer told him. 'So you don't know anything about this place then, presumably, either.'

Was this clown going out of his way to make them appear ignorant, wondered Holland. It was hardly the way to make friends on his first day. 'I know it's a pheasant farming operation,' he said flatly. 'I remember it created a lot of interest among the locals when it first opened up. In one way or another.' He looked at Jejeune. 'It must have been, what, a couple of years ago now?'

'Eighteen months,' said Summer. 'The property was originally part of the estate, but the business is a private enterprise. It's registered with the Livestock Smallholding Agency.' He consulted his notes. 'Holding number 86522, issued in Norwich. No riders or restraints on the licence.'

'Sixty-eight degrees,' said Holland.

Summer looked puzzled. 'I'm sorry?'

'Today's temperature. Might as well put that in your report, too. No point in doing a half-arsed job, is there?'

The new detective constable looked at Jejeune uncertainly, as if to confirm Holland was being sarcastic. But he found nothing in the DCI's thoughtful expression. He was looking at the far side of the compound, where two men and a woman stood at a discreet distance from each other, alone in their responses, unwilling to seek the normal comfort of others at such a time. 'Those are the ones who found her?'

Summer nodded. 'Evan Knowles, the inspector from the LSA, was first on the scene.'

'That'd be the male model,' confirmed Holland, nodding towards the tall, good-looking man with immaculately groomed hair.

'He was en route when he received a text from the victim indicating she was about to take her own life. He contacted Jim Loyal to alert him. Loyal is a gamekeeper on the Cleve estate so Knowles thought he would be able to get here faster. But Loyal was in the local pub, the Board Room, so Knowles arrived first.'

It was as if he was reporting on an incident from long ago, thought Jejeune, rather than on the death of a woman whose body lay less than three metres away. Summer's shoulders had remained faintly hunched as he spoke. His tone was similarly guarded. Perhaps his emotions were, too.

'And the girl?' asked Jejeune.

'Tara Skye. According to uniforms, she's a local activist; animal rights. She was in the pub, too. She gave Loyal a ride here.'

'Do we think we need a female officer, sir?' asked Holland. 'Only with Lauren not being here...'

Jejeune studied the young woman closely. He wasn't sure what the dress code for local animal rights activists was, but he suspected Tara Skye would have opted for the unconventional look no matter what role she had chosen for herself. He told Holland to make the offer, though he expected the woman would decide she would be fine without any support, female or otherwise. It was the older man that concerned Jejeune. He looked so distraught Jejeune advised Holland to check on him first. As he began to leave, Jejeune called out to him.

'Urgent, Sergeant Salter said? An urgent call.'

'Yeah, that's what I thought. I mean, what kind of government department closes at nine in the morning? Must be important though. I've never known her to duck a case due to personal business before.'

When Jejeune turned back to Summer, the constable was staring at the body. But perhaps not quite. 'That's where her gloves were found?' he asked the younger man.

Summer nodded. 'With the phone beneath them. The text was verified, but then the phone was replaced.' He hesitated slightly. 'The uniformed officers said you like to see things *in situ*.'

Jejeune continued looking at the gloves. 'Why not put the phone back in her pocket? Wouldn't that be the natural thing to do?'

'And why leave it on? I would have thought she'd have switched it off completely. Maybe even taken the battery out.'

'As a final gesture, the act of saying goodbye to the world, severing her connection to it,' said Jejeune, nodding, 'I don't see a car, DC Summer. Did you walk here?'

'My B&B is just up the road. I was out for a walk when the call came in. I was already halfway here. It was faster just to continue on foot than to go back to get it. Sir, there's something else.'

Summer seemed to hesitate again. Holland had finished his interviews and was approaching them across the compound. The new detective constable's eyes tracked his approach for a moment. 'The gloves, sir. There's what looks like hessian fibres on them. Only, I've had a look around. I don't see any hessian on the site at all.'

Jejeune looked at the gloves, neatly positioned by the body, just far enough away to have avoided the blood flow from the woman's wounds. He nodded thoughtfully as Holland reached them. 'Loyal confirms he knew the deceased. He said she was up at the estate yesterday. She and her sister had words.' Holland looked over his shoulder at the man. 'He's in a right old state, sir. He might need to see somebody. The girl's all right, though. Seems a bit dazed by everything, but I don't think she's likely to fall apart. Oh, and Knowles would like permission to leave. He has to run his kid to some school programme.' He looked at Jejeune, expecting a nod of approval. But his superior's mind seemed to be elsewhere. 'Sir?'

'What? No, I'd like a word with him first.'

Holland beckoned Knowles over and he came at speed.

'It was you that discovered the body?' confirmed Jejeune. 'Only, sometimes the mind has trouble coping with a shock like that. It can lead to distraction activities, a need to perform some action, just to keep from dwelling on what it has just taken in. I'm wondering if you might have tidied up at all, put the phone beneath the gloves, anything like that?'

'No.'

'You're sure? How about the others?'

'Jim Loyal couldn't go anywhere near the body. He started to approach but as soon as he saw it, he turned away. He couldn't bring himself to look. I told Tara to take him over to the far side of the compound. I said I would wait here by the... here.'

'You knelt beside the body, didn't you? It's when you got that blood smear on your trousers.'

Knowles looked at the stain on his knee as if it was some alien presence. The skin over the man's taut cheekbones coloured slightly. 'I was going to check for a pulse. Tara came and pulled me away. She said not to touch... anything.'

'So just to be clear, you didn't disturb the body at all? Or any of the other evidence? And neither did Tara Skye or Jim Loyal? So we wouldn't find your fingerprints or theirs anywhere, if we were to process the scene?'

'Absolutely not.'

Jejeune nodded to himself. 'Thank you, Mr Knowles. If anything comes back to you that might contradict that statement, please let us know.'

As the LSA inspector departed, Holland turned to Jejeune. 'So what do you think, sir? Wrap this one up?'

'Have you noticed the birds?' asked Summer suddenly.

'The birds?' said Holland.

'The pheasants. They've been so still since we've been here. You'd hardly know there are birds in those pens at all.'

'They're about to be packaged up as somebody's dinner,' said Holland impatiently. 'They probably think the quieter they are, the more chance they've got of making it through the day.'

But Summer shook his head. 'There's an uneasiness about them. It's not natural. The negative energy about this place, the birds sense it.'

'A woman just killed herself here,' Holland pointed out irritably. 'So, yeah, I'd say there's some pretty bloody negative energy about this place.' He sighed impatiently. 'Look, we have a note and once we've been up to the estate to verify the argument with the sister, I'd say we'll have our motive. All the evidence is completely consistent with suicide. Agreed, sir?'

Summer looked at Jejeune, and the DCI read the message. He, too, was troubled by the careful positioning of the phone beneath the gloves. On another day, those hessian fibres might have given him pause for thought, as well. But Domenic Jejeune had other things on his mind at the moment. 9 a.m. in Norfolk was 5 p.m. in Singapore. And that was likely closing time for government departments there.

7

Beneath an uncertain sky of mottled cloud, a new coolness was announcing the Earth's slow transition into its next phase. The fronds of bracken below the stand of dark conifers that lined the driveway up to Cleve Hall were already showing the brown tinges that signalled the onset of the new season.

Noel Summer paused for a moment to look up into the trees. 'Can you feel how still the world is today? No wind, no movement, no birdsong.'

Tony Holland's expression suggested that, as far as he was concerned, the world seemed to be turning at about the usual speed. He wasn't sure why Summer had asked him to park at the end of the driveway and make the long walk up to the house on foot, but at least it gave him a chance to ask a question. 'That comment about the birds up at the Nye, it sounds like you know a bit about them.'

'About birds? Not especially. Why?'

'It's just the DCI is a big fan, that's all.'

'What, of shooting them, you mean?'

'Watching them.'

Summer stared at him. 'He watches birds? Why?'

Holland nodded his head slowly. 'There's hope for you yet,' he said.

The house was of a style Holland had seen many times dotted across the Norfolk landscape. Not on the scale of the baronial mansions, but imposing enough to instil the necessary deference in the estate workers. Two large narrow buttresses scaled the entire height of the building to the roof-line, separating the façade into three equal sections. In the centre one, a towering peak-arched door stood open. The woman standing in the doorway wasn't tall anyway, but she looked almost waifish in the immense space surrounding her. Holland had the impression she'd been waiting there since they pulled up at the foot of the driveway; but, with the pro-tests and counter-protests scheduled to be coming to her gates in the next few days, a bit of extra vigilance would have been understandable anyway. She smiled a guarded greeting to the officers as they approached.

'Lisbet Cleve?' inquired Holland.

'Only when I'm in trouble. Otherwise it's Libby.'

'Police, ma'am, Detective Constable Holland, and this is DC Summer. We have some news concerning your sister, Abigail. I wonder if we could come inside.'

'Actually, it might be just as well if we were to speak out here.' Summer managed to deliver the suggestion more like an addendum than a contradiction. But it didn't really matter where the news was going to be delivered. Libby Cleve already knew why two police officers had made the long walk up her driveway to talk about her sister.

The sun had broken through the cloud cover like a circle of white fire. In its pale light, the dwindling flowerbed in the centre of the forecourt was bravely holding on to the last of its colour. From her seat on the stone bench overlooking it, Libby Cleve stared at the fading foliage, as if somewhere in the labyrinthine tangle of leaves and stems there might be a place where her sister's death made sense. Perhaps Summer's instinct was right, thought Holland. Perhaps it had been better for the woman to receive the sad news out here, rather than in the oppressive silence of some sunless interior, filled with reminders of happier times.

'Your gamekeeper, Jim Loyal, was one of the people who found Abigail. He seems to be in a bad way.'

Cleve flashed a glance at Summer. 'Poor Jim,' she said.

'He said she visited you here yesterday. The estate is yours?'

'It passed to the oldest child on the death of my father, so it is mine – though, as Abbie used to remind me, not by much. We were born in the same year, me on 1 January, she on 31 December.' A short, mirthless smile touched the corners of her mouth. 'Even in that, we were about as far apart as it's possible to be.'

Holland was struck by the similarity between the two sisters. He hadn't dwelt long on the features of the deceased woman, but she seemed to have shared the same body shape as the woman seated beside him. The well-developed muscle tone of both belied the small-boned wiriness of their build.

'I wonder, can you think of anyone who might have wished your sister harm?' asked Summer.

'Not unless that idiot Tara Skye took things too far.' She gave a cold laugh at the men's interested stares. 'I'm not being serious,' she said. 'Her attacks are limited to nasty emails.'

'About?'

'Meat. She believes we should all give it up and become vegetarians. I mean, really? They didn't call our ancestors *grazer-gatherers*, did they?'

'And she specifically targeted your sister's pheasant business in these emails?'

'Tara Skye is opposed to all operations that involve the raising of animals for food. Including this one. We run a beef farming operation here. She is one of the organisers of this protest that's coming next weekend. She's joining forces with the climate activists and the anti-hunting brigade. We run a shoot on the estate every season as well, you see.'

Holland could see how the combination of meat production and hunting would make this place a lightning rod for protesters. 'Mr Loyal suggested you and your sister argued,' he said. 'Can I ask what that was about?'

'Abbie had been exiled from the family for some time. She came to ask to be readmitted. As head of the family, it was my decision. I refused.'

Holland sat forward. 'Exiled?'

'It was her choice to leave, but effectively, yes. She began seeing a man my father disapproved of, Peter Estey. She was given an ultimatum.'

The tyranny of a dead parent's wishes, thought Holland. Even now, this woman had felt compelled to honour them. Unless of course, there were more convenient reasons for her decision. 'How did she take it?'

'Not well, but she can hardly have been surprised. She knew that once she chose Estey over my father, there was no way back for her. She broke our father's heart. He blamed Estey of course, but Abbie never did anything she didn't want to.'

'Did your sister say why she wanted to be readmitted now?'

Cleve shrugged easily. 'Hard times? There are benefits to being part of a well-connected family that go beyond reputation and standing in the local community.'

'Did she say she needed money, then?' asked Summer.

'The conversation never got that far, I'm afraid.' The woman winced as she shifted her position to favour her arm, and Holland noticed for the first time a flesh-coloured brace on her wrist. She raised a hand and began massaging it. 'Time for my needles,' she said. 'An old judo injury. Acupuncture is the only thing I've found that can relieve the pain. I suppose that's one thing my sister has left me to remember her by.'

From the moment they had delivered the news, Holland had found the coldness of Libby Cleve's response to her sister's death disconcerting. When Summer's question came, therefore, it wasn't as surprising as it might otherwise have been. Which was not to say he approved of it. 'Would there be anyone who could confirm your whereabouts this morning?'

'As you can imagine, running an estate of this size is a full-time undertaking. I expect I've spoken to half a dozen people today.'

Holland rushed into the pause that followed, in case Summer was planning a follow-up. 'Can I ask what your father's objections were to this man Estey?'

'He was a criminal. A poacher. Property theft, my father called it. He couldn't abide the romantic notions associated with someone stealing his game.'

'Did you agree with your father's views? About Estey?'

'He knew what he was doing taking up with Abbie. And he knew the consequences. They both did.' She looked at Summer. 'My whereabouts? Someone who might harm Abbie? Are these normal questions when a family member has taken their own life?'

Summer's expression suggested there really was no *normal* in unexpected deaths. But he said no more, and Holland brought the visit abruptly to an end. 'We should be going,' he said, standing up quickly and hovering until Summer followed suit. 'Is there anyone you'd like us to call? To be with you?'

The woman declined with a shake of her head. 'My sister's body…?'

'There are some formalities to take care of,' he told her. 'Someone will be in touch to let you know when you can begin to make arrangements.'

'What the hell was all that about?' demanded Holland as soon as they were clear of the forecourt. 'Asking her to account for her movements this morning?'

The sun had retreated behind denser clouds and the air had turned colder again now that they had entered the avenue of tall conifers.

'In any suspicious death, everyone starts out as a suspect,' said Summer as the two men reached the car. 'You know that.'

Holland leaned on the top of the Audi and looked over it at the other man. 'It's not suspicious. The only suspicions are yours. This was a suicide, plain and simple.'

'A suicide with no hesitation cuts, with lateral ones instead, that bleed out faster. Any reason you can think of that a suicide needs to hurry things along? There's the text, too. *Please tell everyone I am sorry for all the suffering I have caused. Goodbye.*'

'It sounds like Abigail Cleve caused her family more than her fair share of grief over the years,' said Holland. 'Guilt, regrets, apology, it's all there in that message. It's a textbook suicide note to the family.'

'Exactly,' said Summer, opening the passenger door. 'So why send it to somebody else?'

8

They were in the same room as before, with its dingy, life-sapping walls and single square of light shining in through the tiny window high upon the far wall. Selena Lim sat primly on one side of the table. Maik had been handcuffed to a metal loop beneath the other side, but there was enough slack in the chain to allow him to rest his hands on the unadorned tabletop. The scrapes and cuts on his knuckles were fresh and raw.

'First things first,' said Lim solemnly. 'There can be no more of that.' It would have been about him establishing boundaries, she thought, letting the other prisoners know what he would be willing to put up with from them. Her guess: not much.

'I'm not sure you understand what it's like for a police officer in a holding cell,' said Maik reasonably.

'Perhaps not. But if I'm trying to build a case that you are not prone to violent assaults, it would help if you were not actually indulging in any. It would have been a pheasant, by the way.'

Maik's brow furrowed into puzzlement for a moment before realisation dawned. His DCS, Colleen Shepherd, was capable of some astonishingly abrupt changes of topic, but even she would have been proud of this effort. 'On the knife, you mean?'

Selena nodded. 'I looked into it. The national bird of Nepal is something called a Himalayan Monal. It's one of a few symbols they use to decorate their kukris; the flag of Nepal is another, and Sagarmatha – that's Everest to you and me. You didn't you see anything else on the knife, did you? The better the description I have, the more chance there is of tracking it down.'

'Just the bird.' Maik shrugged. 'I didn't get the best of looks, you understand.'

Selena inclined her head. 'I'll bring it up at your appearance before the Criminal Mentions Court, but they'd need us to produce it if it was going to have any impact on the charges you'll be facing. If we could have convinced them of self-defence, you might have been given the chance to plead manslaughter.'

The conditional tense didn't escape Maik's notice. 'So that won't be the charge when I appear?'

Selena left her dark eyes on Danny's face for a long moment. 'Based on the witness statements, they have a compelling case for a charge of murder. I take it you'll be entering a plea of not guilty.'

'I *am* not guilty.' Maik rarely raised his voice, and he reined it in immediately with an apologetic look.

Selena held up a hand. 'In that case, there will be a series of further Criminal Case Disclosure Conferences. At the first, the prosecution case will be reviewed. After that, there will be a second conference, which is our chance to outline the case for the defence. Essentially, this would be our last chance to get the charges reduced or dropped altogether, so this is where we'd need to convince them of our position: that you were defending yourself from an unprovoked attack by an unknown assailant armed with a knife. And that the blow you administered couldn't reasonably have been expected to kill.' The following silence emphasised just what an uphill task that was going be in the absence of any corroborating evidence. 'Once proceedings have advanced to the third conference,' she continued, 'you'd have one more chance to enter a plea, but the prosecution wouldn't be in any mood for generosity by then. The very fact that we were all still there at that stage would be a strong indication that they felt they had a winnable case at trial.'

Like all the sounds in this place, the unlocking of the door echoed jarringly, as if it had been wrenched up from some dark place of emptiness below them. The sudden noise startled Maik and prevented him from dwelling on Lim's comments. A young man entered the room and nodded to the guard, who closed the door behind him.

'Selena Lim?' he asked, extending a hand. 'Ronnie Gunn.' Unbidden, he drew up a chair and sat down beside Selena. For the first time since entering the room, he allowed his eyes to fall on Maik. 'And you'd be Danny Maik, Guy Trueman's friend from the UK.' Maik had been on the alert for any signs of hostility since he'd first been brought into this station, so much so that the effort of constant vigilance was beginning to exhaust him. But he sensed none in this man. Though the delivery was carefully managed, there was still a warmth to it. 'He asked me to pass along his regards.'

'You know Guy?'

Though it was Maik who had asked the question, Gunn addressed his answer to the lawyer. 'I work with him on recruiting. He comes at it from the military side and I represent the police.'

'And he knows Mr Maik how?'

Both looked at Danny.

'He was my commanding officer when I served in the army. One of them, anyway. How is he?'

'Same as always, fingers in a lot of pies, but still finding the time to cast an eye over the ladies. And the occasional leg. You know Guy.'

Maik did. And his reputation. But discussing it wasn't how he wanted to spend this precious time out of the holding cell. Especially when something so significant had caught his attention. He regarded Gunn carefully. 'You were there.'

'There were others, but I was first on the scene, yes. That area is a popular drinking spot for off-duty officers. I was only a couple of minutes away when the call came in, so I got over there as fast as I could. Not fast enough, though. I gave Titus Chupul mouth-to-mouth until the doctor came and took over. But it was no good.' A moment of silence followed and Gunn's features revealed the tortured eloquence of a hard man trying to suppress his emotions.

Selena Lim stepped in before the regret could morph into something more dangerous. 'So why have you come here today, Mr Gunn?'

'Officially, the police have an interest in this death. They want to know why Sergeant Chupul was attacked. Was it tied to an inquiry he was following, or could he be mixed up in something else?' He shook his head. 'I knew him. There won't be anything to find in that regard, but, until they've convinced themselves of that, they feel it's better if someone from outside the department makes the initial inquiries.'

'And unofficially?' Maik was glad Selena Lim had picked up on the point. It was a question he had been prepared to ask himself if she hadn't.

Gunn shrugged easily. 'They're interested in your client. Titus Chupul was skilled in close combat, enough that he trained others. It was his job, and he was good at it. And yet, despite the fact that your client has a few years on him, he was able to best him.' He turned to Danny. 'You see where they're going with this, don't you?'

Maik did, and, if Selena wasn't there yet, she was proving herself to be a quick study, so he had no doubt she wouldn't be far behind. 'It was self-defence,' he said.

Selena shot Danny a warning glance and turned to Gunn quickly. 'We will not be discussing any aspects of my client's defence today.'

Gunn rolled over the comment as if she hadn't spoken. 'Self-defence?' He shook his head. 'What I'm hearing is that none of the witnesses can testify to any provocation by the victim. What they saw was you delivering a lethal blow to an unarmed man. Now, Guy Trueman says you know how to look after yourself, but either you're a lot better than you look or you took him by surprise, as in, it was you who initiated the attack. That's the current line of thinking.'

'He had a knife,' said Maik.

'Danny,' said Selena sharply. But she knew the moment for damage control had gone. Maik had felt compelled to defend himself to this acquaintance of Guy Trueman's against the accusation that he had attacked an unarmed man.

'My client's attacker was carrying a kukri.'

'A kukri?

'It's a ritual dagger with a curved blade.'

'I'm Nepali,' said Gunn shortly. 'I know what a kukri is. I used to own one myself.'

'It had a Nepali symbol on it and regimental colours.'

Gunn turned to Maik. 'I accompanied Titus Chupul's body in the back of the ambulance, but I didn't see any sign of a weapon. Nor was one found at the scene. Have any other witnesses come forward to say they saw one? Because I know the eight witnesses the police have already spoken to didn't. Where is this coming from?' He looked at Danny intently.

'Is this self-defence angle your idea, or did your counsel put you up to it?'

'I'm told Sergeant Chupul had an unregistered phone,' said Selena, ignoring the jibe. 'Is that true?'

Maik realised that, once again, his lawyer had conjured up the question to deflect Gunn's cynicism from hardening into anger.

'A burner?' Gunn nodded. 'It's common practice for a detective to have a backup phone. No cop would want some of the clients they deal with having their personal number.'

'The police haven't recovered a second phone from Chupul's desk or his locker at work. I didn't see any record of one in his personal effects from the hospital, either. Do you know where it is?'

Gunn shrugged, but it wasn't apathy. He was beginning to realise where Selena Lim was going with this and he knew there was nothing he could do to prevent it.

'Okay, enough of this.' She counted the points off on her long, slender fingers. 'We have an unprovoked attack by a man my client has never met, we have a missing weapon, we have the fact that the victim's burner phone has disappeared.' She shook her head and looked at Danny. 'There are just too many unanswered questions here. With my client's permission, you can tell your superiors we are not ready to enter a guilty plea at this time.'

Gunn fixed Lim with a stare and Danny finally saw a flicker of the hostility he'd been expecting. 'Titus Chupul didn't have any weapon on him,' he told the woman flatly. 'I strongly advise you against dragging this out. I know how hard you lobbied to get this case, and I'm sure you think you're helping your client here. But I can tell you, you're not.' He nodded towards the bruises on Danny's hands. 'They can get your client into protective custody, but they're not going to do that unless you cooperate with them.'

'I'd like to get Mr Trueman on record as a character witness for my client, Mr Gunn,' said Selena. 'Do you think he would be willing to do that?'

Gunn was silent for a moment. 'I'll speak to him,' he said finally. 'Maybe he can talk some sense into both of you while he's at it.' He stood up to leave.

'Did he say anything?' said Maik suddenly. 'Titus Chupul. You said you were with him. In the ambulance.'

Gunn shook his head slowly. 'He never regained consciousness. Life was declared extinct at the hospital, but the doctor who gave him CPR is prepared to testify he was dead at the scene. The paramedic in the ambulance didn't even try to revive him. He just sat there with his hand on his chest, looking at me. It was like he was asking me why I hadn't saved him.' He fell silent again for a moment as he fought back the memory, before looking at Danny. 'Guy Trueman says you're a man of honour, Sergeant Maik. You need to do the decent thing here. And you need to do it soon.'

9

The mood inside the Incident Room was rarely set by the people gathered there. Most often it was a reflection of external events they were dealing with: the tragic, the outrageous, even the hilarious. But Colleen Shepherd couldn't ever remember the tone being set by a situation half a world away, one as far out of their control as it was out of their reach.

'By now you will have all heard about this terrible business with Danny,' she began as she stood up to address the group assembled for the morning briefing. 'Understandably, Sergeant Salter is taking some time off. She'll be going over there as soon as she can get things arranged.' Shepherd looked across at Summer, who was leaning indolently against the far wall. 'The sergeant and Danny Maik are… involved.' The news seemed to make no impression on the new recruit. She paused, struggling to find the necessary detachment to consign Danny's troubles to the background as they went about their own investigations. 'As for the rest of us, as much as I know we would like to help, our hands are tied. This is an ongoing police investigation by a foreign police service, and they neither need, nor want, any input from us. It goes without saying Danny couldn't possibly have committed this crime, so we just have to have faith that a full and proper police investigation will prove that.'

'Unless they've already made up their minds,' said Holland dubiously.

'Meaning?'

'Meaning maybe they've already accepted that Danny's guilty. They've got eight witnesses. Instead of trying to find some further evidence, perhaps they're just going to decide they already have enough.' He turned to the room. 'They've lost one of their own. You don't think they're going to be keen to nail this one shut in a hurry?'

'Surely it's precisely because it does involve a colleague that they'll want to get it right,' said Shepherd. 'We have to put our trust in the integrity of the investigative process, Constable. It's what underpins everything we do. If we don't believe it will get to the truth of the matter, we shouldn't be in this job.' Her long, thoughtful pause drew a line under the discussion. The next comment, they knew, would be about matters closer to home. 'This suicide at the Nye,' she said. 'There are questions, I understand.'

'Not really,' said Holland tetchily. 'We've got a note, and a reason. She wanted to be welcomed back into the family, and she was refused.'

'Would that have been enough to cause her to take her own life?'

'We've seen suicides for less.'

'And her reasons for asking to be readmitted in the first place?'

Holland shrugged. 'The sister suggested she might have been in need of some funds for her business. I imagine the prospect of hard cash can make swallowing your pride a lot easier.'

Summer eased upright from the wall and squared himself to the room. For a first contribution, it wasn't going to lack conviction. 'If that note was to her sister, it doesn't make any sense she'd send it to someone else.'

'Unusual, I agree,' said Shepherd, 'but perhaps, if she was estranged from her sister... Domenic, any thoughts?'

Jejeune's preoccupation evaporated beneath Shepherd's expectant stare. 'I find myself wondering why anyone would want to fake a suicide. If you wanted to disguise a cause of death, surely making it look like an accident would be far easier. There are any number of dangerous objects on a site like that. There's even a shotgun. An accidental discharge...?' He shrugged. 'You could understand a family trying to disguise a suicide out of a misplaced sense of shame, perhaps, but not the other way around. The same goes for insurance; a suicide voids any claims that a death by accident might offer. It simply makes no sense that someone would have attempted to make it look like a suicide if it wasn't.'

Since when had something failing to make sense been a deterrent to Domenic Jejeune, wondered Shepherd. Usually, he was the one pitching outlandish theories, thinking outside the box, piecing together disparate elements into some sort of whole and trying to convince the rest of them with the kind of earnestness and conviction Summer was now showing. And yet here he was, instead trying to dismiss inconsistencies and shelve the whole case, as if he saw the matter as a distraction he wanted out of the way, so he could concentrate on what was really concerning him.

'There's also the fact that Evan Knowles was heading up there that day,' said Holland. 'Perhaps she thought the LSA was intending to shut down her operation.'

'Does the Livestock Smallholding Agency even have that kind of authority?' asked Summer.

'When the government privatised that arm of food production oversight, the LSA was granted the same powers DEFRA had previously,' Shepherd told him. She turned to Holland. 'Was a shutdown likely?'

He opened his hands. 'Who knows, but on top of this business with her sister, it could have been enough to send her over the edge. You know how it is, problems keep piling up and all of a sudden there's a mountain of issues facing you that seems impossible to cope with.'

For a man who had always seemed singularly immune to piling-up problems, Tony Holland was demonstrating an impressive understanding of the pressures they could cause. If nothing else, it spoke to just how hard he was trying to oppose the idea of this being anything other than a suicide. Shepherd fixed Jejeune with another long stare to encourage his further participation. Again, he seemed to need to drag his thoughts from some other place.

'Blood-flow patterns suggest Abigail Cleve was alive when her wrists were cut,' he said eventually, 'but the gravel around the body was neatly raked. It showed no signs of a struggle. That means she'd have to have been convinced to walk there and lie down of her own accord. I don't see anybody being that compliant if they knew they were going to be killed.'

'She could have been drugged,' stated Summer resolutely. As new as he was to the team, it was becoming apparent that he wasn't going to be easily deterred when he had a theory to defend.

Holland shook his head. 'As the DCI says, there's no signs that the gravel in that forecourt had been disturbed at all, let alone had a semi-conscious body dragged across it.'

Perhaps Summer could have been excused for not appreciating the significance of Tony Holland's wholehearted backing of his DCI in this way, but the novelty was not lost on Shepherd. Nevertheless, she had become accustomed to accepting Jejeune's judgement in these matters. 'I realise it's hard to come to grips with a death so soon after your return to duty, Constable, but, unless there was anything else that convinces you that there was more to this, it does appear that suicide is the likely cause.'

Summer inclined his head. 'I'd like to look into someone called Peter Estey. He was known to the deceased: a former boyfriend. He might be a person of interest.'

'If there was a crime,' said Holland, 'which there wasn't.' He looked at Shepherd significantly. 'We can't delay the inquest much longer without justification, ma'am. I'm sure the family will want an autopsy done as quickly as possible so the body can be released to them.'

'Can I ask what it is that convinces you this is more than it seems?' Shepherd asked Summer.

He shrugged uneasily. 'The atmosphere there...' He shook his head. 'There was such a sense of unease. It was as if the forces of the natural world were out of balance. Even the pheasants...'

'Here we go again,' said Holland sarcastically. 'What is it with you and those bloody birds?' A thought seemed to occur to him. 'Here, if you really think those pheasants are suspects, perhaps we should get them in here and grill them.'

Even Shepherd managed a faint smile, but Summer left his intense stare in the middle distance. 'An unnatural death disturbs the Earth's equilibrium.'

Holland raised his eyebrows and looked around at the others. 'Know a lot about this stuff, do you?'

'It's central to my belief system,' Summer said. 'I'm a Druid.'

The statement concussed the room into silence for a moment. Tony Holland was the first to recover. 'You're in pretty good nick for somebody over a thousand years old. What's your secret, then? Skin creams?'

'Druidry has been officially recognised as a religion in this country for a number of years now,' said Summer flatly. 'There are more of us around than you might imagine. And the numbers are growing all the time.'

'Here, wasn't it your lot that used to be involved in human sacrifices?' Holland looked at the others and winked. 'I take it you don't go in for any of that side of things.'

'I help them out on weekends, if they're short.' Summer's expression suggested this wasn't the first time the topic had come up.

'Right,' said Shepherd briskly, 'well, as I'm sure you can appreciate, we can't justify an investigation purely on anyone's religious convictions, as valid as they may be,' she added hastily. 'So unless there's anything else…?'

Summer looked across at Jejeune. 'I did find some hessian fibres on the gloves.'

'Surely all her products would be vacuum-sealed in plastic, wouldn't they?' asked Shepherd. 'What would she need hessian bags for?'

'She wouldn't,' he said, 'but a poacher might. Estey has a couple of old convictions.'

'Those fibres could have come from anywhere,' said Holland. 'Half the farming community around here uses hessian bags, I should think. Plus, there's no way to tell how long they've been there. For all we know, they could have been on those gloves for weeks.'

Shepherd exhaled thoughtfully. 'A look into her bank records will tell us whether the motive for seeking readmittance was financial,' she said. 'And a chat to Knowles will clear up whether or not she was facing closure.' She turned to Summer. 'Do you know where to find this Estey?'

'No, but I know where to start.'

She nodded decisively. 'Right. Twenty-four hours. Let's take a look at her finances. We'll talk to Knowles and Estey and, if nothing leaps out at us, we'll advise the coroner we have nothing to contradict a finding of suicide.'

Summer straightened his stooped shoulders slightly and turned to leave, his long, fluid strides taking him off at an unhurried pace. Holland hung behind as the others filtered out until only he and the two senior detectives remained in the room.

'There's no crime, here, ma'am,' he said. 'He's inventing one. He's just looking for a bit of attention. As if being a Druid wasn't enough of a distinction.' He looked in the direction that Summer had gone. 'I suppose I'd better go and check he's not using the kettle to brew up some concoction to cast a spell on us all.'

Shepherd watched Holland leave. 'Is he right, Domenic? Is Summer simply trying too hard here? Just back, it would be understandable, after all.'

Jejeune took a moment to order his thoughts. 'The high wall surrounding the Nye means the road is effectively the only way in and out. The entire area would have been in view to Knowles once he crested the hill, less than a minute after he received that text. There simply wouldn't have been time for anyone to have killed Abigail Cleve, sent the message, tidied up the scene, and then slipped away without Knowles seeing them.'

Shepherd nodded. 'In that case, let's wrap this up. Tensions are running high enough as it is with these impending protests and counter-protests this weekend. Both sides will be out in force and, regardless of the validity of anybody's arguments, none of them will lack for passion. With the potential for things to turn nasty, this is a distraction we don't need. We'll give Summer his head with this Estey, but if nothing comes of it we can sign off on this.' She paused. 'Agreed?'

From his desktop perch, Jejeune shrugged easily, and drifted back to his thoughts. By tomorrow they should have all the answers they needed to put this case to bed. It was just as well, she thought, since any further contributions seemed unlikely from a man whose mind was seven thousand miles away.

10

Though the garden at the rear of Bob Ferris's bungalow showed signs of once having been carefully tended, it was clear nothing had been done in a long time. Weeds had been allowed to grow unchecked between the cracks in the crazy paving pathways, and once-tidy flowerbeds had spilled over their boundaries into untidy tangles of poorly nourished vegetation. Jejeune and Summer stepped through a gap in the low brick wall that separated the garden from the road and followed a concrete path that had been graded into a gentle incline ending at a small patio beside the front door. As they waited for the doorbell to be answered, Jejeune saw Summer looking back along the ramp. It had risen no more than the height of two stone steps, but to the man who lived in the bungalow even those would now have been an insurmountable barrier. Jejeune could almost feel the flinch as Summer's mind recoiled from the thought.

'You're early.' Bob Ferris wheeled his chair back from the doorway to allow the two men to enter. 'By a few days, according to my calculations,' he said over his shoulder as he led the detectives along a narrow, empty hallway into his living room. Ferris wheeled to face the men, extending a hand to offer a seat on the low sofa. 'He comes here every six weeks or so,' he told Jejeune. 'On the special days. When was the last time?'

'The equinox,' Summer told him. 'In September. Can I get you anything? A cup of tea?' He half-rose from the sofa and began to reach for the machine on a fully stocked cart nearby, but Ferris patted him back into place.

'I can do it.' Ferris smiled at Jejeune. 'Like a mother hen,' he said, busying himself with making the tea. 'Comes here, makes me something to eat, tidies up.' He cast a glance around the sparsely furnished room, where everything had been laid out to provide clear wheelchair access to all corners. 'Not that the place needs it.'

'I visit on the eight auspicious days,' explained Summer. 'I like to make sure everything is in order for the coming of each new phase. It's important.'

Beneath the gathering weight of Ferris's fleshy features, Jejeune could see the shadows of world-weariness that life as a street cop brought. It was not the face of a man the DCI would have expected to have much tolerance for the auspicious days of the Druidic calendar. But Ferris seemed to accept his younger visitor's comment at face value. He reached to offer the cups to the men, but Summer sprang up to take them from him. Jejeune would have preferred coffee but he hadn't been consulted, and, since it would have been dispensed from a push-button machine anyway, it hardly mattered. 'Eight days?' Jejeune looked at Summer. 'The equinoxes, the solstices...'

'And the midpoints,' Summer told him. 'Imbolc, Beltane, Lughnasa and Samhain.'

'That's the one coming up, isn't it,' said Ferris, 'Samhain?'

'The traditional beginning of the dark half of the year. Ruled by the goddess known as the Dark Woman of Knowledge.'

Again, Jejeune searched the older man's features for any flicker of cynicism. Again he found none.

'But that's still some time away,' said Ferris. 'So what brings you out here today?'

'We're looking into the death of Abbie Cleve,' said Jejeune.

'Really?' Ferris looked at Summer. 'Interesting case you've landed yourself for your first one back, I must say.'

'The inspector said he didn't recognise her, so I told him you might be able to fill us in on the family history. I know you used to spend some time up at the estate.'

'I see.' Ferris was silent for a moment.

'It's not an investigation, Mr Ferris,' explained Jejeune. 'Just a few background inquiries.'

'Poor woman,' said Ferris. 'Imagine the demons she must have been battling to do something like that.' He slapped the side of his wheelchair with his hand. 'Puts this into perspective, eh?'

Putting things in perspective was what people said to minimise their own misfortunes. Jejeune took in the room with its subtle accommodations. A shelf had been installed beneath a window ledge to allow the plants to be watered from wheelchair height. In the bookcases on either side of the fireplace, the tattered paperbacks were arrayed only on the lower shelves, the upper ones reserved for framed photographs of family members and happier, outdoor days. Jejeune knew there would be many other adjustments throughout the house. Living independently would create challenges for Bob Ferris that the DCI couldn't even begin to anticipate. Perhaps the death of Abbie Cleve would put them into perspective, but it wouldn't alleviate them.

'The constable said you used to hunt with Jim Loyal up at the estate. We were wondering if you knew her.'

Jejeune's question caused Ferris to pause, but it did not seem like the act of a man trying to remember something. Perhaps a memory of a different kind had overtaken him; of a time when he was able to walk through the woodlands on shooting expeditions. 'Not personally, no,' he said eventually. He forced a smile as he dragged himself from the memory. 'I do know Jim always had to be sure he knew where she was before we set off, though. She used to like walking the grounds.' He shook his head sadly. 'He'll be devastated. He thought the world of those girls.'

'Do you know much about the rift in the family?' asked Summer. He cast a glance in Jejeune's direction to see if he wanted to take up the running, but he seemed content to let the other man continue. 'It involved a man named Estey. A local poacher.'

'I know they would have all liked to lay the blame at Pete Estey's feet up there at the estate,' said Ferris, nodding. 'Certainly, Old Man Cleve went to his grave claiming it was Estey that broke up the family. But in his heart he knew better. The solace of self-deception, my therapist calls it. You construct a version of events that you can live with, instead of dealing with what actually happened. In time, your created memory overwrites the truth when you think about the event. You can see why, though, in his case. It would be hard for any father to accept that his darling little girl had abandoned the family because she fancied a bit of rough.'

Ferris reached to set his cup on the cart, but it caught the rim and crashed to the floor, spilling the remnants of the tea on the carpet. Jejeune had leapt up reflexively before he even considered the implications. He seemed to realise it would now be more humiliating if he simply resumed his seat to watch Ferris's laboured efforts to clean up the mess himself. 'I'll get a cloth,' he said awkwardly, retrieving the fallen cup before disappearing into the kitchen.

He set the cup in the sink beside an unwashed plate, still holding the traces of last night's chicken dinner. Dark red streaks of ketchup had dried hard on the rim. Picking up the cup had been the right thing to do, he thought, as he dampened the dishcloth. It had fallen beyond Ferris's reach. He would have done the same thing for anybody. But he didn't need this episode to remind him that doing the right thing didn't necessarily make people feel any better about themselves. From the other room, he heard Danny Maik's name, and realised Ferris was speaking to Summer. 'If you turn out to be half the copper you're replacing, Saltmarsh station will have done all right by themselves. But are you sure you want to be doing this, on your first case back?'

Jejeune returned to the room carrying the wet cloth, and Ferris smiled in his direction. 'I was just saying, it seems like a waste of his talents, chasing Estey. I'm sure Tony Holland could have given him the once-over.' He reached over and patted Summer on the knee. 'I've told him before, this boy's got all he needs to go right to the top. He's in the right place now, too. Colleen Shepherd's a good, solid DCS, and then of course he's got you. Not sure what Tony Holland could teach him, other than how to find women and lose them twice as fast. I hear he's grown up a bit since he got back from London, though.'

Jejeune finished dabbing the carpet and stood up, setting the cloth on the tea trolley. It was clear that Ferris, like many ex-officers, still found himself drawn to the local police gossip. Jejeune couldn't imagine anything that would hold less interest for him if he ever decided to leave the service himself. 'You wouldn't know where we could find Estey, would you?' he asked.

'Last I heard he was living up near Stone Road.'

Jejeune looked puzzled. 'I'm not aware of any properties around there,' he said.

'Estey's living rough,' Ferris told him. 'He did a tour in Afghanistan. It wasn't kind to him. A war never returns the same people who went into it. How could it? Pete Estey was damaged goods when he came back. Not all ex-army types adjust to civvy life as well as Danny Maik.' He shook his head. 'A man with those qualities. It's a good job we didn't lose Danny to any war, eh, Inspector.'

'Estey has post-traumatic stress disorder?' asked Summer.

'He even tried hypnosis to help him.' Ferris pulled his lips into a grimace. 'Not that I could ever see it doing any good. It never did anything for me.'

'Those Stone Road woods border the Cleve estate on the north side, don't they?' Summer turned to Jejeune for confirmation, but his DCI's mind seemed to be elsewhere. 'That wouldn't be too far from the Nye. Is he living there because he was still in a relationship with Abbie Cleve?"

Ferris shook his head slowly. 'She ended that long ago,' he said. 'It was never likely to last between them. I suspect once she'd broken her ties with the estate, she decided her new life didn't have any place in it for Pete Estey after all.'

Summer looked at Jejeune again, but he still seemed lost in thought. 'As a gamekeeper, it'd be in Jim Loyal's best interests to know where a poacher like Estey was living these days, wouldn't it?'

Ferris moved his head slightly. 'Jim might know where he is. I don't see him much these days. 'Never been what you'd call a fan of the indoors, Jim, and, now that I don't get out so much any more, we've drifted apart.' He seemed to realise from Summer's sudden stillness that the comment had wounded him. 'That's not to say I can't get out when I want to,' he said brightly. 'As a matter of fact, I was thinking I might even try to get up to the estate's annual shoot this year.'

Jejeune's attention returned to the present. After his own earlier faux pas, he felt the need to relieve Ferris's obvious discomfort. He stood up. 'We should be going. We've taken up enough of your time today.'

'Not to worry. Time is the one thing I have plenty of these days.' Ferris seemed to regret this remark, too, as soon as he had uttered it. Jejeune smiled his sympathy. If someone felt guilt keenly enough, everything could seem like a reference to it, however veiled.

Ferris manoeuvred the wheelchair along the corridor, backing against the wall to give the detectives room to get past. As they reached the edge of the ramp, he called out to them. 'You know, it occurs to me – if Abbie Cleve did take her own life all because of a wrong decision she had made in the past, how terrible that would be. I mean, none of us would want our lives held to account over one past mistake, would we? Don't be a stranger, Inspector. Any time you've got a few minutes, if you'd like to drop by for a chat, it'd be nice to see you.'

Jejeune looked at Ferris, trying to decipher the reason for the unexpected invitation. But Ferris's pale, unshaven face revealed only the same look of forced good cheer that they had seen throughout their visit. It was still there when he closed the door.

11

The view from Guy Trueman's penthouse office would have been stunning anyway but, to a man who had only been shuffled between a windowless cell and a sterile interview room for the past few days, it was quite literally mesmerising. Maik took a couple of moments to drink in the sweeping vista over Singapore's civic district. Towering structures folded into dramatic curves that seemed to defy the laws of gravity. Concrete canopies appeared to float through space. Banks of windows glittered from all directions in the bright morning sun. Maik had never really considered himself a fan of big cities, but it surprised him to realise just how much he had missed the dynamic appeal of an urban setting.

'For the record, I have strongly advised my client against this meeting,' said Selena Lim.

Trueman acknowledged the statement without comment.

'And obviously, nothing that my client says here today, either in my presence or otherwise, can be used in evidence. Nothing,' she emphasised.

'Don't worry, sweetheart. Anything said in here will stay within these four walls.'

Lim flashed Trueman a glance, but said nothing. She had bigger dragons to slay than the condescending terminology of an ageing ladies' man. 'There's some evidence that Titus Chupul had a burner phone,' she said. 'I wondered if perhaps you had the number.'

Trueman shook his head without checking. 'I might have received a call or two from it over the years, but he's not somebody I'd have in my contacts list.' He raised his arm in a slow steady sweep and consulted a heavy Rolex of the type favoured by officers, both military and police. 'Danny and I have twenty minutes, I believe. There's a hawker food court down on the corner. They do a nice bowl of *mie goreng*. A bit on the lively side, but you strike me as somebody who could handle her spice.'

'I'll wait in the corridor.' She turned to leave, smoothing the back of her skirt, as if to divert the lingering gaze she suspected would accompany her departure.

'Your reputation precedes you,' said Maik as the door closed behind her.

'I'm a reformed character now, Danny. One-woman man. Foreign girl. You'd like her. No kids, though.' Trueman shook his head. 'Might be a bit of an ask, these days, if I'm being honest. For me, at least.'

Maik regarded Trueman carefully. He had the same upright military bearing he remembered, and the same understated self-confidence. The tan he had acquired suited his lean features well. He still looked fit and well toned. Whatever police–military liaison involved, it obviously required Guy Trueman to keep up a rigorous training regimen.

'I can't offer you a drink. They were very clear about that. Water only. And no food either.' He shrugged. 'You know what it's like, they lose a battle, so they pile on the petty conditions to show they're still in charge. Pathetic, really. Still, we've managed our face-to-face, at last.'

It was the reason Maik had come to Singapore. Now that he was in a stable relationship of his own and his life had a forward purpose, it had seemed more important to him to rebuild some past bridges. But though he and Trueman had corresponded by email, this was the first time they had met since the latter had left the UK under the darkest of dark clouds. The last time Danny had seen Trueman, he was bringing about his former CO's resignation from a top security position for negligence in a murder inquiry. He had steeled himself for some lingering residue of the incident, but, like his looks, Trueman's easygoing personality seemed to have survived the intervening years intact.

Maik looked around the lavishly appointed office, taking in the polished wood furniture and large impressionist paintings. Colleen Shepherd had a couple like this on her walls. Maik had never cared for them. He liked a bit of clarity in his art, not something that could be anything you wanted it to be, depending on your point of view. But these works undoubtedly wouldn't have been cheap. 'Not exactly a hardship posting out here, then,' he said.

'For years now, the Singapore police force have had a policy of recruiting Nepali Gurkhas once their military service is over. I use my connections to find the most suitable candidates, and then make the arrangements to get them here. The Singapore police take over from there. I get a nice bungalow up in the Dover highlands, a decent salary and some sunshine. They get elite ex-military personnel.'

Maik acknowledged the wisdom of the policy with a faint nod of his head. The Gurkhas were among the finest fighting forces in the world. Their courage and discipline were legendary. 'So why am I here, Guy?' He nodded towards the window. 'Not that I'm not grateful for the change of scenery.' He was aware that today's meeting had only come about because Trueman had been able to overcome major objections from the police. His ex-CO had never been one to expend energies like that without good reason.

'Your lawyer has made an application to get you into protective custody.' Trueman shook his head gravely. 'It's not going to happen.'

Maik's expression suggested he'd already reached the same conclusion. The police wanted his confession, and they thought keeping him in among the general prison population might help them get it. Both men in this room knew it wouldn't.

Through the glass pane in his office door, Trueman watched Lim as she paced back and forth along the corridor, a mobile phone pressed to her ear. 'Might come as a shock to her. I imagine she's used to getting her own way. I mean, let's face it, be hard to say no to a pair of legs like that, wouldn't it?'

Clearly the reformation of Trueman's character was a work in progress. 'I think there's a bit more to her than that,' said Danny.

'All I'm saying is she obviously knows how to use what she has to get what she wants. Take this case, for example; she lets it be known that she'd be interested and, hey presto, look who's ended up with it.'

It was the second time Maik had heard that his lawyer had specifically requested to represent him. He didn't know if Trueman had brought him here to tell him why, but in his current circumstances, it didn't seem likely he was going to get an explanation from anywhere else.

'Are you saying I should get different counsel?'

'I'm saying there's not a lawyer in Singapore that could get you off these charges. The good ones would know better than to try.'

'All I care about at the moment is that she's asking the right questions. There's a lot that's not right about this, Guy. That man shouldn't have died from the way I hit him. Not somebody with his conditioning.'

Trueman moved his shoulders easily. 'Perhaps you don't know your own strength these days. We get a bit older, maybe we feel the need to overcompensate. At our age, it's the speed that goes first, you know that. The power tends to stick around a bit longer.' He gave it some thought. 'Coming up sudden like that, a bloke who looked like he could handle himself? It'd be more surprising if you hadn't given it a bit extra. I know I would have. Especially if he was carrying, as you claim.'

Not *said*, thought Danny. The word suggested Trueman hadn't fully bought into Maik's account about the knife. Or was this just his old CO trying to keep a foot in each camp, as he normally did?

'If there were any underlying health issues, a well-placed strike could have done for him,' said Trueman. 'This bloke, Chupul, he liked a drink now and then. Plus he was a smoker...'

'You knew him?'

'I ran across him from time to time. His missus is in charge of some birds the Gurkha regiments use as mascots. Pheasants; Monals, I think they're called. Bit of a morale booster for the lads far from home. Chupul did what you used to do, train the young 'uns. Lacked the finesse you had, though. More BFI with him; brute force and ignorance. Bash them all into the same mould, instead of showing a bit of flexibility here and there to get a better end result. That said, his approach did have its successes. Ronnie Gunn turned out okay, for example. He was one of his. I gave him that name, by the way. Chitron Gunteng, Ron Gunn. Ronnie. Couldn't be anything else, could it? He seems to like it, anyway. That's all he goes by, these days.'

'He seems eager to get this over in a hurry.'

Trueman nodded. 'That'll be for the widow. He knows her. He stayed with them when he first came here from Nepal.'

'Gunn is a friend of the family?'

'It's not that unusual. Half the lads I've brought in have stayed with local Nepali families.'

'He has to recuse himself from his role as liaison, though, surely?'

'He's in no position to influence the case, Danny. They don't need him, frankly, they've got you bang to rights on this one. Eight people saw Chupul fall after you hit him. He never got up again.'

He approached Maik and sat on the corner of the desk. It was a posture Maik's former DCI had often adopted and, for a fleeting moment, Danny's mind was transported to the Incident Room at Saltmarsh station. The lights, the sounds, the easy familiarity of the surroundings; they all rushed in on him like a warm embrace. But the vision flickered into nothingness as quickly as it had appeared, and he was back here, in this room, half a world away, with another of his old bosses apparently about to deliver some cold, hard truths.

'A knife like that,' said Trueman, 'be worth a good bit to the right collector. Some of the types that hang around the Geylang, maybe they wouldn't be averse to lifting a kukri in all that confusion if they saw one lying around. It's probably on eBay already.'

'No knife matching that description has been listed for sale on any of the major online sites since the incident,' Maik told him. 'My lawyer checked.'

Trueman raised his eyebrows in what might have been a sign of approval. 'Danny, if you say Titus Chupul came at you with a kukri, I believe you. You say the love-tap you gave him shouldn't have put him down for the count, I'll accept that too. But the truth has no place here. All that matters is whether a jury will believe you killed an unarmed man. And with the evidence the prosecution has got, they will. Listen, that business back in the UK, that's behind us now, water under the bridge. This is me, your old CO, telling you a plea is your best option.'

Maik looked out over the dazzling modern cityscape again. Profusions of carefully manicured green foliage punctuated the relentless man-made busyness like deep breaths. Though he had fought for it in a general sense, Danny had never really given much thought to his own liberty. Like most cherished things, it was only the prospect of losing it that had brought it into clear focus for him. For the first time, the reality that he might go to prison settled on him; not the fact of it, but what the consequences would be. The loss of his career, and the stigma of a conviction afterwards, on the basis of a confession to a killing he hadn't committed. Lauren would say she'd wait, but he wouldn't permit that. He'd end it the day he was incarcerated. She deserved someone who wasn't followed around by the taint of shame he would carry when he came out. So did Max.

'This lawyer of yours,' said Trueman, intruding into Maik's thoughts, 'have you asked yourself why she pushed so hard for this case? I imagine you think it's because having her picture all over the news is the best form of publicity any new lawyer can hope for. I mean, let's just say for the sake of argument she's already accepted what everybody else knows – that she hasn't got a snowball in Singapore's chance of getting you off. Still, to see her out there every day, battling away on behalf of her hapless client, what's the first name that's going to spring to mind later if you're a defendant with a fighting chance?'

Maik said nothing. Trueman always did like an audience, and it never did any harm to let him hold court. Like most people who covered a lot of ground, he sometimes told you more than he intended.

'Only, I'm not sure that's all there is to it in this case, Danny. A little firecracker like that is always going to land on her feet. And that's because she plans where she's going long before she gets there. All I know is, if this doesn't end up going your way when it's all said and done, you're going to have a lot more to lose than she does.'

There was a warning in Trueman's look, but it didn't linger. In an instant, the familiar easy smile was back in place as he gestured to Selena in the corridor and motioned her in.

'You still have a few minutes,' she said.

'That's all right,' Trueman told her. 'I think Danny and I have covered all we need to.'

'Before we leave, Mr Trueman, it really might help Danny's defence if we could locate Chupul's burner phone. You wouldn't have committed the number to memory, by any chance?'

Trueman shrugged. 'Do you know anyone who memorises phone numbers these days, love? It is a lost skill, gone the way of happy endings and fairness and all those other dreams of a better life Danny and me had before we knew any better.' He turned to his old sergeant. 'It's been good to see you, Danny. Remember, don't let your guard down. And promise me you'll think about what I said.'

12

It was so out of character for Domenic Jejeune to be late for a morning briefing that Colleen Shepherd actually checked her own watch as she entered the Incident Room to make sure it wasn't her timing that was off. 'No DCI Jejeune yet?'

Holland shook his head. 'I know he's in the building, though. He was already in his office when I got here.'

'Then I imagine he'll be along any minute to grace us with his presence.' Shepherd looked out at the eager faces of the junior officers scattered among the desks before taking in the two detective constables on the opposite sides of the room. Noel Summer was leaning against the wall once again, shoulders slightly forward, thumbs tucked loosely into his waistband. He looked about as relaxed as it was possible to be. Standing across from him, Tony Holland appeared anything but. With his splayed-legged stance and folded arms, he looked ready for a fight. Clearly, he was not expecting today's update to be a meeting of the minds. Shepherd took one more glance into the corridor for an approaching Domenic Jejeune. Finding it empty, she decided to press on. 'I believe we were going to have a look into the victim's financial position. To see if there was a possible motive for her seeking access to the family fortune.'

'There are enough funds in her accounts to suggest otherwise,' offered Summer. He nodded to a junior officer, who clicked a remote, sending an array of spreadsheets up onto the whiteboard behind Shepherd. He gave them a moment to digest the contents. 'As you can see, there was no financial motive for Abigail Cleve to seek readmittance to the family.'

'This doesn't prove anything,' said Holland dismissively. 'For all we know, she could have been planning a major expansion.' He shot Shepherd a glance as if to remind her of his earlier comment about Summer. The look she gave him in return let him know he hadn't entirely made his own case, either. She believed she understood the reason for Holland's hostility towards the new detective, but pointless obstructionism like this wasn't doing anything for Shepherd's mood.

'Weren't you going to speak to that LSA inspector?' she asked.

Holland shifted his stance slightly. 'Evan Knowles. Yeah, I couldn't reach him directly, but he did forward a copy of the email that prompted him to schedule the visit. And somebody in the LSA offices was able to confirm that a visit could sometimes be a prelude to a closure. So, you know, the theory still holds. A woman under pressure. Sees no other way out.'

Summer eased himself upright. 'Knowles told me that visit was in response to an anonymous complaint.' He waited until it became clear Holland wasn't going to respond. 'And we know there had never been a previous inspection.'

Shepherd nodded. 'So, unless the LSA is in the habit of threatening operations with imminent closure based solely on unsubstantiated complaints from anonymous members of the public, it doesn't seem likely that an impending visit from Evan Knowles would be enough to drive Abigail Cleve to suicide.'

'I'm not sure we can make that assumption, ma'am,' said Holland. 'She might not have been the most grounded of people. There are indications that she had a tendency towards the overly, er… *self-absorbed*.'

Shepherd rolled her eyes. Holland was obviously unsure where references to vanity were on the PC scale these days. She could sympathise. She could hardly keep up herself.

'Constable Holland believes the clue is in the name,' offered Summer. He turned to Holland. 'Something about her birthdate, wasn't it?' His wide-eyed innocence wasn't fooling anyone, but Shepherd was intrigued enough to pursue the point anyway.

'Tony?

'She was born on New Year's Eve,' he said reluctantly, 'so to go and name the place the NYE to commemorate it, I just think it shows she was a bit full of herself, that's all.'

From NYE to narcissism? Summer was clearly not the only one susceptible to a charge of trying too hard. Summer's attempt at payback by bringing up this nonsense was perhaps understandable, given the hostile reception he'd received from Holland thus far, but this kind of antagonism between them wasn't going to help the investigation. Especially when they were the only ones contributing anything at all at the moment. She checked the corridor again, and found it still empty.

'Go and put a rocket under the DCI, will you, Tony,' she said irritably. 'Remind him that, as splendidly as we're progressing without him, his contributions might still be welcome.'

As he left, she turned to Summer. 'So that just leaves Estey. Any joy there?'

'Bob Ferris suggested a possible location for him, over near the Stone Road woods. I'm heading over there later. Erm…' The room waited. Perhaps Summer could be excused for not knowing that Shepherd had a particularly low tolerance for prevarication, but her look suggested he would need to learn fast. 'This location, it's not far from the Nye.

According to Bob Ferris, it was over long ago between Estey and the victim, but…'

'*But…* indeed.' Shepherd nodded thoughtfully. 'What did DCI Jejeune make of all this?

'His mind seemed to be on other things, to be honest,' said Summer. He hesitated once more. 'Er… there is one other thing, ma'am. I had Abigail Cleve's phone analysed. Only, I might have given the impression it had been authorised at a higher level.'

Amid a general stirring among the others in the room, Shepherd raised her eyebrows in his direction. 'As well it might have been, Constable, had you come to one of your senior officers first. I take it you're not confessing simply because you're racked with guilt. Was there anything of interest on the phone?'

'I didn't have the data analysed, only the physical phone. But yes. Forensics found minute traces of silicone on the keypad.'

'A stylus?'

'They think so, yes. But this model doesn't come with one. Not only that, the traces were on top of the fingerprint oils, and…'

There was a sound at the doorway and Jejeune entered, smiling a sheepish apology. 'Sorry, I was just checking into something.'

'A rare bird?' inquired Shepherd frostily.

Jejeune inclined his head in that way of his when he didn't particularly want to go into details. 'Constable Holland tells me there's nothing to warrant further investigation, at least.'

Was it Shepherd's imagination, or did he seem relieved? 'Constable Summer might beg to differ,' she said. 'Forensics found traces of stylus use on the keypad of Abigail Cleve's phone.' She extended a hand to Summer to invite him to continue.

'The thing is, these traces were only found on the letter keys used in the message. *Please tell everyone I am sorry for all the suffering I have caused. Goodbye.* There's no evidence of stylus use on the keys for j, k, q, w, x or z.'

'They're not the most common letters,' said Jejeune uncomfortably.

'W? K? How much texting could you do without using those?' asked Shepherd in a tone that suggested she was losing patience with all these petty objections. 'It's enough to go on, at least for me. I'm prepared to reclassify the death as suspicious.' She turned to Summer. 'This is very good work, Constable. Outstanding. Right, we need to speak to the coroner.'

'That's going to be an awkward conversation,' said Jejeune. 'I already informed the coroner's office we had no objections to a finding of suicide.'

The two senior officers stared at each other like gladiators. 'I was under the impression we'd agreed to wait for answers on Estey, the financials, the LSA visit?' said Shepherd carefully.

Jejeune seemed surprised. 'Had we? I thought we'd concluded we could close it out.'

The strength of Shepherd's willpower was never more evident than when she was visibly attempting to suppress her anger. 'Yes, after twenty-four hours. You were here when I gave Summer the directive to look into Estey, for God's sake.'

'But our conversation came after that. Once Bob Ferris had put Estey in the clear, there was no reason to continue the investigation.'

It was not Shepherd's normal practice to express her displeasure with senior officers in front of the rank and file, but something in Jejeune's calm, unapologetic tone caused her frustration to boil over. 'In the first place, I'm not at all sure Ferris did put Estey in the clear. Did he not tell you Estey now lives less than half a mile from where the body of his former lover was found? Did you not find that something worth pursuing?' She raised her hands furiously. 'Bloody hell, Domenic, you've made us look like we don't know what we're doing here.' She turned to Holland. 'Contact the mortuary right now and inform them we will, after all, need a forensic autopsy as part of a criminal investigation into the death of Abigail Cleve.'

The room waited in uncomfortable silence as Holland made the call. He ended it and looked at Shepherd with something approaching reluctance to inform her of his news. 'The body, ma'am. The funeral director from Allford's has already been in to collect it.'

'What?' asked Shepherd incredulously. 'How is that possible?'

'Some cock-up with the paperwork.' He hesitated. 'Erm, it seems to have come from our end, ma'am.'

Shepherd rounded on Jejeune. 'Wasn't it you that completed those forms?' She held up a hand to still Jejeune's response and turned to Summer. 'You need to get over to Allford's and have them return the body to the mortuary immediately,' she said urgently.

'Can't I just call them?' asked Holland.

'No thank you. We've had quite enough human error for one day.' She turned to Summer. 'Allford's Funeral Parlour, Constable. Quick as you like. You know where it is?'

Summer nodded his confirmation and left hurriedly. Silence returned, settling over the Incident Room like a layer of ice. None of the junior officers seemed willing to look at either Shepherd or Jejeune. Holland's were the only eyes upon them as Shepherd turned to leave. In place of her customary end-of-briefing dismissal, she had a single directive, for one individual.

'My office, Domenic. Now.'

13

Jejeune stared out at the rolling fields beyond the window of Colleen Shepherd's office. It was a view he had taken in many times. Sometimes the sunlight beckoned, lying over the low landscape like a bewitching promise of escape. On other occasions, veils of soft rain drifted in from the coast, swirling into windswept dances over the open fields. The reasons for his visits to this office had been equally varied: to receive praise for a job well done, or to lament a shared failure. But never had he been called in here to discuss his own competence. It had never been necessary. Until now.

Shepherd shut off her phone and looked at him directly. 'According to the mortuary, you misspelled the surname on the admitting form. You added an "a".'

'That's the way Cleave is spelled,' protested Jejeune.

'Over here, it can be either. It's not an uncommon name in these parts, with either spelling. Additionally, though, you transposed the names in the first and middle name boxes: Margaret, Abigail, instead of the other way round. There was already a Margaret Cleave awaiting a release notification from the coroner.'

'Don't they assign file numbers to avoid this kind of... thing?' he asked.

'They try not to revert to them unless they have to. They feel it dehumanises the individual. As you may be aware, there's a lot of scrutiny about treating bodies in police custody with appropriate dignity these days.' She turned a steely look on him. 'Frankly, they don't expect us to make these kinds of mistakes.' She paused and looked out of the window before returning her gaze to him. 'I can't have it, Domenic. With Danny no longer here, and Lauren Salter off on what is effectively compassionate leave, you being out in the ether leaves me with exactly no senior detectives at all. Not to mention I've got a new officer in serious need of some support, but receiving none whatsoever from either you or Tony Holland. Whether you agree or not that Noel Summer is on the right track, he at least deserves the courtesy of having his theories considered, and not just being summarily dismissed.'

'I know. It's just…'

'I know what it is. I suppose I can safely assume this *something* you were checking out earlier wasn't on this continent?'

'I was trying to get direct access to Danny. I told the Singapore authorities we needed his input about a new officer we had employed. I said he was familiar with him from an earlier case.'

'And?'

'And they told me any relevant observations he had made would be in the case file.'

Shepherd nodded. 'Which is exactly what I would have expected them to say. A file that, I might add, you have no earthly reason to consult. So let's put an end to this nonsense now, shall we?'

'I can't sit here and do nothing. It's not looking good for Danny. The evidence against him is piling up. And it's beginning to look irrefutable.'

'Don't you think we all feel this way? We can't help him, Domenic. Of course we all want to. But we can't. As I said, we have to trust in the investigative process.'

Jejeune looked unconvinced. 'The problem is, they're basing everything on the evidence. They're not looking at the rest of it, who he is. The Danny Maik we know doesn't even fit this profile.'

'Are you listening to yourself, Domenic? The evidence is the only guide to what happened, at least for us mere mortals. Unless we believe the evidence can lead us to the truth, the entire criminal investigation system crumbles away. Evidence has to be the basis of all we do, or we have nothing, save a vague mist of impressions and personal opinions. We can't simply tell them what we know in our heart to be true: that Danny Maik is a good man, who would never in a million years kill someone in cold blood.' She slammed her hands on the desk, and drew a breath to gather herself. 'Yes, it's terrible, and I'm pushing as far up the ladder as I can to see if anything can be done, but I'm afraid we have to accept that it's out of our hands at the moment. In the meantime, we have a job to do here, and it's that I need you to be focusing your efforts on. You might start with Lindy. See if she has any insights into Abigail Cleve. After all, she did interview her a few months back.'

'Did she?'

Shepherd sighed exasperatedly. Was he really so preoccupied that he'd forgotten even this? 'Yes, Domenic, she did. Something about the first anniversary of the pheasant farming operation and how well it was doing.'

Holland knocked on the door but didn't wait to be summoned before entering. 'Call from Summer, ma'am. He says he can't find Allford's.'

'Can't find it?' It hadn't escaped her notice that Holland had brought this news personally, rather than leaving the desk sergeant to call her. 'Doesn't he have a GPS in his car?'

'In that crappy old Trabant he drives? He doesn't even have Bluetooth. He'd have been better off taking his broomstick.'

'He's a Druid, Tony, not a warlock. And since Druidism is now officially recognised as a religion, I wonder if it might be time to start affording it the respect it deserves.'

'My profound apologies,' said Holland with the heartfelt sincerity of an officer who wanted to avoid another weekend cultural sensitivity course. 'I'll send him a peace offering. Perhaps I can get him some of that woad they're growing out by Dereham. His mob used to use it to paint their faces blue, didn't they?'

'That was the Picts, I believe,' said Jejeune.

'Also not Druids,' confirmed Shepherd in answer to Holland's puzzled look. 'Call him, Tony, and give him directions.'

She looked at Jejeune as Holland left. 'God help us if the family get to hear of this. Releasing the body for funeral prep and then recalling it. It will be a bloody PR disaster. Google "Police Insensitivity" after this and it will be the first hit that comes up.'

Holland re-entered, staring at a text from his phone. He looked at them, wide-eyed. 'He's on the north side of the river.'

'What?' shouted Shepherd with exasperation. 'Allford's moved from that location a couple of years ago. Does he even know where the new one is?'

'I told him. But the bridge is up to let the boats through now. He's looking at about fifteen minutes at least before he can get across. Only, the thing is ma'am, the funeral director picked up that body this morning. He must be about to begin preparing it any time now, if he hasn't already started.'

'Call him,' said Shepherd urgently. 'We need to stop that process immediately.'

'I did, ma'am. Nobody's picking up.'

Shepherd grabbed her car keys. 'Domenic, with me,' she said as she began running along the corridor. 'We can get there faster than Summer if we take the back roads. We just have to hope the director hasn't got to that body yet.'

The high hedgerows passed in a green blur as Shepherd sped along the country lanes. Despite having been her passenger in other high-speed drives over the years, Jejeune could never remember seeing the kind of recklessness she was showing today. Her cavalier attitude towards crossroads and yield signs would have been unnerving enough in a vehicle with lights and alarms flashing. In an unmarked burgundy Jaguar XF, it represented a level of risk that he would have had trouble justifying in other circumstances. But perhaps equally unnerving was the way Shepherd seemed able to carry on a conversation as casually as if she was sitting beside him on a living-room couch.

'I have to say, that knowledge about the Picts was very impressive, Domenic, even for you. The body art of ninth-century British tribes is not something I'd have expected to come up in the Canadian school curriculum.'

'I've been looking into early British belief systems,' he told her, grasping at a dashboard as she steered around a pothole at speed. 'I wanted to understand more about their views on the Earth's cycles and the forces that control them.'

Shepherd raised her eyebrows. 'Are you considering converting?'

Jejeune shook his head. 'I was wondering what Summer had picked up at the scene that could have convinced him so quickly that this wasn't a suicide.'

'Perhaps it was just good detective work. Like this business of the phone keypad. You have to admit, that's impressive, albeit, unauthorised.'

The inference that Jejeune had not been around to give his consent wasn't lost on him. 'Trying too hard can be a dangerous thing in this line of work,' he said. 'It's easy to read signs that aren't there.'

A blind curve banked more sharply than Shepherd had anticipated and the Jaguar skidded onto the gravel at the side of the road. She whiplashed a correction of the steering wheel and the car catapulted back onto its line, the rear end rocking as the tyres found purchase on the hard surface again. She readjusted her grip on the steering wheel and risked a momentary sidelong glance. 'It can also produce results, Domenic. Don't tell me you still don't believe there is something suspicious about this death?'

'I'm not saying that. I'm just wondering why Summer has fastened on to Pete Estey in the way he has. What does he have that the rest of us don't? What else does he know?'

She put her foot down as a village hove into view in the distance, causing another slight shimmer in the car's rear. It occurred to her that if Domenic had concentrated his recent efforts on the case at hand rather than on his colleagues, past and present, they might not have found themselves hurtling through the north Norfolk countryside like this.

He seemed to read her thoughts. 'I got this wrong,' he said as the small cluster of buildings loomed ever closer. 'There have been things about this case from the start that I should have looked at more closely. I'm not sure they add up to murder, but at the very least they should have been eliminated.'

'I'm not asking you to apologise, Domenic, only to do your job. Forgetting meetings, misinterpreting directives. Even pairing two constables who hardly seem to be getting along like a house on fire to deliver a notice of decease to Libby Cleve. You should have handled something as sensitive as that yourself, especially if there were questions about the death.'

'There weren't,' said Jejeune. 'At least, not at the time.'

'But there clearly are now,' said Shepherd. 'Oh God, don't tell me this means what I think it means.' She had wheeled the XF into the car park at such speed the tyres squealed in protest, causing an inattentive pedestrian to flinch and glower at the car. But by the time the chassis had rocked to a stop, Shepherd suspected there was no need for them to exit the car with equal haste. The pedestrian had just finished locking the doors to the funeral parlour as they arrived, and was now reaching for his own car keys and heading to the only other vehicle in the car park.

Jejeune got out and spoke briefly with the man as she watched. He was shaking his head in her direction even before he reached the Jaguar again. Shepherd banged the leather steering wheel with her hand as he got back in the car. 'Damn it. Why the hell didn't Summer say if he didn't know where he was going?'

'He thought he did. The Allford's location on the far side of the river would still have been in operation the last time he was around these parts,' he said simply.

'So that's it, then,' said Shepherd. She started the car but didn't put it in gear. Instead, she stared at the funeral parlour for a long moment. 'Any evidence that might have existed on that body has now been compromised or removed entirely.'

'There could still be toxicology, stomach contents.'

She shook her head. 'The chain of custody has been broken. Nothing we took from that body, either externally or internally, would be admissible in any case we brought. And without it, I don't see how we could ever prove a crime had been committed.'

Jejeune's expression suggested he might not agree. She knew he felt his distraction had been a disservice to everyone associated with this case. He would want to make amends. But surely, with this kind of a handicap, proving what had happened to Abigail Cleve was a step too far even for him. Wasn't it?

14

As she paused before the gates of the Mount Vernon Camp, Selena Lim reflected on the nature of incarceration. A couple of the long-term prisoners she had met had told her it was all a state of mind. Certainly, the people behind this ten-foot-high fence could come and go as they pleased. But they could hardly be said to be free. Their access and exit points were carefully monitored by security guards. Activities and behaviour permitted in other parts of Singapore without a second thought were forbidden behind this barbed-wire wall. But the people did not seem bowed by the limits to their liberty. They went about their daily lives, greeting their neighbours, pursuing their tasks, as if they had all the freedom in the world. It was a stark contrast to Danny Maik, whose own imprisonment seemed to be gnawing deeper into his soul every time she saw him.

The unsmiling guard admitted her but, though he kept his eyes averted as he escorted her through the compound, others did not. The close-knit Nepali community was in mourning for one of its fallen members, and she was tasked with defending the man charged with causing his death. Children stopped playing football as she passed, women ceased their conversations; all watched her in silence. It was with genuine relief that she reached the lobby of the apartment building she was heading for.

The heavy iron grille protecting the entrance to the apartment was already open when she arrived. A tall, statuesque woman stood inside. 'I am Iniya, Devina's friend. This is my home. She is staying here with me for a few days.' She led Lim into a spacious living room. In a chair by an open window sat a small woman with bright eyes and flawless skin drawn tightly over elegant cheekbones. She was wearing a shawl, despite the heat.

Devina Chupul greeted Selena with that particular kind of gentle smile that seemed to be the shared property of Nepali people everywhere. 'Please sit,' she said. 'Iniya will bring us tea.'

The other woman disappeared into the kitchen and Devina tracked her departure with her gaze. 'We are from the same village back home,' she told Lim. 'We have known each other for many years. She does not wish me to be alone at the moment.'

'Perhaps that's wise,' said Selena. 'Enduring friendships are what sustain us through difficult times.'

She thought about Danny Maik and how little he seemed to have been consoled by his visit to Trueman. He had been so withdrawn and thoughtful on the journey back, he had barely remembered to bid her goodbye when they arrived at the police station.

'I appreciate your agreeing to meet me today, Ms Chupul. Please understand, I am not trying to make things more difficult for you. My job is to make sure my client receives the justice he deserves. I am only interested in finding out the truth of what happened.'

Devina nodded softly. 'There are questions. This I know.' She nodded her head again. 'Ronnie keeps me informed, though I think he doesn't share everything. He, too, is trying to protect me.'

She retreated into a comfortable silence. It was clear she was waiting for Iniya to join them before continuing the conversation. Perhaps it was simply a Nepali courtesy, but assuring an independent witness at a meeting such as this would have been an astute move anyway. Selena looked around the room. The dark furniture and polished wooden floors seemed somehow appropriate for the solemnity of the circumstances. From a small ornate pot in a corner, incense sticks released thin wraiths of pungent smoke to curl heavenward. Iniya returned to the room with a silver tray bearing tea and a small bowl of fruits: rambutan, lychees, mandarin oranges. She set it on the table and began to pour the pale liquid into tiny cups with no handles.

Selena took the proffered teacup in both hands and held it in her lap. 'It is kind of you to let your friend stay here,' she told Iniya. The woman inclined her head. There was no hint of unfriendliness, but it was clear that she wasn't going to be contributing anything to today's discussion between her friend and the woman defending her husband's killer.

'I will return home soon,' Devina told Lim. 'To be with my birds.'

'The monals, you mean? The mascots of the Ghurkha regiment?'

'Guy Trueman has agreed to continue the contract for now. The police survivor's pension would be generous for Nepal, but here it is not even enough to live on,' said Devina.

For a moment Lim thought she saw the shadow of something else behind the woman's sorrow, but it passed before she could identify it. 'I didn't see any birds on my way in here,' she said. 'Or even anywhere to keep them, come to think of it.'

'Pets are not allowed at Mount Vernon. I told the authorities my birds are proud symbols of the Nepali people, our national bird. But they said it would set a precedent. So instead I have a smallholding up in Kranji. While I am staying here, I go there each day to tend to them.' A brief smile ended the topic. 'I am curious about your client, Ms Lim,' Devina said. 'Ronnie says that perhaps he is not a bad man.'

Selena leaned forward to sip her tea, but she didn't sit back afterwards. A woven, multicoloured shawl like the one Devina was wearing was draped over the chair back, and she was keen to avoid resting against it. 'I think there is a great deal of good in him.'

'And yet he will not admit his guilt. Why is this? There are many witnesses to what he did.'

'I can tell you he is very sorry about what happened.'

'He is sorry? Is not a confession merely another kind of apology?'

'In the legal world, it means accepting you are guilty of the crime you are charged with,' Lim said gently. 'My client is not denying he and your husband fought, but he maintains he didn't strike him hard enough to kill him. Certainly that was not his intention. Perhaps we will know more after the autopsy.'

The answer seemed to satisfy Devina and she nodded softly.

'My client says when your husband… approached him, he was carrying a knife,' said Lim.

Outside, the sound of children playing soccer came to them through the open window. Devina seemed to take a moment to listen to it. 'Ronnie told me this also. A kukri.' She sighed wistfully and looked at Iniya. 'These knives hold a great significance for the Gurkha people. Like much else, they remind us of our homeland.'

'Did your husband possess one?'

Devina nodded. 'A ceremonial one. It is at his family home in Pokhara. He gave it to his mother when we came here.' She thought for a moment. 'It has been a long time since I saw that knife. Or my own family back in Nepal.'

'Will you go back now, when this is all over?'

Devina shook her head. 'I cannot. It was always Titus's wish to remain here. He will be buried here. I cannot leave him alone. It will be my duty to stay with him.'

Selena was silent as she explored subtle ways to introduce her new point. She sighed as she abandoned the pursuit. 'The nature of your husband's work. It involved violence,' she said.

Iniya's face remained impassive, but a soft tut escaped from her lips. Outside, the noise of the children playing football had stopped. Selena realised that, despite it being a compound teeming with people going about their daily lives, she could now hear no noise at all outside this cool, dark apartment. It was as if they were all listening in through the open windows, trying to hear Devina Chupul's answer.

'Violence was part of his job. Perhaps also his nature.'

Again, a flicker of something passed behind the words, and again Selena Lim failed to identify it. 'Did your husband ever mention the name Danny Maik? My client feels your husband came there that day to attack him but, since he did not know him, he has no idea why.'

'Perhaps violence does not always need a reason,' said Devina Chupul. And in that moment, Selena Lim realised what it was that she could sense behind the woman's sadness: the guilt that would haunt her all her days, the shame Devina Chupul felt at her relief of being freed from a violent man. Selena hesitated on the edge of taking the point any further, but she looked into the woman's eyes and she knew that even without her friend sitting beside her, Devina Chupul would never dishonour the memory of her departed husband with accusations against which he could no longer defend himself. She knew that to push further would end today's interview. She let the matter rest.

'Why did you come today, Ms Lim?' asked Devina.

'Tomorrow is an important day in the trial. It is the Criminal Mentions appearance. There will be a chance at the end of it for my client to plead guilty. I came here to tell you he will not.'

'Ah.' The woman nodded slowly. 'This is something that Ronnie did not tell me. This is your advice to your client?'

'It is his wish.'

'You say it is your job to ensure your client receives the justice he deserves, but perhaps justice, too, has a different meaning in the legal world.'

'It means receiving what is deserved, exactly that to which he is entitled. No more, but no less, either.'

Devina Chupul nodded slowly and gave another soft smile. 'Ah yes, how can justice deliver anything else and be worthy of the name? Punishment of the innocent is not justice, is it, Ms Lim? If your client truly believes he is innocent, then he can follow no other path. Can you tell him this? From me?'

'I'll tell him,' said Selena. 'Thank you for your time.'

She stood up to leave and Iniya stood with her. At the doorway, she leaned forward and spoke softly to Selena. 'In our culture, life is not a linear progression to a final ending. For us, it is samsara, the endless cycle of death and rebirth. The word karma has been much misunderstood since the West took it for its own, but past wrongs must be corrected, Ms Lim, past debts must be paid, if they are not to be carried into the future.' She leaned closer. 'Please tell your client this, also.' She went back inside and closed the door with a soft click.

Outside the building, Lim waited for a moment to gather herself. Despite the courteous tone, she had found the woman's comments unnerving. She left the estate and walked briskly along Mount Vernon Road, feeling the same sense of unease she'd experienced when she was being escorted through the compound. As she waited for a traffic light to change, she spun around quickly, but the other people on the street seemed to have no interest in her. A sign on a post advised women to report any incidence of molestation. *Outrage of Modesty*, the crime was called. But even in the safest city in the world, no one could protect a woman from an assault by stares, by crossed arms, by silence. Selena Lim was beginning to understand that in this case, the prosecutors of the Attorney General's Chambers were not the only adversaries she would have to face.

15

Lindy wouldn't have expected attending quiz night at the Board Room to be at the top of Noel Summer's to-do list, but she had no doubt Colleen Shepherd, seated next to her, would have stressed the importance of these team-bonding opportunities in no uncertain terms, so it was no surprise he had reported for duty.

He spotted their group from the doorway and made his way over to the table. His habit of holding his shoulders hunched slightly forward gave his gait a curiously guarded look. The observation of what was known as *body language* was one of a disturbingly long list of things that tested Lindy's patience these days, but it was hard to deny the impression that the way this man carried himself reflected a desire to suppress any involuntary gestures, in case they might provide a window into something he would prefer to keep hidden. That said, the shy smile he offered to Lindy on their introduction was not without a certain charm. It suggested to her that there might be an approachable human being in there somewhere, after all.

Tony Holland's arrival completed their team for the night's competition. Shepherd left a lingering look behind him. 'No Lauren?'

'She's not really up to it,' he said. 'Plus, I suspect she's busy making arrangements for Max when she's out in Singapore.'

'Probably just as well,' said Lindy. 'More than five and we'd have needed to divide into two teams. Can you imagine if Dom and I were on opposite sides? You'd have to choose whether you wanted a teammate with four years of university education in the UK, or one who went to school in the colonies. The IQ-shaming is bad enough when we're on the same team. I wouldn't want to rub it in.'

The humour was designed to stop them from dwelling on Salter's destination. It had been tacitly acknowledged that they would all try to use tonight's gathering as a welcome distraction from Danny's situation, at least for a few hours. Summer looked around him as if perhaps he hadn't been out at an event like this in some time. But then, there were still always a few nervous glances whenever Lindy attended any large maskless gatherings these days. She looked at the people at the bar, standing slightly further apart, backing away further when others squeezed past than they might have done in earlier times. 'I wonder if the human psyche will ever heal itself from the scars left on it by the pandemic,' she mused, almost to herself.

'Only the Earth can heal our wounds.' Summer's unexpected comment made Lindy look at him. 'The Druidic view is that viruses are a sign there is a disruption in the natural order of things, that the Earth's system of checks and controls has been compromised in some way. Nothing but the rebalancing of the natural cycles can redress something like that.'

Lindy remembered reading somewhere that language and gesture were part of the same neural cortex, so perhaps it was no surprise that Summer's speech shared the same kind of guardedness as his gait. She smiled to acknowledge the comment but made no reply.

'If you're looking for signs, up-to-date maps wouldn't hurt, either,' said Holland with a sarcastic laugh. The comment didn't mean anything to Lindy but station references often passed her by, so she let it go.

The quizmaster tested the microphone with a series of overloud taps, and announced the start of the quiz. The first category was to be 'Days of Yore'. Captaincy of the team had fallen to Shepherd but, given that the combined age of her four teammates was probably not much over a hundred, she wasn't optimistic that this would be a strong category for them. The first question seemed to confirm it.

'Which 10th-century figure has given his name to an essential piece of modern technology?'

'Harald Gormsson,' said Summers confidently.

The others stared at him

'He was able to connect a lot of disparate tribes in Denmark. He was known as Bluetooth.'

'You've heard about Bluetooth, then?' said Holland.

'I'm more of a tenth-century Danish king's man, actually,' said Summer flatly.

Lindy took up the pencil to write down the answer. The quizmaster judged that he had allowed the teams enough time and moved on. 'Question Number Two,' he intoned deliberately. 'What was the name of the ancient festival traditionally held to welcome the dark half of the year?'

'Samhain, obviously,' said Jejeune with exaggerated nonchalance. He didn't look at Summer, who took the hint and found the tabletop with his own gaze.

Lindy's surprise was clear. 'Are you sure? I've never heard of it.'

Jejeune shook his head gravely. 'Wow, four years of uni and they didn't cover something as basic as that? Do you think it's too late to get your money back?'

She put out her tongue and snatched up the pencil to write down the answer. 'Sam… what is it?'

'…hain,' offered Summer. 'H.A.I.N.'

Lindy flickered a glance his way and then turned her gaze upon Jejeune as the realisation dawned. 'You're despicable,' she told him.

'Now children, let's play nice,' said Shepherd. 'We are all on the same team, after all. Remember?'

Lindy huffed her frustration as she wrote, as Jejeune fastened on one of his most infuriating smirks. The first round ambled to a gentle conclusion without further hostilities between the teammates, and the quizmaster announced a break.

'It's tradition that the new bloke gets them in,' Holland told Summer. 'That is, if you think you can find your way to the bar? Come on, I'm going that way, I'll show you.'

Lindy watched them go, weaving between the tables of other teams, their members now with heads bent over phones, studies in isolation. Technologies like Bluetooth connected us all so seamlessly, she thought, and yet it seemed to her human beings had never been more separated. No wonder Danny Maik reverted to the music of an earlier time, with Motown's redolences of a simpler, more connected era. *Poor Danny*. She pushed the thought away and looked at Summer leaning on the bar as he waited for the drinks. Despite his overall sense of unease in company, he looked comfortable enough in these surroundings. She suspected he'd spent many moments in the corners of pubs in quiet reflection over the past few months. 'Do you think Noel is enjoying himself?' she asked Shepherd. 'I get the impression he hasn't spent much time in the company of other people recently. But perhaps he's just not much of a mixer.'

'Give him time,' said Shepherd, looking at him. 'He'll settle in. He was from around these parts originally, after all. But until he finds his feet, I'm sure he's going to be quite happy concentrating all his efforts on his work.'

She looked at Jejeune to see if the comment had hit home, but his attention was focused on a nearby table, where a man was slathering ketchup over a meat pie. 'Tell me something,' he said, still watching the man. 'People wouldn't put ketchup on a roast chicken dinner over here, would they?'

Lindy and Shepherd looked at him with equal puzzlement.

'I saw something recently,' he explained. 'It just didn't look right. Surely they don't do that, do they, even here?'

'I hardly think you have any room to talk, Mr Canadian,' said Lindy. 'You come from a land where they pour tree juice over everything. No wonder the maple leaf is your national symbol. But to answer your question, I think people put ketchup on pretty much anything these days, both here and over there. I thought you told me there was even a ketchup ice-cream flavour in Canada.'

'That's only at the CNE, the Canadian National Exhibition. It's kind of an annual summer fair. They like to experiment with new foods.'

'Well, as long as they're only testing them out on Canadians and not laboratory animals. That would be cruel beyond words.'

They leaned back as Summer returned and distributed the drinks. Holland made it back to his seat just as the call bell for the second round of the quiz rang, and the team settled in to hear the new category. The quizmaster announced it with his customary deliberate enunciation. 'Words and Phrases.'

'Finally,' said Lindy, rubbing her hands together. 'A proper subject.' But her enthusiasm was dampened immediately by the news that they would be starting with a *Star Wars* question.

'In the film *A New Hope*,' said the quizmaster, 'which character utters the famous line, "May the Force be with you"?'

'Obi-Wan Kenobi.' Holland sat back with a self-satisfied smile.

'Actually,' said Shepherd, 'he says, "Remember, the Force will be with you always." It's General Dodonna who says, "May the Force be with you," just before the *Death Star* battle.'

A moment of silence cloaked the group as Lindy bit back a smile and Jejeune searched for points of interest on the pub walls. Shepherd tilted her head to lower her glasses and fixed the two constables with her patented over-the-rim glare. 'And if either of you ever breathes a word of this, you'll be on desk duties for the rest of your career.'

Lindy wrote the response as the quizmaster spoke again. 'Now you've all heard of a murder of crows, no doubt. But what is the collective noun for a group of pheasants?'

'It's a bouquet, isn't it?' Lindy asked the group. 'I'm sure I heard it somewhere.'

'When flushed,' said Jejeune. 'A group of wild pheasants in flight is a bouquet. On the ground, it's a nye.'

'A nye?' said Holland. 'Spelled...'

'Yes, Constable, the same way,' said Shepherd gently. 'So perhaps not so much to do with New Year's Eve after all, then.'

Lindy looked to Dom for clarification, but he looked similarly puzzled. It wasn't unusual for her to feel this far outside the loop, but it said something about Dom's own recent detachment from station life that he seemed similarly in the dark. 'We'd need more information to answer that question properly,' she said. 'Since he hasn't stipulated, perhaps he'll accept either answer.'

'It's a stupid question, anyway,' said Holland, still smarting from Shepherd's gentle rebuke and even more so from Summer's following expressionless stare, which had said all he needed it to. 'They should just pull it. What sort of question has two completely different answers that are both right?'

Lindy didn't know the answer to that one either. But by the look on Domenic's face, he seemed to feel there were a lot of these kinds of questions going around lately. Both here and in Singapore.

16

Autumn drew so much of its splendour from the sun, thought Noel Summer. On overcast days like this, there were no bursts of colour, no vibrant pulses of reds or dazzling orange hues to catch the eye, only a pale, washed-out light that seemed to drag the sky down towards it and seep into the vegetation, coating the landscape with a sickly pallor.

In front of the detective, a thread of green moss traced a path over the weathered granite face of a stone angel like a teardrop. The statue's grey body twisted in anguish beneath a speckled robe of tiny yellow lichen roses. 'There's so much sadness in funeral statuary,' he said, looking at the angel carefully. 'I've always thought they should show more joy, more celebration of the release from trials of this earthly life. But then, the sadness isn't for those who've departed, is it? It's for those who have been left to deal with their absence.'

Jim Loyal paused in his work and rested on his leaf rake. He looked up at the statue but made no comment. He had swept the fallen leaves away from a plot near a split-rail fence towards the rear of the small hilltop cemetery. The area was in deep shadow and the gloom gave it an aura befitting the sad expression of the stone guardian watching from its nearby plinth. 'That should have been Abbie's place,' he said. 'I'm clearing it in case Libby decides to relent and put up a memorial to her.' He gave a sad shake of his head. 'Doubt she will, though. There's not an ounce of give in that girl. In that, at least, she's exactly like her father.'

'They told me up at the house that I'd find you down here,' said Summer. 'I hope you don't mind.'

'Why would I mind? If it's more questions about the suicide, better to get it over with and let the poor girl rest.'

'You knew her well, you said. Back at the Nye.'

'Her and her sister both. Since childhood. Lovely little girls they were. Peas in a pod, looks-wise. Not so much in personalities, though. In a way, it was good that Libby took over the estate. Beef farming is a difficult business at the best of times. Now the so-called experts are telling people they have to reduce their meat intake by a third if we're going to save the planet. Add that to the calls to optimise land use for crops, pressure from the lifestyle choices brigade, and the climate change protesters, and it's not hard to understand why the industry has been on a downward swing for years. Of the two girls, only Libby would have the vision and the determination to keep the operation going this long.'

'She doesn't seem too upset about the death of her sister. Or is she just one of those people who bottles it up inside?'

'Oh, she feels it all right. But I daresay she's not as broken up as some might expect. They were never close, the sisters. Even from an early age they were always at odds. Usually with me the peacemaker between them.'

'What did they fight about?'

'Everything they could. The trouble is, neither of them could ever let a past slight go. Held on to them for years, they both did.'

'Libby mentioned an old judo injury.'

Loyal nodded and gave a sad smile. 'Ah, that's one of the big ones between them. Was,' he corrected himself. 'I thought teaching them both some self-defence would be a good thing. They could look after themselves if needs be, and it might even draw them closer.' He paused and looked at the newly raked plot for a moment. 'Turns out, it did the opposite.'

Summer waited patiently for Loyal to continue.

'Libby had a lot of success, see, when she was younger. Won a couple of tournaments. There were those that felt she might be on her way to bigger things.' Loyal shook his head. 'I wasn't one of them. Abbie was the one with the more natural talent, only she didn't have the discipline to stick at it. Libby did. Plus, she had that ruthless streak the good ones need. She could have gone further if it wasn't for the injury, no doubt about it, but she'd never have made it all the way to the top.'

'But she blames her sister for that?'

'She'd rather remember things the way she'd like them to have been. The reality is that it was her error. Libby should have never tried to make that grab. She was off balance. Abbie just used it against her and her wrist gave way.'

The solace of self-deception, thought Summer. One other trait Libby Cleve shared with her father. A large black and white bird made a tentative foray onto a nearby headstone and Summer watched it as it jittered about nervously for a moment before retreating to the cover of some nearby trees. It was not like a Magpie to be so furtive. Perhaps it was the atmosphere today that was making it so uneasy. Or perhaps it was just the setting. He saw that Loyal had been watching the bird, too.

'I'm told there were those long ago who believed Magpies held funerals for their dead friends,' said Summer.

'That'd be right,' said Loyal, nodding his head. 'Saw it once myself. A group of Magpies, six of 'em in all, lined up on a roadside fence near the carcass of one that had been hit by a car. Each of them had a small stick in its beak, and one by one they flew down and laid it beside the body. Damned if they didn't. I wouldn't have believed it if I hadn't seen it with my own eyes, but I'd defy anybody to put it down as anything other than a form of marking the passing of the dead one.' He looked up at Summer. 'You'll think I'm half-mad, I suppose.'

'Not at all. The natural world is full of secrets it would reveal to us if we only we gave it the time.' Summer delivered the comment with such solemn earnestness that Loyal left his gaze on him. 'Druid,' said the detective.

Loyal nodded. 'Ah, so you'd understand then, the relationship between a man and the land. I daresay the others would like me to join them up at the house, but it's out here I find my comfort. Let them deal with their grief indoors. In my view it's better to get out, let nature do the healing.'

'It must have been difficult for Abbie, being so close to her sister in age, sharing the same birth year, even, and yet being denied all this.'

'I don't think she ever really cared much about the business. Or the family. But the land, now that she did love. I'd see her walking in the woods every once in a while after she'd left the family home. I never mentioned it to Libby. She'd have had you lot on her for trespassing. But there was no harm in letting her roam.' He looked at the statue for a long moment, letting it transport him back into the past. 'She asked me to go with her, you know?'

'Abigail?' Summer looked surprised.

'When she left. Said we could set up shop together, run some new venture. As soon as Libby heard about it, she decided she needed me here to run the shooting operation. The old man was out of it by then and she said she couldn't cope with both businesses on her own. In the end I chose the land. It needed me too, and it was easier than having to decide between the two of them.'

'But you do still run the shoot?'

'You don't approve?'

'For all those birds to die so wantonly, even if they are raised exclusively for that purpose.' Summer shook his head. 'The stresses it must cause on the Earth's systems of decomposition and nutrient recycling to cope with so much death in such a short space of time. Unless we find ways to reconcile our actions with the Earth's energies, I can't help feeling the natural world will come to show us its displeasure in time.'

'I can't find a way to fit your beliefs into my own way of looking at the world,' said Loyal, 'but you're not wrong. The Earth does have its secret ways, that much I know. I've seen how the animals and birds react to things none of us humans can see or sense.' He nodded thoughtfully. 'It seems to me there was some kind of connection between hunters and their prey in the past, some sense of balance, you might say, that's been lost in this sort of shooting. But then again, the people who come here to shoot are not doing it for the sake of nature, are they? Or the Earth? It's a sport to them, nothing more.'

Summer looked towards the plot, nestled in its pocket of shadow, still and silent. 'The estrangement,' he said, 'it was definitely over Peter Estey? There wasn't anything else between the girls?'

'Estey,' said Loyal with disgust. 'Better he'd never darkened their door. He destroyed that family. And still, he had the nerve to show up at the opening ceremony for the Nye, as if he expected Abbie to welcome him with open arms, when it was long over between them by then.' He looked at Summer. 'You don't think he had anything to do with Abbie's death, though?'

'It's just something we're looking into.'

'Might have trouble asking him. For all his faults, Pete Estey is a son of the land. He knows it like you and I know it, its moods, its ways. If he doesn't want you to find him, you won't.' He shook his head sadly. 'I should have known there was more to it. It wasn't in Abbie to have taken her own life.' His hands began shaking. He stared down at them, seemingly unable to take his eyes away. 'That poor little girl,' he said sadly.

The Magpie was gone now, the swaying branches of the trees beyond the graveyard the only movement. 'Could I ask you something?' said Summer. 'Would you say Abigail Cleve was a truthful person? I mean, could she be taken at her word?'

Loyal looked puzzled. 'I wouldn't trust her to put anybody else's concerns before her own, but outright dishonesty?' He shook his head. 'Sad to say, but she didn't care enough about what other people thought to be bothered to lie to them.'

'If she had no one close to her, what will happen to the Nye now? Will it continue to operate as a pheasant farm?'

'Can't see how. The land is all part of some trust or something, so I understand. I'd imagine the business will just be sold.'

'And the proceeds?'

'I couldn't say. I might get a token, along with the rest of the staff. Abbie won't have forgotten her happy times at the estate when she was growing up. Whatever her other faults, she was generous to those she liked.'

'Any chance it gets left to her sister?'

Loyal shook his head slowly. 'They never put their differences behind them.' He looked at the plot, already littered again with wind-blown leaves. 'She wouldn't have felt anything, at the end, would she? Abbie. She wouldn't have suffered?'

'I imagine it would have been quick,' said Summer. 'Painless, at least.'

'That poor little girl,' said Loyal again. He picked up the rake and began clearing the plot of leaves once more. Summer departed in silence, leaving Loyal to take his solace from the natural world while he performed one of the saddest tasks the detective could imagine: clearing a site for a memorial that would never be built.

17

After Maik's trip to Guy Trueman's office suite, his cramped holding cell had seemed to take on a more claustrophobic feel. For that reason alone, a trip upstairs was a welcome respite. Judging from Selena Lim's expression, though, the content of today's meeting was going to be less to his liking.

She drew a sheet from her briefcase. 'The autopsy report confirms Titus Chupul's injuries were consistent with the type of blow you were witnessed delivering. Cause of death can be attributed to these injuries.'

Maik was silent as he took in the information.

'This is not good news for us,' said Selena unnecessarily. Her features were taut with concern.

'I didn't hit that man hard enough to kill him,' Maik said simply.

'Yes, Danny, you did.' Selena snatched the report from the table to wave it at him in exasperation. 'Bruising to the larynx, broken hyoid bone, swelling of the oesophagus.' She looked at him candidly. 'I'll accept that you may not have intended to kill him, but this report leaves no doubt that you did.'

She tucked the report back in her case and prepared to withdraw another, but she left her hand inside the bag for a moment. Maik looked at her. She knew what to expect from the autopsy report. The news shouldn't have disturbed her this much. There was something else troubling Selena Lim, something that, even now, she was hesitant to share. Finally, she withdrew the sheet and laid it on the table. But instead of looking down at it she looked at him. 'Why were you in the Geylang district that day?'

'There's a shop there selling vinyl. It specialises in the kind of music I like,' he said. 'Motown. Especially from the late sixties. Do you know it?'

'The late sixties? My mom wasn't even born then.' But she showed no surprise that he could have found a store catering to such music. Nostalgia was a journey everybody seemed keen to take to these days, and none more so than well-heeled expats seeking reminders of their youth. The streetwise entrepreneurs of Singapore weren't likely to miss an opportunity like that.

'There's a record I've been trying to get for someone, a single: *You're All I Need to Get By,*' continued Maik. 'I thought they might have a copy.' He tapped the sheet of paper with his fingertip. 'Does this make it important why I went there?'

'Can you confirm that's the address of the shop?'

He studied the paper and nodded.

'The same address was found on a notepad on Titus Chupul's desk at the police station. There's no search history for it on his work computer or phone. Just to be clear – you didn't give him that address?'

Maik didn't answer, but his look did. Still, it wasn't enough to quell his counsel's concern. 'Tell me again, Danny, once and for all, that nothing is going to come up. Not even if they ever found his missing burner phone or got the number and ran a trace on the call log. There would be no evidence of any contact between you and the victim?'

Maik had already answered the question all the ways he knew. His expression suggested they needed to move on.

'He got that address from somewhere, Danny. Who gave it to him, if it wasn't you?'

'If this was my case, I'd be looking at hotel staff. If Chupul was tracking my movements, as you seem to be suggesting, he might have requested them to report back to him. I asked the concierge where the shop was.'

'I've already checked with him.' The look was designed to remind him she knew what she was doing. 'He is adamant he didn't tell anyone.'

Maik shrugged. 'A bystander, then, eavesdropping. I wasn't keeping it a secret.'

'And Chupul knew just which bystander to ask?' Lim shook her head, making her dark hair shimmer. 'As far as the prosecution will be concerned, this demonstrates that there was a connection between the two of you, that you gave him that address, however strenuously you deny it. It helps them build their scenario.'

'What scenario is that?'

Again, Maik saw the reluctance that suggested that, whatever she gave him, there was going to be something much deeper she was holding back. 'They're going to say you deliberately targeted him. You sent him that address to lure him there.'

'Lure him?' Maik's surprise was genuine. 'Why would I want to do that? I'd never even heard of this man before that day. I had no idea he existed.'

'Motive is the one thing they are struggling with at the moment. But this all fits nicely with Ronnie Gunn's earlier point, how you were able to overpower someone so well versed in close-quarters combat himself. They are going to say it was because you were ready for him, waiting for him to show up at the address you'd given him.'

The lock to this door was quieter than the one in the Conference Room, but the noise of it opening, when it came, was still jarring. Ronnie Gunn entered the room, cradling a clear plastic cup filled with a green liquid. He saw Selena Lim staring at the drink. 'Sugarcane juice. Sorry, I should have brought you one.'

'I prefer Starbucks,' she told him. Maik suspected this was a long way from the truth, but neither he nor Lim had missed the message. Here was somebody who had enough pull even in rule-bound Singapore to flout the directive against bringing food and drink into the room.

'So they have their connection, at last,' said Gunn solemnly. 'The plea deal wasn't meant to extend to a brawl between known combatants. I'm surprised they haven't pulled it already.'

'Danny will testify under oath that he didn't tell Chupul where he was going that day. This is still an attack by an unknown assailant. An armed assailant.'

Gunn nodded. 'Ah yes, the phantom knife.' He turned to Maik. 'Guy Trueman says you can be taken at your word. If you say Titus had a weapon, it's because you believe that's what you saw.'

'It was a kukri,' said Maik.

'But it occurs to me,' said Gunn, continuing over Maik's interjection without missing a beat, 'if the prosecution calls Guy, he would also be able to confirm you are familiar enough with those weapons to be able to describe one with your eyes closed. Size, the shape, right down to the danphe and the regimental colours, whether or not such a knife ever existed.'

'Danphe?' asked Maik.

'The Nepali symbol,' said Gunn. 'The thing is, Sergeant Maik, Danny, feelings are running high. More than one officer out there owes their life to the skills Titus Chupul taught them. There's a saying here in Singapore: *When the citizens are in trouble, they call the police. When the police are in trouble, they call the Gurkhas.* That edge they've got, Titus Chupul gave them that. They will want to honour that. They'll want to make sure justice is done here.'

'Devina Chupul said her husband was a violent man,' said Selena Lim suddenly.

'It was the nature of his job. He turned boys into men, gave them the steel they needed to do their job. He was hard on people, yes, but they respected him for it.'

'I got the impression that his activities may not have been restricted to work.'

'I lived with them for a while. I never saw him raise a hand to his wife.' Gunn looked at her through dark eyes, their coldness matched by the flint in his lowered tone. All pretence of courtesy and friendliness had gone now. 'Don't try to put this on him. Any of it. Titus Chupul was the victim here. Your client killed him. Now all that's left is to decide the price he has to pay for it.'

Not a single silky hair on Selena Lim's head moved out of place. She stared back at Gunn, completely unfazed by his threatening tone. 'Why are you here, Mr Gunn?'

'To tell you they are going to up the charges at the First Disclosure Conference.'

'We don't know that.'

'Yeah, Selena, we do,' he said. 'If your client is prepared to enter a plea of guilty now, they will be willing to extend the deal to cover the new evidence. Maybe tack on a year or two, but no more than six, maximum.'

'Six years?' The extent of Gunn's authority was vague to Danny. But one thing was clear: this wasn't speculation. Whether Gunn had come on his own or been sent here by someone higher up, he could deliver on the offer he was presenting.

'You know, I listen to Guy Trueman and he tells me what a stand-up guy this Danny Maik is, and I come here and find his lawyer preoccupied with the idea that a couple of items of evidence have gone missing. But I don't find many people sparing a thought for the widow. I knelt beside Titus Chupul's body and watched a doctor administer CPR that was never going to work, and all the time I'm thinking, I have to tell her this. I have to tell Devina that her husband of twenty years, her only form of support in this world, is gone, killed, and she will have to bury him. Plead it out, Selena. Get it closed. Bring the wife some peace. I have no personal liking for Danny here. He killed the man who was my mentor. But out of respect for Guy, I don't want a worst-case outcome. If your client doesn't plead, the prosecutors are planning to push for a first limb conviction.'

Maik watched the interaction between them, felt the tension in it. He looked at Selena expectantly but she seemed unable to meet his eyes. Maik knew that his earlier instinct had been correct. There was something that she could hardly bring herself to contemplate, let alone share.

'What's the first limb?' asked Danny quietly, as if the others had forgotten he was in the room.

'You have a duty to inform your client, Selena,' said Gunn. 'Don't make me be the one to do it.'

'What is the first limb?' Maik asked again, patiently.

Selena looked down as she began speaking. 'In Singapore, premeditated murder falls under the first limb of Section 300 of the criminal code.' She paused and took a fluttery breath. 'If premeditation can be established,' she paused again, and lifted her eyes to look at Danny, 'say by luring the victim to the scene of the killing, the mandatory sentence is the death penalty.'

18

Bob Ferris's garden might not have been tended in a long time, but that made no difference to the charm of Goldfinches foraging industriously among the overgrown foliage as Jejeune and Summer got out of the car. At the men's approach, the birds took flight, exploding like shrapnel in all directions. They would regroup and return as soon as the intruders had passed, Jejeune knew, likely to remain undisturbed, and even unnoticed, for the rest of the day. He found the thought strangely reassuring.

The detectives heard the sound of raised voices coming from the front of Bob Ferris's house as they approached, and they quickened their pace towards it. They rounded the corner to find Tara Skye in an animated discussion with the homeowner. Ferris was seated in his wheelchair, perched on the top step with the door to the house open behind him. Beneath him at ground level, Tara was leaning forward, one black-booted foot leaning against the bottom step, pressing her white muslin dress to her thigh against the billowing breeze.

'Ah, Detectives,' announced Ferris with an airiness that belied any hostility in the discussions. 'I was just telling Tara here she and her friends are likely to encounter a significant amount of resistance to this weekend's little show of force up at Cleve Hall.'

'It's a legitimate gathering, not an insurrection,' protested Skye. 'We have permits and everything.'

'Strong tradition of shooting in this part of the world, you see. Comes from up there.' Ferris inclined his head inland, in the direction of Sandringham. 'Took their shoots very seriously, did the royals, back in the day. Old King Edward had the idea of turning the estate into the best shoot in England. Succeeded, too. Undertook a massive planting scheme to create habitat, brought in the top land consultants, the best game managers. In the ten years either side of 1900, they were bagging twenty thousand birds a year up there.'

'Four hundred thousand birds,' said Tara, shaking her in disgust. 'Killed for no reason. A tradition rooted in death and suffering is hardly something a community should be proud of,' she added angrily.

'Do you know, the king even changed the time at Sandringham, to allow more daylight for shooting?' continued Ferris blithely. 'It was officially half an hour earlier there than in London during his reign. Stayed that way for thirty-five years, all told.'

Though the information had no doubt been designed to further infuriate Tara Skye, it had been delivered in Jejeune's direction under the theory, he supposed, that someone from the colonies might be less familiar with royal history. In his case it was true, but it wasn't an assumption Jejeune would have necessarily made himself. Some of the most fervent monarchists he had ever met resided on the other side of the pond.

'You could stop this carnage if you wanted to,' Tara Skye told the detectives, 'then there'd be no need for any more birds to die.'

'What can they do?' asked Ferris. 'It's all perfectly legal.'

'There are laws in this country forbidding the release of alien species,' she said firmly. 'Pheasants aren't native to the UK. They're from Asia.'

'I believe they're considered a naturalised species,' said Jejeune. 'They've established thriving self-sustaining breeding populations outside the introduction range.'

Skye's expression suggested she was not best pleased that, after having years of free rein with environmental facts and statistics, she had finally encountered someone who could meet her on her own terms.

'He's a birder,' explained Summer.

Skye stared past Jejeune at the Range Rover parked next to Summer's Trabant on the street beside them. 'Not the most climate-friendly choice, I would have thought. Just another name-only environmentalist, then, I suppose.'

'I like to think my overall carbon footprint is pretty good,' said Jejeune, surprised to find how important it seemed to defend himself against this intense young woman's claims. 'I think most birders would say the same.'

'Really? And suppose a rare bird was to show up here, a Lammergeier for example. What would their response be then?'

'Astonishment, I should think. There is no habitat for them here.'

Jejeune had been in the country long enough to be familiar with the British technique of deflecting uncomfortable questions with dry humour, but no amount of wit could disarm the accusation behind Tara Skye's stare. 'Look at what happened when that Rufous Bush Chat showed up a couple of years ago at Stiffkey,' she said. 'You couldn't see the place for cars.'

'You have to let people see what they are saving,' he said. 'You can't expect people to commit to an abstract concept like habitat conservation unless they can see the birds it is benefitting. Not with the same sense of purpose and engagement anyway,' he added weakly.

If Lindy was the queen of withering looks, Tara Skye was proving herself a worthy handmaiden. 'Did it ever occur to them to just charter a bus? I mean, they are all going to the same place, after all.'

'It doesn't really work like that.' Jejeune dragged his smile back from a condescension he didn't intend, leaving it dangling awkwardly in limbo. 'The time it would take to organise mass transportation, well... With rarities, you need to get there as quickly as possible. The bird might not stay around long.' His finishing smile was even weaker than his previous effort.

'I wouldn't blame it, if it had to listen to tosh like this,' said Tara Skye in a tone filled with contempt. She withdrew her boot from the step and, with a theatrical whirl of her dress, marched away quickly, leaving the men to watch her departure in silence. Ferris shook his head slowly. 'Kids. Everything's so black and white to them.' He turned to the detectives. 'So, twice in one moon phase. Must be important. Want to come in?'

'Not unless you want to go in,' said Summer.

'Nice enough out here,' said Ferris, turning his face towards the weak sun. 'Bit of fresh air will do me good. So what can I do for you?'

'We still haven't been able to find Pete Estey,' said Summer. 'We need to ask him a few questions.'

'About Abbie Cleve's death? Must mean it's been reclassified as a suspicious...' He waited. He hadn't expected either man to confirm the statement, but the fact that they didn't refute it was enough.

'Have you seen him recently?' asked Jejeune.

'Not since before she died.'

'But you don't deny you are friends.'

The hectoring tone seemed to anger Ferris. 'Deny it?' He sat forward in his chair. 'Why would I deny it? More likely, I'd be proud to call him a friend. A good friend. Hard to find in this world where everybody's in it for themselves, somebody who'd be willing to stand by you, no matter what kind of hard times you've fallen on.'

'And would you do that for him?'

'Of course I would. But I'm not protecting him in this case. I don't need to. He didn't do anything to harm that girl.'

'You said he had tried hypnosis,' said Summer. 'Was it you who put him under?'

Ferris moved his shoulders easily. 'I picked up a couple of things during my treatments. But as I say, it never really took with him. Or me.' He shook his head slowly, weighing the evidence like the old policeman he was. 'Bit of a stretch, to suggest just because he'd had a couple of sessions he'd know how to use it on Abbie Cleve. Besides, I did hear that most people can't be manipulated into doing something harmful to themselves under hypnosis.'

'If Abbie Cleve was aware that what was coming would harm her,' said Summer.

Ferris hesitated for a moment, as if he might have more to say. When he continued, though, Jejeune had the impression he had decided on a different direction. He offered the young detective a smile. 'I've told you. You're barking up the wrong tree here. Pete Estey's not your man.'

'Then help us eliminate him from our inquires,' said Summer reasonably.

The detectives waited in silence.

'That place off Stone Road. It's just an old trailer. No electricity, no utilities. Gas canister for cooking, a stream nearby for running water, but that's about it. It's all but impossible to see from the road.' He smiled. 'Pete always said you can hide anything if you put enough effort into it.' He looked at Summer. 'I remember when you were coming up. Good instincts, they said, that was your edge. Same as your DCI here, if you don't mind my saying so. But I'm telling you, you're both off the mark on this one. Just take it from an old scrote who's seen a few things. You need to look elsewhere.'

'A good friend,' Jejeune repeated quietly. 'One who you could call on any time you needed to? That would be hard to do unless you had a way to get in touch with him.'

'Does Estey have a phone up there, you mean? That an old friend might use to warn him about a police visit?' Ferris shook his head and laughed. 'No, Inspector, there's no phone, either.'

'You think he's already told Estey we're on the lookout for him,' asked Summer, halting as the two men approached the gap in the wall to leave the garden.

'Not here,' murmured Jejeune, looking straight ahead without breaking stride. 'After an interview, a suspect will usually watch you leave,' he explained as the two men walked side by side. 'It's a natural instinct. If the detectives stand and chat the moment they are out of the suspect's presence, it tips them off that something they said probably warranted further discussion.'

'But you can't suspect Ferris of anything, surely?'

'Perhaps not, but it's a good habit to get into. Any thoughts as to why he seems so keen to have us eliminate Estey from our inquiries?'

Summer shrugged without breaking stride, as advised. 'Friendship, loyalty. Who knows? It's sometimes difficult to believe someone you're close to could be guilty of anything.' He seemed to realise the implication of the statement. 'I'm sorry. I didn't mean…' He looked at Jejeune. 'Is this one of Danny Maik's tricks, this business about walking away?'

Jejeune smiled. 'He's very good at what he does. You heard Ferris earlier. If there's a more dependable, steadfast person out there than Danny Maik, I don't know where.'

Summer shook his head dubiously. 'Still, it's hard to see how eight independent witnesses could all be mistaken. It has to be true that he killed that man. But there must be more to the story.'

'A lot more,' said Jejeune. 'We'll take your car. You can drop me back here afterwards.'

Summer checked the sightlines and stopped. They were out of view of Ferris's window now, whether he'd been watching them or not. 'The thing is, the weight of all those expectations, being the dependable one, the steadfast one, the one who can be relied on to get it right all the time, they can be hard to live up to,' he said quietly. 'Everybody makes mistakes now and then. Lapses in judgement, in restraint, in attention. It happens. All I'm saying is, you might not want to count out the possibility that it happened in this case as well.'

Noel Summer slid behind the wheel of his anonymous grey car and, as soon as his DCI had squeezed into the passenger seat, they drove off in silence.

19

It was not often that Domenic emerged from a car and found a person adopting exactly the same attitude as him. A momentary pause, to breathe and take in the air, to feel the breeze on one's face. And to listen. While he doubted Noel Summer was taking in the burble of mixed bird calls from the understory of the nearby trees, it was clear his new partner was embracing the natural world every bit as much as he was.

On the horizon, a bank of clouds drifted across the sky like pale fog. Unless they darkened, they would pose no threat to this clear, crisp day. In a landscape like this you could see the weather coming from a long way off. It was a good thing, thought Jejeune. It gave you a sense of your place in the world, reminded you of your responsibilities to it.

They left Summer's Trabant on the side of the road and made their way from the road into the forest. Their footfalls raised soft sighs from the bed of leaves beneath them, and the sour tang of moist leaf litter drifted to them on the still morning air. Jejeune stopped and raised his binoculars. Summer was enough of an outdoor person to know not to speak for the moment. 'Interesting,' Jejeune said, lowering

the bins. 'In this area, I'd expect it to be a Chiffchaff, but …'
He shook his head. 'It presented more like a Willow Warbler,
not as jittery and less tail-flicking. If it is, it's an excellent
sighting for this area.'

Summer pointed to the bins. 'Those can't help you?'

Jejeune gave a wan smile. 'The two species are virtually
indistinguishable. In spring and summer, their calls help to
differentiate them, but they don't often sing this late in the
year.' He raised his bins again as the bird flitted into view.
He noted the slightly elongated shape and clearer yellow
eye-stripe. 'Willow Warbler, definitely.' He nodded with
satisfaction. 'Pleased with that. They're becoming really
scarce in these parts, so it's a good bird, especially for so
late in the season.'

As they advanced deeper into the forest, the shadowy
interior began to take on a more sinister atmosphere. Without
their cloaks of leaves, the trees looked like an army of frozen
warriors, waiting for the order to advance. It became eerily
quiet. A wide stream ran across the path of the two men and
they paused at its bank. Summer looked around, listening to
the silence. 'It's like nature's equilibrium is being thrown off
by something. That bird showing up here, the stillness when
I was up at the estate speaking to Libby Cleve, the strange
furtiveness of a Magpie at the family plot where Jim Loyal
was working.'

'I'm sure it's that way every shooting season,' said Jejeune.
'It's bound to change the activities of all birds, not just the
target species.' It must be hard, he thought, for someone of
Summer's beliefs to accept the concept of an organised shoot.
Harvesting the bounty of the forest no doubt went hand in
hand with a Druidic existence in the olden times. But it
would have been done respectfully, in a way that was in harmony with nature. Killing for recreation would have been

unthinkable back then – and even now – for someone whose belief system was based upon a balanced relationship with the natural world.

They heard the snap of the twig at the same time, and both swirled low and to the side. A shape moved between the trees on the far side of the stream, but it was too deep in shadow to make out clearly.

'Estey,' whispered Summer. 'Stay on this side, in case he crosses.' He eased into the cold, shallow water before Jejeune could reply. He watched the DC scramble up the far bank and tracked him along his own side of the water. Perhaps it made sense for Jejeune to stay on this side and cut off an escape, but he couldn't shake the feeling they should have stayed together.

His phone buzzed and he looked down at the text from Summer. *Eyes on. Possibly armed.*

Jejeune felt a tightening in his chest, more uneasy still at the cavalier way Summer had hurried into his pursuit. Here the woodland was deeper, dappled with pockets of dark shadow and unclear sightlines in every direction. It was hunting season and they were in territory, in pursuit of a known poacher who they now believed could be armed. How could he have let this situation get so far out of control?

Hold, he texted. *On my way.*

Across the water, Summer emerged into a clearing at the edge of the woodland. Jejeune tried to attract his attention, but the constable's gaze was fixed on the interior of the woods, where a shadow of a figure was still moving through with purpose. Summer had turned back and resumed his pursuit of the subject before Jejeune could catch his eye and signal him to stand down.

He heard Summer call out. 'Police. Remain where you are. Do not turn around. Identify yourself.'

From the far bank, Jejeune froze and watched. He could hear the blood pounding in his temples. The figure continued moving. Summer repeated his command, but the shadow showed no sign of obeying. A text pinged on Jejeune's phone. 2. The person had ignored two orders to remain in place, and twice failed to provide identification when requested. It meant a use-of-force provision was now in effect.

Jejeune had just lowered his gaze to find a place to ford the stream when he heard the sounds of a pursuit and a scuffle on the far bank, followed by Summer's shouted announcement. 'Suspect apprehended.'

Then he heard the call of another voice. He plunged into the water and took the far bank in a single vault.

Summer was bending over the figure sitting upright on the bed of bracken when Jejeune arrived. It wasn't likely he had failed to recognise the person he had just tackled to the ground, but he seemed so distraught it was possible.

'You remember Noel,' Jejeune told the victim, looking for a soft opening to address the constable's embarrassment. 'From pub night.'

'I am so sorry, ma'am.'

'Lindy will do fine,' she told him frostily. She took Summer's proffered hand and pulled herself to her feet. 'A little quick off the mark, there, Noel.' She peeled an earbud from one ear. 'What on earth are you playing at? You scared the life out of me.'

He lowered his head. 'I can't apologise enough. This,' he indicated the scene, 'it's unforgivable.'

'He did call out to you, Lindy,' said Jejeune. 'Twice. He asked you to identify yourself.'

'I had my earbuds in. I wanted to get to the end of a chapter in my book. I didn't think it would be a life-threatening decision.'

'Again, I am truly sorry. I'll understand if you want to file a complaint.'

'What?' Lindy looked genuinely shocked. 'This was just a little misunderstanding, Noel. You got a bit overexcited, that's all. I should probably have just phoned Dom instead of coming here anyway. I'm just never sure whether his phone is going to be on when he's out in the woods like this.'

'Still, my conduct was inexcusable.' He looked crestfallen.

'There were repeated police requests ignored,' said Jejeune. 'Officially, it's enough to justify use of force.'

'See,' Lindy told him, 'you were just following procedure.'

'But not good judgement. I should have recognised you, or at the very least considered the fact that you might be wearing earbuds and couldn't hear my commands. And that stick you were carrying. It looks nothing like a weapon. I see that now. There was really no reason for bringing you down like that. None.'

Lindy raised her eyebrows at Dom, looking for help in relieving the man's despair. It seemed so out of proportion with the event. Jejeune gave the faintest of shrugs in reply.

'Listen,' said Lindy, 'let's put this right. It's about time we fixed a date for dinner, anyway. Why don't you come over one day next week? If you'll be willing to listen to Dom's attempts at small talk for a couple of hours, we'll consider that penance enough.'

'Oh, I couldn't,' said Summer. 'Especially not after this.' But Lindy was apparently too preoccupied with picking the last of the bracken fronds from her sweater to acknowledge the protest. Summer relented with a sheepish half-smile of gratitude. 'Well, okay then. If you're sure.'

'Great. How about next Wednesday. Around eight? Now I'm afraid I don't know anything about Druidic cuisine. Forgive my ignorance but is there any particular way you'd like your food prepared. I mean, raw? Charred?'

'They're both something of a speciality of Lindy's,' said Jejeune, to show he too was on board with putting the incident behind them.

'Anything, really,' Summer told them. 'Anything at all. Thanks. Thank you.'

'Settled, then,' announced Lindy. 'You know, if you wanted to head off and get changed into dry clothes, I can give Dom a ride back with me.' She gave Summer a reassuring smile as he hesitated. 'I'm fine, Noel, honestly. And this business, forgotten. Totally.'

But not by you, she thought as she watched him picking his way through the undergrowth on his way back towards his car. 'Now there's a young man who has trouble forgiving himself,' she said.

'It's not his first mistake,' said Domenic. 'Are you sure you're okay?'

'A bit shaken up. It's not every day one gets rugby-tackled in a forest. But I'll be fine. Is this guy you were looking for really that dangerous?'

'We're not sure. He's a known poacher. He may have been armed. All in all, Summer was probably justified acting the way he did.'

But you wouldn't have acted that way, she thought. *And neither would Danny Maik.* She looked across at Jejeune as they made their way back out of the woods, side by side. He seemed to be deep in thought. 'You haven't asked why I came to find you,' she reminded him.

He shook his head, as if disgusted by his own preoccupation. 'Sorry. I'm guessing it must have been pretty important, too, if it couldn't wait until I got home.'

'I received a message from Singapore.'

'From Danny?'

'Yes, but I'm not sure the person who sent it knows what he's telling us. It's from somebody named Selena Lim. She's Danny's lawyer.'

20

Jejeune was sitting on a rock at the shore of the inlet beside the house, cradling a cup of coffee as he watched the sunset turn the clouds to orange smoke. The water in front of him was gradually darkening. It seemed like a long time since the sun had risen over the stand of conifers on the far bank that morning to bring it silvering into life. Even the events in the forest felt like a distant memory now.

Lindy was sitting beside him with her iPad propped on her knees, staring down at an email bearing the address of a legal firm in Singapore. 'I still can't understand why he had his lawyer send it to me,' she said.

'Communications regarding official police business would need to be handled by Singapore police liaison, in case there was sensitive information being transmitted. Personal communications would have to be vetted by the prison service. This message straddles the line between the two, just as Danny knew it would. There's enough ambiguity to allow him to argue to his lawyer that he didn't know where the jurisdiction for this message would lie. He would have told this...' he bent in to check the name, 'Selena Lim that you were a journalist he knew here, and you could be trusted to get the message where it needed to go.'

She read the email aloud again:

> *Verbatim from Daniel Maik*: *It looks like I'm not going to be home for a while, so I need you to have my caseload transferred to someone else.*

'A lot to unpack there,' said Lindy.

Jejeune nodded. There was. For a man sometimes accused of lacking subtlety, Danny Maik occasionally found a deft touch. The message was a case in point. While brief and to the point, it was a model of disguised information.

'*I need you to...*' quoted Lindy. The phrase had jumped out at her the first time she read it, and every time since. 'I mean, when did you ever hear Danny put anything that way? He's in trouble, isn't he, Dom? The fact that he now thinks he's going to prison for this, the fact that he's reaching out to us for help.'

And the fact that he needed to disguise the true meaning of this message, thought Jejeune. On his transfer from Saltmarsh station, Danny had relinquished his old caseload. And, since he hadn't yet reported for duty at his new posting, he hadn't been assigned a new one there. So, for caseload, read *case*.

'It's pretty obvious he doesn't trust this lawyer, for whatever reason – but if he wants a new one, why not just tell her and get her replaced?' asked Lindy pragmatically.

Jejeune shrugged. 'You know Danny. Friends close, enemies closer. If he's come to the conclusion she can't be trusted, he at least knows where he stands with her. If he gets new counsel, he'd have to go through the whole process of sizing them up again. That would take some time.' He pointed to the screen. 'And it sounds to me like time is one of the many luxuries Danny doesn't have any more.'

Lindy shook her head. 'There must be more to all this,' she said. 'You said so yourself. There has to be something out there that can clear him.'

'Danny's only hope of acquittal seems to be this claim of self-defence. But without a weapon it will never stand up. The sheer evidentiary weight of eight independent witness statements is going to be enough for a conviction.'

'So you're saying unless this lawyer who he doesn't even trust,' she slapped the screen of her iPad angrily, 'this Lim woman, can produce the kukri knife Danny saw, he's going to go to prison.'

Jejeune looked at her. It was hard to deliver news you knew would cause pain to those you loved. But, in the end, it was worse to deceive them. 'As things stand, yes, I believe he is.'

Lindy pursed her lips determinedly. 'Well, I for one am not prepared to let that happen while we all mope around wringing our hands and saying how terrible it is.'

He looked out over the inlet. The dark water was reflecting the light from the setting sun. It looked like there was a distant fire burning somewhere down within the water's depths. 'I'm not sure there's anything we can do. Believe me, I've been giving it a lot of thought lately.' In truth, Jejeune's mind had been on little else, including a murder-dressed-up-as-suicide case that was becoming more and more perplexing with every new development.

Lindy stood up and walked to the water's edge. He followed, wrapping his arm around her shoulders. So recently, they had stood here and believed all of their problems were behind them, that only the fresh new untracked trails of a life ahead awaited them. How quickly such visions of the future could turn to dust.

'We can't let Danny go to prison for this, Dom. We almost had him taken away from us once. I couldn't bear to lose him again. You have to find something to clear him. Staying out of it is not an option any more.'

But even Lindy's irrepressible determination wasn't going to get past the facts this time. 'I can't help him, Lindy. Even if I tried, I can't get access to any evidence. Not even Shepherd can. The Singapore DCS in charge of the case will only tell her what he wants to. The specifics, the minor details, those areas where the truth to all this lies, that's where I'd need to look. But I can't get to them.'

Lindy was quiet for a moment, lost in thought. 'I wonder if someone else could,' she said. 'Your brother's out that way, isn't he?'

'Damian? If by *that way* you mean Asia, then yes. He's working his way across the foothills of the Himalayas. He was in Bhutan, the last I heard.'

'There you are then,' said Lindy brightening. 'He's practically next door.'

'Well, if you overlook the half a dozen countries in between, I suppose. But what could Damian do, even if he went there? The UK police service can't get access to information – the Singaporean authorities are hardly likely to make it available to a foreign civilian.'

'He can at least find out why Danny feels he has to disguise messages to us through a lawyer who he clearly doesn't trust. Damian could, I don't know… visit the crime scene, ask around at the hotel where Danny was staying, see if he could unearth any new details, any bits of information you could work with.'

Jejeune shook his head. 'Even if Damian found anything, I wouldn't be able to bring it to anyone's attention. I'm not officially allowed to obtain information pertaining to the case. I'm sorry, Lindy, there's nothing we can do. As Colleen Shepherd says, we just have to have trust that the system will get it right in the end.'

Lindy's expressions were never less than eloquent. This one left him in no doubt how she felt about that approach. 'Domenic, if you needed help, Danny would walk to Asia if he had to. You know he would.'

Jejeune sighed and looked out over the water. The fire had gone from it now, and only a faint twilight glow rested on its calm surface. 'The Thunder Dragon Hotel, Thimphu,' he said finally. He looked at his watch. 'If you call now, you might catch him before he leaves for his day's birding.'

'Can you speak up? I can hardly hear you.' Lindy stuck a finger in her open ear and hopped from one foot to the other as she sometimes did when she was on a phone call while standing. 'Where are you?'

'I'm watching the traffic control system at Norzin Lam in the centre of Thimphu.'

'What an interesting life you lead, Damian.'

'I'll say. This one's human. It's also the only traffic signal in the entire country. It makes a handy spot to meet people. I'm waiting for my ride to take me to Phrumsengla National Park.'

Around Damian, the low-paced shuffle of the big city cum country market that was Bhutan's capital rattled on. The scent of spices from a nearby food cart drifted to him on the dry dusty air. A steady trail of vehicles trundled past. The low-density mix of buses, heavy goods vehicles and Asian-made compacts would have been unremarkable traffic in almost any other urban community on Earth, but here it seemed to give the area a pulsating, big-city vibe its other amenities didn't warrant. The gentle ambience of Thimphu always left Damian with a smile on his face. Bathed in its weak, warm sunshine, with lilting breezes flowing down into the valley from the foothills to the north, it made a perfect place for watching and waiting. Until Lindy's phone call had changed all that.

'So how's the birding out there?'

'Magnificent. Every day is like Christmas Day. There's always new birds to see, often something truly spectacular. I'm heading up into the park for the weekend to try for Blood Pheasant.'

The news was greeted by silence. Even Lindy usually managed to at least offer some kind of interested noise at this sort of announcement. 'I'm not the detective in the family,' said Damian, 'but I'm guessing that wasn't the reason for your call. Is everything okay?'

'Yes.' There was a hesitation on the line, again unlike the Lindy Damian knew. 'Yes, with us, everything's fine.' She seemed to realise the weakness of her response. 'Dom sends his love,' she said in a lighter tone.

'Then everything must be a long way from fine. What's up?'

Lindy looked back to the conservatory, where Dom had retreated to be out of earshot of the call. 'You remember Danny Maik?'

It was Damian's turn for silence. He had only met the man once. He had seemed decent enough, a solid, good person who had helped his brother out in a time of great difficulty. 'I do.'

'He's in trouble, Damian. He's in jail in Singapore. Dom was wondering, well we both were, actually, more me really, I was wondering if you'd fancy a trip down there to see if you can do anything to help.'

Damian watched the row of small cars creep by, the sharp-eyed drivers hunched behind their steering wheels, scouring the dirt side roads for cherished parking spaces in front of old shops that seemed unworthy of the competition for such prized spots. One more thing he knew about Danny Maik was that Lindy owed her life to him, too, on more than one occasion.

'There's almost eight hundred bird species for me to see here, Lindy. Singapore has about a hundred and forty. Dom and I could probably get that many at that twenty-four-hour Springsong event on Pelee Island. You want me to leave here to go there? Danny isn't being held for importing chewing gum, is he? That used to be a $100,000 fine down there. I don't have that kind of money to get him out.'

'Danny is being charged with the murder of a police officer.'

Once more, silence seemed to be the only response Damian could muster. Though he didn't know Maik well, he knew his brother's opinion of him. And Lindy's. It would be inconceivable to either of them that Danny could be guilty of this. But anybody in Singapore who didn't know Danny Maik, like the local police for example, would be forced to go on first impressions. Maik's build and overall demeanour would tell you he probably could kill someone, and his army service records might even tell you that he had. Neither were particularly good news if he was intending to deny the charges.

'Domenic is officially forbidden from getting involved, Damian,' Lindy said into the echoing emptiness on the other end of the line. She had emphasised the word *officially*, but Damian had already realised it wouldn't have been Lindy calling if Domenic could have investigated this himself.

A small black van rattled to the kerb beside him and the driver waved him in with a broad smile. 'My ride's here. I'll tell you what, the Blood Pheasant is held in high reverence among the people of the Himalayas. It's considered a bird of almost mystical powers. If I see one while I'm out there, I'll take it as a sign that I should go. How's that? I'll call you as soon as I'm back in Thimphu and let you know what the birding gods have decided.'

Lindy hung up and stomped into the conservatory, where Dom had his back to her with his bins raised.

'Wigeon,' he said, 'just dropped in.'

'Honestly, that brother of yours,' she said furiously.

'What did he say?' asked Domenic without turning.

'He said it would depend on whether he could find some bird or other in a park. I told him Danny's in trouble, but the message clearly didn't get through. I can't believe he'd be willing to base an important decision like this on some stupid bloody bird sighting.'

Jejeune turned in interest. 'Which bird?'

'A Blood Pheasant.'

Domenic smiled softly. Despite their revered status, Blood Pheasants were considered as Least Concern with regards to their population numbers. They could still be found if you knew where to look. Damian would.

'If Damian sets his mind on finding a bird, he doesn't give up,' he told her. 'He'll spend every minute of his time in that park looking until he sees one. The next time you hear from him, it'll be to tell you he's booked his ticket to Singapore.'

21

'Erm, I'm here to see Constable Holland. Something about an interview.' Jejeune recognised the man who appeared sheepishly at the doorway of the open office area. He introduced him to his DCS, who had appeared from the opposite direction at roughly the same time.

'Evan Knowles, DCS Shepherd.'

It wasn't necessary to add a tag about Knowles being the LSA officer who had been first on scene at the Abbie Cleve murder. Shepherd read case notes closely and had a prodigious memory for detail. She cast her eyes over the man quickly and offered him a thin smile. 'Please wait there, Mr Knowles. Constable Holland will be with you momentarily.' As she turned to Jejeune, her expression suggested that she would shortly be having a discussion with the desk sergeant about his new habit of sending members of the public back here unaccompanied, even ones as easy on the eye as this specimen.

Holland had advised his superiors of Knowles's impending visit at an impromptu gathering in Shepherd's office directly after the morning briefing. 'I'm asking him to come in to explain why, after receiving repeated reports that the premises should be inspected, he allowed Abbie Cleve to continue operating until he finally found the time to get off his arse and get over there. Though I'm pretty sure I already know.'

'Well, why don't we give him the opportunity to tell you anyway,' Shepherd had suggested testily.

The man stood up now as Holland approached. 'Mr Knowles.' The constable hooked a finger in the man's direction without breaking stride. 'With me.'

Shepherd watched them as they left. 'Tony seems dangerously upbeat about his prospects, wouldn't you say? No doubt I'm going to deeply regret this later, but I have to say I'm intrigued to see where he intends to go. Fancy a watch?'

Jejeune hadn't observed another officer's interview for a long time, but the look Shepherd gave him suggested there might be a secondary purpose to her request. He stood and followed her to the Observation Suite.

Holland settled in quickly, hoping the disorientation of being in the interview room would help keep Knowles off balance. He began his questions as soon as he had run through the preliminaries.

'For the record, please state the reason for your visit to the Nye on the morning of the fourteenth?'

'I was going to investigate the conditions and overall operation there. We'd received an anonymous email that there might be some compliance issues.'

'This email, it arrived the day before your visit.'

'It seemed important to investigate as soon as possible.'

'Really? Do you know Tara Skye? She was there that day at the Nye.'

'I recognised the name, as I imagine most people around here would. But I'm fairly sure we had never met before that day. She'd be difficult to forget, frankly, wouldn't she?'

Holland didn't even set off along the path to meet the man's smile halfway. 'You know the name because she sent you three signed emails asking you to investigate the conditions at the Nye. You ignored all of these requests, and yet you suddenly rush out there on the basis of a single email from an anonymous source.'

The smile had disappeared, to be replaced on Evan Knowles's handsome features by a look of embarrassment. 'Ah, yes. The thing is, it was a question of time, you see. My daughter has special needs; there are appointments, after-school programmes. It involves lot of running around. It means I have to arrange my work schedule very carefully. It's worth it, though. She seems to be making real progress.'

He gave another weak smile but, if he was trying for the human connection, Holland's deadpan expression suggested he might be looking in the wrong place. He could sympathise with the man's challenges, but it opened another door for later on.

'Did Abigail Cleve know why you were coming that day?'

'She was aware there had been complaints, and we were required to investigate them.'

'But you weren't going there with the intention to shut her down?'

'Not initially, no. Obviously that would have depended on what I found. I would have taken samples, examined the housing conditions and processing facilities, checked sanitation and disposal practices. But only after compiling a report and presenting it at tribunal would a decision be taken to close a facility. A Cease Operations order is a very serious matter, with grave consequences for the owner and the local community. It's not a step we at the LSA would take lightly.'

'I understand you've done all those checks now, though. Post-mortem, as it were.'

'A thorough audit of the stock and facilities at the suspension of operations is normal practice.'

'Any basis for Tara Skye's complaints? Or the anonymous one?'

People had different ways of equivocating, Holland knew. Knowles's was to purse his lips slightly and tilt his head. 'Yes and no. I mean, were pens a touch cramped and lacking in perches? Perhaps. Could larger outdoor runs have been provided? Yes. But those things were by design. Birds that aren't given perches to fly to and can't roam far are ultimately going to produce more meat for the market. As for the overall condition of the birds, our sampling shows them to be free from disease, farm-raised and hormone-free, as advertised.'

'So just to be clear, you wouldn't have shut the operation down on the basis of your findings?'

'Let's just say I've seen far worse. I'd have written a couple of compliance notices, set a date for a follow-up visit to check it had all been done, and left it at that.'

'So that's consistent with your earlier position, then?'

'What earlier position?'

'A very meticulous woman, Abigail Cleve,' said Holland, withdrawing a couple of forms from a folder. 'Went some way to explaining how she became so successful so fast, I imagine. She kept the thirty-day continuance certificates you issued her. The thing is, Mr Knowles, I'm wondering how you could justify issuing a licence to continue operations three times in a row, when you had emails suggesting the conditions needed to be investigated. Be worth a lot, that, knowing she was going to be allowed to continue to operate without the possibility of being inspected. She could ignore regulations every other livestock farmer had to observe, cut corners, compromise standards, all the while confident in the knowledge that you would not be coming round to check on her. Be how she was able to maximise her profits, how she was able to make so much money so quickly.'

There was a long silence as Knowles assessed the statement, then he held up a hand. 'Okay, look. I'll admit those continuance certificates might look like favouritism. But it was hardly her fault I couldn't make it over there for an inspection, was it? Issuing them was the decent thing to do, the kind thing. No good deed goes unpunished, I see.'

'We'd have to hope not, if that good deed led to a woman's murder.' Holland left the statement hanging and announced a short recess. He gathered up his papers and left the room hurriedly.

In the Observation Suite, Shepherd raised her eyebrows to Jejeune.

'Good time for a break,' he said approvingly. 'It will take Knowles's imagination to all sorts of places we might not know about yet. It might distract him enough to let something slip later.'

Shepherd gave him a sideways glance. This was exactly the kind of insight she'd been hoping he might have been able to pass on to Summer, if his mind wasn't elsewhere all the time. 'I received a call from Lindy, Domenic. A theoretical question about how much trouble a serving officer might find himself in for becoming involved with a defence case in a foreign state. *Theoretical*, mind you.' She gave him a look she reserved for insults to her intelligence. 'Honestly, that girl. At least she didn't say *foreign city-state*.'

'She's just trying to protect you.'

'Protect me? From what? The conduct of one of my officers who ought to know better?'

It had been a poor choice of phrase, one guaranteed to draw Shepherd's ire. Jejeune wished he could have pulled it back, but it was too late now.

'Well, you may inform your young lady that the Police Professional Standards Board has a phrase for any unsolicited involvement in a defence case, foreign or otherwise. Perhaps you've heard of it. It's called a sackable offence.'

'I'm not involved. I'm hoping to suggest a few new directions they might try, that's all.' He raised his hands, palms upward. 'It's Danny,' he said. 'His only hope of avoiding a conviction is this self-defence claim, but without the knife he will never prove it. That's where the defence team's efforts should be going. A fight between two men on a busy street, one of them wearing a police uniform? I imagine it's hardly an everyday occurrence in Singapore. It would have drawn a big crowd. Have they even asked for mobile-phone footage, I wonder?'

'I'm told they have, as a matter of fact. Remarkable as it may seem, even in Singapore defence lawyers seem to be familiar with basic investigative techniques. There is nothing on any of the footage, no sign of a knife anywhere.' She paused. 'So what exactly was it you wanted to pass on, anyway?'

'There's a mobile phone missing, too.' he said. 'A burner. The most likely scenario to me is that it was taken at the scene as well. But what are the chances that the phone and the knife were taken by two separate individuals, and neither act was witnessed by anyone in that crowd?'

'Not high, I'll grant you, but it would have been mayhem there. So you're suggesting the phone and the knife could have been taken by the same person.'

He nodded. 'And if so, locating the phone could lead them to the knife. Danny's defence lawyer needs to be putting everything she has into tracking down that phone.'

Shepherd considered the idea thoughtfully. Her own silences generally boded well for Jejeune. She was not shy about telling him when she disapproved of an idea. 'This and no more, Domenic, am I clear? How are you intending to get this to the lawyer? I'm assuming Lindy's back-door contact over there is some friendly journalist?' She shook her head. 'They're a law unto themselves, that lot. Eric has connections all over the world.'

Jejeune didn't correct his DCS. He'd learned long ago that, when someone was looking pleased with themselves over their deductive reasoning, they rarely welcomed being told they had it wrong.

Holland re-entered the interview room and recommenced proceedings with the same abruptness he had ended the previous session. 'Right, where were we? Oh yes. Your belated inspection of the Nye. You're affiliated with a number of climate change groups, aren't you, Mr Knowles? Planning on being up at Cleve Hall on the weekend, are you?'

'I don't think it would be appropriate, given my position. I limit my involvement to a few talks on the subject. I'm afraid I don't see the connection.'

'Luckily, that's our job. This last email. It came from the account of one of those groups. And yet they didn't sign it. To you, a card-carrying member of their cause. Strange that, if they just wanted you to have a quiet word with her. Not so strange, though, if they were expecting you to do something more. Were you going to shut down her operation, on the advice of your climate-change mates?'

'No.'

'I hear Abigail Cleve wasn't exactly the type of woman to take news like that quietly. Perhaps there was an argument, a bit of a set-to that got out of hand. You killed her and tried to stage it as a suicide.'

'What?' Knowles had been slumping in his chair slightly, affecting disinterest. He raised himself in a hurry. 'No. That's ridiculous. She was dead when I arrived.'

'Was she?'

'I was driving there when I received her text. I called Jim Loyal immediately. You can check. The phone will have pinged off the mast, won't it? It'll give you my position when I made the call.'

'The phone mast can only confirm you were in that area. It can't confirm where you were within it. You could have been a mile down the road when you made that call, as you say, or you could have been kneeling right beside her body for all we know.'

Knowles's voice began to rise in panic. 'I placed the call through my onboard car system. There'll be a record, surely. Besides, what possible motive could I have for killing that poor woman?'

'You tell me. You had multiple requests to investigate and you never went. You issued continuance certificates in the meantime. It must be expensive, that care for your daughter. Be handy to have another source of income.'

'This is crazy. It was nothing like that. You have my financial records. They don't make pretty reading, but it's everything I have. LSA officials don't have secret accounts in offshore tax havens, Constable, at least not the ones I know.'

'If not money, then how about payment in kind? Abigail Cleve was a good-looking woman, unattached. A touch of the upper crust, so to speak.'

Knowles gave a short laugh. 'There are still some things you can't do electronically, Constable. I told you, I didn't have time to go over there; for an inspection, sex, or anything else.'

Holland stood and briskly gathered his notes once again. 'That'll be all for now, Mr Knowles,' he said 'We'll be in touch if we need to talk to you again. Don't go anywhere without letting us know, will you?'

In the Observation Suite, Shepherd turned to Jejeune as Holland left the room. 'The denials seemed believable, but there was something there, wasn't there? Some reason Knowles chose to help Abigail Cleve out with those continuance notices. I'd say there was definitely more to their relationship than meets the eye.'

Jejeune nodded sadly. When murder was involved, there usually was.

22

Fall was such a defined season when he was younger, thought Domenic Jejeune. The trees had leaves, then there was the spectacular display as they moved through their various colour phases, and then the trees had no leaves; and the ground beneath them was littered with a carpet of brittle, sugar-depleted flotsam. Now fall, or autumn as it was over here, seemed such an ambivalent process. Some trees began to turn by August, while others were still holding on to their colour into November. And then there were those like the ones hanging over the narrow pathway ahead of him, a speckled display of intermittent green and yellow, as if the trees had started the procedure of turning and then suddenly abandoned their efforts halfway through. Were things really so much more clear-cut back in his younger days, he wondered, or was it just the snapshots of memory that made them seem so?

Above him, the sky had settled for a subdued palette. On a canvas of the palest of pale blue, trails of thin cloud were shot through with light from the soft, white sun. It gave the day a mood that Domenic Jejeune chose to interpret with guarded optimism as he strolled along the half-leafed track.

He caught sight of a figure approaching from the other direction and was about to look for an alternative trail when he heard a rustle a few metres ahead. He stopped instinctively and trained his bins onto the base of a hedgerow, catching a flash of dazzling gold and scarlet. Suddenly, the bird stepped out onto the path in full view. Jejeune left his glasses on the Golden Pheasant as it calmly inspected the gravel before proceeding at a leisurely pace across the track and disappearing beneath the hedgerow on the far side.

From opposite directions, Jejeune and Tara Skye arrived at the spot at the same time, but, despite careful scrutiny of the tangled vegetation, they could see no sign of the bird. It seemed impossible that such a large, spectacularly coloured creature could disappear without trace, but Jejeune had lost count of the number of times he had marvelled at the way the natural world was able to swallow up its treasures like this.

'Well, that was pretty special,' said Skye. 'I didn't think they were around these parts any more. Do you think it was an escape?'

'Possibly, but you used to be able to find one once in a while around Dersingham, so I suspect there is still a remnant population out there somewhere.'

'Too bad birders can't put them on their lists, isn't it?' She didn't look sad.

'Actually, the UK is the only place in the Western Palearctic where Golden Pheasants are still considered *countable*, for want of a better word. Lady Amherst's Pheasants were, too, though I believe the wild population of those has pretty much disappeared completely in the UK.'

'As a result of Section 14, Wildlife and Countryside Act 1981,' Skye said heavily, 'which banned their release. So if we can do it for those pheasants, why not the ones for shooting? Fifty million pheasants are released into the countryside every year during the shooting season. Fifty million! Plus another ten million Red-legged Partridges. Even if you don't care about the fate of these poor birds, surely everybody can appreciate the catastrophic damage they must be having on native ecosystems. I read a report that said at this time of the year, game birds make up half of the UK's entire avian biomass. Think about that.' She set her hands on her hips in exasperation. 'So many pheasants released that they equal the combined weight of every other bird in the country. It's insane. I mean, how can anybody believe that's not going to decimate habitats and prey species?'

The woman's youthful intensity might have made it difficult to counter her arguments anyway, but Jejeune had no wish to do so. Tara Skye was undoubtedly right. She shrugged resignedly. 'Well, if you lot are not going to do anything to stop the shooting, I suppose I'll just have to resort to my own methods.'

'Meaning?' he asked.

'I'm planning to fly a drone over the estate. I'll try to flush the birds away from the shoot area.'

'I'm not sure that would be wise. For one thing, it would undoubtedly cause the birds a great deal of stress.'

'Really, Inspector.' Skye gave Jejeune one of the contemptuous looks of which she seemed to have an inexhaustible supply. 'You don't you think the birds are already a touch stressed by gunshots and beaters? Unless you can tell me it is categorically forbidden by law, I'm heading off to practise my piloting skills right now.'

She turned to leave, but Jejeune knew interviews conducted in informal settings generally yielded better results. Especially if the person didn't realise they were being questioned. 'You lodged three complaints against the Nye, and Evan Knowles failed to respond to any of them. But you didn't pursue the matter. Forgive me,' he said with a smile,' but you don't seem like the type to let something like that drop.'

She took the comment as a compliment and returned his smile. 'I took another approach, didn't I?' she said proudly. 'I sent some meat samples from the Nye off for independent analysis. I wanted to see if it contained growth hormones or anything else that might get the operation shut down.'

'And?'

'Nothing. The meat was fine. I don't have anything against Knowles personally. I know he has to look after that kid of his and all, but I suspected the fact that a member of the public was doing his job for him might spark him into action and get him out there. And I was right.'

'But only after another, anonymous, complaint from a climate group. Though I have to say, I don't quite understand why they'd be going after operations at the Nye. I would have thought a business that reduces methane emissions and produces more protein might have been something they wanted to support.'

The sun caught rainbow highlights in the hair that hung down the unshaven side of Tara Skye's head as she shook it to show her indulgence at the ignorance of this older man. 'It was. The climate crowd went out of their way to endorse Abbie Cleve's operation when she started up. They already had effective campaigns going against beef farming in other parts of the country and they thought this would be their flagship operation. They held up the Nye as a shining example of today's more environmentally conscious food production practices.'

'So what went wrong?'

'They expected a lot of exposure for their anti-methane, high-yield land use positions. Only, whenever Abigail Cleve did any interviews, TV, newspapers, magazines, she avoided the topics like the plague. It was all about healthy food choices, better sources of protein, promoting her own products and company, basically.' Tara Skye shook her head with a disillusionment beyond her years. 'Still, when a group of idealists pin their hopes on a self-centred opportunist, it's never going to end well, is it, Inspector – Bird!' she shouted suddenly, pointing over Jejeune's shoulder.

He spun and raised his bins to see a raptor dancing over a hedgerow on strong, deliberate wingbeats. In a moment it was gone, but when he lowered his bins he saw that Tara Skye had been thrilled by the sighting, too.

'Lammergeier?' she teased.

Jejeune smiled. 'Goshawk. A really great bird.'

'They're rare, aren't they?'

Jejeune nodded. 'Less so now, but it's a species that's only slowly recovering in numbers. For years, the birds were persecuted by gamekeepers to protect their stock.'

Skye gave her head another grave shake. 'This hunting business has got a lot to answer for, if you ask me.' She looked at him frankly. 'Sorry if I was harsh on you back at Ferris's the other day. I have a tendency to get a bit worked up at times.'

Jejeune smiled his forgiveness. She had just told him Abigail Cleve had not quite turned out to be the campaigner the climate groups had expected. He considered the information she had given him debt paid.

'But I wasn't wrong, was I?' she asked.

He shook his head slowly. 'About birders and rarities? No, you weren't.' He knew of people who had hired planes to see birds, helicopters even, flying in to claim a single sighting. He could understand it, sympathise with it, even. But he couldn't excuse it.

'We're none of us innocent in this, are we, Inspector? Not as innocent as we'd like to be, anyway.'

Jejeune looked at her for a long moment. Was there something she wanted to tell him, out here on this quiet country path on this soft fall day? Something she might not have wanted to share when she was standing near a dead body at the Nye? 'Your alibi for the time before you arrived at the Board Room,' he said casually. 'Can you remind me what it was?'

'I was at home. Tidying my flat. Believe me, it needed it.'

'And it could be verified?' he asked.

'The flat's still tidy, if that helps,' said Skye impatiently. 'What's this all about?'

'Why were you at the Board Room on the day Abbie Cleve was killed? It's not your local, is it? You live a good distance away.'

For the first time since they had begun speaking, Tara Skye shifted evasively. 'They do a good breakfast.'

'But you didn't order one. So why were you there?'

'Okay.' She sighed and dropped her hands to her sides. 'I was planning to screw with some poaching operations, all right? I'd come across some regular runs up there where snares were being set.'

'How were you going to go about that? Like it or not, it is an offence...'

'to damage or remove snares and to disrupt a lawful activity, such as snaring,' she recited. 'Yeah, I know. But fox urine is a naturally occurring substance and, as far as I'm aware, there's no prohibition on spraying it anywhere I want. If rabbits choose to give any urine-doused snares a wide berth, well, that's just too bad, isn't it?' she asked defiantly.

'Would Pete Estey have been one of the people setting those snares?'

'Who cares, they're all as bad as each other, poachers. Worse than hunters even, given the suffering they cause. I can't imagine how many animals there must be out there carrying some sort of injury caused by a snare they managed to escape from. It's heartbreaking to even think about it.'

'So you never saw Estey anywhere near where Abbie Cleve was killed?'

She shook her head. 'He wasn't even around. Jim Loyal saw him heading off towards Cromer, miles away.'

'Loyal did?' The rest of Jejeune's shocked response was cut short by the buzz of his phone. He reached for it as soon as he saw the caller ID, and pressed it to his ear urgently.

'Shots fired, sir. Officer requests assistance.'

He waited for the desk sergeant to confirm the location. 'Stone Road Forest. North side.'

Jejeune didn't need to ask the identity of the officer involved. He sprinted back towards the Range Rover parked at the far end of the track, leaving Tara Skye staring after him in bewilderment. She heard the throaty roar of the Beast's engine firing up and watched it pulling away with the detective still dragging the door shut.

23

Damian peeled off his daypack, feeling the cool air on the sweat patches on his shirt. He slumped to the ground gratefully and took in the view. In front of him, green-clad valleys, draped in wraiths of mist, stretched out in all directions. Red dirt paths like the one he had just taken, beaten into hillside trails by millennia of leaden feet, traced their way through the vegetation like arteries. The valley below, from which he had begun his ascent, shimmered like a vision from a dream. It was a three-hour hike, his guidebook had told him, up here to Paro Taktsang, the legendary Tiger's Nest monastery. He had taken four. An earlier version of Damian would have striven for half that. He would have turned it into a test of his fitness, of his endurance, of himself. But a recent encounter had caused him to re-evaluate his priorities, as so many encounters seemed to do in this Land of the Thunder Dragon.

A ray of sunlight broke through the mist, trapping a spectrum of rainbow colours in the vapour. Damian watched as the diffused light slowly brought the far hillsides to life. He could not remember a place where the light lay so gently on the land. Patches of shade seemed to blend effortlessly into pools of light, giving the emerging landscape a dappled harmony that was mesmerising. He had come to Bhutan to take on the

Snowman Trek, the notorious month-long route along the base of the Himalayas, renowned for being the most difficult trek in the world. That billing alone was reason enough for Damian to want to attempt it. But a mixture of red tape and post-pandemic insurance complications had left him without sufficient time to complete the trek before the winter snows came, so he had abandoned his plans. He had returned to nurse his disappointment in the tea houses of Thimphu, and in one he had spoken to a lithe young American trekker who had recently completed the route. It was the gruelling conditions and challenging trails the man spoke of first, long before the beauty of what he had seen. Damian thought about what the man had missed, head down against the fierce winds and biting cold temperatures, eyes focused only on those winding dirt trails, as he battled his way to the top of the next pass, and then the next one. Was the view from the summits the only prize worth seeking? Or would it have been equally rewarding to choose a gentler route, one that revealed the gradual transition from one elevation to the next? Was the spectacle of those slowly unfurling wonders any less gratifying than a single view from the top? Over the next few days, the realisation had slowly come to him that the only reward he needed was the beauty the world held. If he had to work to see it, travel to remote spots and endure harsh conditions, then that was the cost. But it was no longer the goal.

A shadow passed over his face, and he lifted his eyes to see a single Himalayan Vulture describing a long, graceful arc through the china-blue sky above him. He watched the bird as it spiralled upwards, its outstretched wingtips riffling as it rode the thermals in a flight as silent and majestic as the mountains themselves. Even the scavengers managed to grace this enchanted land with their beauty, he thought. On the hillside across the valley he saw a tiny flicker of activity among the vegetation. He raised his bins and focused on a small group of birds as they emerged from the cover. Though they were mere dark spots from this range, he knew they were Kalij Pheasants. He watched the birds for a few moments as they foraged among the scree and low scrub, then, as if by magic, they melted back into the cover and were gone. So it was with this place, he thought. It momentarily bestowed its gifts upon you before gathering them back in until they could be shared with the next fortunate viewer.

Damian's new approach would affect his birding, too, he realised. He would no longer feel the need to earn a sighting by putting in sufficient effort to seek out the bird. Views of those birds that simply drifted into his realm, as the Kalij Pheasants had just done, would become every bit as rewarding as any tracked down on arduous, solitary travels to remote areas. *Solitary*? Perhaps such a softening of his approach might even encourage someone to accompany him now, too. Because the only way this place, this moment, could have been any better was if he had someone sitting beside him on this cliff face taking it all in with him, someone he cared about, sharing the experience. He had always admired Domenic's relationship with Lindy. Despite all they had been through, they were still together. His clueless brother probably lacked the nous to do the sensible thing and make it official, but surely even he would have enough sense to hold on tightly to the most precious thing he had in this world. Danny Maik had found someone too, according to Lindy. After all this time. She had made it sound as if that only added to the tragedy of all this. And perhaps she was right. To wait this long to find the right person, and then to lose them – no, to have them taken away, unjustly. That alone would have given Damian the resolve to go to Singapore and fight on Danny's behalf, he realised now. To fight for love; if not his own, then someone else's – for the idea of love, even. He shook his head and smiled. He could imagine his brother's eye-rolling disdain at such fanciful notions. Domenic would probably tell him he needed to get out of this country before he found himself in some monastery with a shaved head and a purple robe.

Damian thought about what awaited him in Singapore, the inevitable assault to the senses he faced from the teeming, tightly-packed metropolis. There were quiet spaces there, he knew, and he would seek them out if he could. But his role, to find out and report on the progress in Danny Maik's case, would require him to inhabit mostly the maelstrom of lawyers' offices and halls of justice in the Civic District. He would not dwell on that today, though. Negative energy had no place in this oasis of human happiness. Instead, he would sit here on the side of this mountain, in the shadow of an ancient monastery perched on a cliff edge, and turn his face to the sun. He would close his eyes and listen to the wind, and feel the peace of Paro Taktsang flowing into him.

He opened his eyes again and drank in the views, one more final, longing look at the pristine unspoiled valleys, with the last of the mist clinging to their lush green sides. He would be sad to leave Bhutan. His life had been one of turmoil and upheaval for as long as he could remember, and the country had filled him with the kind of peace he had not known for a long time. But he recognised that his reluctance to move on was not just because of what he would be leaving behind. Lindy had made it clear that he was Danny Maik's last hope. If he could not uncover some evidence, or find some other means to clear him, Danny was going to prison, likely for a very long time. But what could he, Damian Jejeune, do? He had no legal expertise, no knowledge of investigative techniques. Perhaps that was the most daunting thing of all; that so little was expected of him. The hopelessness in Lindy's tone had made it clear his chances of achieving anything were low. Her hollow despair seemed only to add to the weight of responsibility he felt.

The vulture had returned, quartering the sky in a series of low passes that gave Damian a perfect view of its effortless flying skills. He watched the bird until it disappeared behind a crag from which a single cypress tree grew. Hanging out over the valley below, surrounded only by sky, the tree moved like a dancer in the faint breeze, its dark-green foliage shimmering in the feathering wind. The tree's silhouette reminded him of a painting by Tom Thomson, that outlier who seemed to him to capture the atmosphere of the northern Ontario parks in a way that none of the Group of Seven had ever quite matched. Damian had thought of that part of the world as paradise when he was there. Now he felt the same about this place. Perhaps that was what his travels had taught him: that you carried your paradise with you, and along the way you simply found different places to lay it.

Yes, he would be sad to leave Bhutan. Some places became a part of you. They attached themselves to your soul and you took them with you when you left. Perhaps over time the feeling faded, and you were left instead with only pale memories of your visit. But he had a feeling Bhutan would not be like that. It would always be a part of him. It had changed his perspective, shown him a new way to experience the world, and he was convinced he would carry its lessons with him for ever. He was sure, too, that part of his own peace would remain here. The serenity and contentment he had found in Bhutan would linger in the atmosphere long after he had departed, suspended in the air for others to breathe. He smiled again. Perhaps it was the presence of the Tiger's Nest monastery behind him that was inspiring such esoteric musings. But any country that was prepared to offer such blissful moments of reflection had to expect the odd foray into the realms of the mystical. Bhutan was a place to make philosophers of us all.

24

Jejeune skidded the Beast to a halt behind Tony Holland's Audi. Parked in front of them on the road along the ridge was Noel Summer's grey Trabant. Holland was pacing up and down, holding a phone to his ear. Across the field below them, the Armed Response Unit that had been fanned out across the land like creeping black beetles were moving freely now towards a central spot, where their command vehicle was parked. Although Jejeune knew this meant the threat had been neutralised, he would wait for the official word.

'Site secured,' Holland told him as he ended the call. 'No shooter, no weapon.'

'Summer?'

'No injuries reported. The DCS is on her way here. She says to wait and we can all go down to the scene together.' He looked at Summer's car and then at the surrounding landscape. 'Why would he park up here?' he asked. 'You don't need to know the area to realise if you park your car on the top of a rise like this, anybody down below can see it from miles away. He couldn't have given Estey more advance notice of his visit if he'd sent him an email.'

The same thought had occurred to Jejeune. Perhaps it wasn't the right time to be critical of a fellow officer who'd just been involved in a shooting, but Holland had a point. Jejeune raised his bins to survey the land below. The expanse of forest flowed like a dark lake across the landscape. Over on the far side, he could see the road where he and Summer had parked the last time they had come here, and even the faint pathway they had followed into the woods. They had been a long way off, and heading in the wrong direction, when Lindy had inadvertently interrupted their search. Would they ever have found Estey's place coming in from that side? He doubted it. Even now, with Summer's car parked up here as a marker, it was all but impossible to pick out the ramshackle trailer in the woods below.

The men turned at the sound of DCS Shepherd's Jaguar crunching to a stop on the gravel behind them. She remained behind the wheel until she had concluded a phone conversation. 'Summer's fine, thankfully,' she told them as she emerged from the car. 'The commander says he seems remarkably unfazed by the whole thing. Of course that could just be shock.'

'What, at actually finding the place?' Holland held up his hand. 'Joking, ma'am. Of course I'm over the moon that he's okay.'

The three of them descended the slope and made their way towards the trees. As they drew nearer, they could see a line of mixed conifers arcing around in front of a clearing, like the protective arm of a sea wall sheltering a harbour. From any other angle, the stand would simply appear to be part of the forest and the clearing behind it would be completely unde-tectable. They rounded the stand of trees and emerged into a surprisingly large open area. The light from above seemed almost to spotlight it against the dark foliage surrounding it. A shotgun blast would have echoed loudly in this silent amphi-theatre, and the acrid tang of gunpowder, gone now, would have hung long in the crisp, cold air.

On the far side of the clearing, Noel Summer was leaning casually against a leafless birch tree, one knee bent to rest his foot against the trunk behind him. He was deep in conversation with a man Shepherd recognised as the Forensic Firearms Investigator. The officer acknowledged them with a look, but made no move to end the interview. He would be keen to get Summer's account while it was still fresh in his mind.

'Over here.' Holland pointed to the dilapidated old trailer pressed deep into the overgrown vegetation at the back of the clearing. The three officers made their way towards it, ducking their heads as they entered. Jejeune looked around the interior in the dim half-light. It was to such meagre surroundings as this that a damaged man had retreated on his return from a battlefront half a world away, he thought.

Holland crossed to the window and opened one of the wooden slats. Bands of weak light filtered in, trapping spirals of dust in their beams and bathing the sparse interior in a patina of grey. On a hook near the door hung a dead male pheasant, still in its full plumage.

'I see Estey wasn't a pheasant plucker, then,' said Holland.

Jejeune turned. 'Surely you'd only do that prior to cooking it?'

'It's a saying, Domenic,' said Shepherd, 'a tongue-twister in these parts:

> I'm not the pheasant plucker
> I'm the pheasant plucker's son
> And I'm only plucking pheasants
> Till the pheasant plucker comes.'

'Ah,' said Jejeune, his expression falling into that wasteland between bewilderment and pity that he seemed to reserve exclusively for explanations of eccentric English ways.

'Usually recited multiple times, at speed, after a few pints of Greene King. With predictable results,' she said sourly.

'Although, given that an officer has been shot at here, Tony, perhaps now's not the time.'

'He seems to be doing okay, though,' said Holland defensively. He nodded towards the window. 'No shakes that I could see, no after-action jazz, just that same half-arsed leaning about as always.'

Through the window of the trailer, Shepherd could see Summer still engaged in a desultory conversation with the FFI. He was pointing an arm casually in the direction of the cabin. They appeared to be going over trajectories, trying to determine where the shooter may have been standing. But the constable was showing no reluctance to recreate the scene, to relive what must have been a harrowing few moments. If not even being on the receiving end of a couple of shotgun blasts got him agitated, Shepherd began to wonder whether anything would.

'Has anyone checked around here for shell casings yet?' she asked. 'Perhaps you could take care of that, Tony.'

Holland ducked out of the trailer, leaving only Shepherd and her DCI inside. Jejeune undertook a visual inspection to the extent the dim light would allow, but touched nothing. He approached the bird hanging on the hook and leaned in to examine it closely. Something caught his eye and he moved closer to the bird. He opened the trailer door wider to allow more light in.

'Domenic?'

'Hessian fibres,' he said.

'No bag, though.' Both officers spun to find Summer standing in the doorway. 'I've had a look around. There is no hessian bag here.' He pulled on a latex glove and took an evidence bag from his pocket. 'I'll get them off for analysis. See if they match those from the Nye.' His look towards his two superior officers suggested they all knew they would. But as he reached forward, Jejeune called out.

'Wait,' he said. 'Leave them on the bird and bag up the whole carcass. I want to take a look at it in better light.'

'Something in particular?' asked Shepherd.

'Something that doesn't appear to be there.'

The answer seemed to irritate Shepherd. She gave Jejeune leeway to indulge in these cryptic responses because they produced results. That had manifestly not been the case in this investigation, not least because his mind had been elsewhere most of the time. She pursed her lips. 'Right, well if you are all done in here, you can see what Tony's been able to find outside and then the two of you can head back to the station. DC Summer and I will stay on and take a look around.'

If the comment struck Jejeune as unusual, he gave no sign. Summer moved aside, and the DCI ducked through the low doorway. Shepherd turned to Summer as soon as he had gone. 'Are you sure you're okay? You're fit to stay on duty? Normally I'd recommend counselling, but we're stretched so thin at the moment with Sergeant Salter off I don't have the resources to cover you.'

Summer shook his head. 'I'm fine, ma'am. It's not like I was staring down the barrel of a gun. It was more just the sounds of gunshots.'

'But you're certain they were directed at you?'

Summer stared back into Shepherd's eyes. 'Yes, ma'am, I am. Two rounds, as soon as I emerged into the clearing. From somewhere beside the trailer here. They were meant for me.'

She lowered her gaze and nodded to confirm she had received all the reassurance she needed. 'This business would certainly suggest you were right to focus on Estey.' Nonchalance was never Shepherd's forte, and as she got older she seemed to find more and more benefits in getting straight to the point. 'How are things going with DCI Jejeune?'

'Okay.' But there was enough evasion in the response to encourage further inquiry. Shepherd couldn't help the feeling that Summer had intended it that way. She left her gaze on him.

'I suppose I'm just a bit underwhelmed, if I'm being honest. I was expecting quite the show, given what I'd heard. But I haven't seen anything out of the ordinary. Pedestrian thinking, routine, run-of-the-mill questions.' Summer gave a small shrug. 'Nothing any other detective couldn't have come up with. Okay, this case has been anything but straightforward, but I'd been prepared for, well… maybe a bit more.'

Shepherd checked her customary reflex to defend her team. Instead she was forced to acknowledge what had been blindingly obviously to everyone since the start of the case. 'You're not seeing him at his best, Constable. He has other things on his mind.'

'This business in Singapore, with his ex-partner?'

'Danny Maik, yes. Things aren't looking good for him, and Domenic, like all of us, is frustrated that he can't do anything to help.'

'From what I've heard people don't seem to think he could have been involved in anything like this. Do you think they've got the wrong man?'

'That's highly unlikely. But I do think they've got the wrong crime. Danny Maik could never murder someone in cold blood. There has to be more to this. But nobody is likely to get to it from here.' Shepherd shook her head. 'I'm afraid until the DCI comes to terms with that, and starts to focus on the job at hand, you'll likely end up having to do most of the heavy lifting on this case. I wonder, Constable, in light of what has just happened, are you up to it?'

Summer nodded. 'I am.'

Shepherd nodded again. She wasn't quite ready to give her junior officer carte blanche for his inquiries but, unless Domenic decided to reveal what was troubling him about this bird, she couldn't tell if it was genuine progress or further evidence of his distracted mind. And if it was the latter, she might soon find herself with no option other than to turn the entire investigation over to Detective Constable Noel Summer.

25

'Noel, come in. No need for a rugby tackle this time. A handshake will do.'

Lindy's mischievous smile dispelled Summer's momentary look of unease, and she took his jacket and shepherded him past her into the living room. 'We're having pheasant. With redcurrant sauce. I do hope that's okay,' she said uncertainly. 'You did say anything. It's from the Nye. It's been getting raves from the locals, so I thought I'd see what all the fuss is about. Dom will be out in a moment. He's on salad duty in the kitchen.' She leaned in confidentially. 'I wouldn't hold out much hope, to be honest. He still thinks arugula is an island in the Caribbean.'

Summer offered a weak smile and made non-committal noises of approval as she pointed out the features in their home, pausing longest to describe the view from the conservatory that nightfall had hidden from them. The Grand Tour over, she led him back into the main room and sat down on the couch, patting the seat beside her for him to join her. Jejeune emerged from the kitchen and greeted Summer before taking a chair opposite them. She detected a faint guardedness in Domenic. Perhaps it was simply the awkwardness of the superior officer hosting the new recruit in a social setting, but it suggested she might have to take up the running of the conversation, at least in the early going.

'Are you okay,' she asked, 'after that horrible business yesterday? We weren't sure you'd still come. Well, I wasn't. Dom seemed pretty convinced you hadn't been too shaken up by it.'

Summer tilted his head. 'I'm not sure it was a serious attempt to kill me. It seems strange to say, but I never felt like I was in imminent danger.'

'Still, it must have been pretty unnerving. And coming on top of that other business, at the Nye. Having to deal with a body there. On your first day back, too. That must have been particularly hard for you.'

He shrugged. 'At least the DCS seems to feel this shooting incident proves we're on the right track.'

'Are we?' asked Jejeune pointedly. 'With Estey, you mean? Can I ask what it is that makes you so sure he's involved?'

'For God's sake, Dom,' said Lindy, 'you're not interviewing a suspect. How about offering our guest a drink instead.'

'No, it's fine,' said Summer. 'First, Estey showed up at the opening of the Nye despite the fact that Abbie Cleve had ended the relationship. I don't know, maybe he feels partly responsible for her success, having been the one who liberated her from the family, so to speak. Perhaps he thinks he's owed something. Add that to the fact that, of all the places he could set up on his return from his deployment, he chooses one so close to where she lives. It just feels off. Is there any reason you think it couldn't be him?'

Jejeune seemed disinclined to answer, and a beat of uncomfortable silence settled over the conversation.

'Okay, you two, enough shop talk,' announced Lindy, rescuing the moment. 'So, Noel, Druidry. I can't say I know much about it, frankly, but I'm intrigued to find out what it was about it that appealed to you.'

'It came along when I needed it and it offered me what I wanted,' he said simply. 'In this case, that was connections, relationships; with the Earth, with nature.' He shrugged. 'It was a starting point for me to try and recover some of what I'd lost in myself.'

He fell silent, and it occurred to Lindy that he hadn't said whether he had succeeded. 'I hope you don't mind my asking,' she said. 'I imagine it's so misunderstood, many Druids would prefer to keep their beliefs to themselves.'

'I've grown a bit more accustomed to speaking about it over time,' said Summer. 'That said, I should probably have kept it quiet at the station.'

'Not from a fear of ridicule, I hope. I'd remind you Dom's a birder. You'd probably need to get in line for some of Tony Holland's contempt.'

Summer shrugged. 'I suppose he's entitled to his opinion.'

'Nobody is entitled to an opinion,' said Lindy firmly. 'An opinion has to be earned, through research and insight and considered reflection. Anybody is entitled to say whatever occurs to them, but calling such spontaneous drivel an opinion really does a disservice to the process of rational thought.'

'Language is something of an area of interest for Lindy,' said Jejeune, in case the point needed making.

'It serves a purpose, I suppose.'

'Serves a purpose?' Lindy clearly already felt comfortable enough with Summer to treat him to some of her faux outrage. 'The grandeur of Milton's prose? The glorious intimacy of a poem by Keats? The enchantment of a children's nursery rhyme? I'd say language is one of humankind's greatest achievements. And its greatest joys.'

'It does have its limitations, though. I mean, language fares pretty poorly when called upon to express the most important things in life; like regret, for example, or sorrow.'

Lindy seemed taken aback by the level of intensity in this pre-dinner conversation. The oven pinged and she looked across at Jejeune. She had been leaving her email open on her laptop recently, so he could check for news from Singapore even if she wasn't around. The latest update hadn't made for encouraging reading, and she knew he would be anxious to see if anything new had come in. She turned to Summer. 'I'd better get in that kitchen, unless you want to hear some language that expresses my emotions about overcooked pheasant. You can come and give me a hand if you like.'

Summer proved a surprisingly resourceful assistant, instinctively understanding what would be required and where it would likely be stored. Someone who lived on his own, Lindy concluded, and was good at it. 'So is there anyone special in your life these days?' she asked, scooping redcurrant sauce into small bowls and avoiding eye contact. 'I suppose we should have asked earlier, really, so you could have brought them along tonight.'

'There is no one.'

The flatness of the response stunned Lindy for a moment. 'How about family, then? Anybody local?'

'I was orphaned at a young age and my foster-parents both died when I was in my early teens. I seem to be one of those people whose loved ones don't stay around very long.'

Lindy put a hand to her mouth at the matter-of-fact way he revealed such a bereft upbringing. Without looking at him, she reached out and touched his forearm. She felt a faint flinch, suppressed immediately, but there for an instant. 'Still,' she said blithely. 'You have your work. I take it you enjoy that.'

He shrugged. 'It's all I know how to do.' He turned to her. 'Can I ask you something,' he said earnestly. 'You interviewed Abbie Cleve a few months ago, didn't you?'

Lindy nodded. 'On the first anniversary of the opening of the Nye. It was going great guns.' She flashed him a glance. 'Sorry. It was going really well. We thought it might be an indicator of changing attitudes in these parts. You know, choosing foods to benefit the planet.'

'How did she seem? I mean, did she express any contrition? Any regrets?'

'About her choice to leave the family, you mean?'

He inclined his head. 'That. Or anything else. Did she seem like she felt she had to make amends for anything?'

Lindy shook her head. 'Not really. In truth, all I really remember about her was an overwhelming sense of self-interest.' She looked at him. 'If you're having doubts about whether she could have actually taken her own life, I have to tell you she certainly didn't strike me as the kind of person who would. At least, not back then.' She picked up the laden plates. 'I think we're all done here. Come on. Time to eat.'

Jejeune caught Lindy's eye as he joined them at the dining table, and offered a faint head-shake. No news from Singapore.

'What is this?' he asked as she set a plate in front of him.

'Redcurrant sauce. Don't look at it like that, Dom. It's a traditional accompaniment to pheasant.' She looked at Summer. 'This from somebody who comes from a country where they put cheese curds on their chips. And gravy.'

Summer seemed not to know what to do with the information and stared at her blankly.

'We were chatting about Abbie Cleve in the kitchen,' said Lindy, as much to relieve the awkwardness of the moment as to provide Jejeune with any real information. 'I have to say, it was one of my stranger interviews.'

'Strange how?' asked Domenic.

'Despite me repeatedly giving her the opportunity to talk about the climate benefits of reducing methane, or increasing land yield for food production, all she wanted to do was to compare the relative merits of beef and pheasant meat in terms of protein and quality. Honestly, it was like she was on a personal mission to destroy the local beef industry.'

'Perhaps she was. One of the operations at least. Did you point out the support she had received from the climate activists when she started up: the endorsements, the social media campaigns?'

'A few times, yeah, but she wasn't interested. People think an interviewer drives the conversation, but not with the guests who know what they're doing. All you can do is keep repeating the question until it becomes clear to the audience they are refusing to answer it. We can't beat an answer out of them. We're not the police.'

Jejeune rewarded the comment with a smile, but, like so many of Lindy's attempts this evening, it fell on stony ground with Summer. But Lindy was nothing if not persistent, and she fastened onto a new topic immediately. 'I was thinking how nice it was that you two have a shared interest in the natural world,' she said.

'I'm not sure we see it the same way, though,' Summer told her. 'Druidism is about being a part of the natural world, existing within it.' He turned to Jejeune. 'When we were out... that day,' he said awkwardly, 'I noticed how much pleasure you got from identifying that Willow Warbler. It seemed really important to you that it wasn't the other bird, the Chiffchaff, was it?'

Jejeune smiled indulgently. 'It's just that it was an unexpected sighting, a bird that's sadly becoming a rarity in these parts.'

'Still, that need to identify it. It was as if it would allow you to draw the bird into your world in some way, instead of simply having it be one more creature, one more part of nature in a forest.'

Lindy watched in silence as Domenic wrestled with the idea. 'Surely being able to identify anything is the first step to having a better engagement with it,' he said.

'But its identity changed what the bird meant to you, didn't it? It was the same bird, but suddenly, it meant more to you, became a more valuable sighting, once you'd identified it as a Willow Warbler rather than when you thought it was just a Chiffchaff.'

It wasn't often Lindy had seen Domenic Jejeune so completely nonplussed by a question about his birding. Clearly, he was going to have his hands full with his new partner. But perhaps that was no bad thing.

'More sauce, anyone?' she asked.

Lindy slid her arm around Dom's waist as they stood in the doorway of the house, watching the Trabant reverse out of the driveway. 'I don't know, Dom, somebody who can't even find any joy in language. That poor man. He seems so… empty. It's like there's a void inside him, as if the incident hollowed him out, and now there's only a big, gaping hole where his emotions should be.'

'He feels responsible for leaving another man with life-changing injuries. It's a long way back from that.'

'I get the feeling that he hasn't even begun the journey yet. It's a shame. I think there's still a decent person in there somewhere. There have been flickers, tonight and at the pub, as if there's a tiny light inside him, burning still against all that darkness, but he doesn't trust himself to let it out.'

The Trabant's taillights had disappeared now, but Jejeune continued to look into the night for a moment. 'The magazine would have a file on the shooting incident, wouldn't it?'

'Of course. Why?'

'Do you think you could get a copy for me to have a look at?'

'Don't the police have a file of their own? Or do you not want Colleen Shepherd to know you're looking?' She pulled away slightly and looked up at him. 'You can't fix him, Dom. That's not how it works. You might find an explanation or a detail that can absolve him of some of the blame, but that won't help him to forgive himself. We might be able to help him in time. You might. But there will be a lot of barriers to overcome before he'd be willing to shed some of his guilt. Something tells me there are a lot of things still hidden inside that man.'

Jejeune left one final stare out in the darkness. 'Yes,' he said thoughtfully, 'I think you might be right.'

26

'So you got in safely, then?'

Across the miles, Lindy's voice was crystal clear. From the phone connection of the Writers Bar in Singapore's legendary Raffles Hotel, Damian would have expected no less. 'Arrived yesterday.'

'You didn't exactly rush there, mind you, after my call.' Lindy didn't sound upset. She realised what it must have meant to him to cut his time in Bhutan short to head out there to help.

'There's only one flight per week from Bhutan to Singapore. It was either wait a couple of days for it, or head out to Kat and try and book something from there.'

'Kat?'

'…mandu. I love Nepal, but it isn't the place to try to get something done in a hurry. Trust me, waiting for the direct flight from Bhutan was the better choice.'

'And did you by any chance manage to fit in any more birding while you waited?'

'The chance to see wild tragopans is not to be taken lightly, Lindy,' he told her with mock gravity.

'You saw one, I take it?'

'Two. A Satyr and a Temminck's. Displaying its throat patch, no less. It must be among the most breathtaking sights in the animal kingdom. Don't tell Dom, though. He'll be beside himself with jealousy. On second thoughts, tell him. You can say I had fantastic, eye-bursting looks, too.'

'Have you met Selena Lim yet?' Lindy's tone suggested she'd been waiting for Damian to bring the subject up. Like his brother, once he got on to the subject of birds it could be a long way back.

'She's on her way here now. Any wisdom from Dom to pass on?'

'Not directly. But you might want to float the idea that it's likely that the phone and the knife would have been taken by the same person. He says the chances of two people each being able to remove a separate item from the scene undetected are a good deal smaller than for one person taking both without being seen, and I have to agree. Oh, and that business about it being not directly from Dom – that's important, Damian. There can be absolutely no connection between the two of you on this at all.'

'Good to know.' A tall woman in a dark business suit and crisp white blouse strode confidently into the bar, but failed to see him at his table tucked behind the door. 'I think Danny's legal counsel has just arrived. I'll be in touch.'

He hung up and stood to greet the woman. 'Ms Lim?'

'Selena. Damian, I take it? Danny's friend.'

Damian tilted a hand. 'More of an acquaintance, really. A concerned one, though. Thanks for agreeing to meet me.'

A white-jacketed waiter approached and Damian deferred to Selena to order for them. They settled in to wait while the bartender prepared their cocktails. One of the things Damian enjoyed so much about travelling was that it reminded you that some things were universally true. Among them was the concept that beauty was beauty. The woman opposite him would have graced any room she entered, anywhere in the world. It was true that the circumstances behind this meeting were troubling, to say the least, but there was no reason why he couldn't enjoy sitting across from an attractive woman while they talked.

She looked around, as if taking in the surroundings like a tourist. 'I'm curious. Why here?'

'Danny was staying here, wasn't he? The day he was arrested.'

'Guy Trueman had comped him. They were due to have dinner here that night. No other reason, then?'

Damian looked puzzled.

'I thought it might be a subtle hint that maybe we could expect Singapore to treat the descendants of our colonial masters with a little leniency.'

'Being from the colonies myself, I can truly say the thought never crossed my mind.'

'Good,' she said, 'because that won't be happening. There's been quite a bit of pushback among the younger Singaporeans about the myth that Raffles carved this worldwide trading empire out of the jungle with no help from anybody else. The Malays, the Indians and the Chinese all did their bit. Sorry for the history lesson, but it matters. In today's climate, the locals will be expecting that Danny receives exactly the same kind of justice a person of any other ethnicity would. I don't want to sound overly dramatic, but it's probably fair to say the eyes of Singaporeans are more likely to be on this case than most others.'

They leaned back as the waiter set down a tray of pecans and olives and their cocktails. 'Your clarified English milk punches,' he announced.

Damian leaned forward and took a sip. 'Vodka, rum, lemon and something else,' he said.

'Earl Grey tea,' Selena told him. 'You wouldn't think it would work, would you?'

Judging by the speed with which Damian took up his glass again, it was quite clear that it did. He looked around the elegant room. 'So, do you come here often?'

Selena laughed out loud. 'Ah, a classic English pick-up line, befitting the era, I see,' she said.

Damian looked embarrassed. 'No, I'm sorry, I didn't mean...' Selena smiled and he started again. 'I just wonder how comfortable Danny would have felt staying in a place like this, even on somebody else's dime. I mean, a room for one night is probably worth a year's salary to someone where I've just come from.' He regretted the remark immediately. It sounded disapproving and judgemental, not to say hypocritical, since he was sitting here enjoying the room's sophisticated opulence along with the rest of the well-dressed elite.

Selena lowered her eyes slightly. 'I suppose we'll never know whether he might have taken to it or not. He checked in, but he never got to spend the night here.'

Damian leaned in earnestly across the low table. 'I have to tell you, for those who know Danny well, it's inconceivable that he would kill someone in that way.'

Selena's expression suggested this wasn't the first time she'd heard a remark like that from someone close to a client. 'You're not one of them, then, who knows him well, I take it?'

'We've met, as I say, but I can't say I know him.'

'That's the problem. No one here does. The only person who can speak to his character is a hardly a man of sterling reputation himself, and the only testimonial he can give is about Danny's ability to kill with his bare hands.'

The waiter appeared as if he had materialised from the ether to inquire if more service was required. It wasn't. A thought occurred to Damian. 'If Danny checked in, his stuff must still be here at the hotel?'

She nodded. 'In storage. They have agreed to hold on to it until it's clear whether the case will go to trial.'

'Surely it will, won't it?'

'Not if I can get the charges dismissed at a pre-trial Disclosure Conference. If I can show Danny acted in self-defence, it might justify his use of lethal force. It's unclear if it would – it's an area the law has some trouble defining – but it's definitely Danny's best hope.'

'But it means finding the knife, doesn't it? And if it doesn't turn up?'

'Then we have a fight between two evenly matched opponents, or at least opponents with similar skills and training. Except one of them was a serving police officer, in uniform, who's left behind a wife and a community in mourning, and the other was an overseas visitor with training in how to kill people.'

Neither of them felt the need to point out that when it was phrased that way, Danny's prospects didn't look good. 'I've been thinking,' said Damian. 'It's probable that the missing phone was taken at the scene, like the knife. But the likelihood of two people each being able to remove a separate item without being noticed has to be less than one person taking both. It seems likely that whoever has the phone has the knife, surely. Have you given any thought to putting your efforts into trying to trace that phone?'

Selena looked at him carefully, and took a sip of her cocktail, barely letting her lipstick touch the glass. 'So you've been thinking, have you? Any police officers in the family back home in Canada, by any chance?

Damian smiled guiltily. 'If there were…?'

'I also think taking those items was a crime of opportunity. But I don't think there is any way I can find that phone unless someone comes forward with it, or the number. Even if they do, that phone might bring its own set of difficulties.'

Damian looked interested.

'It seems certain now that Titus Chupul tracked Danny to a record shop in Geylang, where the attack took place. There was nothing about it on Chupul's work phone, or on his computer. If it turns out there is a message on that burner from someone, at the very least it would establish a connection between Danny and the victim.'

Damian nodded. He might not be familiar with the grey areas of the law, or the infinitely fine lines of the legal system that so often separated guilt from innocence, but he understood the wider implications of what Selena was telling him. Danny was claiming self-defence against an unknown assailant; it would justify why he had reacted so violently. But if he already knew Chupul was coming, perhaps he knew a lot more about him: his weight and size, for example. And exactly how much force would be needed to kill him.

And that was the very least. 'At most?' asked Damian.

'It could help prove the prosecution's theory that Chupul was lured there by Danny. That could have some very serious consequences for him. Extremely serious.' She seemed to lose herself in thought for a moment. 'But let's not concern ourselves with that yet,' she said, returning to the present.

They watched in silence as their waiter cleared the table next to them. Empty glasses and snack dishes loaded onto a tray, a deft wipe of the tabletop with a damp cloth, and suddenly there was no evidence that anyone had ever been there before.

Selena sighed, and, although they had only just met, Damian could tell she was going to reveal something she had held to herself until now. 'Titus Chupul's attack wasn't random. There were lots of bystanders he could have attacked first if it was just some unhinged rampage. He went after one person specifically, a person who insists they had never met, never even laid eyes on each other. Only one explanation makes sense.'

'A case of mistaken identity?' Damian shrugged. 'From what I remember of him, Danny's a pretty easy guy to recognise. It's hard to believe there would be somebody else similar enough looking he could have been mistaken for. Especially here. Did the wife have any idea who her husband's real intended target might be?'

Selena shook her head slowly. 'I didn't bring the idea up. She knows a man called Ronnie Gunn who's working as police liaison. If she got to know what I'm looking into, so would he. I'd rather the prosecution didn't get wind of any of my lines of inquiry until I'm ready to tell them.'

'How's she doing, the wife?'

'All over the place, as you'd expect. I don't believe it was a happy marriage, but then who am I to judge what that means. If it worked for them, then she's lost her soulmate, her life partner and her source of financial support all in one go. It's a pretty devastating position to find yourself in.' She checked a watch on her slender wrist. 'I have to get going,' she said, 'but let's stay in touch.'

She stood up and smoothed her black skirt, laying down enough money to cover the drinks. Damian thought about protesting, but in the end he simply extended his hand to meet her outstretched one. 'I don't know how much help I can be here, if any, but I thought I'd pay the wife a visit tomorrow, up in Kranji. I can tell her I have an interest in the monals she's breeding up there. It wouldn't be untrue. She doesn't have to know I'm anything to do with Danny. Maybe the conversation could drift towards anybody her husband might have wanted to attack for any reason.'

Selena nodded thoughtfully. 'I think that might be a good idea,' she said. She seemed to be mulling it over still as she descended the hotel's marble steps to the street. Unless, thought Damian, she had something else on her mind.

27

Domenic Jejeune left the Beast at the end of the driveway, looking forward to the brisk walk up to Cleve Hall. Like so many of these estate homes, it had been built on a slight rise, designed to offer the inhabitants a view over their surrounding land. On the weekend, it promised Lisbet Cleve a grandstand view of the protesters who would be gathered at the foot of her driveway.

She was waiting for Jejeune on the top step, with the door open behind her. She closed it as he approached. Perhaps she was of that class that didn't believe in admitting policemen into their homes, thought Jejeune. Or perhaps she simply felt that family secrets were best kept out of sight.

'If you've come to apologise for the mix-up with the funeral parlour, your chief constable has beaten you to it,' said Cleve by way of a greeting. 'I told him I wouldn't be taking the matter any further.' She looked at him frankly. 'What I didn't tell him is that my lawyer advises me bringing a lawsuit would be a long and costly process with an uncertain outcome.'

She seemed no more impressed by Jejeune's contrite look than Colleen Shepherd had been earlier that morning. 'The body is off-limits from this point on, Domenic,' his DCS had told him firmly. 'The CC has made it clear that under no circumstances will we be permitted to go anywhere near it. Since nothing we got from it would be admissible anyway, it would serve no purpose for our investigation, and it would only distress the family further, something we are all now particularly keen to avoid.'

The memory of her lingering stare remained with Jejeune as he spoke to Cleve. 'We still intend to do everything we can to discover the truth about your sister's death,' he told her.

She flapped a hand. 'I would expect no less. I was just heading up to the paddocks,' she said. 'You're welcome to join me if you fancy a stroll.'

Jejeune fell into step and they began their way up the gentle incline to the fields at the top of the rise. 'I noticed you were looking at the stage for the forthcoming show,' she said. 'I take it your people will be here in numbers. I'm hearing now that the anti-foxhunting crowd are likely to join the fray as well.'

'It's hardly surprising,' said Jejeune, 'after word got out that you'd allowed trail hunting on your land last year.'

'It may have happened, but it was not with my permission.' Her expression suggested it was not a distinction she was expecting the protesters to make. Jejeune suspected she was probably right. 'You know, now I come to think if it, your little error may have been helpful in a way,' she said. 'We can schedule a memorial service here the day before the protests. That will hardly play well in the media for them, will it? They'll come across as insensitive, as well as insufferable.'

Above them in a clearing, a Rough-legged Buzzard soared lazily on outstretched wings and Jejeune took a moment to watch the bird until it disappeared from view.

'I trust you are as busy as I am, Inspector,' said Cleve, 'and you seem to be someone who wouldn't be averse to coming to the point. Since your colleagues have already been here, I assume you have some follow-up questions.'

Jejeune wasn't a man who took pleasure in the discomfort of others, but there were still some people he found it more rewarding to put under pressure. 'According to those same colleagues,' he said evenly as they walked, 'you suggested the reason your sister wanted readmittance to the family was because she needed the connection to help finance her business. A look at her bank records would suggest otherwise. I was wondering if there was another reason Abigail came here.'

Libby Cleve's tight smile showed no hint of embarrassment at having her duplicity exposed. 'Of course Abbie didn't want to be welcomed back into the family. Once she'd gone, she grew to despise all this.' She spread her arms to indicate the cattle pastures and, by extension, the lifestyle.

Walking beside Libby Cleve now, Jejeune was struck by the physical similarities between the sisters. Perhaps they shared the same sense of ruthlessness, too. 'Is that why she set up her business so close to you?'

'She was entitled. That property, Bouquet House, had been empty as long as anybody can remember. And a pheasant farm, less than a kilometre away from our front gates – well, that was exactly her type of revenge. Direct, confrontational. Her marketing campaign, as you will already know, was entirely focused on undercutting our operations, drawing direct comparisons between the perceived benefits of pheasant meat over beef.'

'And it was being successful?'

'It was having its effect, yes. The beef industry as a whole has been under pressure for some time, but it was undeniably her fault we were suffering as much as we were. Of course it didn't hurt that she was the darling of the climate-change lobby in the beginning. She could concentrate on maximising profits, while her acolytes trotted out all the usual environmental claptrap associated with beef production.'

'Methane emissions, you mean?'

'And acreage yields. It's all deflection, of course. The whole agenda is being pushed by the fossil fuel lobby. These idiots don't realise they are doing their work for them. You look surprised, Inspector, but it all makes sense if you think about it. Make enough fuss about methane, and it becomes a handy distraction for the oil and gas industries, to deflect attention from their own impacts on global warming.'

She paused at a gate, and chose to climb over it instead of opening it. Jejeune noticed that she favoured her injured wrist as she did so. He suspected she had made the climb precisely to prove that she could, not least to herself. She waited until Jejeune had joined her on the other side of the gate.

'The facts on methane, however, are not quite so cut and dried. For all the media coverage about the evils of the cattle industry, over seventy percent of the world's methane emissions come from cattle in developing countries. These are animals that are not even actively contributing to the food chain any longer. After about three years of useful productivity, they're simply allowed to roam free. With the best will in the world, there's not much the UK beef industry can do about that.'

In the field, a number of cows looked up from their grazing to stare disinterestedly in their direction, untroubled by their approach. 'And what about decomposing food?' Cleve continued. 'Did you know that one-seventh of the food on Earth is wasted, Inspector? That alone counts for almost ten percent of the planet's methane emissions. But, of course, it's harder to put a face to a pile of rotting vegetables. Much easier to fasten on the cattle industry.' She stopped walking and turned to him. 'There's just so little interest in the truth these days, don't you find? Facts, details, they're all mere inconveniences to these people.'

'So the argument you had with Abigail. It was because you asked her to stop targeting you with her campaign?'

'We employ a lot of people, up and down the supply chain. I told her people's livelihoods would be threatened if she carried on the way she was going.'

'But she refused to stop?'

'Point blank. Not a hint of consideration for anybody else.' Libby Cleve touched the bandage on her wrist. 'Just like when she gave me this. Made a joke of it, moved on, forgot it. Someone else's pain you, see, Inspector. It never quite seemed to register with Abbie.'

Jejeune decided to take a shortcut across the fields back to where he had parked his vehicle. Almost without him noticing, a magnificent autumn day had unfurled around him, sun-kissed and bright. And beneath it the soft, musty scent that spoke to him not of decay, but of change, of the Earth moving inexorably through its cycles, to a time when the fresh, tingling feel of the air on his skin would become more constant than the fleeting touches it gave now.

At the edge of a tract where the meadows bordered some scrubby gorse, Jim Loyal was rolling out skeins of barbed wire. He didn't stop working at the DCI's approach, but he addressed him anyway. 'The protesters are allowed to assemble in public places, so I'm told,' he said over his shoulder, 'but the shoot site can be accessed from further along the road, and that's private property. It'll be posted, but this will serve as a reminder in case they forget their manners.' He shook his head. 'Anti-this, anti-that. Makes you wonder if anybody is *for* anything any more.'

'I was hoping I might run into you today,' said Jejeune. 'In your statement, you said you were up at the house when the sisters had their argument. I was wondering if you had heard what it was about. Libby has had a rethink, but I'm not convinced she's giving me the whole story even now. I know you liked Abbie. Perhaps you can help me get to the bottom of all this.'

'One of the rare occasions I was up there, as it happens,' said Loyal. 'Wouldn't call it an argument, though. They never were. Mostly they involved one of them quietly saying the wrong thing to the other at the right time. They both knew which buttons to press without having to go in for all that shouting and screaming.'

'It seems likely that it would have been the last time anyone saw Abigail Cleve alive,' said Jejeune. He seemed to hesitate, and took in the surroundings for a moment. The open spaces and fresh air seemed to embolden him. 'The sisters were about the same build, weren't they? Same height, same weight? Would Libby have been able to best her sister in a fight, if things became physical between them?'

Loyal shook his head firmly. 'Never come to that. As I say, each one knew the other's pressure points well enough. They didn't need to resort to violence.'

'But Libby's judo training, that might have made it possible for her to subdue her sister, correct?'

Loyal shrugged. 'Get your opponent off balance and anything is possible. Judo is all about that, how much force to apply, when, where. Certainly back when they were sparring either one could have easily pinned the other.'

Jejeune's look made it clear he wasn't asking about the past.

'With that wrist injury?' Loyal shook his head. 'Doubtful Libby could have even thrown her sister, let alone held her down.'

Jejeune watched the man methodically unrolling the bales of barbed wire, expertly manoeuvring it with his gloved hands to prevent it snagging the material. He looked back along the land, in the direction of the Nye, less than a kilo-metre away. 'The pheasant farming operation Abbie set up. Weren't you concerned about escapes? The captive birds from the Nye weren't raised for the shoot. They'd be overweight, probably weak fliers if they could get airborne at all. Birds like that on the loose wouldn't do much to enhance the shoot's reputation, I should imagine.'

'You're not wrong there. If word got out we had poor stock, it'd be hard to draw any clients. Very particular about their experience, are shooters. Course, they pay a lot of money for the privilege, so they're entitled to have high expectations, I suppose. But you've seen the set-up at the Nye yourself. Take an army to get through that fencing. No bird is ever going to escape from there. Not that anybody would ever mistake one of them for one of our birds anyway. Ours are raised in enhanced pens, with perches and plenty of room to encourage flying. We set them free at the right time, too, so they can get settled into the habitat before the shoot starts.'

Jejeune nodded. 'So by the time the season opens, the birds are feeling secure enough to venture further from their cover when foraging.'

Loyal nodded. 'Makes them easier to flush. They're more likely to fly, less to run. Delicate balance though, giving them enough time to get used to the habitat, but not so much that they might be encouraged to venture too far afield. All about the timing, see. That's the way it is with most things in nature, isn't it?' He stood up and surveyed his handiwork. Jejeune had the impression he was weighing just how much he was fencing the protesters out and how much he was fencing the land in. 'These protesters, they really don't understand what it means to have a proper relationship with the land, do they?' he asked Jejeune. 'That constable of yours, he understands. And I suspect you do, too. You're a birder, aren't you? To find your birds, you have to know a bit about nature, what habitat they are going to be in, what time of year, their behaviour, their habits. Lot like hunting in many respects.'

Jejeune nodded. The similarities had occurred to him before. 'Bob Ferris was mentioning the shoot up here. Did he ever take part?'

Loyal shook his head. 'Any shooting Bob and me did was what I call proper hunting. Lie in wait for your prey, stalk it, lure it. There's any number of legitimate ways you can bag your game. This business of beating to flush the pheasants your way, or walk-ups, shooting whatever rises before you...' He shook his head. 'These gentrified gunslingers, whatever it is they think they're doing, it's not proper hunting.'

'I imagine it must be hard to do all this work to manage the shoot if your heart's not really in it.'

Loyal looked around. 'Been here at this estate all my life, man and boy. I don't have many possessions in this world, but I have this land. That's enough for me. I know this place, its heartbeat, it secrets, and it knows me. Can't imagine spending my days anywhere else. Might as well add to the estate's coffers while I'm doing it. An estate like this can make thousands of pounds a weekend off shooting. More than one place around here would be on its uppers without its shooting income.'

Jejeune nodded. 'You saw Pete Estey, I understand, the day Abbie died?'

Loyal looked at him, as if trying to assess where the information might have come from. 'That's right,' he said eventually. 'Out on the Cromer road on his bike.'

'He couldn't have returned to the area? Made it back here before you got to the pub?'

'Not the way I came back, over the estate's fields.' Loyal straightened to look at Jejeune directly. 'Listen, Inspector. Nothing would give me greater pleasure than to say Pete Estey

was around here that day, and let him stay on your list of suspects, but I've been firing salt cartridges at his backside long
enough now to know him when I see him.'

Jejeune nodded and smiled his appreciation. 'I'll let you
get on with your work,' he said, turning to leave. Before striking out for the Range Rover, he paused for a moment to take
in the view from the top of this ridge. Pasture and forest swept
down the hillsides in all directions in a breathtaking vista of
unspoiled agricultural land. Jim Loyal said he was content to
have all this instead of filling his world with possessions. On
a day like this, Domenic Jejeune couldn't find any reason to
disagree.

28

Domenic was peering through his binoculars when Lindy entered the conservatory. Although this wasn't exactly an unknown phenomenon, the intensity of his concentration on the treetops across the water suggested he might be on something special. 'I thought it might be a Pallas's Warbler,' he said. 'A few do show up here this time of year. But I never really got good looks. Anyway, if it was one, it's gone now.' He shook his head. 'Pity, I think you would have liked it.'

'Maybe next time,' said Lindy distractedly. She twisted her features into a scowl as she read a text on her phone.

'Trouble?'

'Eric. He's rejected my angle on the upcoming protests. He wants more background on the impact of a vegan diet on climate change, whether going vegan really can make a difference to the planet.'

Jejeune inclined his head 'I imagine for most people the decision to go vegan is at least as much an emotional one as a climate-based one.'

Lindy smiled. 'I suppose that's fair enough, though. Love, trust, loyalty. All our best decisions are emotional ones, aren't they? But it's probably just as well because, I have to tell you, the science is all over the shop on this one. Does switching to a completely vegan diet reduce a person's emissions by three percent, or does simply halving your meat intake cut them by thirty? How is anybody supposed to make sense of such contrasting numbers?'

'It's because they're measuring different things,' said Jejeune. 'Some measure only the impact of cutting animal products out of your diet, while others factor in the climate costs of producing what you'd need to replace them with. Cheese, for example, has a higher carbon footprint than either pork or poultry.'

'You ask a Brit to give up cheese,' said Lindy darkly, 'and I think you'd find most would rather settle for a warmer planet.' She sighed. 'Of course, many aren't even going to Cleve Hall for a climate protest anyway,' she continued. 'From what we're hearing at the mag, it's going to be a right old mishmash up there: vegans, animal rights groups, the anti-hunting lobby. Thank God you haven't already aligned yourself with any of that lot.'

Domenic had been talking about exploring ways to become more involved with organisations whose work he believed in. Finding himself at a point in his life where he was aware of, and thankful for, his good fortune, he had told her recently, what he wanted to do now was to find some ways to give back. He had wondered if volunteering with a couple of environmental organisations might be the way to go. She suspected the more strident approach some were taking this weekend might cause him to revisit the idea.

'How is Libby Cleve responding to the prospect of all and sundry rocking up on her front lawn this weekend?' she asked. 'Not best pleased, I'm guessing, given her, shall we say, notoriously low tolerance for alternative points of view.'

'She thinks the methane argument is being promoted by the big oil polluters as a way of deflecting attention from their own actions.'

'I wouldn't have had her down as a conspiracy theorist.'

'We're all conspiracy theorists when we find one that suits us,' Jejeune told her. 'But she might have a point. I can guarantee no one up there protesting this weekend will be talking about big oil.'

'It's going to be bad, isn't it?'

'The main concern is if outside agitators get bussed in,' said Jejeune. 'If it's just the locals, I'm sure Shepherd and the uniformed officers have enough personal contacts in the community to stop things getting get out of hand.'

Of course, the one person who would have been ideally suited both to work the personal contacts side and to ensure matters stayed well and truly in hand would have been Danny Maik. His absence, and the reason for it, filled the space between them for a moment, as it had done so many times recently. 'Any news?' asked Jejeune when it became clear Lindy wasn't going to offer any.

She shook her head. 'Last I heard, Damian was going to visit the victim's wife. She breeds birds of some kind. Himalayan Monals?'

Jejeune stared at her with interest. 'Really?'

'She supplies them as mascots for the Gurkha regiments. They're the national bird of Nepal, apparently.'

Jejeune nodded approvingly. 'Excellent choice. Damian is going to enjoy that trip. It's not everybody who gets to see the Nine-coloured Pheasant up close.'

Lindy looked puzzled. 'The Nine-coloured Pheasant? Why do they call it that?'

Jejeune shrugged. 'I don't know, maybe because it has eight colours?'

If Lindy's stare didn't turn him to stone, it wasn't from a want of trying. 'I mean the pheasant part. Damian called it a *Monal*.'

'Monals are part of the pheasant family, *Phaisanidae*. The species in it are generally pretty striking. Some, like the Elliot's Pheasant, or the Reeves's Pheasant, are absolutely stunning. But the Himalayan Monal is probably the most spectacular one of all. Some people claim it's the most beautiful bird in the world.'

'Are they rare?'

'Not particularly. There's also a healthy captive population in collections around the world.'

'So why does she need to breed them?'

'I don't know for sure, but, because Singapore was a former hub for wildlife trafficking, it now has some of the tightest restrictions in the world on the movement of animals across its borders. With all the HN51 outbreaks around the world, the importation of birds is tightly controlled everywhere. I'm guessing it would be all but impossible to try to bring any live birds into Singapore these days. If you need a supply of non-native birds there, you'd better be able to breed them for yourself.'

But Lindy's interest in bird talk, ever mercurial, had already moved on to other concerns. Or in this case, back to one. 'Why were you up there at Cleve Hall, anyway? I thought Summer had already talked to the people up there. Was Colleen Shepherd not happy with his efforts?'

'There were a couple of things in Libby Cleve's statement that didn't add up,' said Jejeune breezily.

The evasive nature of his answer encouraged Lindy to press. 'But she does still think Noel Summer is a good detective? His job, you know, it's about all he has.' She thought about the momentary flinch when she touched his arm. 'Certainly, I think it's fair to say it's been some time since he's known the warmth of human contact, anyway.'

'I thought you were the comely old woman who was going to take care of that,' said Jejeune with a teasing smile.

'Old-er, Domenic. It's a subtle distinction but one you might do well to remember. Of course, he'd need to up his game a bit to have any chance of finding romance with me or anybody else. I've seen Christmas sweaters with a better sense of style.'

'Maybe I should give him a few pointers.'

'A birder? Giving fashion advice? Not unless he wants to look like part of the woodland he worships.' She shook her head. 'No, I think it might be better to leave the makeover to somebody with what is known as *dress sense*. I have to say, though, it'd be some challenge. It's almost as if he's deliberately trying to be as nondescript as possible.'

'Attention hasn't been kind to him. When he was on his way up and full of promise, it would have been overwhelmingly positive. But when things went bad, it's almost as if everybody holds you responsible for all those expectations they poured into you, as if it was your fault they built you up, set these impossibly high standards for you. Now you've let them down, and they make sure everybody gets to hear about it.' He paused for a moment. 'Once you've attracted the wrong kind of attention, you realise you're probably better off staying under the radar altogether.'

The tense change hadn't been lost on Lindy, and she knew that, as explanations went, it would be a long time until she heard one coming from a more authoritative source. She nodded at the folder lying on Domenic's desk nearby. It was the magazine's file on the Bob Ferris shooting. 'Are you done with that? I have to have it back by tomorrow, unless there's anything of particular interest you still need it for.'

Jejeune shook his head. 'You can have it. It's mainly background stuff. Plus a few photographs. There is something about one of them though...'

Lindy gave him a sympathetic look. 'I know you wanted to find something in that file, Dom. I know you wanted to help him. But you can't. I covered that case, I remember it well. Summer admitted his negligence. He didn't even offer a defence. The suspension was like a penance for him, but it doesn't mean he wants to leave behind what he's done. Or have any of it taken away. He doesn't seem to want to be relieved of it. He took it on and owned it right from the very beginning.'

'Perhaps he's entitled to a sense of injustice, though. I mean, nobody should be punished for a lifetime for one mistake, one moment of inattention, one momentary loss of self-control.'

Self-control? And now they both knew who they were talking about. But she knew, too, that no amount of displacement activity was going to distract Domenic from Danny's plight. Even if Dom found some area that might help to absolve Noel Summer of his culpability, he wasn't going to be able to help Danny Maik. And that was where he really wanted to be channelling his energies.

Jejeune undertook one more fruitless search for the now-departed Pallas's Warbler and then looked at his watch. Turning up late for the recent briefing had bothered him a lot, and he had no intention of repeating the trick. 'I have to go. But be sure to call me if there is anything new from Singapore.'

Lindy nodded. 'How about that file? Are you sure it's okay for me to take it back?'

He had almost reached the door, but he returned to his desk and picked up the folder to take one more look. He held up a photograph and tapped it with his fingernail. 'This one,' he said, shaking his head, 'there's something about it. I'm sure I've seen this building somewhere before.'

'I should hope so,' said Lindy. 'Don't you recognise it?'

He shook his head.

'It's Bouquet House, Dom, where Abbie Cleve went on to set up her business a few months later. That location, where Bob Ferris was shot, it's the Nye.'

29

The mangrove forest below Devina Chupul's smallholding looked as benign as others Damian had seen over the years. Stands of twisted trees tilted their shiny green foliage over the still, shallow water. Beneath them, shoals of tiny fish quicksilvered their way among the exposed root systems, an occasional flash of light or the stirring of silt betraying their presence. But like many of those other mangrove forests, this one held unseen dangers along its muddy shores, Damian knew. Pit vipers, pythons and cobras inhabited these mangroves, and even estuarine crocodiles lurked in the tea-coloured waters. So when the Oriental Pied Hornbills flew into view, Damian was mindful of where he placed his feet as he manoeuvred himself into a better viewing position.

'You are interested in all birds, I see,' called Devina Chupul from the top of the steep incline behind him. 'Not just mine.'

Damian turned his head and smiled. 'I am. But these are native. I wouldn't expect to see your birds in the wild out here in Singapore.'

The comment seemed to please the woman and she gave a small smile. 'I see many birds here in the mangroves: ducks, herons, kingfishers. But you are right, my birds are special. Now you may help me feed them if you wish.'

He scrambled up the steep slope and together they walked around the breeze-block wall that encircled the property. 'You really want to keep the birds safe, I see,' said Damian.

'The wall is to guard them from predators, not people,' she said simply. 'The snakes, the civets, even the crocodiles would come to take my birds if they could.' Damian looked down the long slope behind him to the glittering water. It would be a difficult climb for a croc, but one they would probably have considered worth making with a prize like an unprotected monal on offer.

They entered the enclosure through a wire gate beside the modest stone house and Devina offered him a bucket filled with seed. Although the pens were ramshackle in appearance, they were well constructed. Corrugated sheeting protected the rooves, and the latches on the chicken-wire doors were securely fastened. The birds had been foraging around on the lower reaches of the enclosed hillside when the humans entered, but the anticipated arrival of food stirred them into action and they swiftly made their way up through the scrubby vegetation onto the large area of bare, hard-packed earth in front of the pens. The woman began scattering grains from her bucket onto the ground and Damian followed suit. The birds began feeding immediately, the sunlight catching the plumage of the males as they moved. Damian was almost dazzled by the brilliance and variety of hues on display. 'Incredible,' he said. 'Just unbelievable.'

The woman gave a contented smile. 'It is strange that someone from Canada would have such an interest in these birds that live so far from your home,' she said.

'I saw some in the wild recently, but I didn't get great looks. When I heard about your facility here, I thought it might be a good chance to see them close up. I have to say, they are every bit as spectacular as I'd imagined.'

'In the mountains near my village, these birds were very easy to see when I was a child,' she told him. 'The local people fed them rice and they came to the paths through the village. I think this is why I became interested in them.'

'The locals do the same thing in parts of Bhutan,' he told her. His mind went back to his own sighting of the species. It had occurred during the earlier Damian phase, as he now looked upon it. He had spurned the chance to see the rice-lured birds at Tharpaling as an easy set-up of semi-tamed creatures. Instead, he had opted for a journey to Chele La, where he had tracked the birds through the silver fir forests at 4,000 metres. He had felt the tightening of his chest in the oxygen-depleted air, and listened to his quiet footfalls on a soft carpet of orange pine needles. He'd shown yak herders photos of the birds on his phone, and learned of their locations through elaborate gestures and pointing. And his efforts had earned him a sighting of a pair of truly wild Himalayan Monals. But it was a momentary glimpse of furtive, fleeing birds, dark shapes in the darker understory of the rhododendron forest. He managed no more than a fleeting impression before they were gone. Here the Monals were less than three metres from him, in full view, every resplendent feather perfectly visible. Was his earlier sighting to be prized over this one, where he could fully appreciate the glory of their multicoloured plumage? At this moment, he would not have said so.

Damian stopped feeding the birds for a few minutes to take in their sheer beauty. 'I can see why the Nepali people hold them in such high regard,' he said.

Devina Chupul nodded. 'The danphe hold a special place in the hearts of Nepali people, but their beauty is not the only reason. They hold much symbolic significance. The sighting of a monal is considered to bring good fortune and protection from evil. It is why the birds must be present at all functions and ceremonies of our local Gurkha regiment, and even at the training camps.'

'So you have a breeding population here to ensure there will always be birds available.' He nodded in understanding. 'Like the Ravens at the Tower of London.'

The woman looked puzzled by the reference, but smiled anyway. 'I have a contract to care for them, and maintain this breeding centre. In addition to supplying them to the Gurkha regiment, I take the birds to schools and community centres so others can learn about them. It is important that people understand the place these birds have in our culture.'

'Are all these birds captive-bred?' he asked.

Devina nodded. 'The original birds were from the stock at the breeding centre of the Great Himalayan National Park in India. But transferring birds to this facility became too unpredictable, so it was decided to keep an active breeding population here in Singapore.'

'I imagine breeding is probably made easier by the fact that Himalayan Monals are monogamous. It would allow these birds to form lifelong pair bonds here, wouldn't it?'

The woman lowered her head slightly. 'The people in my village were always sad when they found a dead danphe, because they knew its partner had been left behind.' She teared up and turned away. 'I am sorry. I lost my husband recently. The feelings are still close to the surface.'

Damian felt his heartbeat quicken as he sensed an opportunity to approach the subject, but his excitement was tempered by the knowledge that it would mean exploiting the woman's sorrow, and he couldn't find it within himself to do that at this moment.

The woman shook off her emotion. 'The birds are happy now,' she said, tipping up her bucket to empty the last of the contents on the ground. 'Come, let us go into the house. We will have tea.'

They left the empty feed buckets outside and she led him into the welcome coolness of the small stone house. He sank gratefully onto the couch while she disappeared into the kitchen to make the tea. After the brilliance of the sunshine outside, it took Damian's eyes a moment to adjust to the darkness. It was a moment longer before they focused on her phone, lying on the table beside him. The recent mention of her husband stirred a thought in him. Would such dedication to him mean that she might have a number to call him on his burner phone?

He thought about how openly she had welcomed him and responded to his interest, despite her recent bereavement, about her hospitality, even now in her kitchen preparing tea for him. He looked at the phone again. Could he betray such trust, such generosity?

It was for Danny, he told himself. And it was nothing, really, a minor invasion of privacy. For a good cause. Perhaps not good, but important. Critical. He heard the kettle coming to a boil and the sound of teacups being prepared. He had only seconds to decide, seconds before the opportunity would be gone. He snatched up the phone and swiped it open. It was unlocked; one more level of trust and openness for him to exploit, he thought sadly. He hit the Contacts tab and saw the names were in Nepali. It had been a stupid idea, anyway. The police would already have checked if she had the burner phone number. He reached to return the phone and hesitated for a moment, cursing his stupidity for not noting exactly where it had been lying. An email came in and a photo attachment popped up, a picture of a Nepali flower arrangement. But in the gallery listing beside it, Damian spotted a thumbnail of something else. He heard the rattle of cups being loaded onto the tray in the next room. He clicked on the image in the gallery.

Before Devina Chupul arrived at the table with the tea, the phone was back in place. But Damian hardly heard her words to him. It had been a long time since he had seen that face, but it had the kind of features that stayed with you. There was no doubt in his mind. The person in the photo, staring out at him from Devina Chupul's phone, trying for a relaxed expression but never quite getting there, was Danny Maik.

Damian hadn't stayed long after the tea. He had struggled to maintain some semblance of conversation, and then mumbled some comment about having to be elsewhere and thanked Devina Chupul for her hospitality with all the coherence that his jumbled mind would allow. Only when he was outside, stumbling almost drunkenly away from her smallholding along the dusty unpaved road, did his swirling thoughts start to coalesce. He didn't know what to do. His own reading of Selena Lim was that she was competent and was acting in Danny's best interests, but he knew there were other points of view on that. Could he entrust this information to her, when it could so clearly work against Danny's interests if it got into the wrong hands?

It was getting towards dusk and he realised he must have been walking a long time. The industries in the area had all closed for the day and the roads were deserted and quiet. Though the heat was beginning to abate with the dwindling light, the moist air from the nearby wetlands still hung heavily around him. He needed a drink, and the thought of a cold beer somewhere where he could sit and collect his thoughts became suddenly very appealing. He consulted his phone and found there was a café a ten-minute walk away. As he stood plotting his route, he heard a gentle rushing sound behind him. He took it at first for a breeze passing through the mangroves, but there was no hint of coolness disturbing the still, cloying air. By the time he had identified the sound and spun around, the fast-approaching bike was almost upon him. He backed away as far as possible, his heels finding the edge of the ditch behind him, but the bike struck him anyway, the handlebars smashing into his ribcage and a pedal gouging into his shins. He flew backwards, putting out an arm to break his fall, his shoulder twisting painfully under him as he landed. As he lay face down in the dirt and debris in the bottom of the ditch, he heard tyres skid to a halt on the dirt road, followed by the slow click of the chain as the bike was walked back towards him. With a move that caused him great effort, he twisted himself onto his back so he could look up at the person he was going to ask for help.

The helmeted bike rider stared at him from the top of the culvert, the last rays of the setting sun reflecting in his dark goggles. He stared for a moment at Damian, but said nothing. Damian painfully stretched out his arm to confirm he needed assistance. After a further moment staring, the cyclist silently mounted his bike and rode away.

30

'Anybody here order the pheasant?' asked Tony Holland jovially as he entered the Incident Room. He set down a large container containing an odd shape hidden beneath a plastic sheet on a desk in front of Domenic Jejeune. 'You said you wanted to see it before we sent those fibres off for analysis.'

Holland was aware his lively entrance had intruded on a tense silence between his two senior officers. Shepherd succinctly recounted the reason for it now. Since Jejeune wasn't in the country when Ferris's shooting took place, he could perhaps be excused for not recognising Bouquet House as the scene of it. But the subsequent change of the property's name to the Nye shouldn't really have been enough to cause the rest of them to miss the connection. It was a collective failure, one more misstep in a case that seemed littered with them, and Shepherd's tone had reflected her frustration.

'It's funny how Summer never mentioned it,' said Holland.

'He knew I would pull him off the case if he did,' said his DCS.

'That's one explanation, I suppose.' Holland said it in a way that suggested he might have another. But if he did, he was keeping it to himself for the moment.

'And now?' asked Jejeune.

'He may as well stay on it. He's already heavily invested. And he, at least, is following tangible leads.'

Holland may have just been clearing his throat, but Shepherd gave him a sharp look anyway. 'Is it right that he is actually proposing hypnosis as a theory for how Abbie Cleve was subdued?' he asked.

'I think he's probably abandoned the idea by now,' said Jejeune. 'For one thing, there's no way Estey could have picked up enough skills just from a couple of sessions of treatment. If you were considering a candidate at all, it would have to be Ferris: the person who taught him hypnotism.'

Shepherd turned to Jejeune. Turned on him would have been closer to the mark. 'You're not seriously suggesting Bob Ferris had anything to do with Abbie Cleve's death?'

'No. Obviously not.'

'Then why the bloody hell are we talking about him, Domenic? Instead of trying to show us how clever you are, how about trying to find us somewhere useful to go on this case?'

Jejeune recognised that her ire was directed more at their lack of progress than at him personally. He wasn't offended, but he suspected he might have to put up with an even worse outburst very soon.

Holland shuffled uncomfortably, like someone looking for a way to dispel the awkwardness of the moment. 'How did it go up at Cleve Hall with the sister?' he asked.

Jejeune shrugged. 'She's not convinced methane emissions are the climate problem everyone believes them to be.'

'I don't know about that,' said Holland. 'I think there's a good argument to be made that the world would be a better place if there weren't so many useless creatures just standing around farting and belching all day.'

'Is this your way of telling us you're putting in for a transfer, Constable?' asked Shepherd tartly.

Jejeune rewarded the comment with a smile, but it died quickly as Shepherd turned her stare on him. 'Still, I'd hardly say that sort of denial raises Libby Cleve to the level of a viable suspect, would you, Domenic?'

'How about Knowles, then?' asked Holland. 'I definitely touched a nerve in that interview when I asked about the relationship between him and the victim. He's right that there's no evidence of a bribe in his finances, but I'm wondering if he could have asked for one, and then killed her when she refused.'

Jejeune shook his head. 'I think a killing under those circumstances would have shown more evidence of rage.'

Holland inclined his head to accept the point. One of the very few things they were able to say with any certainty about the body of Abigail Cleve was that it had been obvious to all who saw it that this had not been a crime of anger.

'So we're back to Estey, then,' said Shepherd. She pointed to the tray on Jejeune's desk. 'Suppose those fibres on this bird do match the ones on the gloves at the murder scene when we send them off. Surely that gives us the connection between Estey and the woman that Summer has been insisting on all along. It is entirely possible that he's right on this, isn't it?'

Jejeune didn't answer. Instead, he removed the plastic sheeting and began to examine the pheasant closely. 'I'd like to know how anybody managed to subdue her without any kind of visible injury. Just like this bird. There's nothing to suggest how it was killed. No shotgun wounds, no snare marks, no sign that it was strangled. Nothing.'

'Maybe Estey hypnotised it,' said Holland. Shepherd's sour look encouraged a more serious contribution. 'Or perhaps he poisoned it.'

'I doubt you'd poison anything you intended to eat later,' said Jejeune.

Holland nodded. 'Fair point.'

'You think the method of the bird's death is connected to Abbie Cleve's in some way?' asked Shepherd.

'At this point, only insofar as something about them has been disguised. Beyond that...' Jejeune held up his hands and shrugged.

Shepherd stared at the bird. As Jejeune said, it seemed to be completely free of any injuries or wounds. While there was undoubtedly good reason for covering up how Abbie Cleve had been made to comply before her death, she couldn't see why anyone would need to disguise how a pheasant had been killed.

Holland looked from Jejeune to his DCS and back again. 'If you're done with it, sir, I'd better get it back.'

'Back?'

'Into cold storage. Here, unless you'd like me to send it off for an autopsy?'

'That might be an idea,' said Jejeune. He looked at Shepherd to show that, even if Holland had been joking, he wasn't.

'I hardly think it's a priority, Domenic. Not with every-thing else we have going on around here. Take it away, Tony.'

As he reached the doorway, Holland lifted up the tray holding the pheasant carcass and moved it through the air. 'Hey look, poultry in motion.'

Shepherd shook her head as she watched him leave the room. 'Those human sacrifices,' she said. 'The ones the Druids are supposed to have been involved in...'

'I don't think they'd take requests,' said Jejeune.

He fell silent and she looked at him, lost in thought, staring vacantly into space. She couldn't remember see-ing him so lacking in direction, flailing around between positions, seemingly unwilling to commit to one line of inquiry over another. Holland may well have a point in criticising Summer's outlandish theory about hypnotism, but at least the new detective was exploring something. All Jejeune had was some shadowy preoccupation with how the crime had been committed. But the why, or by whom, it seemed to her, would have been questions much more worthwhile pursuing.

Holland returned to the room and lifted a folder from the top of a filing cabinet. In the wake of Shepherd's recent tetchiness, it was probably better to at least appear to be pursuing some worthwhile task, and, in the casual art of looking busy, the station had no finer practitioner than Tony Holland.

The desk sergeant tapped on the doorframe and waited to be beckoned in. 'Call just in, ma'am.' He looked at Holland and then back at Shepherd.

'Yes?' she urged. The sergeant's troubled expression suggested his news was not going to do much to change her mood.

'Summer.' The sergeant flickered a look in Holland's direction again before continuing. 'He's found the shell casings up at the site. He's bringing them in now.'

'Found them?' Shepherd turned to Holland, understanding now the sergeant's reluctance to speak in front of him. 'Didn't you do that search yourself, Tony?'

'Where were they found?' asked Jejeune, before he could answer.

'Alongside the trailer, sir. It looks as if Estey was probably standing in the doorway when he fired.'

Jejeune waited to see if the sergeant would add anything further. But, having already been forced to reveal the news in Holland's presence, he clearly felt he'd done enough damage for now and retired in silence.

Holland turned to them before the man was even out of sight. 'They weren't there, ma'am. I'd swear to it.'

'There's a lot of tangled undergrowth out there, Tony, not to mention an entire carpet of fallen leaves. They would have been easy to miss.'

Holland laid the folder on top of the cabinet and looked at Shepherd frankly. 'My last assessment, ma'am. All those nice things you said about me, being meticulous, thorough, competent. Does that sound like somebody who's going to miss two shotgun casings lying on the ground?'

When he'd been accused of errors in the past, Holland's usual response was to get loud in a hurry. The flat, matter-of-fact tone he adopted now only seemed to make his question reverberate all the more forcefully. For a long moment, only silence filled the room.

'Look, I know how this is for you,' he said finally. 'On the one hand you've got the word of a guy who's been here a while. Reliable enough, but nobody really rates him. On the other, you've got the new boy wonder, saying the complete opposite. For you two, it's only my word against his. You can't be sure who's right. But I can. I know those shells weren't there.'

The easy thing would be to write off Holland's position as defensiveness about his own slip-up. But in her heart, Shepherd knew he hadn't missed those shell casings, and she suspected Domenic Jejeune did, too. Officers like Tony Holland did the things they had control over as well as they possibly could, because there was a truth they recognised. Some detectives had an edge that others like Holland would never be able to match. Most went about trying to assemble the big picture from all the fragments. But the really good ones, the naturals, did it the other way. They intuitively knew which missing piece was crucial and which could be ignored. And they knew this because they already had the big picture in their head. Procedure could be taught. You could set exams for it, and sort out the ones who would go on to become good detectives, possibly very good ones. But that gift, that extra intuitive spark that the special ones had, you couldn't teach that. And you couldn't learn it either. Jejeune had it; they'd all known that from the moment he arrived here. But Holland recognised, as she had, that Summer possessed it as well. And Holland knew, too, that no matter how efficient he was, how meticulous and well-prepared, he would never have it, that tiny glimmer of genius that sets the great ones apart from the really good ones and the rest. It would be a hard thing to acknowledge. It would be harder still to accept. But it meant that to compensate, any time Tony Holland was on a case with Jejeune or Summer, he would do everything in his power to make sure he was operating at the peak of his abilities. And that meant not missing spent shotgun cartridges he had been specifically dispatched to find.

Holland shifted uneasily, seemingly aware that his next contribution would likely take them somewhere from which there was no coming back. 'Have you asked yourself what he was doing up there in the first place, ma'am? Why go back to the search site when the report had already been filed and signed off?'

'Just to be clear,' said Shepherd cautiously, 'it's your position that Estey took the original casings with him when he fled, so Summer couldn't have found them? Because, as you know, planting evidence is a very serious charge. At the very least, it would put paid to any thoughts DC Summer had of continuing his time as a police detective. Why on earth would he risk it?'

Holland shrugged. 'Maybe he sees it as restoring the balance in some way, reinstating the natural order and all that cra—stuff. If we can't use any evidence from Abigail Cleve's body to get Estey for her death, it's thanks in large part to that cock-up at the funeral parlour he was responsible for. Perhaps he felt it was up to him to provide some other evidence to replace it.'

Shepherd looked across at Jejeune for his thoughts. The DCI drew in a breath and looked at them both. The time had come. 'Pete Estey has an alibi for the time of Abbie Cleve's murder,' he said simply.

'What?' Shepherd looked at him in disbelief. 'Where did you hear this?'

'Tara Skye told me, just before the shooting call came in.'

'And you're only just mentioning it now?' Shepherd could not keep the incredulity from her voice.

'I've only recently had a chance to verify it. Jim Loyal can place Estey miles away at the time of the murder.'

'Loyal?' said Holland. 'I thought he couldn't stand Estey.' He nodded thoughtfully. 'Which, of course, is all the more reason to give this some credibility.'

Despite her astonishment, Shepherd hadn't missed the wider implications of what Jejeune was telling her. 'So if this is true, you're saying Estey would have had no reason to shoot at Summer, or resist arrest.'

'I'm saying he wouldn't have had this one.'

Jejeune's pedantry was never less than irritating, but she had always seen it as the price of his astonishing powers of deduction. Only now, when he was using it to call forward only more problems instead of solutions, she found her indulgence beginning to wane. 'Right,' she said tersely. 'I need to give this entire situation some serious thought. In the meantime, not a word. To anyone. Either of you. Do I make myself clear?'

Judging by the two men's silence as they left the room, she did. But it wasn't just the implications of what Jejeune was saying that troubled her. It was the timing. *Why on earth didn't you bring this to us earlier, Domenic?* she asked silently as she watched him leave. *Was it really that you were waiting to verify it with Loyal? Or was it perhaps that you decided to hold on to it for a little while longer to give Summer time to dig himself into an even deeper hole?* Jejeune's own contributions to the case were at the moment being outshone by a junior officer. People would do a lot to protect their reputations. She'd never suspected Jejeune of anything like this before; but then, his status here had never been under threat like this. Whatever his motivation, she couldn't let things go on as they were any longer. And by this time tomorrow, after a house call she'd been asked to make, she knew they wouldn't.

31

Lindy was typing intently on her laptop, sitting at a patio table set overlooking the shallows of the cove beside the house, when the car pulled up. She knew who it was, but turned anyway. 'Thanks for coming,' she said as Colleen Shepherd closed her car door and started towards her.

'Domenic's not here?' she confirmed.

'When I chose this time, I'd expected him to be off birding,' Lindy told her. 'But to be honest, his heart doesn't even seem to be in that much these days. He's gone for a drive instead.'

Shepherd joined Lindy at the shoreline of the inlet and looked out over the waters, rippling as gently as a skein of folded silk. 'It's such a lovely spot here,' she said taking a seat in the other patio chair. 'You'd think this would be enough to calm any troubled soul, wouldn't you? Even his.'

'I'm sorry to drag you out here. I know you must be busy with preparations for the protest. From what we're hearing at the mag, it sounds like you might be in for a bit of a rough weekend. I suppose it's too much to ask they might suddenly be willing to listen to each other's positions and reach some sort of common ground.'

Shepherd's look was one of sadness rather than contempt. 'I'm afraid we don't seem to live in those times any more, do we?' she said, shaking her head. She glanced at the laptop Lindy had been working on. It had reverted to a screensaver of a bird. 'What a glorious creature.'

Lindy followed her gaze. 'It's called a Himalayan Monal. It's the one on the handle of that knife Danny saw.' She turned the laptop towards Shepherd, who leaned in for a better look.

'You know, a lot of the birds Eric shows me look a bit samey; a dab of yellow here, an olive eye-stripe there,' said Shepherd. 'I do try, for his sake, but I don't really see what makes them so special. But this one, I have to say, it really is one of the prettiest birds I've ever seen.'

'I know. I mean look at that plumage on the wings.'

'And that patch of turquoise at the shoulder.'

'It's the iridescence on the neck feathers that I find so stunning.'

Both women seemed to recognise at the same time the moment they were in. Lindy laughed out loud. 'Oh God,' she said in mock horror. 'What's happening to us? Can the camo gear and dodgy hats be far behind?'

'And the endless reams of photographs from every conceivable angle?' agreed Shepherd.

'Ah now, thankfully at least Dom's never shown any interest in that side of birding.'

'Well, if he ever does, take my advice. The day he walks through that door with photography equipment, you need to take swift and decisive action, Lindy. Strychnine would be my suggestion. It's colourless and odourless.'

Lindy nodded gravely. 'Sprinkled on his cornflakes, you think?'

'In his coffee,' said Shepherd. 'Harder to detect.'

The mood dissipated as they both silently acknowledged that the fun was about to give way to the reason

Lindy had asked Shepherd to come today. Dom called it her raptor approach, a lot of slow circling before swooping in. 'A few days ago, Danny sent us a message via his lawyer. The way he phrased it suggested he might not have complete confidence in her.'

Shepherd pursed her lips. Danny was a good enough judge of character for her to accept the sergeant's reservations unequivocally, without even knowing the details.

'We thought it wouldn't hurt to have our own set of eyes and ears out there, so we asked Domenic's brother Damian to go. Actually, I did. He was already in the area, well, sort of, anyway,' said Lindy, tossing her hair in case any facts were going to get in the way.

Shepherd tensed a little on hearing this news. 'Damian has met this lawyer by now, presumably,' she said. 'What does he think?'

'Selena Lim. He says she seems nice.'

Shepherd sighed. When it came to the list of qualities Danny's lawyer was going to need for this case, being nice was close to the bottom. She was sure he would have happily traded a few measures of affability for a little extra competence.

'The thing is… Colleen, Danny is in a lot of trouble. There is a photograph on the victim's wife's phone. It's Danny, smiling right into the camera. Damian took a look at the woman's phone when she was out of the room.' Lindy blurted it all out, staring straight ahead, unable to even look at Shepherd as she spoke.

Shepherd fought down her panic and simply lowered her head in thought for a moment. Danny's defence all along had been built on the idea that he had reacted to an unprovoked attack by someone he had never met. But that photograph, on that phone, meant that nobody was going to buy the idea that this was a random incident any more.

Danny had been targeted. And an assailant didn't do that unless they had a reason.

She looked up at the calm, still water in front of her, but Lindy knew she wasn't seeing it. 'I think we need to prepare ourselves for the reality that Danny is going to prison,' said Shepherd finally. 'He no longer has a viable defence. Now that the Criminal Mentions Court is over with, the first Disclosure Conference must be coming up soon. He will have to enter a plea.'

'It will be "Not Guilty". On the advice of his lawyer.'

Shepherd snapped a look at Lindy. 'In light of this? I'm beginning to see Danny's point.'

'She doesn't know about the photo,' said Lindy. 'That's what I wanted to ask you about. Damian doesn't know if he is obliged to inform her about it. You know, legally.'

Shepherd sat quietly, her elbows resting on the table, her hands clasped before her as if in prayer. Lindy couldn't ever remember seeing her mull over a situation quite so intently. 'To be clear,' she said eventually, 'Damian doesn't have a copy of this image. He's only glimpsed it on the woman's phone.'

Lindy nodded.

'And he is only aware of its existence because he unlawfully obtained access to it, which is to say without the owner's permission?'

Lindy could see she was building a defence for not reporting it. But it wasn't coming easily. All Shepherd's training, her instincts, her professional background were arguing their case inside her, dragging her in one direction then another. Wherever she ended up, it was going to represent a compromise in one way or another: of her professional integrity or her loyalties. She was not alone. This case was claiming casualties like that all over the place.

'Lindy, you know I would never, ever, counsel you to withhold evidence from a police investigation, but they have made it abundantly clear they do not want our involvement in this case. Either we stay out of it or we don't. They can't have it both ways.' She seemed to be trying to convince herself that this was the correct approach. It may have been defensible on the shifting sands of police procedure and evidence gathering, but both women knew that whether it was right was another question altogether.

'Given that you've waited until he's out to tell me, I take it you haven't mentioned this to Domenic?'

Lindy reassured her with a short shake of her head.

'He's falling apart on me, Lindy, missing evidence, forgetting things. I've never seen him like this. A case like this one we're working on would normally be meat and drink for Domenic Jejeune. A viable pool of suspects, plausible motives, one or two extremely promising leads. I'm not saying he'd get a conviction, necessarily, but answers – I'd back him to come up with those. The way he's floundering around, you'd think we were dealing with the crime of the century here. He seems to have no idea which way to go.' She paused. 'I don't want to go down that ridiculous "if Danny were here" road, but the undeniable truth is he would be mortified to think his own difficulties are ruining the skills of the best detective either of us have ever known.'

She looked out over the water for a moment, saying nothing. Lindy was prepared to give her all the time she needed to get around to telling her what she already knew was coming. 'Domenic can't be involved in Danny's case any further, Lindy,' she said finally, 'in any capacity whatsoever. Any hint of involvement that could be linked back to him, even through Damian, and we could be looking at a major diplomatic incident between the two police services. It would be a career-ender for him, certainly.'

Lindy nodded to show she understood.

'That means no input, no updates, no further information at all. I need him to be focused on this case at home, but more importantly I need him not to be distracted by any others, here or overseas. So if anything more comes in from Damian, anything at all, it should come straight to me, please. Nothing whatsoever to Domenic.'

She raised her eyebrows to give the air of expecting an answer to a question that really wasn't a question at all. Lindy nodded dumbly. She was giving her word. Sincerely. Unequivocally. She just wasn't sure how she was going to keep it.

32

Selena was sitting at a table beside the window in the trendy Duxton Road café when Damian approached. A man was standing beside her. The interaction between them didn't look confrontational, but it was a long way from cordial. Damian did his best to disguise his injuries, but manoeuvring between the other tables to get to them made him wince involuntarily.

'What happened to you?' Selena asked.

'Slept wrong,' he told her, flickering a glance towards the man. An instinctive caution about providing information to people he didn't know had served him well in the past.

Selena introduced the two men. Neither offered a hand.

'Jejeune,' said Gunn. 'I hear you're interested in birds. Devina Chupul said you'd been by.'

Damian didn't comment, allowing his silence to suggest he was waiting to speak to Selena alone.

'I'd better get going,' announced Gunn. 'Remember what I said, Selena. That phone could mean bad news for your client if it provides evidence of luring. You need to ask yourself if that's a risk you're willing to take. The plea deal is Danny Maik's best hope of avoiding that outcome. But the offer won't last for ever.' He turned to Damian. 'Hope you sleep better tonight, Mr Jejeune. You take care now. Goodbye.'

Damian took a chair and together they watched Gunn making his way past the other eating establishments along the street until he disappeared from view. 'Everything okay? Your friend didn't look too happy,' he said.

'He isn't, and he wasn't,' Selena told him. 'He came to remind me the upcoming discovery hearing is a second chance for Danny to enter a guilty plea. I told him if I needed someone to mansplain how to count to two, he'd be my first call. Have you eaten breakfast?' she asked.

'Sort of,' said Damian, who had discovered to his cost that the 'half-boiled eggs' on the hotel's menu was not the misprint he'd assumed it to be.

'Want one of these?' She indicated a couple of small round cakes on a plate. 'They're tau sar piah, mung bean paste. They come in sweet or salty.'

'Which are these?'

'Oh, salty. I need to do something really good to treat myself to a sweet one.'

It crossed Damian's mind that getting Danny off his charges might qualify. It said a lot about the Singaporeans' reverence for food that a woman who drove a brand new Hyundai Avante felt she needed a reason to reward herself with a sweet snack. He looked through the window, considering the street outside. Even without their louvred window coverings and ornate wrought-iron balcony rails, the street-front rows of two-storey buildings would have made the Duxton Road district an anomaly in a city where land was so highly prized and lavish, multi-dwelling high-rises were the norm. 'Interesting area, this.'

'You don't know where you are, do you?' asked Selena. 'That big grey building you walked past, about a minute away around the corner, is the Bukit Merah East Police Cantonment Complex. It's where Danny is being held.' She looked at him. 'I eat here, watching people walking past, enjoying the sights, the sounds, the fresh air, so I can remind myself of all the things my clients will lose if I can't win their case.'

An overwhelming urge to tell her about the photo on Devina Chupul's phone rose in Damian, but he fought it back. 'You know, given everything, I wonder if it might not be wise to give some thought to a plea, Selena,' he said instead.

'Danny isn't guilty of the crime he's charged with,' she said flatly. 'Justice is about reaching the right verdict, not bargaining down from one unjust sentence to a different wrong one.'

She sounded so convinced of her client's innocence, so determined to prove it, that Damian wondered where Danny's doubts had come from. Lindy had told him the sergeant wasn't a man to rush to judgement. If he had misgivings, they were justified. But if so, Selena Lim must be showing Danny a different side of herself from the one he was seeing. Beyond the spotless plate glass-window a steady stream of people hurried towards their favourite eating places as if they had been evacuated from a burning building. *Keep moving, don't stop, don't turn around.* He shook his head as he watched them. 'I'm told they say if Singaporeans had to choose between sex and eating, they'd have to think about it,' he said.

Selena smiled. 'Judging by the ratio of kids to restaurants here, I don't think they see them as mutually exclusive activities. But food has always been hugely important in Singapore. One might say the place only exists because of it.'

Damian gave her a quizzical glance.

'Singapore grew up because it was the centre of the spice trade route. As far back as the fourteenth century, spices were prized commodities. The term *spice* even has its root in the

Latin word for *item of special value*. It's a word you birders use all the time, actually; *species*.'

'So no spices, no Singapore?'

'Certainly not the Singapore the world has come to know.' She looked at him carefully. 'What did happen to you, really? After all, this is meant to be the safest city in the world.'

'Unless you get wiped out trying to cross a road by people driving on the wrong side.'

'The British were in charge when the Singapore traffic system was set up. You could hardly have expected us to drive on the right. But you weren't hit by a car, were you?'

'Bike,' he said. He told her the details, but left out the part about the cyclist leaving without helping. He thought about the incident now. Everything about the cyclist's actions suggested it was a deliberate attack, but he had no idea why that could be. No one knew why he was in Singapore. And no one besides Selena knew he had planned to visit Devina Chupul that day.

'I guess you wished you'd stayed in Bhutan,' said Selena, drawing him from his reverie. 'Will you go back there once this is all over?'

He nodded. 'I'll make arrangements for the Snowman Trek, get my permits, arrange my insurance, make sure my equipment is all in good working order. And then I'll give myself permission not do it.'

Selena laughed. 'You are an unusual human being.'

'You're not the first person to make that observation,' he told her, 'though you are by far the best-looking.' He looked shocked at himself. 'Oh, I'm sorry, I didn't mean... It was meant to be a put-down of my brother...'

'Are you saying you'd like to take it back?' asked Selena, enjoying the moment.

Damian shook his head. 'No, no. All good. But we should probably, you know, get going. I'm sure you have lots to do,' he said weakly.

Selena nodded. 'Preparing a brief for a Discovery Conference, for one.' She reached for the bill, but Damian stretched out a hand to take it first. The movement made him wince.

'You really should report the accident, you know. It's what a tourist would do, unless they had some reason not to. It might keep Ronnie Gunn guessing a little bit longer. At the moment, he can't be one hundred percent sure why you're here. We don't have much going for us in this case. Keeping the opposition off balance is one of the few advantages we can give ourselves.'

Damian said he would consider it, which in Selena's experience was what men said when they didn't want to receive any more advice. She stood up to leave. 'Try that tau sar piah,' she told him, 'you'll like it.'

Damian had fished his phone from his pocket even before Selena was out of sight. As he listened to the unfamiliar UK ringtone, he thought about how quickly he had ricocheted from his gloriously uncomplicated existence of a few days ago to the world of turmoil he was experiencing now. He knew part of the change could be traced to his decision to remain offline while he was hiking in Bhutan. Had there been calamities while he was out there on those quiet trails – natural disasters, political upheavals? Undoubtedly. The world's problems hadn't ceased to exist just because he had chosen to disengage himself briefly from the web of information that entangled him when he was home. But for a short time, his life had been free from the day-to-day catastrophes that existing on this planet seemed to bring. And then, less than twelve hours after reconnecting with the world by switching on his phone once he arrived back in Thimphu, Lindy's call had come through.

Lindy answered her phone and he heard the concern in her voice immediately. 'Are you okay? How's the pain this morning?'

'I've known worse. I've heard Domenic sing Leonard Cohen tunes after all, remember?' He became suddenly serious. 'The first Discovery Conference is coming up shortly. You know Selena Lim won't be entering a guilty plea on Danny's behalf. It's a big risk they're taking, Lindy. Ronnie Gunn just told her as much. There's a lot of pressure coming from the other side. They're still offering a deal, but it's likely to be withdrawn at any moment.'

Lindy was silent for a moment. 'Did you tell her about the photograph?'

Damian thought about the moment he almost had. 'No, but I think we should. If it comes out, she's going to be blindsided in a way she may not recover from. Whatever that photograph means, I think Selena should be in on it.'

The use of the woman's first name hadn't slipped by Lindy. Nor had the level of personal connection it signified. 'Domenic doesn't know about the photo either, Damian, and it has to stay that way. But I did speak to his DCS, Danny's old boss. She would do anything in the world to save him, but her advice is to keep the news about the photograph to yourself at the moment.'

Damian thought for a moment. He watched the crowds of happy, carefree people drifting by outside. 'Lindy, can you find out what difference it would make if the prosecution could prove Danny had lured the victim to the scene? I'm not saying he did, but the scenario seems to be hanging all over this. When I walked in on a meeting between Selena and Ronnie Gunn just now, that's what they were talking about.'

Lindy told him she would look into it and, with a further warning for him to be careful, hung up. After the call, Damian stayed at the table for a few moments, distractedly sampling the tau sar piah but not really tasting it. As far as he was aware, only two people would be in a position to know how that photo had ended up on Devina Chupul's phone. Damian wasn't really in a position to ask the woman herself about it just now. So that left Danny Maik.

33

Jejeune had parked a short distance from Bob Ferris's place, having been unable to find a space among the unbroken chain of cars lining the street in front of his bungalow. During the last of the increasingly frequent energy crunches the UK seemed to keep finding itself in, Lindy had made noises she no doubt considered subtle about the suitability of a large, fossil-fuelled vehicle like the Beast. In truth, he had been seriously considering going electric for some time now. On its own, the switch wouldn't help him find parking spaces any more easily, but if he downsized at the same time there might be more available spots for him to squeeze into. One more change to consider, he thought ruefully. These times seemed to be bringing about so many.

Jejeune entered the small, underlit living room of Bob Ferris's bungalow to find some redecorating had been done. Specifically, with food. Beside a tall bookcase, tear-trails of brown gravy had dribbled down the walls, amid splatters of unidentifiable food that pockmarked the creamy paint like a shotgun blast. Around the bookcase's base, the carpet was littered with the shards of a broken plate.

'Temper tantrum,' said Ferris matter-of-factly. His tone betrayed no remorse for his actions, nor any embarrassment that his guest had witnessed the aftermath. 'I thought I was over this sort of thing, to tell you the truth. If any good has come of this, it's that I've rid myself of that terrible temper I used to have. I'm more philosophical now, I suppose. I realise it's not worth getting too upset over things. Usually.'

After the last time, Jejeune knew better than to offer to clean it up. He looked at the bookcase again. On the higher shelves, ornaments and photographs had toppled over. A ceramic figure of a hummingbird was broken.

Ferris saw Jejeune looking at them. 'From the impact,' he said simply. 'Don't worry about them, Inspector. I'll get around to cleaning it all up after you've gone. Keep me busy. Give me something to do.'

'I suppose it's one way of dealing with the dishes,' said Jejeune lightly. 'That first time I came, you'd left the one from the previous night's meal in the sink.'

'Daresay you're right,' said Ferris airily. 'Housekeeping's not my strongest suit sometimes.'

'Do you remember what it was you'd eaten?'

'Can't say I do.' But the way Ferris shifted when he said it told Jejeune that he did.

'I think it was pheasant. With redcurrant sauce.'

Whether it was a question or a statement, Ferris greeted it with silence.

'Did Pete Estey bring you that dinner?'

'I used to enjoy a bit of pheasant, but,' he slapped the sides of his wheelchair, 'seeing as how I can't get out to shoot any more, he brings me some every now and again. He told me he'd come across a brace recently. He brought me a plate over.'

'So he didn't dress it here? You never saw the bird yourself?'

'Did it at his place. Plucked fresh and cooked right away. He knows what he's doing with a pheasant, let me tell you. Why do you ask?'

'Did he say how the bird had been killed?'

Ferris looked surprised. 'Snared, likely as not. He used to shoot them, but he doesn't do that any more. He has a physical aversion to any kind of violence now. Literally. It makes him sick since he came back.' He looked at Jejeune frankly. 'He's erratic, Pete, since he returned from the war. Damaged goods. But he still knows right from wrong. That Summer is a good one,' he said. 'He had Abigail Cleve's death nailed as a murder right from the start. But he's wrong about Pete Estey.'

'The pheasant he cooked for you,' said Jejeune. 'Was it from the Nye?'

'What? No. It was a wild one. Well, one raised by the estate, or some shoot, anyway, but you take my meaning. You'd never get Pete Estey eating a farm-raised bird. Not enough flavour. He likes a bit of gaminess to his bird, does Pete.'

'You're sure?'

'You can tell a farm-raised bird from a free-roaming one a mile off. Those birds at the Nye are basically packages of meat. No flight muscles, no sinew, nothing that gives a wild bird a bit of taste.'

'Has he ever brought you birds from the Nye?'

Ferris's unshaven jowls creased into a smile. 'Pete is a poacher through and through. He's been an outdoorsman all his life. He'll only ever take birds off the land. It'd be an insult to him to even suggest buying a farm bird.'

Jejeune fell silent. Over the man's shoulder, he could see the garden. Despite the gloominess of the room, or perhaps because of it, it seemed particularly bright and sunny outside. If Ferris was to put up a feeder, this tiny oasis would see more than its share of birdlife in the coming winter season. Blue Tits and Chaffinches would come by in good numbers, possibly Long-tailed Tits and Siskins, too. But how much effort would it cost Ferris to fill those feeders every day, to wheel his way out of the front door and down the ramp alongside the house, to navigate over the cracked, uneven paving stones of the back garden on the narrow tyres of his wheelchair? He looked at the traces of the dinner Ferris had thrown and realised he had no idea of the challenges this man must face on a daily basis. Tears, be they of brown gravy on walls, or frustration on cheeks, would be an ongoing part of a life like this, he knew.

Ferris eased himself around in his chair like a man looking for a comfortable position he knew he wasn't going to find. 'He'll get it right in the end, you know, Summer, but he'll get no satisfaction from it. Most coppers, they get an answer, it's enough. But for some, like him, it just drives them somewhere deeper. They can keep looking as hard as they like, they're never going to find the light.' He tapped his chest. 'It's in here, see. It's about forgiving. Yourself, others, for what's been done, what can't be done.'

His look at Jejeune told the DCI that they both knew they weren't talking about Summer any more.

'Was he at fault, that day?'

Ferris tilted his head and smiled, as if he had known all along this would be where the conversation was going to end up. He scratched an unshaven cheek with his fingers. 'Some kids had been getting sick from a new drug that was on the streets,' he said quietly. 'One of them damn near died. We got a lead that the dealer, a local low-life named Calvin White, was operating out of a residence, and we applied for a warrant to enter his room to search for the drugs. Clear and present danger to the community; the judge didn't bat an eye. White had previous for violent resistance, so we thought it might be best to execute the warrant when he wasn't at home. Summer was sent out to check. The homeowner was just on the way out, but confirmed White wasn't home, and agreed to leave the door unlocked until we got there, as long as Summer stayed on to keep an eye on the place. He retreated to a safe distance to watch the house until we arrived, so he could let us know if White had come back.' Ferris paused and looked at Jejeune. 'At least, that was the plan.'

'But White was there when you went in?'

Ferris stayed silent for a moment. Outside, the garden remained empty, the bare stems and seed pods basking in the glow of bright sunshine. 'What happened? Did Summer leave his post at some point?'

'Not according to him,' said Ferris bluntly. 'Claimed he'd been there the whole time. The conclusion was that sometime during his watch, White must have returned and gone in unnoticed.'

'And there is no chance the homeowner was mistaken, and White was in the house all the time?'

Ferris shook his head. 'Adamant the house was empty. White didn't say one way or another. Refused to cooperate, even at the end.'

The end had come the previous June, when Calvin White, riddled with end-stage cancer, had finally died in prison. Jejeune might want to go back to the beginning of the story, but some of the avenues were closed. Permanently.

'It happened just the way everybody said it did, Inspector. Guilt like Summer's, you don't carry that around unless you know something was your fault. He never offered any excuse, you know, never tried to deflect any of it. He said he was sitting there the entire time and he didn't see him enter. End of.' Ferris turned to look out the window at the untidy garden going to seed. He didn't turn back when he spoke again. 'Can I ask you something, Inspector? Can you tell him not to come any more?'

'I think he needs to.'

Ferris wheeled round to face Jejeune. 'You could just say it's distressing for me to see him. A reminder of... whatever.

You could make something up. I told him life goes on. He needs to start getting on with it.'

Jejeune stared at the food-stained walls, at the man's greying complexion, with a sun-filled garden just the other side of the window behind him. Yes, life does go on, he thought, but for some it is just an endless series of sadnesses punctuated by the occasional ray of hope.

'I don't mean to put this on you, Inspector. I would have asked Danny Maik if he was around. He's got the touch for this kind of thing, hasn't he?'

For telling people difficult truths, he meant. Jejeune didn't disagree. He realised it was his place as Summer's senior officer to speak to him, whether he felt ready to assume responsibilities like this or not.

'Danny Maik's a good man. Despite all that evidence against him, what they're saying, what they're accusing him of, he won't have done it. We both know that.'

Jejeune shook his head in agreement. 'No, he won't have.'

'But he's beyond your help, now. You've got to let the world take its course, Inspector. Trust me. It's the only way.' Ferris shook his own head sadly. 'He's innocent. All we can do is hope that's enough, can't we?'

Again, Jejeune nodded. But when he stood up to leave, Ferris's sad expression suggested he felt the same way he did. Namely, when had innocence alone ever been enough to save anyone?

34

A faint line of morning clouds had formed pink mountains on the horizon, and Jejeune shielded his eyes from the low glare that reflected off the sea. Along the shoreline to his left, a small knot of backlit shorebirds foraged among the seaweed at the water's edge. Low waves rolled gently against the rocks, sighing to their deaths with a sound like desire. Domenic Jejeune would not have considered himself a creature of habit, but it was undeniable that at certain times in his life he defaulted to particular activities, and places. When he was troubled, he often found himself gravitating to this stretch of shoreline. A drive in the Beast would bring him here, the high hedgerows going unnoticed as they passed until he crested the rise and the sight of the sea unfurled before him. And as he emerged from the car the sensations would rush in upon him, as they did now, the light playing on the open, limitless expanse of the water, the freshening breeze on his face, the sweet-salt tang of the air.

The ringing of his phone broke into his thoughts, and he answered it quickly.

'Is that Inspector Jejeune?

'It is.'

'Detective Chief Inspector Jejeune, of the Saltmarsh Constabulary?'

Jejeune decided to circumvent any further attempts by the caller to definitively establish he had reached his intended audience. 'Dr Jones, what can I do for you?'

'I have on the desk in front of me the carcass of an adult male *Phasianus colchicus*, together with a form requesting that I perform an autopsy on it. The form bears your signature.'

Jejeune didn't get his hopes up. Mansfield Jones was infuriatingly meticulous even with his human subjects. It could take days to prise from him information that other MEs would have willingly parted with in hours. He could not believe Jones would have changed the habits of a lifetime to fast-track an examination of this bird for him.

The ME cleared his throat. 'Due to the, erm, somewhat unusual nature of the subject, I thought it best to confirm the request with DCS Shepherd. I trust you don't feel I acted inappropriately.' He sounded concerned but it was an understandable course of action. In truth, Jejeune might have expected no less from a person of such legendary caution.

'And did DCS Shepherd green-light it?' he asked, though by now he already knew the answer.

'She did not. She told me I was to stop immediately. She even used the word *forthwith*, which is a term one doesn't get to hear very much these days, isn't it? She suggested my time might be better used clearing my backlog of other outstanding tasks,' he said. 'Of which, I admit, there are quite a few.'

Jejeune sighed inwardly. He was on the verge of thanking Jones for his courtesy in letting him know and ending the call when the ME offered another comment. 'I did notice a puncture mark in the bird's neck.' He hesitated. 'A needle comes to mind.'

Jejeune recognised the man's uncharacteristic speculation as an apology for having checked with Shepherd behind his back. As reparations went, it wasn't bad.

'You're sure?' he asked. 'I didn't see anything when I looked.'

There was a polite pause. 'Yes, well, I imagine it helps if you have some experience at this sort of thing. It's unlikely it was the cause of death, though. It was only a cursory glance, you understand, but it did appear that the puncture might be post-mortem.'

For Jones, this was a veritable fountain of conjecture. It was a sign of how truly contrite he must have felt about his actions. Jejeune considered the information in silence. Perhaps the ME could hear the wind and the sea through the phone, because he inquired after a few moments whether Jejeune was still there.

'I don't suppose you could take another look to verify that,' said Jejeune by way of an answer.

'The moment I receive authorisation from DCS Shepherd, I would be happy to. Until then, however...'

Jejeune smiled. Mansfield Jones's maverick streak had reached its limit. He thanked the man for the call and hung up.

As he walked back to the Range Rover, the birds lifted from the shoreline and began to spin out over the sea, swirling in the air like wind-blown leaves. Even without his bins, Jejeune could pick out the features he needed now to identify them as Sanderlings. Was Summer right? Did it bring him any more joy to know the name of these birds? He wasn't sure, but it was his instinct to identify, to recognise, to understand. That meant, too, finding out what had happened at a pheasant farm in north Norfolk, on a sad October morning just few short days ago. And he had just taken a step closer.

Lindy looked up at the sound of Domenic's car keys hitting the bowl on the hall stand. 'Everything okay?' he asked. 'You look a bit down.' He paused. 'Not bad news from Singapore, is it?'

Lindy shook her head. 'Eric again. Now he thinks the piece needs to acknowledge the other side of the hunting angle. He wants me to point out that shooting brings in revenues of around two billion pounds a year to the UK. That's equivalent to about seventy-five thousand jobs. He says it's hard to ignore an economic impact like that, especially in these parts.'

'It really is.'

'Maybe,' Lindy conceded, 'but if he's looking for me to make some sort of an argument that this is justification for shooting living creatures for sport, he's got the wrong girl.'

'Would it be better if another reporter handled the story altogether, I wonder,' asked Jejeune gently.

She looked up at him. 'It's been mentioned that if I can't strike a better balance, the story could get taken away from me. I think we all know that won't be happening,' she said in a tone that sounded like it might be a dress rehearsal for a conversation she may soon be having with her editor. 'You're just lucky you get to stick to your straightforward, uncomplicated view of hunting without anyone asking you to compromise it.'

Was it? he wondered. Uncomplicated? Not so long ago, he would have been able to give an unequivocal answer about where he stood on hunting. But just lately, that clarity had disappeared, and it was now one more issue, like methane emissions and carbon footprints, surrounded by subtleties and caveats and exceptions in a mist of uncertainty that made it difficult to take a steadfast position one way or the other. There were, after all, undeniable benefits to preserving habitat for hunting. Back in Canada, organisations like Ducks Unlimited worked hard to conserve wetlands where a number of threatened species, not just birds but reptiles and amphibians too, thrived. It was questionable whether those habitats would have avoided the developers' tentacles without the hunting group's efforts.

And yet, some species undeniably paid the price for any uneasy coalition between hunters and conservation groups. Hen Harriers had been systematically persecuted to the verge of extinction in this country, he knew, by gamekeepers who wanted to preserve their grouse stocks. All around the world, other raptors were often similarly targeted and killed. And what of the birds who were actually shot by the hunters, those individuals sacrificed for the greater good? No, Lindy, not uncomplicated. Not any more. 'So no news from Singapore today, then?' he asked.

Lindy shifted uneasily. 'Can you think of any reason I would keep it from you if there was?' she asked.

'I keep hoping you're going to tell me they've managed to trace that phone and it's led them to the knife.'

From her seat on the sofa, Lindy could see their dining room. Danny had sat at that table with them, chatting, drinking, sharing a joke. How much she wanted to tell Domenic that what he should be hoping for now was that the phone was never found at all. She'd done as Damian asked, and looked into what it would mean if Danny could be shown to have lured the victim to his death. She wanted to tell Domenic that if the phone ever did resurface, there might be enough evidence on it to lead to a death penalty conviction for their wonderful, loyal friend. She wanted to tell him that the absolute, solid-gold, best-case scenario for Danny now was that all he received was a long prison sentence instead. But she couldn't.

A flicker of movement over Lindy's shoulder caught Jejeune's attention and he grabbed his binoculars from the desk. 'It's the Pallas's,' he said excitedly. He shook his head delightedly as he watched the bird. 'Want a look?'

He handed the bins to Lindy and she swivelled in her seat to focus on the distant trees. She locked immediately onto a small bird hovering as it picked off insects from the underside of a dying leaf. The lighting was perfect and she could see the plumage details clearly: the bright greenish tint, the whitish undersides, the bold, dark stripes and yellow bars. 'It's a beautifully marked little bird,' she said. 'So what is this again?'

'Pallas's Warbler. They call it the seven-striped sprite.'

She watched it for another moment. 'Oh, it's just flown off,' she said. 'You know, I think there might be something to that observation of Noel Summer's. Knowing what that little bird was called didn't make any difference to my enjoyment of it at all. It was just as pretty before I knew its name as after.'

Domenic couldn't see any movement with his naked eye, but he took back the bins back for another look of his own just in case. After a brief search, he concluded that the bird had gone. 'So what were we talking about before it showed up?' he asked.

'Your case, wasn't it?' said Lindy quickly. 'How's it going? Any new developments? Are you still looking at Peter Estey, or do you have anybody else in your sights just now? If I can be of any help, just let me know.'

Jejeune was silent for a moment. It had been a long time since Lindy had shown this kind of interest in a case. And she knew better than to ask for details he might not be in a position to share. 'I'm making some progress,' he said guardedly. 'I'm still a long way from understanding everything, but some small parts of the picture are beginning to come into focus.'

'Such as?'

'Such as, you told Noel Summer at dinner that night that you'd interviewed Abbie Cleve on the first anniversary of her business opening.'

'That's right. We wanted to highlight the success she had managed to achieve in just one year.'

'Can you remember the date of the interview?'

'Not off-hand, but I could look it up. It'd be six months ago, more or less to the day, I think. Why?'

'One more part of the picture,' said Jejeune simply. Her downbeat tone disturbed him. It was so out of character for the vibrant, optimistic woman he knew. 'Listen, I have to go back out, but stay positive. I know it's hard, but Danny could still get out from under this. There is still a chance that it could all turn out okay.'

No, Dom, thought Lindy as she watched him leave, *there isn't.* Not any more. His earlier comments suggested that perhaps a tiny chink of light had opened up for him in his own case. But for her, the knowledge of what the discovery of that phone could mean had filled her world with darkness. It was a thought so terrible she couldn't even bring herself to pass the news on to Colleen Shepherd. It was as if she was afraid that even speaking about it might make it come to pass. So for now, all she could do was keep the secret to herself, locked away inside, where it could do its damage only to her.

35

The days of incarceration had done nothing to diminish Danny's powers of observation. With barely a glance in the man's direction as he entered, he gave a brief flicker of a smile. 'Damian, good of you to come.'

Damian knew enough about Danny to forgo the usual inquiries as to how he was doing. 'Not the brother you were expecting, I imagine.'

'I wasn't expecting him,' said Danny matter-of-factly. 'He'll have been advised not to come, and for once he'll have had the sense to listen.'

'Still, with it being you...'

'You've not met our DCS, but she has a way of getting her point across.' Danny allowed himself another short smile at the thought of how the conversation between Jejeune and Shepherd might have gone. 'In this case, her point would have been that he could not get involved without a specific request from the investigation team here.' He paused significantly. 'That won't be coming.'

Selena Lim watched the interaction between the two men. Both had admitted to only the briefest of previous contact, but there was a bond between them in spite of that. Whatever, or

whoever, their mutual link was, it must have been an extraor-
dinarily strong one.

'I hear you went up to see the wife,' said Danny. He shook
his head. 'I'm not sure I'd have chosen a pheasant as a mascot
for one of the fiercest fighting regiments on Earth.'

'It is a strange association,' conceded Damian, 'but then
the relationship between humans and pheasants goes back a
long way. It's probably fair to say there is no family of birds
more deeply ingrained in human culture than pheasants.
There's probably not a nation on Earth that doesn't have some
connection with them.'

'I suppose that's one word for a relationship that involves
blasting them out of the sky by the millions back home this
time of the year,' said Danny ruefully. At the mention of
autumn in the UK, his eyes dimmed slightly.

'I can't speak for anybody over there, Danny, but the way
things look,' Damian inclined his head, 'I don't know, I think
they might advise you to take the plea.'

Selena sat forward abruptly, drawing her legs together as
if she meant to stand up. She decided against it but spoke anyway. 'There is still time for another piece of evidence to turn
up, another lead to develop...' Whether her reluctance to continue was because she couldn't think of any specific examples,
or because she simply thought better of sharing them, Damian
couldn't have said. All he knew was, if it sounded as uncon-
vincing to Danny Maik as it did to him, it wouldn't be doing
much for the other man's confidence.

'The more I learn about this case, the more convinced I am
that you've been set up by somebody,' Damian told Danny earnestly. 'The address of the shop, the knife going missing, the... the
rest of it.' His own faltering to avoid mentioning the photo might
have had more purpose than Selena's, but to the listening Danny
Maik, he was sure it simply sounded like more vapid uncertainty.

'If somebody else is involved, they will have made a mistake,' said Selena. 'Trust me, if there is anybody out there I will find them.'

'This charge the prosecution are considering, the first limb...' Perhaps even Damian wasn't sure where his tentative opening was going, but he knew he needed to move the conversation in a specific direction. He paused and tried again. 'A first limb conviction would have to be based on some evidence that Danny knew the victim, or at least knew of him. Or vice versa. Is that correct?'

'It would be implausible for them to suggest Danny could have lured Titus Chupul to the scene without establishing some evidence of prior contact,' said Lim. 'Or at least a prior connection between them. Why?'

Damian ignored the question. 'But if something did come up that could establish a link between Danny and Chupul, then they'd definitely have all they needed?'

The silence suggested to Damian that he had overplayed his hand. Perhaps Selena was approaching the question at face value, carefully assessing what she knew before answering. But Danny's suspicions were aroused. The way he was looking at Damian now went a long way beyond casual interest.

'Did you have anything particular in mind, Damian?'

'Just trying to get a clear understanding of the situation.' He shrugged as non-committally as he could. Whether a life-long watcher like Danny Maik was buying it, though, was another matter. 'Oh hey, I forgot to mention, Lauren Salter has been in touch. She's made all her arrangements for – Max, is it? She'll be flying out in a couple of days. In the meantime, if there's anything you'd like me to pass on to her, I'd be happy to do that.'

Maik left his hard stare on Damian for a long moment before allowing himself to be dragged off into the new subject.

In a world of restricted opportunities, you had to choose carefully which ones you pursued. 'You could just tell her the name of that song I was searching for. That pretty much says it all.'

Selena leafed back through her yellow pad for the notes from their earlier conversations. She gave a small gasp when she found it. '"You're All I Need to Get By". Oh, Danny. How I wish that were true,' she said. There was as much sadness in her voice as Damian had ever heard.

They all looked up at the sound of the door opening. There had been no knock, Damian noted. Privacy might be guaranteed in a prison meeting between a client and his lawyer, but privileges like courtesy weren't included. Ronnie Gunn didn't look particularly surprised to find Damian in the room, but he didn't look overly pleased either. 'You again. You like birds and you know Danny.' The silence that followed made it clear Damian wasn't going to accept the invitation to respond. 'Guy Trueman said he recognised your name,' Gunn told him.

'We've never met. He must be thinking of somebody else.'

'Mr Gunn is an acquaintance of Danny Maik's old CO,' said Selena into the uncomfortable void that followed.

'Guy Trueman. He's taking an interest in Danny's case,' Gunn told him. 'Moral support, mostly.'

'I wouldn't have thought he had any to spare,' said Selena sourly.

Gunn made a face. 'I wouldn't be too dismissive. It looks like your client is going to need all the help he can get.' He turned to Maik. 'Your lawyer's put you in a bad situation, Danny. That not guilty plea at the first Disclosure Conference…' He shook his head gravely. 'That was a mistake. The prosecution is reviewing their case. Sometime within the next forty-eight hours, they're going to decide they have all they need for a conviction. After that, all deals will be off the table.' He tapped on the door to let the guard know he was ready to leave. 'I won't keep you. I'm sure you all have a lot to talk about.' He looked at Damian. 'Oh and it might be better if you didn't visit the wife any more. Trouble just seems to follow some people around, doesn't it, and she's got enough to deal with right now. From now on, you want to study danphes, you should do it at the Mandai bird park. They have a nice display of them there, I'm told. You'd like it. The public gets special access on Wednesdays at noon.'

Maik sat forward. 'Danphes?'

'Birds. Himalayan Monals,' said Gunn. 'That's the local Nepali name for them.'

'I thought it was the word for symbol,' said Danny.

Gunn nodded. 'Yes, they're a Nepali symbol. The national bird. It's why they were chosen as the mascot of the regiment. Remember, Danny, forty-eight hours. You might not think I'm acting in your best interests here, but I can assure you I am.'

The guard unlocked the door and Gunn slipped out without saying goodbye.

Damian regarded Maik carefully. Something seemed to have changed in him. He was looking a little greyer in complexion, a little emptier, as if a light had gone out somewhere inside him. The news that the prosecution were confident they had enough for a conviction seemed to have extinguished the hope within him now, and he looked hollowed out by his ordeal.

'We don't need updates every five minutes telling us what dire straits we are in,' he said quietly. 'Let's end the liaison as of now.'

Selena looked puzzled. 'He has proved a useful source of information up till now,' she said. 'But it's your call, Danny. Everything is. It always has been.'

'I should be going,' announced Damian. 'Leave you to discuss your strategy.' He wouldn't say any more to Danny in front of Selena about entering a plea, but the long, meaningful look he gave the sergeant as he stood did it for him.

'Again, thanks for coming, Damian,' Maik told him. 'Remember me to everybody back home when you're talking to them. I can't tell you how reassuring it is to have an intermediary you can trust to get the right messages across.'

Selena Lim's head was buried in her notes and she didn't seem to notice anything particularly significant about Maik's parting words. But to Damian it seemed like a lot more than a simple goodbye. He just didn't know what.

36

The sense of unease around the station was palpable to Colleen Shepherd, and, if Summer seemed to be oblivious to it, that could perhaps be put down to the fact that he wasn't aware of how things had been in the past: the easy familiarity, the swapping of banter, the casual air of productivity, carried on by colleagues who were comfortable in each other's company. And who trusted each other. Still, for someone who professed such a connection to ethereal forces, it was surely almost an act of will for Summer not to have picked up on the sense of tension that greeted his presence these days. On the other hand, perhaps his frequent absence from their company was a sign that he did.

The desk sergeant tapped and poked his head around the door. 'Handsome Hughie's back.'

Shepherd shot him a quizzical glance.

'Knowles. DC Summer has brought him in.'

'Because?'

The sergeant shrugged. 'All I know is he had a sheet of financial statements with him when he went into the Interview Room. He asked me to show Knowles straight in when he got here. Only, given… everything, I thought I'd just run it by you first, ma'am.'

She looked at Jejeune and Holland. 'Didn't we have a look at his financials?'

'We did,' confirmed Holland. 'And conducted a pretty tight interview with him, if I do say so myself. Covered some good ground, shook him up a bit.' He did not look best pleased that his sterling work seemed about to be upstaged by a second round of questioning.

'So why does Summer want to go over them again?'

'Who knows? Perhaps he found something in them that everybody missed the first time. There's been a lot of that going around lately. Amazing, isn't it? His number one suspect gets discredited and he brings in somebody else without missing a beat.'

'What are you trying to say, Tony?'

He shrugged. 'I don't know. He just seems in a hurry to get this bloke in. A big hurry.'

The desk sergeant gave a short cough to remind them all he was still there. 'The thing is, ma'am, Knowles has brought his daughter with him. He said he had no choice because her alternative education programme has been suspended. Only, she can't stay out in Reception.'

'No, of course not. Bring her through. One of us will look after her.' Shepherd's gaze fell on Holland. She dismissed the thought as quickly as it had come. 'It'll have to be you, Domenic. I'm heading down to the Observation Suite.'

'Me?'

'Just keep her entertained for a short while. I'll make sure you get a transcript of the interview.'

'I suppose I could show her some bird photographs,' he said. 'Explain a bit about them.'

Shepherd sighed. She could never forgive herself for subjecting the poor child to that. As far as she was concerned, it was tantamount to child endangerment. 'On second thoughts,

Domenic, you can come with me to watch the interview. Tony, go and ask someone from Family Liaison to come up here and then you can join us.'

Summer had wasted little time in getting the preliminaries out of the way and, by the time the two senior officers had settled into the small Observation Suite, the interview had already begun.

'So to confirm,' the detective was saying to Knowles. 'You were actually already on your way to the Nye when you got a text?'

'Yes. Luckily, I have hands-free technology in the car, so I was able to take it.'

'And you called Loyal?'

'Yes. Right away. Immediately. As soon as I received it. There's a record of both the incoming call and the outgoing one, with the times. I told the other officer I thought there would be. I've checked since.'

Holland had squeezed into the suite and was leaning in to watch the monitor. 'Smug prat,' he said.

But Summer seemed uninterested in the detail. 'But you weren't going there to shut down her operations, were you?'

'Not initially, no.'

'Not ever. Because no matter what you found, you would have let her continue to operate. And that's because you had a reason for leaving Abbie Cleve very much alone, didn't you?'

With long pauses, there was sometimes the temptation for watchers to wonder if the monitor had frozen. It had been known. But the observing officers could tell from Knowles's posture that he was simply not offering any response. Summer waited patiently.

'I never took any money from her, if that's what you're implying,' Knowles said eventually. He was a long way from being calm and collected, but he was making a fist of pretending. 'You can check my bank records. Or hers, for that matter.'

'I have them right here, as a matter of fact,' said Summer, producing the spreadsheet. 'As you say, there's nothing in them to indicate she ever gave you a penny. Your own bank records appear to confirm this.'

'There you are then,' said Knowles, trying for a defiant tone that was betrayed by the nervous smile he flashed.

'One thing that does come up, though, is a series of cash outgoings. The totals and regularity suggest they might be donations of some kind.'

Knowles shifted uncomfortably in his chair. 'It's perfectly legal to make cash donations. I assume she wanted them to remain anonymous, which of course is her prerogative.'

Summer nodded as if accepting the point. He reached into the folder and produced another set of records. 'There's an exact match for those totals and dates in these records.' He tapped the top line, where a name appeared in bold font. 'Harmony Hill. That's the after-school programme your daughter attends, isn't it?'

Knowles didn't look down at the sheet for a long time. Instead, he simply stared at Summer with an unblinking intensity that made it seem like he was trying to look right through him. The detective matched his gaze until Knowles finally relented and looked down at the sheet.

'It doesn't look like that much,' he said unconvincingly. 'Probably just enough to cover the utilities and a few supplies each month, I should think.'

'But without it, the programme couldn't survive, could it? That's why it's suspended now. So the deal was, as long as you gave Abbie Cleve a free pass on any inspections, those donations would continue.' It wasn't a question. At this point, it didn't need to be.

Knowles seemed to spot an opening and smiled smugly. 'If there was anything to this ridiculous scenario, then it does seem to suggest it would be in my best interests for her to stay alive, doesn't it?'

'It does,' said Summer. He paused to shuffle the papers in front of him. 'So what happened? Did you get cold feet, start to feel the pressure of all those ignored inspection requests? Tara Skye had even sent some meat off for independent analysis, hadn't she? That can't have looked good to your superiors. Did you call Abbie Cleve to say you weren't going to be able to continue your special arrangement?'

'No, I did not.'

'And did she tell you that unless you did, all donations to your daughter's programme, the ones that were actually keeping the place going, would stop?' The detective looked directly at Knowles again. 'There was no anonymous complaint against the Nye, was there? Normally, everything that comes in to the LSA goes through the general admin account. This one went straight to your email. You sent that note to yourself, didn't you? To give you an excuse to go out there and plead your case to Abbie Cleve.'

Knowles spent a long time staring down at the table. Finally, he looked up and fixed Summer with a defiant stare. This one was genuine. 'I didn't harm that woman, Constable. I give you my word. But I'm not surprised somebody did.'

Summer raised his eyebrows. 'Why do you say that?'

'Because Abigail Cleve was a woman who knew how to make enemies. She was skilled at finding your pressure points. And when she knew them, she was an expert at using them against you.'

Summer stared at Knowles for a long moment before gathering up his files and standing up. 'Thank you for coming in, Mr Knowles. You're free to go. For now.' He left the room without a backward glance.

Holland looked at the others as soon as Summer had exited. 'Impressive,' he said in a way that made it clear it wasn't a compliment. 'No doubt about it, the connection between the donations and the school programme, uncovering the fact that Knowles had sent himself the email. Stellar work, all of it. All that research, all that background. Takes the kind of effort only a truly dedicated detective might put in.'

Shepherd was waiting for him to get to the point, but Jejeune looked as if he might already be there. 'Or one desperate enough to cover something up.'

Which made you wonder, thought Shepherd, if someone was prepared to invest that much effort, what other lengths might they have gone to? She looked at Jejeune and then at Holland. Her look gave him permission to continue. But it made it clear that he was on a short leash.

'You saw him talking to the FFO at the site, ma'am. Did he look to you like somebody who'd been in the line of fire of two shotgun blasts?'

'Perhaps he's just someone who doesn't show his emotions all that much.'

Holland was normally careful with his verbal responses to his superiors. He sometimes found it harder to control his expressions. 'You think so? Because to me, it looked more like somebody having a casual chat about football down the pub. Didn't the AR commander comment about how relaxed Summer seemed about the whole thing? And he's been around enough shooting victims to know the difference.'

The abruptness of Holland's pause suggested he wasn't going to go any further until asked. Shepherd stared at him frankly. 'To be clear, we're now talking about an officer filing a false firearms report. That could lead to a custodial sentence, Tony. Why in God's name would he do that?'

'To get Estey to run would be one possibility.' Holland looked across at Jejeune to see if he was going to go along with him. He wasn't sure he had his DCI's support yet, but he could tell he was prepared to listen. 'Let's say Summer finds out from somewhere that Estey has an alibi,' he continued. 'It's not looking too clever for him now, is it? Here he is, putting all this energy into trying to find his number one suspect, insisting to anybody who would listen that it had to be Estey and nobody else who killed Abigail Cleve. And now, it turns out it couldn't have been him after all. Hardly the impression you want to make on your first case back, is it? On the one hand, you could look at botching Estey's arrest by parking in plain sight as just incompetence. But that doesn't seem to square with somebody who has the insight to pick up on the hessian fibres, or the stylus used for the phone message. So what if it wasn't a mistake? What if he parks at the top of the hill at Stone Road just to let Estey know he's coming?'

He paused, as if he had expected to find some resistance. But Shepherd simply continued to leave her even gaze on him. 'So why did Estey run, then, according to this theory of yours, if he's not guilty of shooting at Summer?'

'He's probably guilty of something. Poaching most likely. But now, if Estey gets wind of a possible charge that he's been shooting at police officers, we'll be lucky if he ever shows his face in these parts again.' He shrugged. 'Let's face it, the speed Summer whipped Knowles in here, it's a pretty clear indication he doesn't think Estey is going to be resurfacing any time soon.'

The silence that fell over the room was testament to the gravity with which the senior officers were treating Holland's comments. Neither one wanted them to be true, but, while Shepherd's reaction was shock and dismay at Holland's accusations, Domenic Jejeune, it had to be said, didn't seem very surprised by them at all.

37

Though she would have been loath to admit it, Colleen Shepherd had become used to death. This was not to say she had lost the capacity to be moved by it. The loss of any life still affected her profoundly. But death, sometimes senseless, violent death, was part of her job, and she was able to view it with a greater detachment than most people. Quite why this one affected her as much as it did, she couldn't have said, but no doubt it had to do partly with the troubling thought that, had Abbie Cleve's case been handled more efficiently, they might not be standing here now, waiting for Mansfield Jones to complete his preliminary examination of the late Peter Estey.

It didn't help that the body had been discovered in such an idyllic setting. They were standing in a clearing on the edge of a small forest, beneath a benign sun that was casting a warm, gentle glow. All around them, blades of soft light filtered through the stands of bare trees, falling in tiny pools on the leaf-strewn ground, setting the entire forest floor glittering like an orange jewel.

Shepherd let her eyes rest on the ruins of the old hunting blind nestled in the trees. 'All we have on this one, Domenic,' she said. She realised her tone had been sharper than it needed to be, and she tried to soften it with a look. The connection between the two killings, if indeed there was one, remained unclear. Perhaps it would have made no difference to have had a fully focused, fully engaged Domenic Jejeune looking into the Abbie Cleve death. But until they had solved both cases, she would carry this gnawing feeling that perhaps it might.

They looked up as Noel Summer approached. As usual, he had his shoulders slightly hunched forward, carrying his arms in front of him loosely. Given the circumstances, the bearing made him look even more funereal than usual. 'The identity has been confirmed,' he told them. 'One of the uniforms is a local lad. He's known Estey since they were at school together.'

Shepherd nodded. 'Cause of death?'

'The ME seems a bit reluctant to commit to conclusions at this stage, ma'am.'

Shepherd and Jejeune exchanged a knowing look. Mansfield Jones was not a man who liked to be hurried. But even he understood the detectives needed to be given something to work with. 'Is there anything specific he isn't prepared to commit to?' she asked.

'Estey appears to have died as a result of internal injuries and blood loss resulting from shotgun wounds to the lower lumbar region. Indications are the shots would have come from close range while the victim's back was towards the shooter.' They understood the reason for his long pause. It was the same way Bob Ferris had been shot. Except, Estey had died from his injuries.

Shepherd stared at the blind for a long moment. 'Nasty way to go.'

'I don't think Estey was shot here,' said Summer. 'There's not enough blood.'

'And does the ME concur?'

'He says it's not beyond the bounds of probability that the body was moved here post-mortem.'

She looked at Jejeune. 'To be concealed, presumably?'

He nodded. 'An unstable structure that might discourage anybody from exploring it, the body inside covered by debris and piles of leaves. If it hadn't been for that single flash of orange jacket lining, it's doubtful even a close pass with a drone would have picked anything up. Somebody went to a lot of trouble to ensure this body wouldn't be found.'

'Agreed,' she said. 'Any similarities between this death and the one at the Nye?'

Jejeune shook his head. 'None that I can see.' He paused and looked at Summer to see if he had anything to add.

'One body laid out carefully on display, killed almost gently, you might say. The other about as callous and brutal a murder as you can imagine, the body hidden from view. You probably couldn't find two deaths more different.'

Shepherd nodded solemnly.

'Close proximity suggests it may have been someone he knew,' said Jejeune, 'someone he was comfortable approaching, even though they had a loaded shotgun. If he was trying to flee, it would indicate he only realised he was in danger when it was too late. A meeting, perhaps, one he wasn't expecting to turn violent. A negotiation of some sort, maybe?'

Why couldn't he be like this all the time, thought Shepherd sadly. She cast a glance out beyond the trees. 'That's the Cleve estate over there, isn't it?' she asked. 'Is this property part of it?'

'It was formerly,' said Summer. 'They set aside a couple of small areas and put them in trust for future generations. It's been treated as part of the shoot lands for as long as anybody can remember, though.'

'So why, then, was Tara Skye flying a drone over it?'

The officers looked towards the border of yellow tape fringing the trees on the far side of the clearing, where Tony Holland was in discussion with the young woman. She had one hand up to her half-hair, and the other wrapped around her ribcage, as if she was trying to hold her chiffon dress in place. She seemed more stunned by this death, somehow, than when Jejeune had seen her at the Nye.

'When I ran into her the other day, she told me she was planning to fly drones over some sites in the area,' he said. 'To try to flush the game birds away from the shoot.'

'Are we buying that?'

He shook his head. 'This body's been here a while. If that was to lay the groundwork for this *accidental* discovery, it was an impressive piece of foreplanning.'

Shepherd nodded. 'I'd agree that she strikes me a bit too impulsive for that kind of thing. Still, this is two deaths now where she has been first on scene or close to it. Is there any reason to think she might have been involved? I imagine she was no fan of Estey's poaching activities, after all. Ask Tony to bring her over, would you?'

Summer gestured to Holland, and they watched Skye follow him over, her heavy black boots pulverising the dried leaves beneath them into powder. In a way Jejeune couldn't have explained, her thoughtful expression seemed to heighten her eccentric appearance almost to the point of pastiche. But there would have been nothing amusing about the discovery she had stumbled upon among the decaying timbers of the collapsed blind.

Shepherd clearly thought the same thing. 'Are you all right?' she asked. 'I imagine that must have been quite a shock for you, finding the body like that.'

'Ya think?' said Skye impertinently. 'I mean, I knew the saddo lived out here by himself in some dump somewhere, but I never expected to find him like this. Still, live by the sword, I suppose.'

'Meaning?'

'Meaning, not to speak ill of anyone or anything, but he took enough lives of his own over the years.'

'You're referring to his poaching activities, I assume? Those were game animals. Surely you can't equate them with this.'

Skye shrugged. 'Killing is killing,' she said simply.

Shepherd bit back a response. She was beginning to lose patience with this woman. For all his sins, Estey had answered his country's call to duty, and returned a man broken by his service. He may not have led an exemplary life, but he deserved better than the disdain Tara Skye was showing him.

'So you disapproved of his poaching activities,' said Holland. 'That might be considered motive.'

'What, you mean this?' She flung a hand backwards towards the blind. Jejeune realised for the first time that she was wearing white fingerless gloves. 'Are you mad?'

'Just to confirm, you're stating that you didn't kill him,' clarified Holland.

Skye looked at him mockingly. 'Are you seriously suggesting that I would?'

It wasn't a denial, thought Jejeune. Skye didn't want it to be. She wanted to tease Holland, to punish him for his preposterous suggestion. He'd heard a similar reply recently, someone else who'd chosen to take refuge in ambiguity of phrasing, rather than say something they wanted to avoid. But he couldn't remember where.

Skye put her hands on her hips and stared at Shepherd defiantly. 'Listen, lady, I didn't kill Pete Estey, and I don't know who did. But there are more than enough other crimes going on at this estate. Crimes against the planet, against poor innocent birds and animals. Take it from me, they're all guilty of something here, every last one of them.'

Shepherd regarded the young woman intently. Tara Skye could wear all the outlandish outfits she liked, but the DCS still had the feeling she wasn't as eccentric as she looked. 'One more thing, before you go, Ms Skye. There is talk that a number of outside agitators might be planning to come to join your rally this weekend. I take it you are aware of your responsibility to report any potential illegal acts you might hear being planned?'

Skye snorted derisively. 'Yeah. As if.' She turned on her heel and marched away to collect her backpack.

'She's a strange one, all right,' said Holland. He flickered a glance at Summer. 'And around here, that's saying something.'

Summer ignored the remark. 'If it's all the same to you, ma'am,' he said, 'I can be the one to inform Bob Ferris. I think he's the closest thing Estey had to a friend, and I know he has some good memories of the times they spent together before Estey shipped out. The news won't be any easier to take coming from me, but I still think I should be the one to tell him.'

Shepherd looked to Jejeune, whose slight shrug suggested he could see no reason the task shouldn't be taken on by Summer, especially since he was volunteering for it.

'Very well,' she said. The three of them watched in silence as the solitary figure of Noel Summer departed through the sun-painted glade.

'He's partly responsible for this, you know,' said Holland, leaving his gaze on him. 'Putting Estey forward as a suspect and then persisting with it even after it became clear there was nothing to support it. It was only a matter of time before somebody took him at his word and decided to avenge Abbie Cleve's killing.'

Jejeune had been looking at a message on his phone. He shook his head slowly at Holland's comment. 'I don't think so. The truth is, as terrible as it sounds, no one seems to have cared enough about Abigail Cleve's death to have wanted to avenge it. Perhaps Jim Loyal might, but he's the one person who knows beyond a shadow of a doubt that Estey didn't do it. I think this death is about something else.' He raised his phone. 'The lab have matched those hessian fibres from the pheasant at Estey's place to the ones on the gloves. Since Estey was nowhere near the Nye on that day, somebody must have given him that bird, somebody who was there, at the scene of Abigail Cleve's death.'

'You think it may have been the killer?' asked Holland. 'So maybe Estey knew something, and this pheasant was a pay-off for him to keep quiet about it?'

'If so, the price of Pete Estey's silence came pretty cheaply, Domenic,' said Shepherd dubiously.

'Perhaps too cheaply,' said Jejeune. 'Maybe he decided he wanted more, and went to a meeting to ask for it.'

A meeting with someone who had brought along a shot-gun.

38

There was something about the way the light fell in the enclosure at Mandai Bird Paradise on this morning that put Damian in mind of a fall day back in Ontario. There was a golden quality to it as it filtered through the overhead netting that was redolent of days he had walked through leaf-strewn woods with Domenic, looking for late-fall migrants. Considering it was about twenty degrees warmer outside this climate-controlled building than it would have been in those Ontario forests, it said something about the power of a setting to recall a past experience in the human memory, thought Damian ruefully.

'Doesn't look like it's carrying the weight of an entire nation on its back, does it?' said a voice at his shoulder. 'Holds a lot of symbolic significance for the people of Nepal, this bird, so I'm told.'

Damian turned to see a tall man with clear eyes in a battle-hardened face staring at him. He had not given much thought to what Guy Trueman might look like, but he supposed he fit the type well enough. The man offered his hand and Damian shook it. It felt as hard-worn as the rest of him.

'Glad you could make it,' said Trueman.

'An invitation that subtle? How could I resist?' said Damian sarcastically.

'It seemed to make a bit more sense, meeting here, rather than somewhere more public. There are lots of eyes on this case, Mr Jejeune. Not everybody is going to have Danny's best interests at heart, either, if you know what I mean. I don't remember running into you when I was out that way,' he said cautiously. 'Are you a friend of Danny's?'

'I'd met him, but I'm mostly here because my brother can't be.'

'Not officially, anyway,' said Trueman. 'So he sends you to report back, see what strategies he can come up with, and then you can whisper them into Selena Lim's ear as a quick thought that has just occurred to you. Smart boy, that one.'

It wasn't the way things were working any more, but Damian saw no reason to share that with Trueman. It had been this man's idea to have Ronnie Gunn deliver his cryptic request for a meeting, keeping both Danny and Selena Lim out of the loop. Damian would be very careful about what he gave away until he knew why.

'How's your brother doing, by the way? Him, I did meet. He likes birds, too, as I remember. Never saw the appeal, myself, but even I have to admit these monals are real stunners.'

Damian nodded. The plumage on the males was catching the light every time they moved, emitting electric pulses of shimmering iridescence.

'I understand you've seen them in the wild. Where was that? Nepal?'

'Bhutan. But they're just as revered there.'

They both watched the birds for a moment more, strutting slowly around their enclosure, scratching and foraging for food among the leaf debris.

'Not much to their life in the wild, I should imagine,' said Trueman. 'Find something to eat, somewhere to sleep, try to avoid getting killed by something in between. Hardly the sort of existence to inspire a nation, is it? Makes me think there must be more to this symbolism, like maybe people trying to see qualities in the bird they wish were there, instead of what really is.'

'Monogamy is one of the qualities of the Himalayan Monal,' said Damian. 'Mrs Chupul got a bit teary-eyed when that one came up.'

'Loyal people, the Nepalis. Marriages mean a lot. Lose your husband… it's hard on a woman.'

Damian turned and looked at Trueman directly. 'I wondered if there might be more to it.'

The other man gave an easy shrug. 'Chupul was a hard man in a hard job. It wouldn't be a surprise if he threw his weight around a bit at home as well. Maybe she's thinking how unfair life is, to put up with that for all these years and then still to end up with nothing to show for it, now that he's gone.'

'She told Selena Lim she still has the contract to care for the monals for the regiment.'

Trueman nodded. 'That's true. Mean a lot to those lads, these birds do. Carry all sorts of importance for them, memories of home, some connection with their history. Like all symbols, I suppose. Course, the bits about them representing longevity and invincibility didn't work for Chupul, did they?' Trueman nodded thoughtfully. 'That's the thing about symbols, isn't it? You can pile all the significance on to them you like, but if they fail to live up to your expectations, well, that's no fault of an innocent bird like this, is it? So what has he come up with, that brother of yours, to get Danny off the hook?'

'Not much, other than he's convinced the knife and the phone were taken by the same person. He thinks if the phone can be located, it's likely the knife will be as well.'

Trueman nodded slowly. 'All the more reason to suspect it will never show up, then. Even if that knife was to surface somewhere, do you really think the police would be willing to turn over evidence that might help Danny get off a charge of killing one of their own? After everybody and his brother saw him do it in broad daylight.' He paused. 'The Gurkhas are well respected in Singapore, as is the Nepali community as a whole. But they're a small community within another culture, and Singapore is as good as anywhere at making a minority feel like one. If this was a Singapore officer that had been killed, the authorities would be moving heaven and earth to get a death penalty. This is their chance to show that they value the life of a Nepali policeman just as highly. Trust me, they're not going to give Danny any breaks.'

The two men watched as a flurry of activity erupted in the monal enclosure. A male charged a potential suitor for his mate and drove him away. In the dangerous, unpredictable world of nature, monogamy had its benefits. But it also had its responsibilities.

'The irony is of course that if Titus was handy with his fists around his wife, and Danny had found out about it, he is exactly the one who would have stepped in. Violence towards a woman, or a kid?' Trueman shook his head ruefully. 'About as low as you can go in Maik's estimation. He'd have moved in to put a stop to it.'

'By force?'

Trueman shook his head again. 'Not at first. Probably just a quiet word, make the bloke see the error of his ways.'

'And if he didn't?'

'Most people would have enough sense to pay attention when Danny was advising them to do something. He has a way of getting his point across.'

'But if not? If Chupul had persisted?'

Trueman inclined his head. 'Then Danny would have, what's that phrase they use out here, *done the needful*.' He turned his cold-eyed stare on Damian once again. 'I'm hearing that the prosecution's deal is going away the second they feel they have a strong enough case for a first limb conviction, and I am hearing that day is coming soon.'

'Are you hearing all this from Ronnie Gunn?'

'Ronnie doesn't want to see Danny get topped for this any more than you or me. He's no friend of his, I'll grant you. Whatever else he was, Titus Chupul was Ronnie's mentor. Gave him a lot of skills that have served him well in life. Danny Maik took someone important away from Ronnie. But he's come to recognise that Danny is a good man at heart, and he knows it would be a tragedy to lose him over this. There aren't that many about these days, frankly, truly good men.' He looked at Damian squarely, one man who knew about the world recognising something of the same in another. 'It's time to face up to the truth, Damian. I know your brother's good, but even he can't get Danny off this one. Somebody needs to make him see that pleading out is the only option he has left. And Selena Lim is not the one to do it.'

'She doesn't want him to plead because she believes he is not guilty.'

'Does she? I wonder. Suppose she talks Danny out of taking a plea, and he ends up getting found guilty anyway. Instead of just doing a few years inside, the man who killed a serving officer gets his just rewards instead. A lot of people would be very happy with an outcome like that. Grateful, too. When you've been around the block as many times as I have you understand that a favour done in the right place, at the right time, can take you a long way in a hurry.'

Trueman shrugged, and turned his eyes on the birds. 'It's a scenario,' he said. 'Here's another one. There might be legitimate reasons somebody with her inexperience was awarded such a high-profile case, but the fact that she got it suggests someone wanted her to. Perhaps she was chosen simply because she could be counted on to lose. She's young, over-confident; those are weaknesses that can easily be exploited. We both know that.'

Damian set his own gaze on the monals. Selena could tell everybody she tried her best, and perhaps even believe it herself. But it would still be her up on Duxton Road, free to drink her sugarcane juice and eat her tau sar piah, after Danny had gone. Damian wasn't sure he was buying it, but he wasn't sure that he wasn't, either. The uncertainty left him with nothing to say.

'Listen, perhaps it's neither of those things,' said Trueman easily. 'But one way or another, Danny is being led down the longest, loneliest one-way road there is. The only way to stop that is if somebody can convince him to enter a plea. Danny's a stubborn bugger. That sense of right and wrong he has, it won't allow him to confess if he thinks he's innocent. But in this case, right or wrong has got nothing to do with it. He needs to save his own life. Nobody else can do it for him. Maybe that DCS of his, Shepherd, can convince him. He's got a lot of respect for her. He might listen to her. Or your brother, he's got a lot of time for him, too. It doesn't matter who gets the message across. But somebody has to. And they need to do it soon.'

He extended a hand as a prelude to leaving. 'I can't be of any help in this, not any more. And I don't think Ronnie can, either. Take Selena Lim out of the equation as well and, as far as I can see, that only leaves one person here in Singapore that Danny can pin his hopes on.'

He took a long, lingering look at the monals as he departed. Damian watched them, too, after Trueman had gone. He thought about the symbolism these birds carried for the Nepali people. And about where the responsibility might lie, if the burden of all those hopes and expectations proved too much.

39

The Incident Room had been many things to them over the years; a place to ponder developments, to vent frustrations, to grieve the departed, even. But none of them could ever remember it feeling like such a strange, alien space. It was as if all the camaraderie, all the teamwork and collective thinking that had gone on in there, the shared experiences, the collaborative efforts, were a thing of the past, and now they were all just a collection of disconnected individuals, each pursuing their own separate agendas. And that included the ones not in attendance.

'I see we're down a Druid again,' said Holland, looking around the room. 'Was it something we said?'

It was something they did, Shepherd knew. Or did not do. Specifically, look in the directions he was suggesting. His understandable lack of faith in Domenic Jejeune's leadership on this case seemed to be leading Summer to believe they would get nowhere unless he began running his own investigation.

'Is that the ME's autopsy report on Peter Estey in your hand, Tony?' asked Shepherd.

Holland looked down as if surprised to find it there. 'Oh yeah. I ran into old Jones on the stairs. He was on his way to bring it to you. I told him I'd save him the trouble. It puts time of death at between six and midnight four days ago.'

Shepherd was less concerned with the fact that Holland had read the report on the way up here than with the clear implication that was causing his self-satisfied smirk. 'As in before Summer reported the shooting,' he said.

Jejeune nodded towards the report. 'Does it mention the stomach contents?' he asked. 'I'm wondering if Estey's last meal could have been pheasant. And redcurrant sauce.'

Shepherd took the sheet from Holland and consulted it closely. She shook her head slowly. 'If you are going in for clairvoyance, Domenic, could you let us know? It would save us a fortune in forensic lab fees.'

'He cooked a pheasant and took a plate over to Bob Ferris. Estey told him he had come into a brace. I think the other bird was the one we found at his trailer. Ferris insisted the pheasant they ate wasn't farm produced, but the fibres tell us that other bird had definitely come from the Nye.' His puzzled expression made it clear he had no explanation.

'It's not beyond the realms of possibility that those fibres were planted on that bird to implicate Estey. I mean, after all, Summer does have previous.'

Shepherd's expression told him the jury was still out with regard to the discovered shell casings. The look Holland gave her in return told her otherwise. 'He was first on scene at the Nye. He could have pocketed a couple of fibres from the gloves then.'

'For what reason? He didn't even know about Estey then, did he?' She looked across at Jejeune, who was staring into the distance, deep in thought. She sighed in exasperation. 'Domenic,' she said sharply, to attract his attention. 'There's no evidence of prior contact between Summer and Estey, is there?'

'Between him and Estey? None that we know about.' But the way Domenic Jejeune answered the question didn't discount the possibility. He seemed to take a second to gather his thoughts, but somehow Shepherd could tell it wasn't the case in Singapore that was troubling him this time. 'When we first discussed Summer's return,' he said, 'you told me he had been off for two years.'

Shepherd nodded. 'That's right. Suspension, counselling and sabbatical.'

'About two years, or exactly two years?'

'To the day,' she said. 'You know what insurance companies are like. The clock ran out on Summer at midnight, and he reported for duty the following day. Why? Do you think he met Estey during that time?'

Jejeune shook his head thoughtfully. 'No, I don't think he did.'

'Then where are we on his death?' she asked, tiring of her DCI's cryptic ways. 'Are we any closer to coming up with a motive? I think we've pretty much eliminated the idea that Estey was murdered in revenge because somebody thought he had killed Abbie Cleve. So do we have anything else?'

'I don't know about a motive,' said Holland, 'but as far as I'm concerned that wingnut Tara Skye is not in the clear yet. I mean anybody who can't make the distinction between snaring a rabbit in a wire loop and the murder of a human being might be capable of anything. I had another look at those emails last night. There's some pretty toxic language in there. This is a woman who knows how to get worked up.'

'Flying drones is a pretty ineffectual way to go about trying to flush birds,' said Jejeune. 'It's a petty, naïve activity designed to annoy rather than to achieve any real purpose. The same with spraying fox urine.'

Shepherd raised her eyebrows.

'Long story,' he said. 'The point is, I think those emails were simply more of the same. She's just an angry young woman, raging against the machine.'

'Since you seem so intent on defending Ms Party Frock, Domenic, I think you should know she has returned the favour by dropping you right in it,' Shepherd informed him. 'She's saying she spoke to you previously about flying her drones, and you told her it was legal.'

'I didn't say it wasn't. I'm not sure that's the same thing. Besides, she didn't say she'd be flying them over private property, even if it was being held in trust.'

Shepherd shook her head sagely. 'They say you should choose your friends wisely, Domenic. You don't have to worry about your enemies. They will seek you out all by themselves. Anyway, it's in her official statement now. A matter of public record.' She looked at him over the rim of her glasses. 'Counselling antisocial behaviour, or at the very least failing to report prior knowledge of it? It'll have consequences. My advice is to propose some form of community engagement. Proactive penance goes down very well with the brass these days.'

'All the benefits of a punishment without the trouble of having to issue one,' said Holland, who could see a few benefits to this approach himself. Choosing your own punishment was something he'd be seriously looking at the next time he found himself in trouble. Perhaps he could get a local group of troubled youths together for a remedial five-a-side tournament.

'So I'll tell them you're looking into ways to engage with the local community, shall I? Good.'

It occurred to Jejeune that Shepherd's ability to phrase decisions as if you might have had even the faintest input of your own was one of her most impressive leadership skills. But he saw no reason to offer any resistance in this case.

Holland stirred slowly. For someone who was never shy about offering his thoughts, it was a sign that what was coming might be particularly significant. 'You know, there is one possibility we've been overlooking in all this,' he said deliberately. 'We thought Estey had done a runner and that's why he wasn't around. But why did we think that? Because we were given a reason to.'

He paused. Neither one of his superior officers was going to need leading by the hand from here, but it was clear from the way they were looking at him that they were going to make him say it anyway. 'Estey lived alone, but there are still people who would have noticed if he'd gone missing. Bob Ferris for one. But with a plausible explanation for running, after shooting at a police officer, nobody is going to go looking for him, including us.'

Shepherd's complexion had darkened ominously. 'Tony, this is preposterous,' she said angrily. 'I'm not prepared to listen to any more of this nonsense.' But she would.

'We now know for a fact that Estey couldn't have fired those shots at Summer. And I know that nobody fired any shots at all. So why go to all the trouble of staging that shooting if not to make us think he'd run away? And there's only one reason you'd want us to think that.'

Shepherd's anger took on a different form now. It was no longer directed at Holland, but at what he had placed before her. Because the simple truth was, as he said, at this point she couldn't really offer any better explanation. And that meant she was forced to consider this worst of all possible scenarios at face value. She asked Holland to leave the room, and waited until he was long out of earshot before she spoke.

'There's a lot that fits, Domenic. The motive is weak; the need to save face – but Summer is a troubled young man, and his police career is all he has. If Estey knew that, and found a way to exploit it… Tony couldn't possibly be right about this, could he?'

'The world has a way of reflecting what you believe,' said Jejeune. 'If you think it's full of joy, you will see examples of it everywhere. Look for injustice, and that is what you will find. Tony Holland has had his mind set on Summer being a part of this since the beginning, but that doesn't mean he is right.'

'Then who else, Domenic. If not Noel Summer, where else can we look for our suspect?'

'No one saw Estey after he left Bob Ferris's that night. That makes Ferris the last person known to have seen him alive.'

He would have more, she knew. A thought had been troubling him, and she knew now there would be some link to Bob Ferris in there somewhere. She shifted uneasily. 'You need to be very careful, Domenic. Investigating an ex-officer, one who was injured in the line of duty at that, is a way to make a lot of enemies in a hurry in this service.'

Jejeune nodded slowly. It was. But just because it was an unpopular thing to do didn't mean it wasn't necessary. Because one other thing he now knew was that, at the very least, Bob Ferris had some difficult questions to answer.

40

Jejeune parked the Beast in front of the gates to Cleve Hall and got out. On the far side of the road, a stand of hornbeams were weeping the last of their russet leaves away, a gentle breeze sending them into a spiralling, wind-blown dance as they fell. Golden sunlight lay like honey across the fields beyond them, beneath horsetails of soft white cloud streaked across a pale sky. He knew the landscape here would soon see less peaceful times. A PDF of the deed to the estate was open on his phone, and he scrolled through it now as he surveyed the driveway and the road running in front of it, checking where the property lines ran. There was not much room for an assembling crowd between the areas of public access and the private land. The wide approach road leading up to the property would provide a natural gathering spot for supporters of both sides, but the shape of the driveway would serve as a funnel, channelling them ever closer as they approached the gates. It was not an ideal setting for a protest by two opposing camps, and the potential for conflict was high. Things could turn nasty in a hurry.

He thought about other protests he had been embroiled in, the roiling, jostling chaos when the crowd began to press in, the confusion and disorder that made control impossible. In such a situation, how easy would it have been for someone to remove a knife or a phone undetected, with all attention on the crush of the crowd, on the action unfurling all around them? In those circumstances, would anyone really have noticed one individual stooping to pick up one item, and a different person grabbing another? Especially if the distracting action was as compelling as someone striking a police officer. He tracked the sequence in his mind's eye: Maik's clenched fist, the sharp, swift blow, the fall. The stillness. It seemed impossible that eight witnesses could be mistaken in what they'd seen. Was Danny, like so many others, indulging in the solace of his own self-deception, he wondered. Had he killed this man in a moment of unrestrained ferocity, with a blow that he was now trying to convince himself had been only a controlled, proportionate response? If it was someone else, Jejeune asked himself, someone he didn't know so well, would he have believed their version of events, despite all the overwhelming evidence to the contrary? He knew the answer, even as he shied away from it. And it hardened a position he had found himself slowly sliding towards over the past few days. He didn't doubt Danny Maik's honesty. He never would. But he was just possibly coming to doubt his innocence. With one last, lingering look at the scene of the impending protests, Domenic Jejeune got back into the Range Rover and drove away.

The pair were standing near a fence under a magnificent oak tree that had already taken its final bow for the season. Beneath its tangled basketweave of bare branches, a carpet of golden leaves lay like a discarded gown. The young girl saw Jejeune walking towards her and ran to cling to her father's trouser leg. Evan Knowles had been unaware of Jejeune's approach and his daughter's actions startled him. He turned and smiled a greeting.

'Inspector Jejeune, isn't it?

'I'd like a word with you, if you have a moment.' Jejeune tried a reassuring smile and it worked well enough for the girl to disengage from her father and resume her play among the leaves.

'Here? So it's not a formal interview then?' The man tried a smile of his own, but it was a lot more hesitant and uncertain. 'Only, the other officer, the constable, he suggested there might be a follow-up.'

'This is not it, but I can come back later. I hadn't realised you would have company.'

Knowles looked at his daughter as she gathered handfuls of leaves and raised them above her head, letting them fall on her like petals. 'Yeah, it's not ideal, having Rosie accompany me to work. Unfortunately, her instructional programme has been temporarily suspended. We had hoped it might soon qualify for funding, but continuous operation was one of the stipulations, and now, with the donations having suddenly come to a stop...' He shrugged and spread out his hands. 'Well, you know all about that.'

'You're a single parent, I understand.'

'Rosie's earlier needs would have taxed the best of parents. Unfortunately, we turned out to be far from that. Her mother found she simply couldn't cope. It's sad, isn't it, that so often we don't discover our failings until it's too late.'

And yet, here you are, thought Jejeune, carrying on anyway. Sometimes our failings are all we have left. 'If you're sure we can talk?'

Knowles nodded. 'Rosie tends to prefer her world to ours most of the time anyway.' He turned to give his daughter an affectionate smile. 'And she is nothing if not discreet. So we don't mind, do we, Rosie?' he said, adopting the shared persona Jejeune had seen in so many parents of children with similar challenges.

Knowles leaned in confidentially. 'Can I ask, do you think I'll be charged with anything?'

'Dereliction of duty is normally a matter between employees and employers, unless it results in criminal negligence. As far as I can tell, that isn't the case here, but perhaps you can help me clear that up. I wanted to ask you what the procedure would be if you received a report that a farm product had been shown to contain toxins or other contaminants.'

Knowles tilted his head. 'We would have the authority to go to see if it was the result of the animals in question being maltreated or kept in unsuitable conditions. But even if this wasn't the case, we'd immediately conduct testing on all the stock.' He looked at Jejeune frankly. 'I can assure you, there would be no difference between our response and the way DEFRA would have handled things when they had oversight of this area. We would take such a report very seriously.'

'Would you shut down the operation?'

'If further problems were found?' He nodded. 'Temporarily at least. Even if it was only an isolated case of a poisoning, we'd want to identify the source before the operation would be allowed to continue.'

'And that operation, that search, it could take a long time, I presume.'

'There are literally hundreds of pathogens out there, Inspector, and hundreds of potential sources for them. Depending on what this one was, we'd have a few likely candidates to check first, but yes, in theory, it could take a long time.'

'And the facility would be forced to remain shut the entire time?'

'People are trying to make lifestyle choices to be better citizens, to affect the planet in a positive way. They have to be able to trust the products they choose, and they're entitled to know they're safe. Can I ask if you have any particular facility in mind, Inspector?' But something in the way Knowles averted his eyes to watch his daughter as he asked the question told Jejeune the man already knew.

'You said you tested the stock at the Nye,' said Jejeune.

'There was no evidence of any toxins in the samples we took. It's not a guarantee, of course, but we did take a very wide sampling. We hadn't been there before.' He tried his luck with an embarrassed grin and, perhaps because the sun had come out, or perhaps because the man's daughter was now fixing Jejeune with a wide-eyed stare, the DCI gave himself permission to return it.

'And no birds from there were ever previously submitted for testing?'

'Not to LSA. There are of course other agencies that can do the initial screening. Only positive test results would come to us.' He looked at his daughter again, playing happily among the leaves. 'It was the issue of funding that did it, you know? Abigail Cleve had found out Rosie's programme might be receiving it, and she was astute enough to know Harmony Hill would no longer be reliant on her donations when it did.'

'Which would mean she would no longer have any hold over you,' said Jejeune. 'So it was the quid pro quo you were on your way to see her about that day?'

Knowles nodded. 'She wanted assurances that I'd continue to issue the operating licences and defer inspections. I intended to tell her that I couldn't. The constant postponements were being noticed – remarked upon, even. I wouldn't have been able to defer an inspection for very much longer. But of course I never got the chance to tell her all that.' He looked at his daughter again for a moment. 'Abbie Cleve was dead when I arrived, Inspector. I swear to you she was.'

Jejeune nodded thoughtfully. He turned to watch Rosie. She was sitting in the middle of the leaves, stirring them into a pile with her feet. He suspected it was a prelude to burying herself in them, a task for which she was going to have to ask for her father's assistance. Evan Knowles would be willing to end this interview to help.

'This process to submit a sample for testing,' said Jejeune. 'Is it complicated?'

'Actually, it's quite straightforward. You submit a tissue sample or even an entire carcass, provide a few details and wait for the inevitable bad news.'

'Inevitable?'

'People don't submit an animal for analysis if they can find any other explanation for its death, Inspector, however tenuous.'

'Can it be done anonymously?'

'Of course not.' Knowles thought about it for a moment. 'But you might get away with falsifying the address the sample came from. The results would be sent to the email account you designated. You understand I'm only talking about a hypothetical situation here. I am not aware of this ever having actually been done. Why would it? If you have a suspicious bird death on your hands, you'd really want to know the results as soon as possible.'

Unless you already knew what killed it, thought Jejeune. Because the toxins you knew the testing would show were the ones you had injected into the bird in the first place.

Knowles turned to watch his daughter playing contentedly beneath the tree. It was some time before he spoke. 'I hope I've been of some help,' he said eventually without looking back. But he received no answer. By then, Domenic Jejeune was halfway to his vehicle, deep in thought.

41

'You're looking thoughtful,' Selena told Damian as the two of them waited in the Conference Room for Danny to be brought up from the holding cells. 'Off in your happy place again, I presume? In Bhutan?'

Damian could not disagree that he had been quieter than usual around Selena since his meeting with Trueman. It had left him unsure of things on a number of levels, and, with Danny clearly uneasy about sharing information with Gunn any more, silence seemed the safest option. But talk about his happy place was safe enough. And it was not entirely untrue that his thoughts had been there, partially at least.

'I guess I'm still just having trouble adjusting to the intensity here. The information, the decisions, the consequences, they all seem so monumental if things don't go our way. It's hard to keep your thoughts straight.'

'And thinking about Bhutan helps?'

'There's a mountain pass called Dochula; thirteen thousand feet high, in the foothills of the Himalayas. I arrived in the early morning when there was not another living soul to be seen. There was still mist in the valley and the call of unseen birds seemed to be coming at you from all directions. The air was so cool and still you felt like you could hold it in your hand.

And then, all of a sudden, the mists parted and the Himalayas appeared like a vision of heaven; seven peaks, snow-covered, majestic, perfect. The feeling, the peace that came over me… I can't ever remember experiencing anything like it.'

Selena nodded. And now, it seemed like he never would again. Such experiences were as much about a time as a place, she knew. They came to everyone, and for the lucky few they lingered. But for most people the sensation was fleeting, and the constellation of perfect conditions that created it would never quite align again in the same way. It made her sad to think that Damian would never recapture that moment. Even when this was over, and the cards lay where they had fallen, there would be consequences from this case that would last a lifetime.

'I've been thinking about what you said, about Danny being set up. It would have to be by someone who knew him well: his habits, his preferences, his likelihood of defending himself in a certain way against an unprovoked attack. I wonder, can you think of anyone who fits that profile?'

Before Damian could answer, the heavy metal door clanged open and Maik shuffled in. He managed a weak smile.

'Selena was just asking me whether I think Guy Trueman is responsible for setting you up, Danny.' They had learned to be economical with the niceties, given the number of meaningful topics they were forced to cover in their allotted time. 'I have to say, his fingerprints are all over this.'

Maik shook his head. 'Not Guy. Why would he do it?'

'Could there be anything between him and the wife, Devina Chupul?' asked Selena. 'They know each other better than they are letting on. I'm sure of it. With his track record, you could hardly rule it out. I didn't find anything on social media, but that could just mean they've been discreet.'

Trueman had never been known for his discretion – but then, Maik had never known him have the need to be. His eye ranged far and wide but, as far as Danny could remember, his ex-CO had never strayed into the territory of adultery. 'If it was me, I'd probably start with the CCTV from Raffles,' he said. 'Guy always did like a bit of luxury. It'd be just his style to take a woman there.'

'I'd need a court order,' said Selena, 'and I'd never get one. When you've been around as long as that place, you accumulate a lot of secrets. There are plenty of powerful people in this town who'd be very uncomfortable about Raffles opening its video footage to scrutiny.'

'What happens in Raffles...?' said Damian.

'Exactly.'

He paused and drew in a breath. He was aware that from the moment he next spoke, nothing would ever be the same again. For any of them. 'A connection between Danny and Titus Chupul is what the prosecution needs to make their first limb case, isn't it?'

'It is,' confirmed Lim warily.

He turned to Maik. 'A photo of you on Devina Titus's phone, that would be enough to establish that connection, wouldn't it?'

He had been prepared to say more, to explain the reason for his question, to flesh out the inquiry with other details. But something in his delivery had made it unnecessary. Maik and Selena were both staring at him, eyes wide.

'You saw one?' Damian couldn't tell if Selena's horrified expression was because she feared the answer or already knew it. He nodded anyway.

She turned a questioning gaze on Maik, but he shook his head slowly to tell her he had no explanation. None at all. 'What was I wearing?' he asked.

'What?'

'In the photo. What colour was my shirt?'

'Erm blueish, maybe. Grey? It had a collar. And a little crest, I think.'

Maik nodded. 'It's blue. I have it with me. That photo must have been taken since I've been here.'

'Then who else could have taken it besides Guy Trueman?' asked Damian. 'You don't know anybody else here.'

'But I hadn't seen Guy until that day at his office. We'd been meaning to get together, but it never happened.'

'That doesn't mean he hadn't seen you before that day. Most mobile phones today are quite capable of capturing high-quality photographs from a long distance. Think about it, Danny. He forwards the photo to Devina Chupul. She leaves it around for Titus to see. He comes for you, and after you take care of him those two get to live happily ever after.'

Danny was shaking his head again even before Damian had finished. 'Not Guy. He wouldn't risk having me face a sentence like this.'

'You were never meant to.' Damian's involuntary glance in Selena's direction did not go unnoticed by Danny. 'You were supposed to plead out to a lower one. His boy Ronnie has been pushing you to from the moment you first met him.'

'And now you are, too,' said Selena.

Damian addressed Maik directly. 'The rules have changed, Danny. You have been set up. You can't win this by fighting fair. A plea is the only hope you've got.'

Selena stood up quickly. 'That's not true. You're innocent, Danny. That has to count for something. We have another line of inquiry to pursue now. I'll see what I can find out about Trueman, see if anybody remembers seeing him and Devina Chupul together. In the meantime, there's still that knife out there somewhere. Somebody must know something. I'm convinced I can find that person if I only keep looking.'

'That knife is not going to show up, Selena,' Damian told her. 'Guy Trueman as much as guaranteed it.'

Maik looked at him in a curious way, as if he was convinced that what Damian was telling them was true, but he had known it already. 'Did he say how he could be so sure?'

'He said the police would never hand it over, even if it surfaced.' He paused, as if recognising that only the brutal truth might smash a way through Danny's defences now. 'They want the death penalty, Danny, and they are determined to get it.'

There was a long silence. 'If the knife and the phone aren't going to show up,' said Selena, 'then going after Trueman is all we've got. We need some way to prove he is behind this.'

'If that photo was tagged,' said Damian, 'it might show that it came from Trueman's phone. Would that be enough?'

'It could be,' said Selena, 'but there's no way we could get to it to find out. At the moment, the prosecutors clearly don't know that photo exists. Without being sure there is metadata tied to it that can help our case against Trueman, we'd be taking a huge risk in alerting them to its existence.'

'Perhaps it's a risk worth taking,' said Damian. 'It doesn't matter what you did or didn't do any longer, Danny. The truth is irrelevant now. The only thing that matters is the opinion of those who will decide your fate: a judge, a jury. You need them to believe you were set up. And that means presenting them with evidence that Guy Trueman sent that photo to Devina Chupul.'

Danny shook his head slowly. 'As Selena says, there's no way of knowing that it holds the information to help us to do that.'

'And if it doesn't, it will without question be the final piece the prosecution need to make their case.' Selena turned to Danny. It was her turn to be blunt. 'It will be enough for a conviction.'

'Then the only thing left is for us to find out what the metadata could tell us before making a formal request for the photo.'

Selena's look left Damian in no doubt that they both recognised there was only one way they could achieve that. Damian would have to get to the phone and take a look at the photo data for himself. And since he couldn't alert Devina Chupul that he already knew the photo existed, he'd have to find some way of getting into a private citizen's home uninvited, and taking a look at the contents of the phone without the owner's permission. And that wasn't just risky. It was illegal.

'I'm sorry,' said Selena, 'I can't listen to any more of this.' She tapped urgently on the door and squeezed through as soon as it opened from the outside, escaping quickly into the corridor. Maik watched her leave. Did he believe in the system of justice? Maybe if it had been given the chance to decide his case on the facts, it might have come up with the right decision. But the system had no mechanism to compensate for evidence that was insufficient, or incorrect, or falsified. It could only function if it was given the truth to work with. And he knew that wouldn't happen in this case. So no, Danny didn't believe the system would work for him. He knew it could not.

He sighed deeply. All his adult life he had followed the rules: at school, in the army, the police. No bending them, no cutting corners, no making exceptions. Accepting the rule of law was the cornerstone of his character, it was who he was. And now he was being forced to turn his back on all that. Unless he intended to go to prison for a very long time, or worse, he had to sanction a crime to be committed on his behalf, to publicly declare to Damian that he no longer had any faith in this system of law and order he had worked in, and defended, and upheld for all these years. He knew he had no choice. It was his last hope.

But he wouldn't do it. Because what would be left of him if he chose to abandon a lifetime's beliefs, and sanction an illegal act? He would lose the only thing he still had. He would lose himself.

'Your brother and I never put away anybody who didn't deserve it, Damian. And we never let one go who did.' Maik shook his head slowly. 'I can't give you permission to break into that woman's home. Not for my needs, not for anyone's. We get the information on Guy Trueman the right way, or we don't get it at all.'

Damian looked at him sadly; a man sentenced to his fate by his moral code. He couldn't think of any greater contrast than the one between Danny Maik and the person who had set him up, a person who was prepared to break any rule, make any choice, to achieve their ends. Damian knew towards which end of the spectrum his own moral code could be found. And although his brother's friend couldn't know it, that was good news for Danny.

42

The garden was empty. A small rowan bush was still heavily laden with berries, and along the fence tendrils of ivy offered yet more food for wild birds, but none had come. Perhaps they were finding food elsewhere, thought Jejeune, in more hospitable spots where sadness and despair didn't seem to hang in the air as they did around this neglected plot.

Ferris was sitting outside on the front porch in his wheelchair when Jejeune rounded the corner. 'I've heard,' he said. 'Noel was here.'

Jejeune offered his condolences. 'I know you were close.'

'For a time, yeah. Not so much lately, but still…'

Yes, thought Jejeune. Still…

'There's to be a service, as soon as you lot have released the body. I've just been trying to round up some of the old gang.' He looked at Jejeune's expression and smiled. 'But you didn't come here today to talk about Pete, did you?'

'In a way,' said Jejeune. 'He has a connection to a place you're familiar with. The Nye.'

'Ah,' said Ferris with a slow nod of his head. 'Well, if we're going back that far, you'd better come in and have a cup of tea.'

In the living room, Jejeune cradled a faded mug holding a thin, milky brew, moving it around occasionally to disguise the fact that he was trying to avoid drinking it. 'I'm wondering if you'd be willing to tell me what happened on that day. I haven't really had any justification to pull the file, so I thought perhaps I could hear it from you.'

Ferris shook his head. 'There's not much to tell. By the time my partner, Paul Tong, and I rolled up with the warrant, Summer had been there a couple of hours. We checked in with him and he reported no activity. As far as we knew, the house was empty. It was unlocked and we had the home-owner's permission to enter, so we just went in. Quiet as the grave,' he said, letting his memory take him back to that time. 'Even Paul said afterwards he could never remember a house sounding so empty. We cleared the downstairs and went up to where the bedrooms were. We weren't deliberately being quiet, you understand. That came up in the inquiry later, why had we been creeping around in silence, if we really believed the house was empty. But we just didn't have anything to say to each other. We'd done a few of these, Paul and me. We knew what we were about. We didn't have to chat about it.'

He paused at this point, as Jejeune had suspected he might. This was the point at which normality had disappeared from Bob Ferris's life. For ever. It would have occurred in an instant in real time, but in Ferris's memory everything would be in slow motion, happening all at once, and at the same time separated out into tiny, discrete flickers of action. No matter how many times he revisited the scene in his mind, the sequence would never change.

'And then' – Ferris sighed – 'well, it all kicked off, didn't it?' We entered the bedroom and there he was sitting on the bed; White. With a load of cash spread out all around him, and a suitcase full of pills resting on the pillow. And a shotgun. The first blast caught Pete in the vest and he went down.' Ferris looked down. 'I tried to run, Inspector. That's not what the report will say. It'll tell you I turned my body to try and protect Pete from the second blast. But I didn't. I tried to run, to get out of that bedroom. I've never told anybody that before. The second blast caught me in the spine and I went down. I couldn't move but I didn't know at the time my legs were gone. It was just pain flooding through my whole body. Like blood, that's what it felt like, like it was just pouring out inside me and spreading all over.'

'And Summer?'

'Got White on the stairs. I heard the commotion and I remember thinking he must have moved a bit sharpish, to get in here from his car that quickly. But of course, White had taken the time to pack up his cash and grab his suitcase, which gave Summer the time to get in there and bring him down.'

'He wasn't armed at that point, White?'

'Left the gun on the bed. Summer secured him to the banister and came up to the bedroom. He saw us and called it in immediately. He stayed with me and Pete until the ambulance arrived. Held my hand. Didn't say a word, though. Not one.'

Jejeune exhaled. He felt as if he'd been holding his breath for a long time.

'And the rest you know. It was the gun that did for Summer. If we'd have stumbled in on a low-value target like White and it had simply turned into a punch-up, it'd have just been a reprimand. A short inquiry, a bit of finger-pointing and a couple of months cooling his heels. But White doing us with that gun – two officers down, one permanently injured, all down to Summer's negligence – well, he was never going to come back from that, was he?'

'Until he did.' Jejeune looked out over the empty garden again. From this angle, it was devoid of any splash of colour, cloaked only in a washed-out sepia. Brittle brown leaves shrivelled on bare branches and the stems of pale, dried grasses, bent and broken, leaned forlornly across the overgrown path.

'It seems to me this entire tragedy all spins off one piece of information,' he said.

Ferris gave a sad smile. 'That the house was empty in the first place.'

'I've been checking some dates recently. Noel Summer came back to work two years to the day after the shooting.'

'You think it's significant that he came back when he did?'

Jejeune wasn't saying yet. But he would soon. 'About six months ago, Abbie Cleve was interviewed about the success of her business. That interview was timed to coincide with the first anniversary of her opening. So that would be about eighteen months ago now.'

'That'd be about the time I remember it opening up, yeah,' confirmed Ferris. 'I presume this is all going somewhere, Inspector.'

'Peter Estey was at that opening. He was already back from a six-month deployment in Afghanistan. You said it was over between him and Abigail Cleve before he was deployed, so that takes us back further than twenty-four months, to the time they were together, the time she was exiled from Cleve Hall.'

'By my reckoning, that'd be about right,' Ferris told him indulgently. But there was an edginess about him now, as if he could perhaps tell, finally, where Jejeune was heading.

'I've been looking at the deeds to the Cleve estate. Libby Cleve said something strange when I was there. I asked her about Abbie setting up shop on a property right beside the estate and she said she was entitled. I thought she meant entitled to do it, but she really meant Abbie was entitled to the land. It was hers in trust, a former part of the estate that had been left to her. The thing is, I can't find any records of Abigail Cleve having lived anywhere else when she moved out. I think she went straight there, to that property, Bouquet House. She didn't start the Nye straight away, but she was living there for at least twenty-four months. That means she would have been the homeowner at the time you were shot, Mr Ferris. It was Abbie Cleve who told Noel Summer the house was empty that day.'

Jejeune had never noticed the ticking of the clock before, but it seemed overloud now. It filled the room, echoing into the silence in every corner. 'When I began to think about it, I realised you were very careful to avoid using a name or even a gender when you were talking about the homeowner earlier,' he said. 'It was the same just now. And we both know there was a reason for that.'

It was the same reason Noel Summer had not mentioned his connection to Abbie Cleve when he had first come upon the body at the Nye that day. Because the inference was all too easy to make. 'Did he blame her for her part in the shooting?'

'Does she have one?'

'If White was in the house all the time, she'd bear some of the responsibility for what happened to Summer, wouldn't she? That would be a hard thing to forgive.'

Ferris shrugged. 'She told him point-blank the house was empty. Only she knew whether she was wrong or not. And now she's gone, so I don't suppose we'll ever find out, will we?' He looked at Jejeune. 'Leave it be, Inspector,' he said. 'It doesn't matter any more. You can't undo what has been done. You can't put things back the way they were, not for me and not for Summer, either. He never offered any defence. He believed he was to blame and he believed he deserved to be punished for it. Leave him with his guilt. He needs it. It's the only way he can come to terms with what happened, and it's all that's keeping him going. He doesn't want to be relieved of his burden.' He offered the DCI a mirthless grin. 'You never did have that talk with him, did you? About him coming to see me.' He tilted his head. 'It's okay, it's a difficult one. I'll take care of it. But I'll leave it up to you to bring up the business of Abbie Cleve with him. He'll not hear anything about it from me. Thanks for coming by, Inspector. I don't suppose I'll be seeing you again, so take care.'

He didn't see Jejeune to the door this time but, when the DCI rounded the house to walk back to the Beast, he caught a glimpse of Ferris watching from the living room window. He didn't pause or slow down, just as he had instructed Summer that day that seemed a lifetime ago now. Bob Ferris hadn't been a suspect at the time, but a lot had changed since then. Because it occurred to Jejeune that Ferris had been very careful not to point out one other obvious fact. If Abigail Cleve did get it wrong about the house being empty that day, Noel Summer wasn't the only one who'd be justified in feeling some resentment towards her. Her error, if that's what it was, had cost Summer two years of his life. It had cost Bob Ferris a great deal more than that.

43

Colleen Shepherd had just closed her front door and was digging around in her bag for her car keys when she looked up to find someone at the end of her driveway.

'Lindy.'

'I was wondering if you'd have a minute. I wanted to talk to you.'

Here, noted Shepherd, not at the station, not anywhere more public. At her own home. 'I've just had a call that the protest organisers want to meet with me up at Cleve Hall. Want to join me? It shouldn't take long. We can grab some lunch afterwards and I can drop you back here.'

Lindy slid into the passenger seat, sinking into the opulence of the grained leather that cinched round her like a tailored glove.

'Domenic hasn't sent you up here on his behalf to ask if he can get out of that community service, I hope,' said Shepherd as she reversed out of her driveway.

Lindy shook her head.

'I'm afraid he's going to be stuck with it. Tara Skye has made sure of that. Honestly, I don't know what he sees in that girl,' Shepherd told her. 'Idealism? Conviction?' She shook her head. 'Whatever it is, he seems quite taken with her.' She offered Lindy a smile. 'But then, he always has liked his women a touch on the unconventional side.'

Lindy returned the smile but, to Shepherd's trained eye, it looked a touch forced. 'Yes, he'd mentioned her comments had made life difficult for him. I imagine he'll plump for an outreach programme or something with one of the environmental groups. But of course he'll want to wait until this weekend's furore is over and done with.'

Shepherd shook her head. 'All this fuss over meat. It's enough to make me want to turn vegetarian.'

'I suppose it would at least help me to shed some of this flab,' said Lindy. She hefted a non-existent bulge of flesh around her midriff and Shepherd smiled again. As far as she could tell, Lindy still possessed the same enviable figure she'd always had. But she was aware that Tara Skye sported a particularly streamlined look. It wasn't always those we admire, she thought, that inspired us to improve ourselves.

'What has me concerned the most,' said Shepherd, 'is that so many different agendas are going to be pushed. You get a single point of contention and it's easier to address. Neither side has to concede, necessarily, but you can at least see what's before you and work towards a compromise. A protest like this one is going to have so many differences, grievances and points of view being aired, addressing them would be like playing a game of whack-a-mole.'

Her phone trilled and she clicked her Bluetooth connection to answer it. 'Go ahead. On notice. I have a civilian in the car with me.' Nothing sensitive, she was saying, nothing for police ears only.

'Things have kicked off a bit up at the Cleve estate, ma'am.'

'I'm just about there now,' said Shepherd. 'I'll see what it's all about.'

'Do you want me to send backup?'

She looked at Lindy and raised her eyebrows. 'A couple of squad cars rolling up might just inflame the situation. I'll see if I can calm things down on my own first. If I need any assistance, I'll let you know.'

'If you're sure, ma'am.' The duty sergeant's tone managed to convey both his dubiousness at her decision and his awareness that he was in no position to challenge it. Shepherd ended the call and pulled a face. 'Honestly, these bloody people…'

'I thought the protest wasn't until the weekend,' said Lindy.

'It isn't, but these things have a way of taking on a life of their own. A few people show up early, eager to stake a claim, there's some pushing and shoving, and before you know it things have got out of hand. It can happen in a hurry.' She paused. 'This business you wanted to have a word about. You haven't told Domenic any more about developments in Singapore, have you?' Lindy was made of stern stuff, but she had a special bond with Danny. Other allegiances, to gentle requests, to the greater good, might go by the wayside in testing times.

Lindy shook her head. 'That's what I came to tell you, though. I can't do this any more, Colleen. I can hardly stand it, the look that comes across his face when he asks for updates and I say there are none. I can tell he knows I'm lying. And now there's something I need to tell him about the situation, tell you, too—'

'Hello, what do we have here?' said Shepherd suddenly. She wheeled the Jaguar to a stop at the gates of Cleve Hall. Through the windscreen, Lindy could see signs and flags being brandished on both sides of the driveway. Many were suspended from wooden stakes or wire frames; it wouldn't take very much effort at all to repurpose them for other, more sinister means.

'Sorry Lindy, it'll have to wait,' said Shepherd, unbuckling her seat belt quickly. 'I'd ask you to stay in the car, but I might need a bit of help getting my point across, if you're up for it.'

The two women got out of the car and Shepherd straightened herself to her full height. 'Right, let's sort this out, shall we?' she said. She flung an arm out to her left. 'You lot over there on the grass.' Her other arm came up to point in the opposite direction. 'And you can go back over to that side.'

'We have a right to gather here,' Tara Skye told her. 'You don't have any authority to move us off.'

'A legitimate gathering on public land is one thing,' Shepherd told her, projecting her voice enough to make sure everyone was getting the message. 'Disobeying a direct order from a senior police officer is another. My assessment of this situation is that there is clear and ongoing threat to public safety, and, as long as that remains in place, you two groups will stay on your own sides of the driveway. Understood?' She eyed both groups. It was clear she would wait as long as she needed to until she received an answer. She eventually received a grudging acknowledgement from each side, followed by a reluctant shuffling back towards the grassy edges of the driveway.

'Lindy, while I talk to the organisers, and only the organisers,' she emphasised, 'I'd like you to get your phone out and focus the camera along this driveway. If anybody from either side comes into shot, I'll need you to send me the file. Anyone who disobeys a police public safety order is liable to arrest. Since the resources obviously aren't available to do it here, uniformed officers will be dispatched to that individual's home or place of work later on.'

Subjecting them to the judgement of their families, neighbours and co-workers, thought Lindy, a court of public opinion that would rush to a verdict before the squad car had even left the street. Shepherd gestured the organisers to one side and moved over to speak to them. Untypically, Tara Skye and a man Shepherd knew from previous encounters as Tom Makepeace were already to be found on the front lines.

'If I deem that this protest cannot proceed in a safe manner, I will cancel the permit,' Shepherd told Skye bluntly.

'You can't do that. We have people coming from all over the country for this.'

'I understand that. So it's up to your group to ensure they are allowed to gather once they get here.' She rounded on the man's smirk. 'And in case you're thinking of inciting anything that might cause that cancellation, if there was any trouble we would need to undertake an exhaustive investigation. It's hard to say how long it would take, but it's a safe bet your members would miss out on a number of shooting sessions.' She paused and gave them both the thinnest of thin smiles. 'Right, now that we've established what won't be happening, let's try to get to the bottom of this, shall we.'

'Usual rubbish,' said Makepeace dismissively. 'This lot think they're the only ones who've got the right to voice their opinions.'

'And his lot feels the need to make theirs known with a gun.'

Shepherd froze. 'There's a firearm here?' she asked cautiously. She looked as if she deeply regretted asking Lindy to be a part of all this, and tried to signal to her to get back in the car. But if Lindy noticed her attempts to catch her eye, she gave no sign. Shepherd surveyed the crowds carefully, concentrating particularly on the one to her right. 'Okay,' she said gently. 'So where is this gun now?'

Makepeace turned and beckoned. The crowd parted and a man sheepishly stepped forward, holding a shotgun broken across his forearm. He approached them and handed it to Makepeace before melting back into the crowd.

Shepherd leaned in towards Makepeace, speaking so quietly even Tara Skye could not hear her. 'I happen to know you did six months not so long ago, Mr Makepeace. A custodial sentence of more than three denies you a firearms licence for five years.'

The man said nothing.

'If you ever want to see a licence again, you'll come with me now and put that gun and any cartridges you have in the boot of my car. You can come by the station later and collect a receipt.'

She turned to address both groups, who had all fallen silent to watch the proceedings. While they couldn't hear what had gone on, it was clear to them now that the situation had been defused. 'Your protest permits are for Saturday. Until then, none of you have any good reason for gathering here, so I suggest you all go home.'

The crowds didn't begin to disperse immediately, but it wasn't long before the first people began to drift outwards from the fringes of the groups. Once the process had started, Shepherd didn't feel the need to watch any longer. She led Makepeace to her car, where she popped the boot latch remotely and stood aside while he leaned in and carefully laid the weapon inside. He reached into his pocket and laid a scattering of shells beside the gun. Shepherd counted them. Six in all.

She closed the boot and called Lindy over to her. With one final glance toward the thinning crowds, the two women got in and closed the doors.

'It was amazing how that all got out of control so fast,' said Lindy as Shepherd pulled away.

'Mobs like that, they have their own energy. They become something distinct from the individuals in them. Distinct and dangerous. Now, lunch, I think we said. Anywhere special you fancy?'

'The prosecution in Singapore are trying to make the case that Danny lured the victim to the site.'

Shepherd hadn't been driving very long, but the XF was already moving along the country lane at a good clip. It didn't matter. Shepherd took her eyes off the road and gave Lindy a long, hard stare.

'Chupul had the address of the shop written down. They're going to claim Danny sent it to him on his burner phone.' Lindy was trying to keep the wavering in her voice to a minimum, but even to her it sounded as if she was about to burst into tears at any moment.

'The phone that's missing?' Shepherd had returned her eyes to the road, but was staring at it so hard she seemed to be trying to see through it.

'If they can make the case, Colleen, Danny is looking at the death penalty.'

Shepherd let the car drift to a halt at the side of the road. She turned in her seat to look at Lindy, but it was a while before she found herself able to say anything. 'Without the phone, I don't think they can prove luring. Not unless they have something else.'

Her eyes questioned Lindy, and she could tell she didn't know. 'If they do,' she went on, 'Danny's only hope would be for his lawyer to create reasonable doubt by showing somebody else might have given the victim that information. The same person who sent the wife that photo, perhaps.' She shook her head. 'Frankly, from what I've heard so far, I doubt this lawyer has the competence to do that.'

'Somebody like Guy Trueman?'

For the second time in as many minutes, Shepherd was left momentarily without words. 'Guy Trueman is in Singapore?' she asked finally.

Lindy nodded. 'It's why Danny went there. Damian thinks there might be a connection between Trueman and the wife. They seem to be particularly close. You knew him, didn't you – Trueman? When he was over here?'

Shepherd nodded thoughtfully. 'I did. He's trouble, Lindy. So he's in Singapore, there's a woman involved, and there's all that previous history between him and Danny?' Her eyes focused on the dashboard. 'A good, hard look at Guy Trueman would have been one of the very first things on my to-do list if I was Danny's lawyer.' She shook her head, thoughtfully. 'And yet he trusts her?'

'He seems to, now. Selena Lim knows about the photo, and Damian is beginning to wonder whether telling her was the right thing to do. But Danny is prepared to stay with her. He wants to fight this. Even with everything stacking up against him, she seems to have convinced him he can still win. I'm so afraid for him, Colleen. I don't know what to do.'

Shepherd was silent for a moment, and then a thought seemed to come to her. 'And you've been carrying this around, on your own, all this time?' she said. 'Oh Lindy, I'm so sorry.'

But while she was grateful for the sympathy, and the little hug that went with it, Lindy didn't receive the one thing she'd come for today. Not then, nor during the muted drive back, nor even when Shepherd dropped Lindy back at her car. Not once did Colleen Shepherd ever say what she was going to do to save Danny. And Lindy knew that was because, like her, she couldn't.

44

Mangrove stands had a way of sucking the moonlight into them, leaving only a milky twilight suspended over the low trees. The sweet, moist smell of decaying vegetation took on a salty tang in these swamps, a heavy, cloying fragrance that added to the oppressiveness of the warm night. Crouched low at the edge of the stand, Damian reflected that it was just one more reason, among many, that he didn't want to be here any longer than he had to be.

The noise of something moving through the dried leaves nearby startled him, but then he relaxed; it was so loud and clumsy it could only be a Malayan water monitor. Creatures that carried the real threats in these mangroves, the spiders, the scorpions, the snakes, were far stealthier than the giant lizard. It was what made them all the more dangerous.

He was grateful that he'd had the chance to visit this place before, in daylight. It helped him to visualise the layout now that the land lay cloaked in the shadowy darkness of nightfall. He assumed many burglars and housebreakers took the time to reconnoitre a property during the day, before returning to complete their work later on. Damian allowed himself a brief smile. The insights into criminal behaviour you could gain by sitting in a Singapore mangrove in the middle of the night, he thought.

Not for the first time, he found himself wondering how he had ended up here. A few short days ago he was wandering among pristine mountain valleys, as far from worldly problems as at any point he could ever remember. But the simple answer to his question was that he had been asked. By a woman he couldn't say no to, on behalf of a brother he would travel to the ends of the Earth to help. It was not either of them he was here for tonight, though. Not directly. It was for Danny Maik, a man he had barely known until he had arrived in Singapore. Now, he was preparing to commit a crime on this man's behalf, multiple crimes, against his wishes. Damian shook his head in wonder. He was under no illusions about the danger he faced. He could go to prison if he was caught, likely would, and, while his pre-crime vigil here suggested the break-in would go smoothly enough, it was still his own liberty he was risking, out of the sense of commitment and loyalty that other people felt to Danny Maik. Devotion, once removed, he thought wryly.

He started to move, but froze again at the sound of a gentle splash at the water's edge behind him. Crocodiles entered the water with a sound like that. If it was in the water, he was safe enough for now. But it was time to move anyway. The clouds shrouding the moon were beginning to drift on the tropical night winds, and he couldn't rely on their cover for much longer.

The window would offer little resistance, he thought, and he was still nimble enough to climb through it with ease. He would be in the tiny living room then, almost within touching distance of the table on which, if his luck held, Devina Chupul would have laid her phone. She had seemed careless with the device when he was there. She was not one of those people who seemed to draw comfort from its feel, cradling it as she sat and carrying it with her whenever she left a room. He hoped it meant she wouldn't have taken it into her bedroom. She had no reason to now. Perhaps if her husband was still alive, out on night duty, she might have wanted it nearby, as reassurance that she could be reached in the case of an emergency. But that emergency had come and gone, and now there was no one for whom she needed to hold a night-time vigil.

But what if it was in her bedroom? Damian would hesitate. He knew it now, even as he approached the low window. If he had to enter her bedroom, and risk having her wake up to find a man looming over her? He didn't want to be responsible for the shock he would cause her. Or the uproar that would undoubtedly follow. No, the phone would by lying there waiting for him, on that table. He would open it, send the photo and attached data to his own phone, shut it off again, and leave. Close the window? As long as he could do it quietly. But even an open window wouldn't cause her any great concern when she woke the next morning. Not if she found her phone lying there on the table. Right where she'd left it.

The little house was in darkness apart from one small bulb over the rear door that cast a feeble yellow light in a tiny pool around the doorstep. Less a deterrent, it seemed to Damian, than a beacon declaring that life existed out here amid this dark, still silence on the edge of the mangrove. He had watched the other light go out an hour earlier. Just before that, he had seen Devina Chupul emerge from the house, a shadow, shuffling slowly towards the monal pens in the enclosure. A final check before bedtime. Apparently satisfied, she had murmured something to her birds and made her way back to the house, shutting the door with a soft click. The bedroom light had gone out a few moments later.

He eased the window open and lifted himself to the ledge. He was ready to step down inside the house when he realised the dogs had gone silent. Ever since he had arrived just after sunset, there had been a steady chorus of distant barks. Yaps, angry retorts, the normal back and forth of a rural Asian community after dark. But there were no dogs barking now. The sultry air was heavy and still. As he perched on the ledge, only the incessant calls of night insects came to him.

The floor creaked. Not much, but overloud in the other silence. Why hadn't he noted this on his last visit? Because he'd had no intention of coming back here in the dead of night to break in, that's why. Not until he had casually picked up a woman's phone, and seen a photograph on it. That had changed everything.

It wasn't there. Even in the dim light of the house's interior Damian could see the phone wasn't lying where it had been the last time he was here. Of course not. Why would it be? There were any number of other surfaces in here Devina could have chosen to lay it. It had been irrational of him to expect that she would casually select one random site to set it down when he was here, and then place it in exactly the same spot every time afterwards. Panic began to rise in his chest. He didn't want to spend time looking around. He had wanted to be in and gone by now, already on his way back away from this house at the edge of the mangroves to the safety and anonymity of the bright lights of the Civic District. Instead, he now had to take precious minutes, dangerous minutes, to search around here for the phone. He calmed himself. It was a small space. There weren't many places she could have set it down. Had she had it with her when she went out to see the monals? Likely not. He hadn't seen her look down when she was outside, hadn't seen any bright rectangle of light from a screen glowing against the night's darkness. Almost certainly the phone was in this small room somewhere. There. On a shelf near the bedroom door, he saw the familiar shiny profile of a black phone case. He reached for it gently and eased it from the shelf. The bedroom door was slightly ajar, so he crept away towards the window before switching the phone on, in case the light was too bright. He opened it; as before, no lock, no password. The phone of someone who trusted the people she invited into her home. The thought pierced him like a knife blade.

The noise startled him so much he almost dropped the phone. A footfall, from the bedroom. A noise of rustling fabric; blankets being folded back. Devina Chupul was getting up. He snapped the phone shut and froze. There was another footstep and a faint creaking from the bedroom floor. Where was the bathroom? In his panicked state he tried to recall if he had used it when he was here. Or noticed where it was. Could he stand here in the darkness, unmoving, not breathing, and hope he went unnoticed while she shuffled off in another direction? Or was he in its direct line? A light flooded part of a narrow hallway, falling in a broad path across the floor of the main room, right at his feet. She was moving in the other direction now, away from him. But she could not fail to see him on her return trip from the bathroom. He couldn't be here then. Stuffing the phone in his jacket pocket, he inched across the room to the window, climbed up, and eased himself back out into the night.

Did he see the shape first, or sense it? He couldn't have said. All he knew was that someone was there waiting for him when he emerged from the window. And now, he had to run. He sprinted towards the back of the lot, towards the slope that led down into the mangroves. The figure that had been lurking by the side of the house burst into life, running after him, footsteps pounding loudly on the packed dirt. Damian reached the fringe of the first mangroves and hurtled in among them, not checking his speed at all. His feet slipped precariously on the slick wet earth, while gnarled roots snatched at his ankles as he passed. He pressed on into the darkness, ducking the low-hanging vegetation, holding his arms up to protect his face from the whiplash of branches. He didn't know where his pursuer was. Had he fallen back? Gained on him? Had he veered off to approach him sideways on? At the speed Damian was moving it was impossible to detect the movement of other shadows among the mottled, patchy darkness of the mangrove stands. But he knew he couldn't let up. Until his balance made him.

With the incline and slick surface and his speed, it was only a matter of time before his feet slipped out from under him but the fall, when it came, was far more violent and jarring than he expected. He flipped forward head first and rolled down the muddy slope, bouncing a couple of times and slithering and tumbling through the tangle of branches, until he crashed to a stop among the roots of a large tree at the water's edge. He lay still and listened, suppressing his laboured breathing and sucking in against the pain in his ribs. His pursuer must have heard the noise from the fall, but surely he couldn't have pinpointed its exact location in this ethereal darkness? Damian listened again. Nothing. He felt wetness in his shoe and realised his feet were lying in the water. He wanted to draw them out, but he couldn't risk the noise if his pursuer was still close. He craned around slowly to see how far into the water his legs were, and saw a sliver of shiny darkness gliding towards them. A snake, by its size a large one, a King Cobra perhaps, moving slowly and purposefully along the water's edge. He tensed every muscle into stillness. If it detected the warmth of his body, it might strike out of instinct. If there was even so much as a flicker of movement here on the snake's hunting grounds, so close to its head, it certainly would.

He lay in frozen silence, watching the snake, listening for movement from above. Even the vibration of a single heavy step from his pursuer coming down the slope towards him might be enough to startle the snake into a strike. He watched it carefully, waiting for the moment it meandered far enough away from him to allow him to inch upwards. What awaited him at the top of the rise was uncertain. But he would flee towards it to escape the certainty of the danger down here. The snake took to the water, quicksilver switchbacks catching the light as it swam. It was all Damian needed. He scrambled up the bank, using the moist mangrove roots to haul himself up the slippery terrain until he reached the top. He had been as quiet as he could, but he didn't know if that was quiet enough. He sat still for a moment and listened. But the night only gave him back the sound of the mangrove, the gentle rustle of leaves, the occasional lapping of the water, the buzz of insects. Whoever had chased him in here had gone. All that was left now was to take a quick inventory of his injuries and then he could make his way home. He had a cut on his forehead and a nasty gash on the back of one hand. He was covered in mud and the smell was barely tolerable. But it was the pain in his ribs when he breathed that concerned him most. Tentatively he touched two fingers to his side just above his jacket pocket. And that was when he realised the phone had gone.

45

It was a day that took Jejeune back to the fall seasons of his youth in Canada. The wind was gentle, stirring the fallen leaves with a sound like soft rain, and a watery sunshine bathed the fields behind Cleve Hall in its soft light. Autumn was beginning to fade into an emptier, more placid time. The gradual shedding of leaves that had set the air alight with their swirling, multicoloured hues had given way to a mass moult after the last cold spell, and now layer upon layer of tawny, crisping leaves lay scattered across the ground like scales that had been shed by some giant mythical creature.

Noel Summer stood beside him, taking in the landscape, as he had done that day at the edge of the Stone Road forest. But Jejeune had the impression they were not seeing the world the same way any more. If they ever had. Summer had asked to accompany his DCI when he heard he was coming to see Libby Cleve again, but they had barely spoken on the journey up here. The silence had suited both men then, each locked in their own thoughts. But it persisted now as they walked side by side up the driveway. It was if a veil of mutual distrust had descended between them. For Summer's part, it may just have been that he felt his efforts in the case had not been suffi-ciently appreciated or valued, thought Jejeune. Certainly, they had not been supported by his DCI, and Jejeune was willing to concede that they were justifiable grievances. But he had his own reasons for his silence. He had taken things as far as he could with the available information, and his investigations had left him in a kind of twilight where two, three, possibly even four people had motives to kill Abbie Cleve, and all had opportunity, too. But he was still unable to make that final link to any of them, the one that answered the two questions he had been asking all along: why was she killed the way she was? And how? Pete Estey's death was just the opposite. There was no question how he had been killed, or why the body was left as it was. But suspects were in short supply. He was convinced the two deaths were linked, but he could only find one connection between them. And that was the man walking beside him now.

But he was here to conduct police business, and Summer was still officially his assistant. And that meant that whatever shadows lay between them had to be set aside for now.

It was Summer who broke the silence. 'I take it the DCS talked to you about that autopsy you ordered on the bird.'

Jejeune turned his head sharply. 'She told you about that?'

'I was there when Mansfield Jones called her to approve your request. And she declined. What were you hoping to find?'

Jejeune was silent for another moment as he weighed how much to share with Summer. Only the sound of their footfalls on the driveway filled the space between them.

'There was a puncture mark in the bird's neck. From a needle,' he said finally. 'It seems something was injected into it.'

'Do you know what?'

Jejeune shook his head. 'But I think it would be something that would show the birds were unfit for market.'

Summer nodded. 'Which would give the LSA enough cause to shut down Abbie Cleve's operations,' he said. 'But now that Shepherd has vetoed the autopsy, you have no way of finding out.'

'Not yet,' said Jejeune.

As they approached the house, the report of twin shotgun blasts from over on the far side of the estate shattered the stillness of the morning air. Jejeune felt a pang of sadness for the birds that were paying the ultimate price for somebody's desire for a morning's sport. *The greater good.* Was that enough to justify the killing of individual birds? The value of a single life never came into question in his job. But how would he assess it, he wondered, if he was asked to weigh one life against many? In truth, he didn't know.

Libby Cleve was standing in her customary spot at the front door as they came up the driveway. Jejeune intended to approach the interview with openness, but he would keep in mind that the woman had been given two previous chances to tell the police the real reason for her argument with her sister, and had passed on the opportunity both times.

'Have you found out who killed my sister yet?' she asked candidly as they arrived.

'No,' he said. 'The case hasn't been given the attention it deserves up till now. And for that I apologise.'

'You make it sound as if it will now. Is that because Pete Estey is dead, too?'

'Both deaths are being considered as related,' he confirmed.

'And will that lead you to the killers, do you think?' She directed the question to Summer, but he simply looked back impassively.

Jejeune thought for a moment before answering, but he did not look in Summer's direction. 'Yes, I believe it will.'

The woman bent and busied herself pulling dead leaves from a plant in a pot near the door. But her heart wasn't really in it and she abandoned the task after a few moments. The plant looked as if it might already be dead anyway.

'We've already established that Abbie wasn't looking to be readmitted to the family. And her marketing campaign against the beef farming operation here effectively ended months ago.' Jejeune's tone suggested that denial would be futile. 'So why did she come here that day?'

'Because I asked her to.' Libby folded her arms across her chest. The pink support bandage crept into view but she did nothing to hide it. She looked at Summer again. 'It was, as I told you the first time, to do with the tawdry world of finances.'

'Our examination of the company's books and her own personal accounts show that she was in a strong financial position,' said Summer.

'Not hers, ours. The business is in trouble. In fact, the entire estate is. We're being propped up by the shooting revenue, but frankly, if farming profits don't pick up soon, I'm not sure how long even that is going to be able to keep us afloat.'

'So this protest the coming weekend has the potential to be very damaging.'

'Catastrophic. Which is why we cannot allow that stupid Skye woman to disrupt the operations here. We've made arrangements to accommodate the shooters elsewhere for the weekend, but if this nonsense drags on they'll simply lose patience and cancel with us altogether.'

'Was Abbie going to be supporting the protests?'

'I don't know, but I very much doubt it. She'd got what she wanted from that crowd. Her business was well established and revenues were, as you point out, extremely healthy. The simple fact is I invited her here to ask her to share some of it.'

'You asked her for financial help?'

'I told her I could sell her a stake in the business, or even take it as a short-term loan, however she wanted to structure it. Just enough to ensure we made it through this season and next, with enough left over to invest in the technologies we needed to stay ahead of the pack.'

'And she said no?'

'She said she couldn't.'

'Couldn't?' asked Summer.

Another shotgun blast rang out in the distance and Libby looked to the empty sky as if perhaps she might be hoping to see a bird fall. 'Bring herself to, I suppose.' She shrugged. 'Perhaps she'd become a believer in that methane nonsense after all. Probably, though, it was just the satisfaction of saying no.' She cradled her wrist, as she had done the last time Jejeune had been here, when she told him her sister had made a joke of the injury, moved on, forgotten it.

'I'm wondering,' said Jejeune. 'Your acupuncture treatments. Did you ever teach anyone else the techniques?'

She shook her head. 'There would be no point. Each treatment is unique, so you simply have to become an expert for your own case.'

'Did it surprise you?' asked Summer suddenly. 'Abbie's refusal to help? After all, if there were past wrongs to put right, this would have been a chance to make amends, wouldn't it?'

Libby Cleve looked down at her bandaged wrist for a moment. 'You know, I have to say it did. I always thought deep down that she really did love the estate. Not the people, of course, or the farming operation, but the land itself. She did really seem to enjoy that. But if she did, in the end the feeling wasn't strong enough to overcome her loathing of the family. Me,' she added, in case there was any doubt. 'I had hoped there might be enough decency in her to recognise her familial obligations. But then the notion of family loyalty is such a frail thread to bind us to our responsibilities, isn't it?'

'The property the Nye is on belongs to a trust,' said Jejeune. 'It reverts to the estate on Abigail's death, doesn't it?'

Libby nodded. 'It does. But not the business. That is a separate entity. The estate has no claim on that.'

'And I take it you are not expecting any money from the sale of the Nye operation.'

The woman offered a soft smile. 'You have a reputation for being perceptive, Inspector. I trust it was built on greater leaps of logic than that. I think it's fair to say Abbie would have gone out of her way to ensure I received nothing from her will. Perhaps some of it would have gone to Estey. She always did have a soft spot for him, I think. But of course, he's gone now, too, isn't he?' She shook her head. 'No, whoever gets the proceeds of the business, it will do nothing to help the finances of this estate. Abbie will have made sure of that.'

Jejeune suggested that they had no further business, and thanked the woman for her time. As the detectives turned to leave, Summer seemed on the verge of saying something, but he hesitated.

'Something else, Constable?' Libby Cleve asked him.

'Your injury – your sister would have felt remorse over it. However she chose to deal with it, silence, denial, she would have carried it with her. Always.'

'You didn't know her,' she said coldly.

Perhaps not, thought Jejeune. But Summer knew the burden of regret, of things done, things not done. And Jejeune did, too. He felt it now, in his inability to help Danny Maik. And he knew, once it worked its way inside you, that kind of remorse never left you.

Silence overtook the men again on their walk back down the driveway. They were almost at the car before Summer spoke. 'I could talk to her if you like – Shepherd. About the autopsy on the Pheasant. It might be useful.'

Jejeune shrugged. 'It couldn't hurt.'

'If she agreed, how quickly do you think you could get the results back?'

'I'd ask Mansfield Jones to fast-track them, so, twenty-four hours, I would think?'

Jejeune looked at him. What was it about those results that interested him so much? Was it because, like him, Summer realised it might be the final piece needed to pull it all together? Did he see it as that last step, the one Jejeune recognised from his own previous successes, that one piece of information, not to give you the answer but to confirm it, to finally make sense of everything? Or was it because Noel Summer already knew what those results would reveal, results that he desperately did not want his DCI to see?

As they reached the car, another shotgun blast came from the shoot site, rocking the air with its concussive roar. Jejeune thought once more about the bird that had likely just died, about the value of a single life. What was the value of Danny's Maik's life, he wondered. How was that to be measured against the greater good? Wherever the truth lay in his case, Danny Maik was about to face his fate with no contribution from his DCI at all. Jejeune could do nothing to help him. All he could do was wander hopelessly through this landscape dwindling slowly towards winter, and wait for whatever outcomes it might hold.

46

There were deaths that had caused her great sadness, and some that had caused anger, but Colleen Shepherd could not recall many that elicited as much pity as this one. She sensed it among the rest of the officers in attendance, too. They went about their business beneath the glaring floodlights arranged around the forecourt of the Nye, securing the site, preserving the scene, identifying and marking the evidence, but most took the opportunity to steal a glance back at the body lying on the ground, and continue on only after a sad shake of the head. As he stood beside her, Domenic Jejeune's features were not betraying any emotion at all. But she knew, behind those quick-flicking eyes, taking in every detail of the scene, he was feeling it too.

A thin grey line on the horizon promised a coming dawn. But there was plenty of ground to cover before the light of day chased the darkness from this site. Shepherd let her eyes rest on the bloodstained, flaccid shape lying on the gravel, the tired-looking wheelchair skewed just off to the side. Mansfield Jones was kneeling beside the body, using a flashlight. The night had shielded many of the details from her when she'd arrived at the scene, but she'd seen enough. First impressions:

shotgun blast, the ME had told her unnecessarily. Chest neck, face. He'd asked her not to hold him to it, until he had the body back at the lab with some proper lighting. But she would. There would be no other cause of death. Not with the violence of this one.

She saw Summer approaching. He looked distraught, wandering around almost as if he'd lost his sense of direction. The death of Bob Ferris would have affected him for reasons that went beyond the obvious. 'If you feel you're too close, Constable, we can manage here,' she said as he arrived. It wasn't clear from Summer's reaction whether he had even heard Shepherd's offer. He simply stood looking at the body.

Tony Holland approached and stopped before them, feet splayed slightly, shoulders squared. 'The team is prepared to do whatever it takes on this one, ma'am. Regardless of the hours.'

She nodded. 'I'll see what the overtime budget will stretch to.'

Holland shook his head. 'They'll give you this one for free. The fact that Ferris was retired doesn't change anything. He was one of us. One of our own.' He looked back at the body and shook his head. 'Do we know anything yet?'

Jejeune looked thoughtful. They *knew* nothing at this stage, but they could infer a few things. 'It occurs to me that for Ferris to come out here, unarmed, to meet someone in the middle of the night, it must have been someone he knew. And trusted.'

Shepherd nodded. 'As with Estey.'

'He was killed with the same type of weapon, by the looks of it,' said Shepherd. 'Same killer?' She was telling them she wanted to hear that they didn't have a third person out there taking lives. Two was already two too many. But Jejeune nodded in confirmation. 'I think there is a chain of causality here. Abbie Cleve's death necessitated Pete Estey's. And Estey's led to this one.' He turned to Summer. 'Do you remember seeing any injection sites on Abbie Cleve's body?'

Summer looked up, dragging himself from where his thoughts had been. 'Needle marks, you mean? I didn't get a good enough look at the body. If there were any on her arms, they could have been covered by the blood from the cuts on her wrists, I suppose.' He paused. 'There was a lot.'

Shepherd saw that Jejeune had been watching the detective's face closely. He'd have taken into account the man's distress, but been alert for any signs of evasion or deception anyway. Like her, it seemed that he had detected none.

'I spoke to the funeral director who prepared Abbie Cleve's body,' Jejeune told the group, 'and he says he didn't remember seeing any puncture wounds either, but he couldn't absolutely rule it out.' He seemed about to ask something of Summer, but Shepherd shook her head and he turned to Holland instead. He gestured him to one side and lowered his voice.

'The brake is still on the wheelchair. Either Ferris didn't feel he was in any danger or, if he did, he was already unable to move at that point. Can you ask the ME to check the body for needle marks? He'll tell you to wait for the post-mortem report, but ask him if he can see anything obvious now. And ask him if he found any on Estey.' They both knew there was no mention of them on the autopsy report but, as meticulous as Mansfield Jones was, he wasn't infallible.

'Needles, sir. That's what they use in acupuncture, isn't it?' said Holland. 'That could make somebody immobile.'

'Yes, Constable, it could.'

As Holland walked away, Shepherd caught Jejeune's eye again. She gestured towards Summer. He had gone back to staring at the body: transfixed, silent. There was a terrifying stillness to him, as if something cold had taken possession of him from the inside.

'Constable,' called Jejeune. 'Noel, let's go and see if the house search has turned up anything.'

Summer left a final, long look on the bloody corpse of Bob Ferris and turned to accompany his DCI. They walked to the far side of the compound and stood before the house, staring at the black, empty windows.

'This was the darkness you felt,' said Jejeune, 'when we first met here. It wasn't some spiritual sense of foreboding. It was memories. It must have been difficult, revisiting it, dealing with it all again. And yet you never mentioned it.'

'I suppose I just expected you would make the connection. You have a reputation for that sort of thing.'

Jejeune felt the burn of humiliation. Casual remarks could cut so much deeper than criticism.

'Besides, there was no similarity between the two incidents,' continued Summer flatly. 'Ferris was shot in the house. And lived. Abbie Cleve died out in the driveway. There was no connection between them at all.'

But both men knew there was. 'Abbie Cleve was the connection,' said Jejeune. 'This time the victim, but before that the homeowner.'

Summer flashed him a glance and then looked towards Shepherd. Jejeune gave a slight shake of his head. He hadn't said anything yet. He wouldn't until he was sure where things might lead. 'Your B&B is very close to here, isn't it? Tony Holland thought it was why you were first to the scene.'

Summer let his body slump, the weight of secrecy finally lifted. 'I was already on my way. I wanted to see if I could deal with being here again. When I got the call, I knew I didn't have a choice. I had to come.'

Jejeune shook his head ruefully. 'For this case, of all cases, to be the first one you landed on your return. This place, that victim...'

'My first day.' Summer gave a mirthless laugh. 'It was waiting for me, saving itself for when I got back. How can anybody deny the Earth's forces, the way they shape our lives?'

'Maybe it was just happenstance. Sometimes it's no more than that.'

But Summer rejected Jejeune's theory with a shake of his head. 'No. This was the way it was meant to be. An event occurs to disrupt the natural order, and another comes along to restore it. This was why I was brought back. But everything is settled now. Nature's rhythms, its cycles, they're all back in place, now that I've returned here this time.'

Jejeune looked around. This place had taken Bob Ferris from Summer once, and then taken him from him again. Where was the balance in that? As far as he was concerned, only solving these murders could address the one disparity that mattered, the one between the living and the dead. He hadn't done that yet. But he felt like he was closing in.

'It must have been something powerful to draw Ferris back here after all this time. Was he looking for the same thing as you, do you think? Some kind of closure?'

Summer shook his head. 'He told me it wouldn't work. He said he'd been here a couple of times. Trying to exorcise his demons, he said. But they stayed with him.' He looked at Jejeune. 'He called me, you know. He said he didn't need me to come over any more, that he would be fine from now on.' The constable gave a small ironic smile, and turned his eyes back to the house. 'The sad fact is, I wasn't going for him, not at the end. In truth, I wonder if I ever really was.'

Jejeune flinched inwardly again. It must have been an excruciatingly difficult phone call for Ferris to make. And for Summer to receive. He could have prevented it, if he had found the time – no, taken the time from somewhere else – to talk to Summer himself. Danny Maik would have done. It was why Ferris would have entrusted it to him in the first place. If he was here.

The sky was lightening to reveal an overcast, cloud-laden morning. It would be a day without shadows, the low, flat light painting the world with a drab lifelessness that seemed appropriate to the mood here at the Nye. And it had not been improved by the news Shepherd had just received. She beckoned Jejeune and Summer back, watching them carefully as they made their way over. There was a distance between the two men that she could see even in the way they walked beside each other. It was a million miles away from the bond Jejeune had shared with Danny Maik, and she knew these two would never bridge that gap, no matter how long they worked together.

Summer's eyes sought Ferris's body as they approached, but Mansfield Jones had concluded his preliminary examination, and SOCO officers had moved in to sift through the evidence, blocking the constable's view. Holland joined them as they arrived to listen in on the briefing.

'This business about Ferris coming out here unarmed,' Shepherd told them. 'That may not be the case. There is a shotgun licensed to him, but the search team at his house can't find any sign of a weapon.'

'He couldn't hunt any more,' said Holland. 'Could he have got rid of it?'

'As of a few days ago, he was talking about maybe joining the shoot up at the Cleve estate,' said Jejeune. 'He made it sound as if he still had a shotgun he could use.'

They looked at each other. The news that there might be a stolen shotgun out there somewhere changed things. Time was even more of a factor now. They needed to find the killer as quickly as possible.

'Next steps, Domenic?' asked Shepherd.

'I'm going to need you to authorise that autopsy on the bird,' he told her flatly.

'At a time like this? What on earth are you hoping it will show?'

Jejeune looked at Summer, still staring at the backs of the SOCO officers, beyond which the body of Bob Ferris lay. He thought about the constable's similar question at the Cleve estate, and his keen interest in the answer.

'I'm not sure.'

'You're not sure?' said Shepherd in exasperation. 'Hardly the finished article then, is it, this bloody theory of yours?'

The harshness was out of character for Shepherd, but Jejeune recognised it as a reflection of her frustration. She'd been asking him to become engaged since the beginning of these cases, and now he seemed to be telling her his price was those autopsy results. She was in no position to refuse.

'We'll need to put a top priority on them, as well,' he said.

47

A man with Danny Maik's life experience must undoubtedly have seen his fair share of disappointment, thought Damian, but it still etched deep lines in his world-worn face. Worse for Damian, though, was the knowledge that it was not that he had failed that troubled Danny so much, but the fact that he had even tried.

The silence that greeted his news had hung in the room since. Selena had put her hand to her mouth but not uttered a sound. Danny simply stared at a spot on the floor: dejected, saddened, empty.

'I want it made clear, Selena, if this ever comes out, Danny was absolutely against it. This was one hundred percent my idea. He had no knowledge that I was going there, no involvement in this at all.'

Selena's look suggested that such considerations were going to be among the least of Danny's problems. 'I don't know if you realise how much damage you've done here, Damian,' she said. 'As soon as Devina Chupul reports the theft of her phone, the police are going to wonder what on earth could make it important enough for somebody to break into her house to steal it. They're going to request the call log and data records, and, as soon as they get their hands on them, they're going to see that photo. If it doesn't tag to Guy Trueman, we will have just handed the prosecution everything they need for a first limb conviction.'

Damian had made no offer to go back to look for the phone. He hadn't mentioned the snake, but Selena Lim had lived here long enough to know the conditions in the mangroves meant there would be little chance of him finding it again anyway.

'She might not report it,' said Danny thoughtfully, in a way that had the others turning to look at him. 'If Guy did send that photo, he won't be too keen on the fact coming to light, either. It might establish a connection between Chupul and me, but the fact that he sent it to the wife would leave him with some awkward questions to answer.'

Selena brightened slightly. 'I'll monitor the incoming police incident reports over the next few hours. If Trueman does pressure her not to report it, I'd say it's as close as we're going to get to an admission of guilt on his part. It wouldn't get us any closer to proving anything, but knowing he's behind it might give us some leverage.'

Her phone buzzed and she frowned contemptuously as she saw the caller's ID. She read the text in silence. 'Gunn. He wants to see me. I'll be back in a few moments.'

As soon as she was out of the room, Damian turned to Maik. 'It wasn't a random passer-by who chased me, Danny. Whoever it was, they were waiting for me. They knew I was coming.'

Maik realised what Damian was going to say next and was already beyond it, processing what it meant for him. And his case. But he let the man continue.

'Only two other people were in this room when I talked about trying to get that phone. And only one of them would have had the opportunity to tell someone else. You saw her, she couldn't get out of here fast enough after I brought it up.'

'She's an officer of the court. You were about to ask me to counsel you to commit an illegal act. If she became aware of intent to break the law, she would have been duty-bound to report it.'

'If it wasn't her, how could anybody else know I was going to be there?'

'Perhaps it wasn't you they were watching.'

'Come on, Danny. Why would anybody be watching Devina Chupul's place?'

'It's a close-knit community. The Nepalis here look out for each other. Or maybe it was a routine security patrol.'

'Out there? You don't believe in coincidences any more than my brother.'

A faint smile touched the corners of Maik's mouth at the number of times a suspect had tried to sell Maik and his DCI on one. It had never gone well. 'All I'm saying is there could be other explanations.'

'And all I'm saying is you seem to be looking for ways to avoid the main one.'

The men sat back as Selena returned to the room, followed by Ronnie Gunn. Damian saw Maik's features tighten. Somewhere along the way Danny had lost his trust in this man, and, if he didn't know why, he knew enough to trust the sergeant's instincts.

'Ronnie has something to tell you, Danny.' Lim's expression suggested she hadn't forgotten Maik's previous directive either. For her to choose to override it now suggested that whatever Gunn had to say, it must be important.

'All deals are off,' he said. 'The prosecution are going for a first limb conviction.'

There was no note of triumph in his voice, no sense of satisfaction that his prediction had come true. Maik looked at Selena Lim for confirmation he didn't need. For a moment he was still, as the reality seeped into him. He'd had his chance, the prosecutors were telling him. They did not want his help any more. They didn't need it. They already had all they needed for a jury to convict him of murder under the first limb of Section 300 of the Singapore criminal code; a crime that carried the death penalty.

The silence lingered like it would never be broken, until it all became too much for Selena. 'It's not over, Danny. We still have other things we can look at. You know that. Guy Trueman,' she said desperately. 'We still have that.'

'Guy Trueman?' Gunn's voice rose in surprise. 'Guy had nothing to do with this. What reason would he have to be involved?'

'That day he went to see Devina Chupul to offer his condolences,' said Selena. 'I'm guessing he didn't need to ask you for the address.'

'If you are suggesting he knew where she lived, of course he did. He's been doing business with her over the birds.' Gunn looked puzzled for a moment, and then realisation began to dawn for him. 'Guy Trueman and Devina Chupul? That's your other thing?'

The sarcastic, taunting delivery angered Damian and he sprang to his feet. 'He told Danny he'd only seen Titus Chupul once or twice, at official functions,' he said. 'And yet he's the one who arranged for that plot up in Kranji where his wife could raise those birds.'

'You can't be serious.' Gunn looked at Selena. 'This is what you're looking at to get your client off a capital murder charge?'

Again, the mocking tone seemed to raise Damian's ire. Maik realised that all the younger man's frustration, all his humiliation and feelings of helplessness over the incident with the phone were beginning to pour out now. 'Trueman has been all over this thing from the beginning,' shouted Damian.

'He set it up, and, for all we know, he sent you in here to see it all went to plan. He's involved, and I'm going to find a way to prove it. There will be something out there, and you can tell him from me I'm not going to stop looking until I find it.'

Gunn seemed to realise the effect his tone was having. He became serious and turned to Selena again. 'The woman whose home you visited when you met Devina Chupul up at Mount Vernon, Iniya. She's Guy Trueman's partner. She's also one of Devina's oldest and closest friends. They're from the same village back home. They've known each other since they were children. Having an affair with a friend's partner is about the greatest betrayal there is, even in Western society. For the women from their village, it would be unthinkable. There's a concept in our culture known as *Atoot Rishta*. It means a bond between friends that is unbreakable.' He shook his head. 'For Devina Chupul to take up with Trueman behind Iniya's back would be to abandon everything she has ever believed in: her values, her integrity, her morality. There would be nothing left of her as a person. No matter what was happening in her marriage, Devina Chupul would never have cheated with Guy Trueman behind Iniya's back. Never.'

It wasn't an argument designed to drive a point home, to convince a sceptical audience, to deflect suspicion. It was a simple statement of fact, and it resonated around the bare, stark walls of the room like the report from a gunshot. There was more silence now, deep and profound. Danny's last hope had disappeared. All that was left was the sorrow that came with accepting it.

But Selena wouldn't. 'We can still fight this, Danny. You're not guilty. That has to count for something.'

'Danny,' said Gunn, 'look at me. Selena can't save you now. She never could. Now that her last argument has collapsed, she's back to basing all her hopes on your self-defence plea.

317

But for that, you'd need to produce that kukri. That knife is gone, Danny. It's gone and it's never coming back.'

Danny stared hard at Gunn. He had been looking into people's eyes for long enough to know when someone was telling the truth. This was a man telling him that he knew beyond any shadow of a doubt that the knife would never be surfacing again. As evidence or anything else.

'There's only one option open to you now, Danny,' said Gunn reasonably. 'Don't listen to your counsel any more, or your birdwatching friend here. You need to listen to me. A long drawn-out first degree murder trial is going to cost the Singapore taxpayers a lot of money. A guilty plea would prevent that. You'd do life, but Selena could get them to take the death penalty off the table. It's an argument they'd listen to, I'm sure of it. But only today. As soon as you walk through the doors of that courtroom tomorrow to begin the Second Disclosure Conference, it'll be out of their hands. Once they've shown they have what they need to seek the death penalty, they'll have no choice but to proceed. The politicians will want it, the public will demand it.' He paused. 'Whatever happened that day, Guy Trueman says there's a good man inside you. He wouldn't want to see you die for this, Danny. Nor do I. Not even Devina Chupul wants that. Tell Selena to make the call.'

Danny looked across to Selena, who was as close to tears as he had ever seen her. *Do you trust me*, her look was asking him. *Enough to risk everything?* The worst part was that he had considered Damian's offer. Despite the answer he had finally given him, Danny's faith in the legal system had been shaken to such a degree that he had been tempted to break the law. He had wanted to, welcomed the idea, even, been prepared to abandon any belief he'd ever held that the system could deliver justice for him. But like Devina Chupul, it would have left him empty of who he was, no more than a shell of cynicism and despair. And, for all his faults, that was not Danny Maik.

Do you trust me? What did he have left to lose? Only his life, and what is a man's life worth if he is not prepared to hold on to the things he believes in?

'I'm not guilty of the crime I'm being charged with,' he said. 'And that's what we'll tell them.'

48

Colleen Shepherd didn't like her team to make a fuss when she spruced herself up a bit, but she didn't mind if they noticed. She waited an extra beat or two before concluding that Holland probably wasn't going to comment. Since they were the only two in the room, she would need to ask. 'This should be all right for the cameras, I imagine?' she said, gesturing towards her outfit.

'More than perfect, ma'am,' Holland reassured her. 'Press conference, is it?' He couldn't imagine why. It wasn't like they had any progress to report in any of their open cases. He would have thought the last thing Shepherd would want to do was face the media.

'I'm going to advise the public that I'm cancelling the permits for the protests this weekend.'

'That won't go down well, ma'am,' he said gravely. 'They've been planning this for months.'

'I agree the police will get vilified for this, and I'm sure the DCI's new BFF Tara Skye will be front and centre with the objections. But unless we are able to guarantee public safety, it would be irresponsible to allow a large gathering of any kind in this area. And let's face it, with a double murderer out there and a missing shotgun, we simply aren't in a position to guarantee anyone's safety at the moment.'

The appearance of the desk sergeant at the doorway rarely meant good news these days. But he looked untroubled today. 'Member of the public in reception, ma'am. A Mr Thomas Makepeace. Says he's here to collect a receipt from you.'

'That bloody shotgun,' she said quickly. 'I'd forgotten all about that. Tony, can you go down and remove Mr Makepeace's shotgun from the boot of my car and get it over to Firearms? There are six shells in there, too.'

'Sorry, ma'am. My firearms certificate has expired. I've been meaning to get it renewed, but...'

She stared him into silence. Since hers had too, she really had no comeback. 'Ask Firearms to come and collect it, would you, Sergeant?' she said. 'Tell Mr Makepeace he can have his receipt tomorrow.'

As the sergeant left, Holland looked around the empty room. 'I've got used to Summer being AWOL, but where's the DCI today?'

Shepherd was quiet for a moment. 'Tomorrow is Danny's hearing. If I know Domenic, he'll be looking for some last-minute piece of evidence to get him off.' She paused. 'He won't find one. I've been over the Singapore police reports myself with a fine-toothed comb.' She paused. 'It's going to go to trial.' She seemed to be having trouble bringing the next thought out into the light, and the words caught in her throat. 'A conviction is a formality.'

Holland took a moment to digest the reality of what he had probably known for a long time. 'There would always be an appeal, surely?'

She shook her head slowly. 'There will be no grounds. The prosecution have a flawless case, and Danny won't hear a word against his own lawyer's efforts.'

'There must be something we can do?'

'Only wait. And hope. And stay busy.' She drew in a breath and composed herself. She offered him a look, but could find no other words.

'Ma'am. I need to say something.'

Holland fell so silent so quickly Shepherd looked at him. It was unlike him to be so cautious about sharing his ideas, especially since she was the only one around to hear them.

'Tony?'

'The DCI is right, ma'am,' he began slowly, 'about there only being a few people Bob Ferris would have trusted to meet out at the Nye in the middle of the night.' He found enough inside him to look at Shepherd now. 'Summer would be one.'

'Summer? Kill Ferris? That's outrageous, Tony. He was obsessed with making amends for what his carelessness had caused. You saw him, he was in bits over Ferris's death. Inconsolable.'

'Regret will do that, too.'

She'd been interpreting Tony Holland's meanings for long enough to know the word he was looking for was *remorse*. 'But why? What possible reason could Summer have for killing a man he felt he owed so much?'

Holland hesitated again for a moment before answering. 'Inspector Jejeune, ma'am, he's not really been at the races on this one, has he? Bob Ferris always was quick on the uptake. He knew a lot about Pete Estey, and he knows Summer much better than we do. As far as background on the two of them, he was streets ahead of us. Perhaps something the DCI told him in one of their little chats was all he needed to put it all together and realise it was Summer who had killed Estey.' He sensed her doubts. 'Bob Ferris was an ex-cop on a disability pension, ma'am. Who else has a motive to want him dead, other than somebody he's about to expose as Pete Estey's killer?'

'If Ferris had worked it out, then why not come to us? Why meet Summer out there alone in the middle of the night?'

'Perhaps he wanted to give him one last chance to convince him he was wrong. What he faced next wouldn't have been an easy step to take.'

Holland was right. Because the only thing she could think of that could compare to the pain of losing a fellow officer, *one of their own*, thought Shepherd, would be having to turn one in. For murder.

She thought for a moment. 'We need to clear this up right now. Get Summer in. Where is he anyway?'

Holland shook his head. 'All I know is that he got a set of results back from the lab first thing this morning, and went haring out of here right afterwards. I'll have him pinged.' He texted the request and fixed Shepherd with a look that told her there was more coming. More she wouldn't like. 'He's spent a lot of time trying to pin Abigail Cleve's murder on people, hasn't he? Right from the off. Starting with Estey and then, as soon as it became clear he couldn't have done it, Evan Knowles.'

'He's been following the evidence. It's what we do.'

'Maybe. But what if there's another reason?'

'To deflect from the fact that he did it himself?' Shepherd looked incredulous. 'Tony, that's not possible, is it? Summer responsible for all three murders? They're all so different: Abbie Cleve was a staged suicide, Estey was hunted down and shot. Poor Bob Ferris appears to have been executed. Not even the weapons are consistent. There was no shotgun in the first murder.' But she sounded far from convinced by her own objections.

'That chain of causality the DCI talked about. It all starts with the first murder.'

'But what would his motive have been for killing Abbie Cleve?'

'Revenge. Not for ruining his life, but Ferris's. It's all this restoring the natural order business he talks about, re-establishing the balance. There's a reason, too, he chose to do it that way. You remember the DCI asking who benefits? Who has anything to gain from setting up Abigail Cleve's murder like that? Well, the answer is, the Earth does. I've been reading up on it. Those human sacrifices, it was all about replenishing the Earth, letting the blood of the victims soak into the soil.'

Shepherd sank slowly to sit on the corner of her desk, never taking her eyes off Holland. Where was Domenic Jejeune to scrutinise this, she wondered, to subject it all to his relentless logic and announce that it was all rubbish, that it couldn't possibly be true because of this, or this, or that? Where he had been for the entire case, she thought bitterly? Nowhere at all, absent in mind and now in body, too.

'No other explanation works, ma'am. Even the date fits. It's coming up to Samhain, that one he talked about at the pub quiz that night. Remember; the opening of the season of darkness?' Holland lowered his head. Despite what she was probably thinking, he got no joy from this. Though it was nothing like Danny's situation, or Bob Ferris's, it was still another police officer whose career would end in tragedy.

Shepherd thought for a moment. She looked at her watch. There was still time to make the press conference if she left now. She reached for her phone to inform the press liaison office she wouldn't be coming.

Holland's phone chimed. 'Summer's on the road to Cleve Hall, ma'am,' he told her. 'He's not responding to the dispatcher.'

She cancelled her call and looked at him. 'Why there?'

'Cleve Hall.' Holland nodded. 'It makes sense. He still needs somebody to lay this all off on if he's going to get away with it. It's the only person he could use.'

'Libby Cleve?'

'No ma'am, Jim Loyal. He's going to say Estey murdered Abbie Cleve, and Jim Loyal killed him for it. And then Loyal did Bob Ferris, too, because he had worked it out.'

'But Loyal gave Estey an alibi for Abbie Cleve's murder.'

'All we have is hearsay. From Tara Skye and the bartender. According to the case notes, Summer never got Loyal to make an official statement. He will simply claim Loyal denied seeing Estey when he asked him about it.'

'Claim it?'

'It'll be a deathbed confession, ma'am. The only way Summer gets away with it all now is if Loyal is not around to dispute it.'

Summer stood up. 'We have to call Loyal, to warn him.'

'I'll try, but his phone will be off. It always is when he's working on the estate. He doesn't want it ringing just as he's lining up a pheasant in his sights, does he?'

'Then we have to get up there. We can call DCI Jejeune on the way and you can tell him what you've come up with. He can meet us on site. And let's get an Armed Response Unit dispatched, too. If you're right, Summer may have Bob Ferris's shotgun with him. And Loyal will certainly be armed himself. It could end up being a bloodbath out there. Come on, let's go. We'll take the Jag, it's faster.'

49

The conifers on the far side of the water looked darker, as if they had drawn in their colours to protect themselves against the coming winter. The other trees around the inlet stood leafless and bare. All around Domenic Jejeune the landscape was beginning to slip towards muted shades of ochre. Soon the water would lose its light beneath cold steely skies, and its surface would become glassy and grey. The air would turn cooler, and on mornings like this, birders would be able to see their breath. The last of the autumn migrants would be gone by then, and the land would belong once again only to the hardy winter species that chose to remain.

Through the window of the conservatory, Lindy watched Domenic for a moment, not wanting to disturb him. She knew what he was thinking as he sat there, the same thought that had occurred to her as soon as she had opened her eyes, the last thought that been with her when she closed them the night before. Today was Danny's last day. She knew Domenic was rebuking himself for all the things he had not done to save his friend. But in truth, there was nothing he could have done. There was nothing any of them could have done. She saw him look up at the sky. The sun would rise tomorrow, too, and the day after that. Life would go on. But it would go on knowing Danny Maik's fate had been decided. She pushed the unbearable thought deep down inside her, and drew back the French doors to join Domenic.

She rested a hand on his shoulder for a moment and sat down on a rock beside him. 'We won't give up, Dom. Not even afterwards. We'll appeal for clemency.'

'He will have been convicted of killing a serving police officer,' said Jejeune, his eyes still on the skies. 'He hasn't pleaded guilty, hasn't accepted responsibility for the crime he is supposed to have committed. The public outcry would be too great for them to grant it.'

Lindy shook her head defiantly. 'I won't let this happen. I won't.'

Nor would she, he knew. It would happen anyway, but not because Lindy had allowed it to. She would have fought it with every fibre of her being, in every way she could. Her efforts, her tears, her frustrations, would all have been in vain. But she wouldn't have given up. Not until the final curtain had fallen on Danny's fate.

He stood up and handed her his coffee cup. 'Maybe I should just go in to work,' he said, 'see if I can be of some use there, at least.'

There was a noise beneath the pines on the far bank and Jejeune looked up to see a brace of pheasants, both male. They had been driven out of their normal habitat by the shooting, and now they had found themselves in unfamiliar territory, vulnerable, nervous, afraid. At some unseen threat, the birds exploded into flight with a flurry of wingbeats that shattered the morning calm. They headed in opposite directions and he concentrated on one bird, watching its busy, whirring wings lift it into an ungainly climb as it spiralled upwards, before settling into a glide as it came to ground near a cluster of low shrubs.

He looked down at Lindy and saw that she had been watching, too. Despite his sadness, his heart had thrilled at the birds' unexpected appearance. He wondered what the sighting would have meant to others. The Pheasant was possibly the most recognisable bird in the country, but what would they have seen? For some, no more than a sporting trophy, for others a polarising symbol of the countryside and conservation issues. Others still might have seen only an entrée-in-waiting, or even an undesirable invasive species. But how many would have seen the bird he had just watched, the magnificent creature with its vibrant red face and glistening green neck, trailing its twenty-inch tail feathers like a bridal train as it flew? But he had seen something else, too. The sighting had crystallised his world for him in a way he couldn't explain, and in that moment he knew where he stood, on hunting, on Danny Maik's innocence, and on the value of a single life. Any life.

'I think that was your phone buzzing,' said Lindy gently.

'It's probably the lab,' he told her as he reached to open it.

'That needle mark on the bird. Do you think there is a connection to Libby Cleve and her acupuncture treatments?'

'I did,' he said, reading an email as he spoke, 'but according to this report the needle bore was too big. Acupuncture needles are extremely thin. The puncture mark on the bird was from a syringe.' He shook his head as he read, gradually cradling his jaw with his hand. 'Of course,' he said.

Lindy looked up from her rock seat. 'Does it say what was injected into the bird?' she asked.

'It does. Nothing.'

Lindy couldn't understand. He had seemed to believe the entire case, all the cases, came down to the contents of this report. And it had come up empty. So why was he not looking crestfallen, or defeated?

'This wasn't about what was injected into the bird,' he told her. 'It was about what was taken out. The syringe was used to draw out a blood sample.'

Lindy was puzzled. 'But does that tell you anything?'

'Everything. The bird was infected with HN51. And somebody knew it.'

'HN51. Avian flu,' said Lindy. A virus. *A sign there is a disruption in the natural order of things.* 'My God, Dom, this is bad, isn't it?'

He nodded. But there was something else in his expression. He knew now. He had his answers. Finally. All except one. He stared out over the inlet. But Lindy knew his thoughts were elsewhere.

'I should have seen this a long time ago.'

'You only just got those results.'

'No. I should have seen who killed Abbie Cleve, the only person who would have had a reason to.'

Not the *why*, she noticed, not the *how*. For him, it was the human aspects of murder that mattered most; the ones who had died, the ones who had killed them, the ones who were left behind, to endure the heartbreak.

'But you know now? Who did it? Who killed Abbie Cleve, and the others.'

'I do.' He thought for a moment and turned to her. 'Lindy, when Danny claimed he didn't kill that man, it was because he knew he hadn't hit him hard enough, wasn't it?'

She hesitated.

'I know you've been told not to discuss the news from Singapore with me…'

She opened her mouth to protest but saw no point. She had given her word to Shepherd, but she didn't suppose it mattered any more. Nothing did. 'He said he had enough combat training to incapacitate somebody without killing them.'

Jejeune nodded. 'Pressure points. It was what Evan Knowles said about Abbie Cleve. She knew how to find your pressure points. But she would do, wouldn't she? She'd had judo training. Both girls had.' He nodded again thoughtfully. 'I need to call the station,' he said. 'Right away.'

As he raised the phone to dial, it began ringing in his hand. The caller ID was one he'd seen many times. 'Domenic, it's Colleen. You need to get over to the Cleve estate now,' she told him breathlessly. 'Noel Summer got some results from the lab this morning and went rushing off out there immediately. He's not answering his phone. We're in pursuit. Tony Holland is with me.'

'He saw the lab results?' Jejeune took a heartbeat's pause. 'He's going for Jim Loyal. We have to stop him.'

'We've already worked it out, sir.' Although Holland's voice from the passenger seat was less distinct through the Jaguar's hands-free system, Jejeune could still hear that it was charged with nervous energy. 'About the human sacrifice,' Holland continued, 'about laying Abbie Cleve down like that, letting her blood seep into the Earth.'

The solace of self-deception. Of course. It was the final piece. Jejeune cast his eyes over the waters of the inlet once again. He understood it all now, why Abbie Cleve had been killed in the way she had, how it had been done. And by whom.

Now the voice was Shepherd's again. 'If you get there first, Domenic, wait for us. Do not go in there alone. There's an Armed Response Unit on the way. We believe Summer has Bob Ferris's shotgun with him. And we know Loyal will be armed. This has the potential to end in more loss of life.'

'It will,' said Jejeune firmly, 'if we don't get there to stop it. I'm leaving now. I'll meet you there.'

There was silence on the other end of the line for a moment before Holland's voice came through one last time. 'Summer, sir, he has no intention of bringing Jim Loyal in, does he?'

'No, Constable, I don't think he does.'

50

Lindy had gone inside after Domenic rushed off, but the house felt claustrophobic, and the ticking of the clock into the emptiness seemed to be counting down towards Danny's fate. She went back out again and walked down to the rocky shoreline at the mouth of the inlet. She often came here when she was troubled, where she could pour her emotions into the wide, open skies and endless horizons, and they would gather them in, reassuring her that even in the vastness of the universe, her problems mattered. But today, even here her mind would not let her escape the reality lurking in the house behind her. They were going to lose Danny.

A murmuration of Starlings swept in over the coast, and she watched them twisting and curling in harmony, connected as if by telepathy, each knowing the other's flight path instinctively. The dark cloud of birds billowed and waned as it danced along the shoreline, as elusive and ephemeral as justice. She knew others wanted to trust the system, to believe in it, and she understood. They had to, Domenic and Shepherd and the rest, it was all they had to hold on to. But Lindy didn't even have the comfort of that. She knew the real world was an unjust place, where innocent men died for crimes they hadn't committed, and guilty ones went free. Danny needed to prove a man he had never met had come to kill him, he needed to find a weapon that would never resurface. He needed to prove a death blow he had delivered in full view of eight witnesses hadn't killed the man. And unless he did, he was going to be convicted of murder and sentenced to death. She blinked back tears as she thought about him sitting alone in a cell, awaiting a fate that had already been decided.

But it was not just Danny she was going to lose. His death would change Domenic, she knew. He would never recover from the knowledge that he had been able to do nothing to save his friend. She thought about how much the human aspects of murder meant to Domenic, how keenly he felt the losses of the ones who were left behind. It would be them soon, Danny's friends and acquaintances who were left behind to endure the heartbreak of losing a loved one. But Domenic would be no more able to repair their broken lives than he could those of any other survivors. When Danny was gone, he would take part of Domenic with him, and Lindy knew she would lose that part of the man she loved for ever. As she stood out here on this rocky point, gazing out over a wild sea with not another human being in sight, a fresh wave of sorrow engulfed her.

The Starlings continued to swirl out over the sea, downwards and upwards, past thin white clouds that scarred the pale blue sky like the faint claw marks of something that had tried to escape from within it. Perhaps it was the truth. She realised as she watched the birds that she probably knew more about Danny's case than anyone else in the country. She had microscopically examined every detail, twisting her mind over it, through it, around it, looking for something that might offer hope. But there had been nothing. And she knew that if even she, who had subjected the evidence to such forensic scrutiny, could not find a chink of light, no one else would.

The murmuration drifted over the glittering sea, folding in on itself, soaring, swooping, and all the time with a synchronisation that defied understanding. Danny would never see this sight again, never feel the world filling his senses with its joys and wonders as it unfolded. Tears welled in her eyes at the thought and it was a moment before she could see the birds clearly once more. How could so many disparate bodies remain interconnected so seamlessly that they seemed to move as one? One explanation she had heard was that the behaviour was meant to confuse predators, but it seemed impossible to her that a ballet of such mesmerising beauty as this could have such a prosaic motive. And yet, she thought about the brace of pheasants she had seen with Dom earlier; how they had taken to the wing and immediately scattered in opposite directions. They could not have made a hunter's job any easier. She had to concede, watching the Starlings now, picking out one individual from this interconnected mass would have been a far more difficult task.

She gave a short gasp as the thought came to her. Was it possible? If so, why had no one else thought of it? Why not the brilliant Domenic, or the equally clever DCS Shepherd? Because they weren't Lindy. They were not in her unique position of knowing the facts, and watching these birds, and putting all these threads together now. She stood there for a moment, staring at the birds but not seeing them any more as she focused instead on the idea slowly taking shape in her mind. It was thin. Too thin, probably. She suspected it would not survive the scrutiny of either Dom or Colleen Shepherd. They would undoubtedly point out all the flaws, tell her all the legal ways it could be challenged, could fail. But Lindy wasn't bound by legal requirements or admissible evidence, or the logic of police procedure. When she took out her phone to ask it a question, it told her the idea was at least plausible. And that was all she needed.

So what to do about it? Would the hospital authorities even agree to release the records? Of course they would. They were in the business of saving lives. Surely they would never face a more compelling appeal than this. But even if they did, could Selena Lim be trusted to make the proper use of them? Shepherd had questioned her competence. Damian had suggested something even more ominous might lie behind it. Once, even Danny had seemed to have his doubts about her. But now he had decided to entrust her with his life. Could Lindy trust her with it, too? Did she have any other choice? Yes: she had one.

The humid evening air in Singapore was no friend to haste, and anybody running at full speed through the busy streets of the Civic District was bound to attract their share of attention. Damian's damp hair was sticking to his forehead and the sweat was soaking through his shirt. But still he ran, sprinting, bobbing, weaving between the knots of startled onlookers on the pavements until he reached his destination: the imposing grey monolith of the Bukit Merah East Police Cantonment Complex.

He might not have expected such air-conditioned relief in the visiting room, but families of those inmates awaiting trial didn't deserve discomfort, and the guards themselves had to spend long hours here. Damian gratefully welcomed the cool air beginning to return his body temperature to normal as he sank into his plastic seat at the table. Danny shuffled in, his face grey and drawn. There was a hollowness behind his features that Damian had not seen before. He had clearly been contemplating his fate, but Damian knew from looking at him that he had been doing so without hope. Danny had already resigned himself to what would happen at tomorrow's disclosure conference. A committal to trial, to be followed by a foregone verdict, a swift sentencing, and...

'Not sure there was any need for all that rush,' he said, nodding at Damian's glistening skin and sweat-dampened hair. 'I'm sure Selena could have managed five minutes prior to the hearing tomorrow for any last-minute instructions.'

'Selena doesn't know I'm here. I just received a message from Lindy.'

'Something?' Maik sat forward. Despite his resigned attitude, he could not suppress a flicker of hope.

'I don't know, Danny. Truly, I don't.' It took barely a minute for Damian to outline what Lindy was suggesting. The silence with which Maik greeted the idea lasted almost as long. Around them the hushed conversations from other tables swirled, like the voices of ghosts echoing off the grey walls.

'It's a possibility,' said Maik. 'No more than that. The hospital won't need a court order, but they'll still need authorisation from somebody in administration before they'll release those records to you. At least two sworn statements from experts in the field would be needed, three would be better. There'd be the three affidavits to collect as well. I'm not sure it could all be done in time. Selena will need to get on this right away.'

Damian's hesitation went beyond the sketchiness of the plan. Danny Maik waited patiently, like a man who had all the time in the world. 'You need to think about this, Danny. If Selena Lim is not who you think she is, she could make sure this doesn't work.'

Around them, the hands of inmates and visitors stretched as far as possible across tables, testing the boundaries of the no-touch restriction. Urgent conversations continued in hushed murmurs. But in the orbit of Danny Maik's table, silence reigned.

'If she's not who I think she is,' said Danny finally, 'it's over for me anyway.'

Immersed in their own dramas, no one else was paying attention to the two men, giving them all the anonymity they needed. But Damian still leaned forward and lowered his voice. 'There's still time to dismiss her. You could request new representation. If nothing else it would give you a little more time, put off this conference for a few more days.'

Maik's grey features creased into a wan smile. 'Never really been my style, putting off what has to be faced.'

The buzzer announced the end of visiting time. All around them there was the scraping of chairs, as people stood up and waved tearful goodbyes with brave smiles. Damian and Danny stared at each other until a guard approached the table.

'I need to know what you want to do, Danny.'

Maik drew in a deep sigh and stood up. 'If Selena is going to have everything she needs to present this by tomorrow, she's got a lot of work ahead of her,' he said. 'I'm sure she'd appreciate your help.'

51

The Jaguar slewed slightly as it skidded to a stop on the gravel. Holland scrambled out almost before it had stopped rocking. Even by Shepherd's standards it had been a fast drive. Despite the winding country lanes and narrow roads, she had taken minutes off the time he could have achieved in his Audi. Jejeune was waiting by the Range Rover, staring anxiously into the stand of trees just beyond the fields in front of him. On the far side of the Beast, Holland could see Noel Summer's grey Trabant. And in front of that, Jim Loyal's quad bike.

Autumn lay across the fields like a tawny blanket, its muted beiges and browns dotted with the dark skeletons of leafless shrubs and bushes. It seemed like such a benign stage to hold the bloody drama that was promising to unfold. But Shepherd knew the tranquillity of this setting would soon be shattered by the arrival of the Armed Response team. How soon?

'Five minutes, ma'am,' Holland told her.

From somewhere, a shotgun blast rang out and rolled across the sky. She flinched. 'Hunters,' Jejeune said. 'On the far side. Not here.'

She looked again at the dense woods and popped the boot of her car remotely. 'Domenic, take the shotgun out of there and grab the cartridges.'

He looked at her questioningly.

'Neither Tony nor I are licensed to handle firearms at the moment,' she told him. 'You can keep it broken for now. I don't expect you'll need to use it, but we can't wait for the AR team to get here. There is an imminent threat to life in there. We have to go in now, but I am not letting my team walk into a potentially hostile situation unarmed. Grab it and let's go.'

Jejeune leaned in and reluctantly removed the broken gun and shells from the boot. Shepherd locked it again and the three of them began making their way towards the trees. The silence of tension was heavy around them as they walked, the only sound the faint shuffle of leaves and faded grasses beneath their feet. The wet-leaf smell rose to them, and a freshening wind tinged their skin. With each step, a faint puff of white breath escaped into the still air.

As they reached the edge of the woods, another shotgun blast barked out. 'Hunters again,' said Holland. But he didn't sound convinced. This one had been closer and, in truth, none of them could be certain where it had come from.

They entered the stand of trees and halted for a moment, filtering out the sounds of the forest, straining for anything else. The faint murmuring of human voices? Somewhere off to the right? Shepherd laid her hand on Jejeune's arm and looked down at the shotgun. It was time to arm it. He inserted the shells and clicked the gun closed, holding it downwards and pointing the barrel away from them. Before they moved off again Shepherd looked at him intensely. 'I have to be able to say I fully understood this situation, Domenic, before I led you both into it. Just so I have things clear, it was the lab results from that bird that finally drove Summer to this?'

'Yes,' he said flatly, knowing that she needed certainty and not his usual guarded caveats. 'Abbie Cleve found two dead pheasants when she was out walking on the estate lands as she liked to do.' He looked around. 'Perhaps it was even around here, somewhere. I imagine she suspected avian flu when she couldn't see any other cause of death for the birds, so she took blood samples and sent them in for analysis. But she didn't submit the samples under her own name. The Nye being so close, she knew it would mean the suspension of her own operations and culling of stock as well if the results came back positive.'

'Her stock would have meant nothing to her,' said Holland. 'The birds were no more than a source of income. She would have received compensation.'

'I suspect she wanted to buy herself some time to put herself in the best position to exploit the situation, perhaps take out some extra insurance.' Jejeune shrugged. 'More importantly, though, positive cases would have resulted in a three-kilometre exclusion zone. It would have cancelled the shoot here as well. Without the revenues, the Cleve estate would not survive. Jim Loyal couldn't allow that.'

'Wait, said Shepherd, 'so it was Loyal that killed Abbie Cleve, not Summer?'

'But you said it was about human sacrifice,' said Holland.

'No, you did, Constable. But you were right. It is now.' Before he could answer their unspoken question, another shotgun blast rang out. And there was no doubt about where this one came from. 'To the right,' shouted Shepherd. 'Deep in. Go, now. Now.'

They crashed through the undergrowth, dodging fallen branches and hurdling tree roots, weaving between the stands of trees that seemed to grow denser the further they went. The others moved faster, Jejeune trailing as he carefully held the weapon across his chest to protect it from snagging on a loose branch as he ran. He was aware, too, that a fall with a loaded weapon could prove fatal. The others had paused at a small clearing when he caught up to them. They were breathing heavily. And watching.

In front of them, two men were standing at a distance talking. The awkward, stretched conversation space between them had been a familiar sight when another virus had gripped the land, but now Noel Summer faced a far greater threat. The man facing him was holding a loaded shotgun, pointed directly at his chest.

'I saw you coming, and I knew why,' said Loyal. 'I thought I'd be able to hide out from you easily enough in here. Know these woods like the back of my hand. Been walking them all my life. But wherever I went, you seemed to sense it. This is your world, too, this forest, isn't it? Don't come any closer. The next one won't be into the air.'

Summer took a couple of steps towards Loyal. 'Tell me, how did Pete Estey get those birds? Did Abbie Cleve give them to him?'

'No, she gave them to me. Handed me them in a hessian bag and told me she was going to let me report it, for old times' sake. If there was any other way, she would have let it go, she said, but two dead birds, here on the estate, there'd be others out here somewhere. They'd shut her down, too, she said, but she'd be able to open up again sooner or later. In the meantime, the compensation would see her right. But if it came to light she'd known there was flu here, that she'd sent off the samples and got the positive test results back, and she hadn't reported it, she'd never be allowed to open again.'

Loyal shook his head slowly, and a look of something flashed across his grizzled, unshaven face. Anger? Defiance? 'I couldn't let them close down the shoot. It was all that was keeping the estate going. I told you, no closer. I mean it.' He levelled the weapon to his shoulder, balancing it unsteadily in one hand as he wiped his brow with the other. From their vantage point, the watching officers could see it was trembling violently.

'He's slipping, ma'am,' whispered Holland. 'The way he's shaking, he could discharge that weapon at any moment, whether he meant to or not.'

Shepherd leaned towards Jejeune and looked at Holland to make sure he was witnessing it. 'Domenic, as your commanding officer, I'm issuing you an emergency field directive, superseding all established protocols. Until Armed Response arrive, I want you to train your firearm on Jim Loyal, who is the suspect in three murders. I'm going to try to engage him but, if he brandishes his weapon in a way that you judge puts Detective Constable Summer's life under imminent threat, a kill shot is authorised.'

Jejeune nodded. As desperately as he did not want to obey the order, he knew it was the right one. He raised the gun to his shoulder. Through the barrel's sights he could see Summer clearly. But only a shadow of Loyal's jacket was visible. 'The trees, I don't have a clear line of sight to Loyal.'

'Then get one,' she hissed.

'Sir, here.' Holland backed up a step to let Jejeune move in front of him. He raised the gun to his eye again. As long as Loyal stayed exactly where he was, Jejeune had a bearing on him. But if he moved a step in either direction, he would lose him behind the trunk of a tree again. Jejeune blinked a bead of sweat away and drew a deep breath. He felt the adrenalin rising in his chest. It was making his arm shake. He took another, shallower breath to steady it.

Shepherd made a move to step into the clearing, but froze before calling out. A faint noise off in the distance told her the AR team was arriving. She looked at Jejeune, still focused on Loyal. *Hold on, Domenic. Help is here. One more minute.*

Summer stepped forward a pace and was now out of view of all of them behind a tree. Only his voice came to them.

'So you killed Abbie Cleve. You set it up to look like a suicide, and went to the pub with her phone and sent the text from there.'

'I knew Knowles would contact me as soon as he got the message. I was the closest one. I was planning to be back before everyone else, so I could put the phone back in her pocket. But while I was in the pub, Estey stole the quad bike. He saw the birds in the basket and thought he'd help himself and have a bit of a joyride into the bargain. Not another step, Constable. Not one more. I will shoot, I mean it. I'll put these shells right into you. I've been shooting things all my life. Don't think I'd hesitate to do it now. It doesn't matter any more anyway. Nothing does.'

He took a step towards Summer and Jejeune lost him behind the screen of trees again. In panic, he moved to the left, the right, swivelling the barrel to try to get a sighting. From behind him he heard the sound of shouting now, and equipment clattering, as the Armed Response team moved into the woods. They knew there was no need for stealth. Speed was all that mattered.

The sound of Loyal's voice came again. 'When Estey dressed that first bird he saw the needle mark, but it was only when he checked the other pheasant that he realised neither one had any other signs of a kill. He knew what it meant right away. Avian flu, found in my birds. He came up here to tell me he was going to report it. Smiled when he said it, too. He knew it would ruin the estate, Libby, me, all of us up here.'

He stepped out from behind the line of trees and Jejeune had him in his sights again for a moment. Was the threat imminent? Jejeune knew it was. He knew what was going to happen. But he couldn't justify the shot. Not yet.

Loyal stepped towards Summer, no more than five metres away now. Jejeune tensed for the shot, blinking away more sweat from his eyes. But Loyal's final step took him behind another tree, and he had only his words to focus on once more. 'I couldn't let Estey do that to us. After I shot him, I went up to his place to find that other bird. But then you arrived. I only shot at you to scare you off. I never meant to hit you. But I realised I had used my gun, so I picked up the shells and took off with Estey's gun. Fired a couple of rounds from it later and took the casings back there for you lot to find. Better if you thought he'd done a runner after firing at you. Maybe stop you looking for him.'

Summer kept advancing. 'You'll spend your life behind bars for this. You know that, don't you? But that's what is needed. The Earth's cycles have been disrupted by all these deaths. Balance needs to be restored. Your imprisonment will do that, Mr Loyal. It's what society calls justice.' It struck Shepherd for the first time how calm Summer sounded. There was no fear, no concern, just a light conversational tone. She realised with horror what it meant and turned sideways to Jejeune. 'Now Domenic, take the shot. Take it, now.'

'I don't have it.' He shuffled sideways, but Loyal remained a half-profile at best.

'You need to take a look around, Mr Loyal, at the sky, the trees, this land,' Summer said in the same even tone. 'Look at it and listen to it and drink it all in, the sights, the smells, the sounds. You'll never get to enjoy them again, not for as long as you live.'

'I won't be going in any prison. Stay where you are. I'm warning you for the last time. Not one more step.'

Summer stepped towards him, in full view of Jejeune. 'It's over, Mr Loyal. I'm arresting you for the murders of Abigail Cleve, Peter Estey and Robert Ferris. I'm going to take you in now. You'll spend the rest of your life locked up in a room. Four bare walls, concrete walls.'

'No closer.'

Summer took one more step. There was a shimmer of movement and Loyal flickered into view for an instant. He had his gun out in front of him, raised to the shoulder.

'NO.'

Both men spun to see Colleen Shepherd burst into the clearing, sprinting towards them. Loyal recoiled in surprise, the gun flailing in the air as he stumbled backwards. Summer looked at Shepherd and she saw an expression lost in a million emotions: sadness, pain, regret, relief.

Loyal drew down the gun to level it on Shepherd, and Holland called out. 'Ma'am, look out.' His voice implored Jejeune from behind. 'Sir, the shot, the shot. Take the shot.'

Summer turned and advanced on Loyal one more time.

A shot rang out.

52

The sheen had disappeared from Selena Lim. Her black hair was missing the glorious, shimmering lustre it normally had when she moved. Her clothes, too, lacked the crisp, clean, out-of-the box neatness Danny had come to associate with her outfits. Today, they looked as tired and drawn as her features.

'Not too close,' she said as she slumped into the seat beside him. 'No shower.'

At first Maik though she was commenting on his personal hygiene, but, when she hefted her briefcase onto the table and reached in, he saw a half-eaten energy bar. He realised it constituted breakfast for someone who'd had other priorities.

'I came straight here from the office,' she whispered. 'I was there all night.' She reached for the bar and broke a piece off, shielding her mouth with a hand as she chewed it.

'Was it worth it?'

'I don't know, Danny. Honestly, I don't. There are two hurdles today. The first is whether the judge will even permit me to present our position. Unless I can convince him we have a valid argument, he may not allow me to proceed.'

'But if he does?'

'Then I have to demonstrate that our evidence would be enough to convince a jury to acquit. If he feels there is not a sufficient likelihood that the prosecution would win this case, he won't allow it to go to trial.'

She rested her fingertips on his forearm and her touch felt like electricity. Apart from that brief handshake at their initial meeting, it was the first human contact he'd had since he had been imprisoned, he realised. Even Guy Trueman had not shaken his hand that day at his office.

'Our position is fragile but, whatever happens today, you must let me handle it,' she told him earnestly. 'Even if it sounds like things are going off the rails, don't object, don't interrupt, don't say anything. Please Danny, it's important. I only have one chance to get this right, and the slightest interruption could upset the whole thing.'

'Can't you at least request an adjournment so you can get something to eat and a change of clothes?'

She shook her head. 'No, that's the whole point. I don't want to give the judge any excuse to delay this morning's proceedings. Any recess, any break at all, and the prosecution might learn what I'm about to present. I don't want to give them time to counter with any one of about a dozen plausible objections. I need to blindside them.'

The judge's entrance and seating were accompanied by the formality and dignity Maik might have expected, though with considerably less pomp and circumstance than he'd seen in the UK. Perhaps they saved all that for the trial itself, he thought.

The clerk ambled through the preliminaries. Selena was watching intently and Maik saw a flicker of something cross her face when the prosecution confirmed they were ready to proceed.

'Were you expecting them not to be?' Danny asked quietly.

'Hoping,' she whispered. 'But they'd only ask for more time if they didn't believe they already have everything they need to win their case at trial.' Selena noticed his look. 'You won't be asked to speak today but, even if I were to make a formal request to enter a guilty plea, it won't make a difference at this point. The charge is murder under first limb. That's what you'd be pleading guilty to.'

Maik nodded his understanding. No more deals. Everything was off the table now. The last of his bridges had been burned. Now everything rested on today's decision.

The judge looked at Selena gravely. 'This is the Second Criminal Case Disclosure Conference, Ms Lim. It is the court's understanding that the defendant is still intending to enter a plea of not guilty.'

'Those are my instructions, your honour.'

'Very well. And the grounds for this plea?'

'It is our position that evidence exists that is critical to the client's defence, but this evidence has been made unavailable to us.'

The prosecution lawyer rose, looking to possess all the polish that Selena Lim so notably lacked today. He strolled around to the front of the table to address the judge. 'The defence is referring to a kukri knife, your honour. It is our position that it is incumbent upon the defence to prove the existence of this knife. We would suggest that it cannot be demonstrated that something is missing if it cannot be established that it ever existed in the first place.'

'And may I remind the counsel for the prosecution that there is neither a jury nor a gallery present today,' said the judge. 'You may remain seated throughout the entire performance.' He drew his mouth into a short grin that no one was expected to mistake for mirth. 'Given the gravity of the charges, I intend to give the defence every opportunity to establish their position. But I have to say I find myself minded to lean in the direction of the prosecution.' He addressed Lim directly again. 'Such a defence as you are proposing would need proof that the knife does, or did, indeed exist. Can the defence produce any witnesses to say they saw it, either at the scene or elsewhere?'

'No.'

'Or any photographic or documentary evidence to attest to its existence?'

'No.'

'And does the defence anticipate being able to produce it at trial?'

There was a long pause before Selena Lim answered. She seemed to be composing herself for the battle that would follow her response. 'No, your honour, we do not.'

'Then, Ms Lim,' intoned the judge gravely. 'I would suggest that the defence's position is untenable. Unless you have anything further, it is my intention to refer this case for criminal trial on the charge of murder under the first limb of Section 300 of the Singapore criminal code.'

Maik grabbed the edge of the table with his hands and pulled himself forward. Beside him, Selena Lim was standing now. Her arms were dangling loosely at her sides. He could see her fingers were trembling. She seemed to become aware of it and drew her body straighter. But she could not disguise the slight tremor in her voice when she spoke. 'The missing evidence I was referring to was not the kukri, your honour. What we do have are records that prove other evidence existed. We are requesting the opportunity to present these records to you now.'

Selena Lim's body became still as the judge took a long time to consider the request. Maik looked up at her, standing beside him. In an effort to keep her face impassive, it seemed to him, his counsel might be holding her breath. The first hurdle, Maik thought; were his hopes to die at this stage? Was he?

'I am interested to hear what you have, Ms Lim, and I have no doubt the counsel for the prosecution will be as well. But these records must offer unequivocal proof of the existence of this missing evidence. Unequivocal, Ms Lim. Furthermore, it must be clear that the disappearance of this evidence is clearly detrimental to your client's case. High bars, I understand, but if your submission fails to clear either of them my earlier decision will stand.'

Selena expelled a breath. 'Understood, you honour.' She reached into a manila folder and extracted a sheaf of papers. She handed copies to the clerk to be distributed to the judge and the prosecutor. 'These are printouts of activity for the connectivity device commonly referred to as Bluetooth. They are from the trip log for the ambulance that transported Titus Chupul from the scene of the encounter between my client and the victim to the hospital. As you will see, a large number of devices are shown as being available to connect with the ambulance's system at the scene. These would be devices belonging to individuals and businesses in the Geylang area, where a large crowd had gathered. But after the ambulance left the scene, only four devices are shown to be consistently available. The first three numbers on this list are for phones belonging to, respectively, the ambulance driver, the second attending paramedic and Officer Chitron Gunteng, who accompanied the body in the ambulance. This leaves us with one other, unidentified device showing as being available to the Bluetooth system: device ID 25:A1:73:5B:C9:14. Each of the three occupants has made a sworn statement that no other phone in the ambulance belonged to them. We believe it's reasonable to assume this can only have been in the victim's possession.'

'Your honour, there is no evidence to support this,' said the prosecutor.

Lim looked at the judge. 'We are not trying to establish this as a fact, we are merely pointing out the obvious.'

The judge offered her a thin smile. 'When you've been doing this a little longer, Ms Lim, you'll appreciate that, sadly, the obvious seems to have precious little place in a court of law. I take it what you are trying to establish as fact is that there were four phones in that ambulance.'

'Two independent experts in the field of Bluetooth connectivity technology have provided affidavits that the fourth device must have been present in the ambulance for it to have registered as available for the entire journey.'

The prosecutor stood up sharply. 'An unregistered phone by definition cannot be linked to an individual,' he said, his voice rising in exasperation. 'We would therefore contend this phone cannot be proven to be the victim's, and is therefore not relevant to the case.' If the prosecutor's agitation was a sign he felt Selena might be making progress, she gave no hint of complacency herself.

'We would respectfully suggest that it is not the prosecutor's place to decide the relevance of this evidence, your honour.' She hurried into her next point before the judge had a chance to respond. 'Document 2A is a copy of the police report listing the items found in the victim's possession upon his admittance to the hospital. As you will see, there is no phone on that list.'

'You honour,' pleaded the prosecutor, 'I would suggest there is a fundamental flaw in logic here. The fact that the phone was not listed among the victim's possessions is not in any way evidence that it is missing. The reason this phone was not listed among his possessions was because the police had no evidence that this fourth phone did indeed belong to him. Since this error renders the defence's entire argument invalid, may I respectfully suggest we move on to a confirmation of the ruling that this case may proceed to trial?'

'It does appear that you have failed to demonstrate the phone belonged to the victim, Ms Lim,' said the judge gravely. 'I can see no reason to change my earlier decision.'

Maik gripped the arms of his chair, as if he might rise. Selena's words stopped him.

'So where is it, then?'

Selena Lim's question seemed to stun the entire courtroom, but no one more so than the prosecutor. 'I'm sorry?'

'The paramedics can testify that there was no time to lay down an evidence sheet beneath the victim before he was put in the ambulance. Because of this, the vehicle was impounded after its arrival at the hospital and held in a secure police lot until forensics could go over the interior to check for any evidence that the body may have left in there. The last sheet in your package is a copy of the inventory the police supplied to the hospital, itemising the objects found in the ambulance. As you will see, there is no phone on there, either. We know it was in the ambulance when it reached the hospital, we know it does not appear in a list of the victim's possessions, and we can see it is not included in an inventory of the ambulance contents. So where is it?' Selena Lim paused and gathered herself. 'Your honour, we believe we could demonstrate to a jury beyond reasonable doubt that a fourth phone made the trip from the scene of the encounter to the hospital. We further believe we have sufficiently proven that this piece of evidence must have later been intentionally removed from a vehicle being held in a secure, guarded police facility. The only inference that can be reasonably drawn is that this was done to deny the defence the opportunity to present this phone as evidence in this trial. We contend that a jury's inability to consider this evidence would render any conviction in a trial unsafe, and require any sentence to be set aside.'

Selena didn't look at Maik as she sat down. It was as if she didn't trust herself to meet his eyes. Would it be enough, he wondered. Could she have made a more compelling case to tie the missing phone to the missing kukri? Could she have done more to remind the judge, just in case he had missed the connection, that one piece of evidence removed could mean more? Would it have been better to have spelled it out for him, beat him over the head with it? What would there have been to lose; a judge insulted by such a condescending approach couldn't do any more harm than one who found against them anyway. Maik had been in enough courtrooms to know that you couldn't read anything from a judge's expression, but the prosecution didn't seem unduly concerned. If this was all the defence had, they seemed to be thinking, if it all hung on one slender thread of missing evidence that could not be proven to be related in any way to the victim, then that was a case they would be happy to contest.

Selena for her own part looked worried. Perhaps she too was now rueing the fact that she'd missed her chance to connect the missing phone to the missing knife. It was the knife, after all, that was at the centre of Maik's self-defence claim, not the phone. Her unsubstantiated assertion that the phone contained evidence vital to the defence's case had gone unchallenged by the prosecution, whose faux outrage seemed to have been exhausted by then. But it wouldn't have been overlooked by the judge. *Fragile*, Selena Lim had said. It was an apt description of their claims. But too fragile? Only the judge knew what that threshold was. But as he looked at the young woman sitting beside him now, Danny Maik could be sure of one thing. Selena Lim had produced a defence in an indefensible case and nobody could have tried harder to clear him. She had been on his side since the beginning and her belief in him had never wavered. Whatever the result, he'd always be profoundly grateful to her for that.

53

Jim Loyal had been crying, but you would have had to look closely to know it. There was no sound, no gasps for air, no sobbing. Just single crystal tears that leaked from his eyes and ran unchecked over his hard, lined face. He had alternated between tears and silence since he had been brought into the station. As the time went on, it found him crying more often. But the earlier silence had not been defiance, merely reflection; a man coming to terms with the lives he had taken, and perhaps, too, the pain he had caused.

Domenic Jejeune was seated opposite him. 'DC Summer never asked you about Bob Ferris,' he said. 'Did you tell him about that earlier, before we arrived?'

Loyal shook his head. 'Didn't have to. He'd worked it out. He was a sharp one. He knew Estey had told Bob where he had got the birds, and how. When Bob heard from you lot that I'd given Estey an alibi, he knew I was lying, and he started to ask himself why. He had the background and the know-how to come up with some answers. So he arranged for us to meet.'

'Did Ferris choose the Nye, or did you?' Jejeune asked.

Loyal looked at his interviewer for a moment. 'Because neither one of us would have had much love for that place, is that what you mean, Inspector? Same as that poor lad.'

'Summer,' said Jejeune. 'His name was Noel Summer.'

Loyal nodded silently. 'Bob chose it. I suppose he thought it was as good a place as any to solve one last case. The strange thing was, he wasn't intending to take me in himself. He wanted to call Summer, have him come up to the Nye and run me in.' Loyal thought for a moment. 'To be fair, if there was one person I would have wanted to, it would have been him. He understood, how it all fits together, humans and the Earth, the land. He knew no good could come of walking birds up to the guns to be slaughtered, cheating the cycles of life and death, upsetting the balance of nature.'

Only the Earth can heal our wounds, Summer had said at the pub that night. Were they healed now, wondered Jejeune. Had Summer's blood sacrifice restored the balance? Or had the hunting season simply claimed one more victim?

'I knew he would work it out, that young lad, that first time I met him,' said Loyal. 'If anybody was going to figure out what I had done to poor Abbie, it would be him.' At the mention of the woman's name, Loyal began to weep again, and this time it looked like it was settling in for a long run. Jejeune paused the interview and left the room.

'For goodness' sake, Domenic, wrap this up,' Colleen Shepherd told him irritably as he entered the Observation Suite. 'We don't need chapter and verse on every aspect of his thought processes. Jim Loyal is not going to be studied at one of those serial killer seminars in years to come. He's just a gamekeeper who killed three people to protect a pheasant shoot on his land.'

'Four people, ma'am,' corrected Tony Holland gently.

'He didn't kill Noel Summer to save the shoot, Constable.'

'No ma'am.'

Nobody said anything into the quiet of the room, although they all knew why Loyal *had* killed Summer. He had already provided all the details of that one: chapter, verse and epilogue. Jejeune understood that part of Shepherd's impatience to get the other three cases wrapped up now was because they already had the whole story on the one murder she was most invested in: that of Noel Summer.

'He just kept coming,' Loyal had told them when he finally found it within himself to talk. 'He knew a man like me couldn't go to prison. Some men weren't meant to survive inside walls. I swear to you, I would have spent the rest of my life trying to atone for what I'd done, but I couldn't go to prison. But he just kept coming, even after I levelled the shotgun. It was like he knew what was going to happen, wanted it to.' Loyal had nodded dumbly to himself. 'That was it. It was like he wanted me to shoot him. Like he was choosing to die there, on that day, in that forest.'

He was. And they all knew it. Shepherd had sighed when Loyal finished speaking. She'd identified it, finally, the other expression in that look Summer had given her as she burst into the clearing: peace, finally, release. He had solved the murders of Abbie Cleve and Peter Estey, but he had not done so quickly enough. And that meant he had failed to prevent the murder of Bob Ferris, failed him for a second time. Ferris was his only reason for existing any more. With him gone, Summer's life had ceased to have any purpose.

Shepherd looked at the monitor now. Loyal sat with his head bowed, tears streaming openly down his face as he thought about Abbie Cleve. The others remained convinced he would have taken his own life after shooting Summer, rather than face up to this kind of reckoning. Perhaps, if Shepherd hadn't reached towards him in an attempt to grab the weapon after he had shot Summer. In the time it had taken for Loyal to wrestle the gun away from her, an Armed Response officer was there, exploding into him with a sickening body-check from behind that sent him hurtling through the air. By the time Loyal's senses had started flowing back to him, the officer was on him, knee in his back, yanking his arms behind him roughly into handcuffs. While Colleen Shepherd had run to Summer and sunk on her knees beside his body. And wept.

They shouldn't have ended up with this case. Shepherd had battled tooth and nail to hang on to the investigation, with everybody from the chief constable on down suggesting they were too close, too involved, to be able to do it properly. She had listened patiently to their arguments, taken all the objections on board, and then made it clear, in the way that only she could, that nobody would be taking the murder investigation of her young detective constable off them. Her team would see it through, and they would do it right. Noel Summer deserved no less than their best. And they had delivered it. Now, she wanted no further part in the matter. She turned away angrily from the screen. 'We have all we need from this man,' she said. 'Get him out of my sight.'

Though he had never seemed to be there, Noel Summer's absence left the Incident Room feeling cold and empty. Shepherd suspected it would be a long time before she once again heard the laughter and easy companionship she used to associate with this place. If ever. She looked at Domenic Jejeune, perched on a desk at the back, his feet on the chair in front. If it was an attempt to establish some sort of normality again after the horrors of the last few days, she was ready to welcome it.

'I'm wondering how Noel Summer was able to be so far ahead of the rest of us on all this.' She looked at Tony Holland, seated in the front row, looking pensive. 'You said that Bob Ferris had the background on Summer and Estey, and that gave him an advantage over us, but what advantage did Summer have?'

'He had the advantage of knowing he was telling the truth about the shells,' said Jejeune from the back of the room. 'We couldn't be sure those shots had ever been fired, but he could. Once he knew it couldn't have been Estey, he started looking at who it could have been. Loyal would have been one of those people. And then when Evan Knowles mentioned pressure points in that interview, that led him to judo. Not the girls who knew it, but the man who had taught them. Loyal would know about the pressure points as well. And who else would Abbie Cleve trust to let them get close enough to put a sleeper hold on her?'

'So Loyal laid her down and cut her wrists?' Holland nodded. 'And because he couldn't face the truth of what he was doing to her, he staged it as a suicide.'

'It's how he needed to remember it,' said Jejeune. 'It was the only way he could cope with the memory, to recall it as a gentle, peaceful death without struggle, without pain. As if she had chosen to take her own life.'

Shepherd nodded thoughtfully. *The solace of self-deception.* How we could all do with a little bit of that at times. She looked at Jejeune in a way that told him something was coming that he might not want to hear. 'There's to be an inquiry, Domenic. The Armed Response commander feels you may have had the opportunity to shoot Loyal before he killed Summer. You were authorised to take a kill shot. They want to know why you didn't.'

'Couldn't.' It wasn't Jejeune who answered. It was Tony Holland. 'I was directly behind the DCI, ma'am, exactly the same line of sight. He never had a clear view of Loyal through those trees the entire time. A flicker here and there maybe, but never anything that would constitute a kill shot opportunity.

I'm a hundred percent sure of that, ma'am, and I'm prepared to testify to it before a Board of Inquiry.'

Shepherd noticed Holland hadn't turned to glance in the DCI's direction while he was speaking, and he didn't now that he'd finished, either. She looked at Jejeune and he met her gaze across the room. Would he have taken the shot if Loyal had been in the open? Some people could shoot another human being, for others it simply wasn't possible. But to save a life, the life of a promising young detective whom Jejeune knew was innocent? Would that have been enough to compel him to fire a kill shot? She looked into his eyes, but as usual nothing came back. As in most things when it came to Domenic Jejeune, she simply couldn't tell.

Her reverie was broken by a polite tap on the door jamb by the desk sergeant. 'Your phone, sir,' he said to Jejeune, 'it's still switched off after the interview. Somebody has been trying to reach you. From Singapore. Says his name is Jejeune.'

54

Illusion. The night-time skyline of Singapore was so dazzling it looked like a field of lights into which the occasional dark hole had been punched. Brightly lit towers soared into the blackness above, and away in the distance the shimmering presence of the Marina Bay Sands hotel floated like a glittering boat across the night sky. Below it, the empty black ribbon of space that was the Singapore River drifted along silently. Danny Maik took it all in slowly. He knew he was seeing it for the last time.

A soft breeze stirred the palm trees in the corners of the open rooftop and offered a welcome respite from the warm night air. Danny took a moment to savour it. All those days standing on the north Norfolk coast, and it had never occurred to him to fully appreciate the feel of fresh air on his skin. On the table in front of him was a box, tied with a ribbon. Inside were four sweet tau sar piah with a gift card, in Damian Jejeune's handwriting. The box wasn't for him.

It was early evening, and it would take Illusion some time to build to fever pitch. Danny would be gone from the rooftop bar by then. One beer, he had agreed to, a muted celebration, and then back to his hotel room to pack. On a small hardwood square in the centre of the rooftop, beneath a string of tiny white lights, Damian and Selena were doing a good job of demonstrating why dancing should be left to the professionals. But they were clearly enjoying their misadventures, and their laughter was infectious. The man sitting next to Danny turned to him with a grin.

'I'm surprised she agreed to let me come tonight, after, you know... everything,' said Ronnie Gunn.

'You were looking out for my best interests. I think she recognises that now.'

Gunn's eyes followed Selena. 'A lot of people misjudged her, including both of us, for a while I think. But she did brilliantly. Nobody else could have got you off, Danny. You were lucky to have her on your side.'

Lucky? Perhaps. He had his freedom and his career, still. And over time, his life would return to some sort of normality. But this incident had taken something from him, something of who he was. He wondered if that could ever be recovered.

'Guy sends his best. He's obviously delighted with the outcome. He'd have been here himself but he's got something else on.' Gunn shrugged. 'You know Guy.'

Yes, Maik knew Guy.

'Did he know it was your knife Chupul had that day?' Maik's eyes had not left the dancers as he spoke and they stayed resolutely on them now as Gunn turned to stare at him. For a moment, neither man said anything.

'Not at first. I told him as much as I had to. When did you know?'

'When I found out danphe was the word for the birds, not just symbols. I'd told Selena there was a bird on that knife, but she only told you there was a Nepali symbol on there. It could have been a flag, a regimental crest, some even have Everest on them, don't they?'

'Sagarmatha, yes.'

'But you knew it was a Himalayan Monal, the symbolic bird of Nepal. And you mentioned you'd had a kukri. Once.'

Gunn's mouth tightened. 'It meant everything to me. My father gave me that knife. Chupul took it from me not long after I first arrived. He told me when I was man enough, I could come and try to take it back from him. Titus Chupul was a bastard, Danny, a cruel, sadistic bastard.'

'Did you take it from him during the ambulance ride?'

Gunn shook his head, but he, too, left his eyes on the dance floor now. The music had changed to a slow song. Damian and Selena were doing better with this one. 'As soon as I knelt beside him, I saw it in his belt. I knew my body was shielding my hand from the crowd, so I just unsnapped the scabbard and slid it and the knife inside my jacket. I swear I thought he was already dead.'

Maik's beer paused halfway to his mouth. 'He wasn't, though, was he?' His voice was quiet, but his relief was evident. Although he had maintained this all along, he wondered now if he had ever been quite sure.

Gunn looked at him and shook his head. 'When he opened his eyes I saw that look in them, the one that I always saw, challenging me to be man enough to take my knife back. Only now, I had. And he knew it.'

'So you killed him.'

'He was in a pretty bad way, Danny. You must have hit him a lot harder than you thought. Honestly, I don't know if he would have made it anyway, even with immediate medical assistance.' Gunn was quiet for a long moment. His eyes went back to the dancing couple, but he seemed to be listening to the sound of the soft breeze rattling the fronds of the palm trees rather than the music. 'You know, it's always struck me how close a responder's hand is to a person's windpipe when they're giving mouth-to-mouth.' He paused again, but this time he was listening to something Maik couldn't hear. 'Bending low, feigning mouth-to-mouth, just squeezing the hyoid, how long would it take?' He shook his head slowly. 'If the victim was already struggling to breathe, from a blow to the larynx, say, thirty seconds maybe. And he'd be gone.'

The two men had been hunching forward slightly. They leaned back now and fixed on smiles as the others joined them from the dance floor, collapsing into their chairs in a whirl of breathless laughter. Damian grabbed his Tiger beer bottle by the neck and took a long drink. Selena gratefully sipped her Singapore Sling through a straw.

'So I suppose it's back to Bhutan for you now, Damian?' It was easier for Gunn to switch gears; he had been living with the news he had just delivered for a lot longer than Danny.

'As a matter of fact, I'm going to be staying on here for a while. Selena is going to take a couple of days off to show me around. We're heading over to Sentosa Island tomorrow. You're welcome to join us if you like, Danny,' Damian said in a tone that made it clear that he wasn't.

Maik shook his head anyway. 'I've been away too long as it is. I'll be on the first flight out in the morning. But you two enjoy yourselves. You've earned it, both of you.' He looked at them earnestly. 'I wouldn't be here tonight if it wasn't for the two of you. I know that. And I won't forget it.' He raised his beer in their direction and offered them a smile. There wasn't much a man could say to two people who had saved him from a death penalty, beyond the thanks he'd already offered. But they had been admitted into his circle of protection now, those for whom he would lay down his life if he had to. Whether or not they realised it, Danny Maik was repaying them with everything he had.

'Don't forget Lindy, too,' said Damian.

Danny's expression told him he hadn't.

'Probably wise to be getting out of here, though,' Damian told him. 'I imagine there will be a few cops in town less than happy with the outcome.'

Maik shook his head. 'A few, maybe. But most will trust that the system got it right. They'll live with the result.' Maik's thoughts seemed to drift for a moment, but the DJ announced a song and it brought him back with a soft smile.

'I can't believe he agreed to play it,' said Selena.

'You think he's going to refuse a request from the hottest lawyer in Singapore?' This time, Damian made no attempt to walk the comment back, and, as Marvin Gaye and Tammi Terrell began to tell each other they were all they needed to get by, he grabbed Selena's hand and led her back onto the dance floor.

Maik turned his eyes back to Gunn. He didn't need to persuade him to tell him the rest. Gunn wouldn't have been able to prevent himself, now that he had started.

He reached for his beer and leaned back in his cane chair. 'In a way, I suppose you could say Guy was responsible. At least, in the beginning. He and I would have lunch at Raffles every once in a while, and when he started seeing Iniya she joined us. One day, she brought her friend, Devina Chupul, my old landlady. Now, as you know, Guy is a man who enjoys being in the company of women, and he's good at it, but it was all perfectly innocent. Just lunch, you know. Only I guess Devina decided Titus didn't need to know. A few weeks ago, Guy starts telling me about his old friend from his army days who is coming over here to see him. Only maybe it wasn't just me listening to these tales about this good, brave man who could slay all the world's dragons. Maybe on that lazy afternoon, with the sun streaming in through the windows in that elegant Raffles dining room, there was someone else listening, someone vulnerable and helpless, who lived with a dragon of her own, one who had her cowering and flinching whenever one of his moods came calling. And maybe this person came to see this valiant dragon slayer of Guy's as the man to end her nightmare.'

'So she asked you to set it up so I could kill her husband?'

'Me?' Gunn shook his head. 'The first I heard of it was when she called me to tell me Titus Chupul was on his way to confront you. She'd made sure he'd seen the photo on her phone – she had left a couple of receipts from those afternoons at Raffles lying around. It was all a jealous, twisted mind like Chupul's needed. I headed down to the Geylang to try to stop him. But you'd already taken care of that.'

'And that's why you took the phone. To stop them from finding the address of that record shop on there.'

'She followed you to the shop and then texted her husband to say she was meeting someone there, just vaguely enough to raise his suspicions. If he hadn't written that address down, perhaps it could have all looked the way she had planned it to.' He looked at Maik frankly. 'You have to know, Danny. She never meant for any of this to happen to you, the murder charge, the luring angle. She didn't want Chupul dead. She wanted him in prison. All she needed was for him to attempt to kill you. But she needed to know he would be attacking someone capable of defending himself. There aren't many who could.'

Maik regarded Gunn carefully. Was it true? All of it? Any of it? Or, like most crimes he investigated, just partly true, the rest blurry fragments, like those ephemeral prints on the walls in Guy Trueman's office, a vague impression of what might have gone on, with most of it left to the imagination? It crossed Danny's mind that if he had died in the fight, Titus Chupul's lengthier sentence would have brought Devina even more freedom. Instead, Chitron Gunteng, Ronnie Gunn, had delivered her the most permanent kind of freedom of all.

'I would never have let them put you to death, Danny. The knife would have shown up, or a witness who had seen it that day. Selena would have had something to give them before they sentenced you.'

Danny looked at her out on the dance floor, pressing in close to Damian as the music swirled around them. Would she? Or would it just have been better to let sleeping dogs lie? Gunn would never have had to confess to Maik about killing Titus Chupul. No one would have ever known. Ronnie Gunn could have carried that secret to his grave. But he would not be going to prison for his crime anyway. Because he knew something, too.

'He never drew that knife, did he, Danny? That's why none of the witnesses saw it. When I took it from him, the kukri was in the scabbard.' He nodded. 'You were right, he had a weapon, and he was coming to attack you with it. But you saw him reaching for it and you reacted before he could draw it. Now, I'm no lawyer, as I keep saying, but it seems to me, a knife in a scabbard, that's not brandishing, is it Danny? That's not threatening, or approaching with intent. That's not assault with a deadly weapon. Whatever happened between you two, you weren't defending yourself against an armed attack. Not when you hit him.'

Did the timing matter? Was it important that Danny reacted seconds before he had to, that Chupul's hand was on the hilt of the knife when he hit him? Did it make any difference that the blow, and the force of it, would have been the same whether Chupul had the knife in his hand or not? Or was it like Guy Trueman had told him, and Damian after; the truth didn't matter in this case? Perhaps it never had.

Damian and Selena returned to the table, holding hands still. 'There's a lot to be said for that old Motown music, Danny,' said Damian. He looked at his watch. 'They'll still be at work in the UK but I imagine they'll be tearing the roof off a few places tonight to celebrate the release of an innocent man, eh?'

'Yes,' said Danny quietly. 'Yes, I imagine they will.'

Ronnie Gunn raised his glass. 'To Danny Maik; an innocent man.'

'An innocent man.' Selena and Damian raised their drinks. And Danny could do nothing but raise his own to join them.

55

The Board Room had never seemed so lively and boisterous to Lindy, but perhaps that was just in contrast to the solemnity at the table she was approaching. It was the same one the group had occupied for the trivia contest just a few short days, and a couple of lifetimes, ago. The three figures sat in their same seats, each locked in their own thoughts. But her approach seemed to lift them from their reveries and it was with genuine pleasure that Tony Holland announced her arrival. 'Here she is,' he said.

Colleen Shepherd stood up and embraced her in a tight hug. 'You, girl, are a genius,' she said holding her out afterwards at arm's-length. 'Bluetooth. Brilliant,' she said, shaking her head. 'Just brilliant.'

'I guess we know where the brains of this outfit has been all along,' said Holland.

It seemed to Lindy that Domenic's smile was a touch forced. Though the euphoria over Danny's release would help, she knew it could not overshadow the other reason they had gathered here today, in this pub, at this table. But Dom had already told her he was proud of her, and she knew he would be trying hard to set aside any other feelings he might be harbouring to celebrate her stunning achievement in bringing Danny Maik back to them.

'Okay, enough of this nonsense,' she said. 'Just thank God he's on his way home. When does his flight arrive?'

'Couple of hours, I think. Lauren is already on her way to the airport to pick him up.' Holland stood up. 'I'll get them in. Tonight's on me. What are you having?'

They gave him their orders and Shepherd watched Tony Holland as he approached the bar. She saw Jejeune looking at Holland and knew he, too, was thinking about the case that had taken Noel Summer's life. Tara Skye and Jim Loyal had both sat at that bar in the moments before Abigail Cleve's death was announced; one knowing, the other not. Now they were facing two very different futures. Tara Skye would continue to roam the countryside of north Norfolk, celebrating in its glories and lamenting its challenges as she battled to protect it from the ravages of humankind. Jim Loyal faced only the numbing mundanity of the same four prison walls each day. He wouldn't last long. Shepherd had ordered a suicide watch on him from the moment he was taken into custody, but she suspected he wouldn't even make it as far as his trial date. Perhaps it would be for the best, some said. But Shepherd wasn't interested in what was best for Jim Loyal. The endless possibilities that had seemed to lie before a young man named Noel Summer that night of the trivia contest had left her full of hope. Now the memory was as sharp as a knife wound. For all the sorrow Loyal had caused, all the pain, but most of all for cutting short the young life of a promising officer, a damaged young man who they might have healed in time, Loyal deserved nothing more than to see out the rest of his days in prison. Perhaps that was what society called justice, too.

Holland returned from the bar with the four drinks clasped in his hands. He distributed them carefully and raised a glass of yellow beer. 'Glad as I am about Danny, I think the first one should be to somebody else. To our fallen colleague, Detective Constable Noel Summer, may he rest in peace.'

'To Noel,' they chorused. The raised glasses flickered orange as they caught the reflection of the flames from the nearby fireplace. The fire would be a fixture in this room now the colder weather seemed to have settled in for the long term, a haven of warmth and quiet comfort. It occurred to Shepherd it was just the kind of place Noel Summer might have made his local.

Even for him, Domenic had been quiet to this point. His relief at Danny's release had been evident, as was his sadness about Noel Summer's passing, but there was something else. Shepherd knew he felt that in both cases he should have been able to do more. He had been a passenger through it all, no more than an observer, right down to the shooting of Noel Summer, watched over the sights of a shotgun. In Danny's case, the result meant Domenic could quickly get over the feeling of failure, but she knew the regrets over Noel Summer's death would linger with him a lot longer.

Lindy could see it too, and, although she addressed her question to the group, it was clear she expected an answer only from him. 'Why do you think Noel came back to the force? As a way of finding closure?'

'I think he came back because Bob Ferris suggested he should,' Jejeune said. 'He probably told him it made him feel guilty to see the talents of such a good officer going to waste because of what had happened to him. Summer would have done anything Ferris asked of him.'

'I wonder if it would have ended any differently, if his first case hadn't been at the Nye,' said Holland, sipping his beer slowly. 'I mean, it could hardly have been a worse place for him to start his career all over again, could it?'

Jejeune shook his head thoughtfully. 'I believe he started off wanting to solve the Abbie Cleve case precisely because of where it happened and who it involved. That's why he was so driven to find the killer in those early days.'

Holland lowered his head. 'I feel bad that I ever suspected him of those murders. I should have known better.'

'You were following the evidence, Tony,' Shepherd told him. She smiled softly. 'It's what we do.'

'I tell you what,' he said, brightening, 'when you stop and think about it, he was a bit good, wasn't he? Those fibres, for example, he had them right away, five minutes after he got to the scene. And the text, that business with the stylus, top-drawer that was. Not to mention checking out Abbie Cleve's finances and finding those donations to that programme of his daughter's.'

'Harmony Hill,' said Lindy, looking at Shepherd significantly.

'Yeah,' said Holland. 'I'm not saying he'd have been another Danny Maik, but he could have been right up there. A bloody shame,' he said sadly. 'To lose a good officer like that, all for the sake of a few days of madness.'

Shepherd shook her head ruefully. 'It was a death two years in the making, Tony,' she said. 'Even though he came back, his heart was never really in it. In the end, he was never going to be able to shake off the remorse he felt over Ferris.'

Lindy nodded. 'That night he came to our house for dinner, I had the feeling he didn't even want to. His life ended that day at the Nye. It hollowed him out, and the guilt was all that was preventing the shell of him from collapsing in on itself. I think when Ferris told him he didn't need him to come by and see him any more, he was unable to find any further purpose to his life.'

'And when Ferris was killed, it was just a matter of time until he found some way to end it.'

Jejeune's comment felled them all into silence for a moment. He looked around the bar. It was not just emotional landscapes that had been reshaped by the events of the past few days. Other terrain would change in the coming days and months. The Nye would not reopen after its enforced quarantine from the nearby HN51 outbreak. And without the revenues from this season's shooting season, the beef farming operation at Cleve Hall would go into receivership. You would have to look hard to find any winners from the events of the past few days. But true to form, Lindy believed she had unearthed one.

'We'd better get going,' she said, standing, 'Dom's got a big day tomorrow.'

'Lindy's got some surprise planned for me,' Jejeune told them. He managed a wan smile. 'Though it's probably too much to hope it's got anything to do with birding.'

'Oh, I don't know about that,' said Colleen Shepherd, suppressing a faint smile of her own.

At the realisation that she already knew about it, Jejeune turned to Lindy. 'Colleen has graciously agreed that you can have afternoons off for the next month. You'll be helping out at the after-school programme at Harmony Hill.'

Jejeune's eyes opened wide. 'The one that Rosie Knowles attends?'

'Among others, yes. They have applied for funding, but it'll take a few weeks to come through, so they won't be able to hire staff until then. I said we would cover the outdoor activities curriculum until they can.'

'I can't do that. What do I know about teaching children?'

'It's three hours a day, Dom. We can take them on nature walks, or down to the beach, have them learn about birds and animals and plants. We'll do crafts, drawings. It'll be fun. I'll teach them how to be obnoxious, and you can show them how to be self-absorbed. Together we'll be turning out perfect little citizens for the next generation.'

Jejeune looked at Shepherd helplessly while Holland did not very much at all to hide a smile. 'This will satisfy the community outreach you committed to as well,' his DCS told him, 'and be very well-regarded by the brass into the bargain. And honestly, Domenic, if you can't find anything fulfilling about introducing the world of nature to a bunch of wide-eyed infants, then I fear for your soul. I really do. We'll manage without you for those couple of hours each day.'

'It's three,' he said. But they could all tell by the way he said it that he had already given up his resistance to the idea. He had lost someone recently, as they all had, and almost lost someone else. In the end, he hadn't been able to help either of them. It would take some time for him to come to terms with that. In the meantime, he needed to surround himself with people who would need him, whom he could help. It would give him time to heal. It would give them all time to heal.

THE HIMALAYAN MONAL

Possibly no group of birds has a longer and more complex relationship with humans than those in the family
of Phasianidae. The striking appearance of these large, charis-
matic birds has been admired throughout human history, with
depictions of the Silver Pheasant (*Lophura nycthemera*) found
in Chinese art and poetry dating back as far as five thousand
years. But even among the brightly coloured members of
the pheasant family, one species stands apart. The stunning
plumage of the Himalayan Monal (*Lophophorus impejanus*)
has earned it a reputation among many observers as the most
beautiful bird in the world. Also known as the Nine-coloured
Pheasant, the Himalayan Monal is native to Himalayan forests
and shrublands at elevations of 2,100–4,500 m. Held in reverence across its range, it is the national bird of Nepal, where it is
known as the danphe, and is mentioned by name in a number
of traditional Nepali songs. Sadly, however, the bird's beauty
has also been directly attributable to a decline in numbers over
many parts of its range. The crest of the Himalayan Monal is
a prestigious trophy among a number of local communities,
such as the Kullu of Himachal. The set of feathers is thought
to bring status to its wearer, and thousands of birds have been
killed so their plumage may adorn the Himachali *topi* caps.

The crest feathers are given to goldsmiths to be set in silver or gold mountings to be affixed as pins on the traditional headgear. They are considered valuable family heirlooms and are worn on auspicious occasions such as festivals or marriages. Though crests are still occasionally recovered from poachers and goldsmiths in the area, it is hoped that a recent ban by the local authorities on wearing these caps may finally be discouraging this long-held traditional practice.

Like many pheasants, the Himalayan Monal also faces other increasing anthropogenic threats from hunting and habitat loss. Of around forty bird species around the world bearing the name Pheasant or Peacock Pheasant, four are listed as endangered, including the critically endangered Edwards's Pheasant, while a further ten species are categorised as vulnerable. To find out more about the valuable work being done by the International Union for the Conservation of Nature to save the beautiful, iconic birds of the family Phasianidae please visit www.iucn.org/our-union/commissions/group/iucn-ssc-galliformes-specialist-group.

ACKNOWLEDGEMENTS

My thanks once again go to Juliet Mabey at Oneworld for her ongoing commitment to the Birder Murder Mysteries. At Oneworld, too, my editor Jenny Parrott kept her usual steady hand on the tiller as she guided me through the treacherous waters of libel law and other inconsistencies in the early drafts. I am also grateful to Beth Marshall Brown, Jacqui Lewis, Paul Nash, Laura McFarlane and the rest of the Oneworld team for their expertise and encouragement in bringing this book to publication.

Meg Wheeler at WCA remained as helpful, resourceful and indefatigable as ever in keeping this project on track. Michael Levine and Bruce Westwood also weighed in with timely and much-appreciated advice. I am genuinely appreciative of the fact that my writing career is in such capable hands.

My time in Bhutan was immeasurably enriched by the knowledge and expertise of Sonam Sonam, Duptho Rinzin Dorji and the latter's son, Mila. My thanks to all of you in the Land of the Thunder Dragon. I was also fortunate to enjoy the expert guidance, and wonderful company, of Agia Kaur on my excursions in Singapore, while Sita Dhillon made sure every aspect of my visit went off seamlessly. My thanks to you both, and also to my good friend, Danny Catt, for the initial introductions.

And finally, no set of Birder Murder acknowledgements would be complete without an expression of gratitude and love to my wife. She rejected my suggestion that she should jot down her predictions for the book in note form this time. Pity, really. I had been hoping I could say I'd finally found something that made Resa write.